Praise for

An Introvert's Guide to Life and Love

"The slow burn of Mallory falling for Daniel as well as Florida is full of lush and lovely scenes, and Mallory is a pleasurable narrator who readers will root for. Like a good soak in a hot tub near the beach."

—*Kirkus*

Rachel Weiss's Group Chat

"*Rachel Weiss's Group Chat* hits the sweet spot of modernizing *Pride and Prejudice* in the vein of *Bridget Jones's Diary* and *Clueless*. Hilarious, charming, and as comforting as a warm hug, Appelbaum's debut proves she's a rising powerhouse in the world of contemporary romance."

—Sara Goodman Confino, bestselling author of *Don't Forget to Write*

"It is a truth universally acknowledged that a book with such a sharp, witty heroine, a swoon-worthy love interest, and laugh-out-loud hijinks must not be missed. Watching Rachel Weiss figure her life out was an absolute delight. Reading this book felt like making a friend."

—Amanda Elliot, author of *Love You a Latke*

"Lauren Appelbaum's charming debut is a laugh-out-loud romp filled with all the best ingredients: sharply drawn female friendships, hilarious social observations, a reluctant appreciation for JDate, and a slow-burn, opposites-attract romance between a lovably chaotic heroine and the tech bro next door. It's the perfect pick for readers who crave a good belly laugh with their romance."

—Lindsay Hammeroff, author of *Till There Was You*

An Introvert's Guide to Life and Love

Also by Lauren Appelbaum

Rachel Weiss's Group Chat

An Introvert's Guide to Life and Love

LAUREN APPELBAUM

FOREVER

NEW YORK BOSTON

This book is a work of fiction. Names, characters, places, and incidents are the product of the author's imagination or are used fictitiously. Any resemblance to actual events, locales, or persons, living or dead, is coincidental.

Copyright © 2025 by Lauren Appelbaum

Cover design and illustration by Elizabeth M. Oliver

Cover copyright © 2025 by Hachette Book Group, Inc.

Hachette Book Group supports the right to free expression and the value of copyright. The purpose of copyright is to encourage writers and artists to produce the creative works that enrich our culture.

The scanning, uploading, and distribution of this book without permission is a theft of the author's intellectual property. If you would like permission to use material from the book (other than for review purposes), please contact permissions@hbgusa.com. Thank you for your support of the author's rights.

Forever
Hachette Book Group
1290 Avenue of the Americas, New York, NY 10104
read-forever.com
@readforeverpub

First Trade Paperback Edition: September 2025

Forever is an imprint of Grand Central Publishing. The Forever name and logo are registered trademarks of Hachette Book Group, Inc.

The publisher is not responsible for websites (or their content) that are not owned by the publisher.

The Hachette Speakers Bureau provides a wide range of authors for speaking events. To find out more, go to hachettespeakersbureau.com or email HachetteSpeakers@hbgusa.com.

Forever books may be purchased in bulk for business, educational, or promotional use. For information, please contact your local bookseller or the Hachette Book Group Special Markets Department at special.markets@hbgusa.com.

Library of Congress Cataloging-in-Publication Data
Names: Appelbaum, Lauren, author.
Title: An introvert's guide to life and love / Lauren Appelbaum.
Description: First trade paperback edition. | New York : Forever, 2025. |
Identifiers: LCCN 2025013476 | ISBN 9781538757864 (trade paperback) | ISBN 9781538757871 (ebook)
Subjects: LCGFT: Romance fiction. | Novels.
Classification: LCC PS3601.P6628 I68 2025 | DDC 813/.6—dc23/eng/20250414
LC record available at https://lccn.loc.gov/2025013476

ISBNs: 9781538757864 (Trade paperback); 9781538757871 (ebook)

Printed in the United States of America

CCR

10 9 8 7 6 5 4 3 2 1

*In loving memory of my grandparents:
Rafi, Iris, Carol, and Richard*

An Introvert's Guide to Life and Love

Chapter 1

I was a real-life Gollum. You know the meme, right? Gollum darting out of his cave to retrieve his packages? That was me. I got a little too comfortable in my work-from-home lifestyle—undoubtedly a shock for anyone who knew me before—and online shopping became my main joy in life. My cozy apartment progressively got cozier with my online shopping addiction. West Elm, Pottery Barn, Anthropologie. The packages piled up, each one a little dopamine hit. I lived in a safe cocoon full of scented candles, chunky throw blankets, and Netflix binges. (So many Netflix binges—one might say I became more Claire Fraser than Mallory Rosen.) But I'm far from the Scottish Highlands now. And I'm far from my Seattle apartment. In fact, I'm the farthest from home I've been in over two years, surrounded by more people than I've seen in just as long.

I'm in a beachside hotel on the Gulf Coast of Florida, sitting on the bed to apply my makeup as my twenty-year-old cousin sobs in the shower. She's been in there for forty-five minutes.

It's weird being here, and not just because I'm so far from home. It's my family. I haven't spent this much time with my aunts and uncles and cousins in years. The last time I was with them, I was twenty-four. My post-college plans hadn't exactly panned out the way I'd dreamed they would, but I made the best of my remote, entry-level tech job by traveling as often as possible. I was suntanned, arms stacked with leather bracelets from my travels, casually referencing places I'd recently been, like Koh Lanta, Oaxaca, and Rome. The difference between the Mallory back then and the Mallory of today is, apparently, noteworthy, based on the not-so-veiled comments I've received so far. My uncle Ron, at least, seems to find it hilarious ("Guess you don't see much of the sun anymore up there in Seattle! You're like a vampire now!").

I've laughed off their comments, because, honestly, I'm comfortable with who I am now. When I think of the Mallory who took advantage of her remote job, toting her laptop around the world, stubbornly ignoring the risks she was taking until it was too late... Well, the point is that I enjoy being a homebody now, and I don't need to travel to far-flung locales to find joy in life.

I squint at my reflection and dust some bronzer onto my cheeks (maybe Ron's vampire comment did get to me) as my sister Maeve knocks on the door of our room. She's staying down the hall with her husband and their baby.

"Are you guys ready?" Maeve asks. I nod my head toward the bathroom, where the shower finally turns off. A wail emanates from behind the closed door. Maeve gives me a look of mild surprise. "Guess that's a no."

My sister raises a tentative hand, poised to knock on the door, when it opens. Maeve takes a hasty step back from the onslaught of steam.

"Aren't you guys even *sad*?" Ellie clutches a towel around her body and glares at us with mascara running down her cheeks. "Lottie is *dead*."

I flinch. Maeve places a protective hand on my shoulder. Our grandmother—who insisted that we all call her Lottie—died two weeks ago. I'm stung by the question. And by the presumption. Do I have to sob in a hotel shower to prove that I'm sad?

"Of course we're sad. And we better go. We're supposed to be on the boat in ten minutes." I stand and smooth the black linen shift dress I'd borrowed from Maeve. It was a puzzle trying to decide what to wear to a Florida boat funeral in April. On one hand, I want to be respectful; on the other hand, it's hot as balls. My online shopping hobby mostly runs toward furnishing my apartment; I never really buy clothes for myself. I mean, most people only see me from the shoulders up on Zoom. Luckily, my older sister has some fashion sense and a job where people have to see her in person, and she's generous with her wardrobe.

Ellie runs a brush through her wet hair and raises an eyebrow at me as I give my lipstick a final touch-up.

"Who are you trying to impress?"

"Trying to look nice for... Lottie, I guess." I'm not literally trying to impress my dead grandmother. But Lottie cared about appearances. She told me once that she liked to wear makeup because it was a reminder to herself, and to the world, that she was trying.

A memory swims to the surface of the last time I visited my grandparents, when Lottie asked me to do her makeup for her. The cancer was already taking its toll. I remember marveling at the deep creases and folds of her eyelids as I gently swiped on a dark-gold eye shadow.

"This is a pretty color," I'd said, guessing that the palette was well over a decade old. "Maybe we can go shopping for new makeup together. That could be fun."

She'd given a little smile and patted my hand. "Maybe next time, sweetheart. Maybe next time."

There it was: the sadness. Less of a loud wail, more of a hard fist clenched in my chest. I let out a loud exhale and followed my sister and cousin to the elevator.

Outside the hotel, we find Maeve's husband, Blake, sheltering in a thin strip of shade underneath an awning as though the sunny pavement is lava. He cradles baby Adam in a thin white blanket and keeps checking to make sure his face is covered by the brim of his baby sun hat. Maeve gives them each a peck on the side of the head.

"It's too bright." Blake holds a hand out in the sun and glances skeptically up at the blinding blue sky. A true Seattleite, my brother-in-law. "I don't know. Should we put sunscreen on him? They say not until six months, but, I mean…"

Blake's talking becomes background noise as we make our way across the marina. The walk over to the unmistakably loud group of people can't be more than a hundred yards, but I'm covered in a sheen of sweat by the time I get there. The air is like hot clam chowder.

"Mallory, hi," my aunt says with an exaggerated pout, drawing me in for a hug.

"Hi, Trish." I rub her back in what I hope is a comforting way.

A man who I assume is the captain starts trying, gently, to herd us all onto his vessel. A few people—my dad, me, and my unfailingly polite Gen Z cousin Max—follow the captain's orders.

Eventually, my great-aunt Lenore bellows at the top of her (sizable) lungs: "GILBERSTEINS! ALL ABOARD!" Within two minutes, everyone has taken a seat on the boat.

Mom settles in between Trish and Lenore. The three of them hug one another as the boat's engine roars and we take off into the Gulf. My gaze slides past them to the tall, reedy man sitting with his arms crossed, his white hair blowing in the breeze. Gramps. He's surrounded by family but looks impossibly alone. I swallow, feeling like maybe I should go talk to him. It's just that he looks like he doesn't want to be bothered.

I cross my own arms and look out toward the horizon. The boat is zipping along now, bumping gently over barely there waves. Now that we're moving, the weather feels perfect. Warm sun, cloudless sky.

The buzz of my family's chatter is rather pleasant when it's not directed at me. My younger cousins are laughing together. My mom is murmuring with her sister, their curly heads bent together. Lenore has asked Maeve and Blake about the baby, and now Blake is expounding on the miracle of infant gas drops.

"He would be crying, and then we'd give him the drops and"—Blake snaps his fingers—"like that, happy again. We went through an entire bottle in—" I tune him out. I've heard this story before.

After ten minutes or so, the captain slows the boat to a stop and the chatter fades. Everyone looks around to see what's supposed to happen next. We all stand and make our way to the front of the boat. Gramps walks unsteadily forward, clutching an urn that I realize with a lurch must be full of Lottie's ashes. Suddenly, the mood feels unbearably miserable.

"Look! Dolphins!" My twelve-year-old cousin leans over the side of the boat. Three dolphins are crisscrossing in the water mere feet from us, their silvery backs shining under the sun. Everyone swarms forward, oohing and ahhing.

"Do you see the dolphins, Adam?" Maeve coos, holding him up. Blake hovers with his arms outstretched like he thinks there's a chance Maeve might accidentally drop the baby overboard.

I turn to smile at my mom. She pulls me in for a sideways hug.

"Mom loved dolphins," she says.

"This is her," Trish says, tears coating her cheeks. "She's sending us a sign."

Gramps scoffs—probably because *signs* are not, scientifically speaking, real. But he's smiling too, showing his surprisingly white teeth for the first time today.

"Thank you, my darling." His voice is so quiet, I don't know if anyone else hears him. And then he hands the urn to my mom. She looks down at it and her face drains of color; she looks like a scared kid, which is painful to see because my mother is a sturdy, fearless woman.

Lenore takes charge. "We should all say a few words." She straightens her rainbow-colored shawl and pulls her shoulders back. "Lottie. When you met my brother I thought, well, what does a fine woman like you see in *him*?" Everyone laughs. "But I'm glad you saw whatever it was that you liked. You became my sister, and I always wanted one of those. You showed me that a woman could be obstinate, and still tender. Glamorous, and still rugged. You were always up for a girls' trip to Geneva at the drop of a hat, even when your daughter was four weeks old." At this, Lenore cackles as the rest of us laugh (and Mom and Trish groan). Lenore gestures to her husband, Paul, who keeps the toasts going.

Everyone says something that elicits some laughter, some tears. Are they all speaking off the cuff? I wasn't prepared for this, and I am, to put it mildly, not the world's best public speaker.

Maeve talks about how grateful she is that Lottie got to meet Adam, her first great-grandchild, before she died, and everyone is dabbing their eyes or downright sobbing. (My mom. And Blake.) I figure I should keep my story light and funny to bring the mood back up.

When Maeve is finished, everyone turns to me.

"Lottie." I'm still unsure where I'm going with this. "You were the most incredible grandmother. You were all the things everyone has already said. But also, you were kind of mean sometimes." I chuckle lightly. "Like, I'll never forget, at Eddy's second wedding when I was fourteen, you told me I walked like a basketball player in heels. As if I didn't feel self-conscious enough already!" My smile widens. Nobody else laughs. *Okay.* "Um...And there was that time you told my sister to suck in her tummy. Because she had a pooch? She still sucks it in to this day." Maeve glares at me. "And, Dad, remember the time she told you that you were losing your hair? Before you even realized it?" Dad just looks at me, his bald spot gleaming under the sun. Everyone else is staring at me, too. I had envisioned moving everyone to tears of laughter. Clearly, my social skills are rusty. Or maybe not so much rusty as nonexistent. I decide to shut my trap. With an awkward little bow, I cede the floor to Trish's husband, Ron.

After the rest of the toasts (all of which are normal, unlike mine), Mom and Trish lower their mother's ashes into the water, urn and all. I'm pretty sure the urn wasn't supposed to go in unless it's biodegradable. But despite the captain's subtle shrug, it's silent on the boat, apart from some sniffling and muffled sobs.

And then Lenore breaks the silence. She clears her throat and spreads her arms wide. I know what's coming before it happens. My great-aunt was a mezzo-soprano for seven years in the Cincinnati Opera, and she's never let anyone forget it. The first note of an aria pierces the air, sweet and melancholy and very, very loud. I can't take my eyes off the perfect O of her mouth, rimmed with shimmery brown lipstick. The song is beautiful, really, and it's a touching display, but it's just...a lot.

"For Pete's sake!" Eddy, Gramps and Lenore's brother, bellows at the top of his voice. "Not this again!"

Lenore just sings louder, her arms sweeping from side to side in a graceful arc.

"I told you at Papa's funeral," Eddy shouts at his sister, spittle flying, "it hurts my ears!"

"Leave her alone!" Paul steps up, apparently to defend his wife's honor. Maeve catches my eye from across the deck, her expression deadpan.

"Paul, I've been dealing wit' her for twenty years longer than you have and I've had enough!" Eddy says over the swell of "Ave Maria."

"Well, I've had enough of your macho attitude! Let my wife sing; we're in mourning here!"

The two men move toward each other and I wonder if we're about to witness some senior-citizen fisticuffs. The captain, apparently at a loss for what to do, decides to motor it. As the boat roars ahead, the two men wobble and clutch each other's arms. Some struggling and grunting ensues. Are they fighting or helping each other keep their balance? It's unclear.

The tension drains from the scene and Lenore continues her performance as we zip back toward the hotel.

I take a seat at the front of the boat and close my eyes. In a few hours, I'll be on a plane back to Seattle, headphones on, watching a movie—*alone*.

Well. *Alone* is a relative term. My parents and sister are on the same flight as me. I thought they were coming home tomorrow, but no. At least I'm a few rows away, and baby Adam is being mercifully quiet. But as luck would have it, I'm sitting beside a Chatty Cathy.

I'm curled in my seat, headphones firmly clasped over my ears, my face hidden behind a mask, and yet the woman beside me rattles on.

"We were here for my niece's graduation. It was so wonderful." She beams at what is, apparently, a cherished memory. "Eckerd College! Have you heard of it? We are just so proud of her. And to think, they nearly held it all *online*." She says it like it's a dirty word. "A virtual ceremony. How awful. Oh, I hope you didn't have one of those. Did you?"

I give a short shake of my head, hoping she takes the hint.

"It's so wonderful to be around people, isn't it?" the woman continues. "It's so important. Nothing can replace actually being with the people you love. Zoom can go to heck!"

I lean into the window, slightly taken aback by this zealous proclamation. From a few rows back, I hear my brother-in-law's voice, undoubtedly directed at some innocent passenger: "Have you heard of gas drops?" And then, quite clearly, from the other side of the aisle I hear the sound of my father snoring like a jackhammer.

"Yes," I murmur. "So wonderful." And then I turn on my tablet and hit PLAY on *Bridget Jones's Baby*.

Chapter 2

It's a relief to get back to my normal routine. It's not like I love my job, but I appreciate the structure of having a nine-to-five that allows for me to work from the comfort of my home and with minimum human interaction. Also, I just appreciate that I *have* a job. Something I'll never take for granted again.

Monday morning, my alarm goes off at seven fifteen. I change into some leggings and a cropped tank, unroll my yoga mat in the middle of my living room, and flow through my virtual yoga class. I've been doing the same class for two years now. They play pop music and I get to work up a little sweat first thing in the morning.

After a quick shower, I scrunch mousse into my hair and put on enough makeup to make me look presentable on Zoom. I make a peach spinach smoothie in the Vitamix blender I got for an insane deal at Goodwill, and an oat milk latte with the Nespresso machine Maeve got me last Hanukkah. The day passes in a comfortably familiar blur. Emails, Slack messages, and a couple of meetings—making it two too many meetings, in my opinion. I only hit a snag near the end of the workday, during my one-on-one with my manager, Kat.

Kat's face dominates my screen, her expertly highlighted hair flipped over one shoulder, delicate lines etched around her eyes and between her brows. She fiddles with her clear-framed blue light glasses as I fill her in on my trip.

"I'm so sorry, again," she says while staring into the screen.

My mind spins, hopelessly trying to think of a work topic to change the subject to. But Kat beats me there, allowing me to escape from the awkwardness.

"So, listen, Mallory. Something came up earlier in my meeting with Dominic. He pointed out that your last status report was formatted incorrectly. Not a big deal, but you know we have a goal this year to provide consistent status reports across the org."

My heart skips unpleasantly. *Really, Dominic? Throwing me under the bus to our manager?* But, God, he was probably right. I always mess up something or other. One week I forget to communicate a deadline to an engineering manager, the next week I mess up on status reports. No wonder I haven't been promoted yet.

Kat has already moved on to another topic, and I feign listening as I pull up the status report in question and compare it to Dominic's. He's right, they're not the same format. But I do these every week—I must have had a brain fart, I guess.

"Is there anything else you wanted to chat about today?" Kat glances down at her phone.

"No." I'm still flustered. "I think that's it. Sorry about the goof, by the way. Won't happen again."

"No worries. Talk to you later, Mallory." She leaves the meeting, and for a moment I'm just staring at my red face on the screen.

I never react well to making mistakes at work. It triggers some sort of impostor syndrome in me. I scroll through my emails from last week, and then I see it. There had been a whole email chain with some of the engineering managers about what they would prefer to see in the status reports. Another project manager on my team, Andi, had come up with the new format. I didn't have a brain fart.

I click over to Slack and start typing a message to Kat: "Hey, so regarding the status report…" And then Kat's status changes to a little bubble that says: "In meetings for the rest of the day."

I delete my message. I can tell her later. It's fine.

By five thirty, I'm so ready for my walk. In true millennial fashion, I've dubbed it my Mental Health Walk, and it has lived up to its name. I started taking a daily walk when my gym closed during the pandemic. It helps me transition from work mode to relaxing mode at the end of the day.

I do my usual loop around my hilly, tree-lined neighborhood. Truth be told, this isn't technically my neighborhood—it's ritzy Upper Queen Anne, the quiet streets full of stately single-family homes, homes full of people who, I assume, are better at life than I am. I have to huff up a big hill to get here. I could walk around my own neighborhood, but instead of lush trees and well-tended gardens, it's full of tourists and people camping under bus stops.

There's a new episode of my favorite podcast, *Elementary*, so I listen to that as I walk. It's hosted by two elementary school teachers—one current, one former—who chat about TV shows and dating and life. They have a core of dedicated listeners who've bonded in the comments, where we chat about the episodes and tangentially related topics, like which face cream to buy and the latest shows to stream. It's like having a group of like-minded friends—something I haven't felt in a long time. I know that sounds pathetic, but it's true.

As I walk under a row of blossoming pink-and-white cherry trees, a fellow walker passes by in the opposite direction. She's a bit older than I am, bundled up in a black down coat despite the mild evening, also listening to something on her earbuds. I give her the requisite Seattle greeting: a tight-lipped nod. I accidentally do a weird, noncommittal form of eye contact where I briefly glance at her face and let my gaze slide away just as her eyes meet mine. She surprises me by murmuring a barely audible "hello."

We walk past each other every day.

For dinner, I heat up a frozen pizza and toss together some spring greens and vinaigrette. I can't stop my mind from drifting back to the status report incident. It's like a bruise that I keep poking just to see if it still hurts. I don't know what's worse: the idea of my manager and co-worker discussing my mistake behind my back, or the fact that I accepted the reprimand without question. Someday, perhaps, I'll grow a backbone. But today I'll carry on being my nonconfrontational self. I'll message Andi tomorrow and ask her to remind the team about the new status report format. That way, Kat and Dominic will realize that I was right and I won't have to say anything.

I take my dinner—and a generous glass of red wine—to the couch, where I spend the next two hours watching *Outlander*. Is there anything in this world better than living vicariously through Claire Fraser? If I could give up twenty-first-century comforts in exchange for loving a man like Jamie, I'd do it in a heartbeat. Well…I glance around my cozy, dimly lit apartment, from the glowing Anthropologie candle burning on my coffee table to my beloved gadgets charging on the console table against the wall—my iPhone, Kindle, and MacBook. Maybe it would take me longer than a heartbeat to leave these comforts behind. But still, I get it. Jamie Fraser is the man we all deserve.

Around ten, I draw a bath, dumping in a capful of lavender-scented bubbles and a sprinkle of Epsom salts. I'm feeling pleasantly loose from the wine and can't wait to sink into the hot water with the novel I'm reading.

Just as I'm dipping a toe into the bathwater, my phone buzzes on the counter. It's probably Maeve sending the latest photos of baby Adam. I glance quickly at my messages, my skin pimpling in the chilly bathroom. It's not from my sister. It's from my ex. *Crap.*

I haven't heard from him in months. I almost delete it without reading it, but curiosity gets the better of me.

I've been thinking of you, Mallory. If you're comfortable, I'd love to get a cup of coffee sometime. Let me know what you think.

I stand there stark naked, re-reading the message three, four times. If I'm comfortable. *If I'm comfortable.* My stomach clenches. I was comfortable a minute ago. I was perfect. In my element. And now? Extremely uncomfortable. Irritating memories threaten to swoop in and ruin my relaxation time.

If I don't think about him, the memories don't plague me. I've grown to be pretty good at living in the moment, appreciating each day for what it is. I let my thumb hover over the BLOCK CONTACT button. But I can't seem to block him. I just won't respond.

My bath is shorter than usual; I can't focus on my book. I do my skin-care routine and pull on my pajamas. As I'm closing my pajama drawer, I catch sight of my bright-purple vibrator. I'd usually be in the mood after two hours of Jamie Fraser, but I'm unsettled now, after the text message. *Shake it off, Mallory.* And I will; I always do. I leave Big Purple where she is, shut the drawer, and turn off the light.

Chapter 3

The next day, Mom has invited us all over for Shabbat dinner. I'm in the back seat of Maeve and Blake's SUV, next to baby Adam. From the passenger seat, Maeve chirps on about how happy she is not to have to cook tonight. My nephew starts to wail but Maeve keeps talking, stopping every few breaths to make shushing noises, which Adam does not seem to find soothing. My ears hurt.

It takes half an hour to drive to our parents' house on the Eastside. I try to psych myself up for the inevitable high energy of the next couple hours. My parents are talkers. I love them, and my sister and her cute little family, but spending time with them wears me out. What can I say? I thrive on alone time. Fortunately, a lot of their conversation revolves around the baby and lawyer stuff. My parents, Blake, and Maeve are all attorneys.

I frequently remind myself that most parents would be proud of a child who makes a decent living as a project manager at a big tech company. And I think my parents are proud—technically. But it's not exactly a secret that I'm the disappointment of the family. My dad's dad was an attorney. Lottie was a public defender—one of only two women in her law school class. My parents met in law school. Maeve and I grew up knowing that we would be lawyers, too.

It sounds silly when I spell it out like that. I've gotten a few weird looks from people over the years when I explain that my parents are disappointed that I never went to law school. But it's just how things are in my family. My parents had certain expectations; one daughter lived up to them, and the other did not.

If I'm being honest, I had those expectations, too. I enjoyed the certainty of knowing what I wanted to be when I grew up. Some friends held similar certainties, knowing they wanted to be teachers or nurses. And then there were those who floundered and flip-flopped through college, changing majors two or three times, some opting for grad school just to put off making a decision for a few more years.

Grad school: That's where it went wrong for me. I didn't get in. I applied to three law schools: one reasonable choice, one reach school, and one where I thought I'd be a shoo-in because my parents went there. But I didn't get into any of them.

My parents were crushed. But they tried to hide it by reading through brochures for different graduate school programs with me and sending me online job listings. My mom encouraged me to consider other options, like medical school. My dad wanted me to work as a paralegal and reapply to law school the next year. I couldn't face any of those options. Deep down, I'd grown up feeling like the awkward daughter—less social and less intelligent. Getting rejected from law school while Maeve was halfway through her program seemed to reaffirm this belief. So I applied to some random jobs and accepted the first one that offered.

It was a data entry job at a local tech company. It wasn't as prestigious as my sister's budding law career, but the pay was okay for someone fresh out of college, and it had one thing going for it that most people didn't have at the time: It was remote. So I made lemonade from the lemons life had dealt me. I traveled as often as I could afford to, bringing my laptop with me. Not only did it help me heal from my disappointment, but the tales of my travels also seemed to impress my family, something I was desperate to do. I had some incredible experiences, like biking through the Dutch countryside with a couple of my friends from college, and spending a solo week in Paris, living out my Parisian dreams. But after nearly two years, I'd lost touch with almost all my friends—I guess that happens when you're out of town so often that you miss all the happy hours and girls' nights. And then I guess I got too comfortable phoning it in to my job, because my lack of work ethic caught up to me. I was fired.

Just like that, I had no paycheck on the horizon, and I was stuck in my apartment lease with an embarrassing amount of credit card debt from my travels.

The conversation that followed is burned into my memory. I confessed it all to my parents, and we sat down at their kitchen table and went through my finances in painful detail. They coached me through breaking my lease, and loaned me money to pay for that and for all my debt. Of course, this was only after we'd agreed to a strict repayment schedule. At the time, it felt like my life was over; I was positive no one would ever hire me again. Who would want to?

My parents let me stay with them—asking me every other day if I was planning to reapply to law school—and after four long months of camping out at their neighborhood Starbucks applying to hundreds of jobs, I finally got one. An entry-level project manager job that I will never take for granted. The day I got the keys to my (second) very own apartment was one of the best days of my life.

And now that I've settled down and have a job that I take seriously, I can actually contribute to my family's conversations about working life. So that's something.

When we arrive, there's the usual hubbub as our parents fuss over the baby and give each of us a hug. One thing I didn't mind about the pandemic was the moratorium on hugging. I enjoy a hug now and then; it just seems excessive to have to hug every single person on arrival and departure for every social event. But maybe that's just me.

My mom ushers us into the sitting room and encourages us all to help ourselves to the veggie platter. She returns a few minutes later with gin and tonics for everyone. Soon we're all settled on the sofas. Dad is bouncing Adam on his knee, and Mom is updating us on a case she's been working on. Maeve and Blake gulp down their drinks with looks of muted glee, like they're high on the freedom of—what? Being in someone else's house? Having another adult hold their child? I'm not sure, but clearly they're enjoying themselves more than I am. There's nothing wrong with having dinner with my family, really. I'm fortunate to have family nearby and to be on good terms with them. It's just that I feel like I'm invisible half the time.

I sip my drink as Maeve peppers Mom with questions about her method of gathering evidence from someone or other. Blake and Dad are talking animatedly about a baseball game. I make eye contact with Adam and give him a little smile. He stares at me and then farts. This catches everyone else's attention. They all laugh and then remember that I exist.

"Mallory, how's work?" my mom asks.

"Fine. Good. I'm working on…" I try to think of something interesting to tell them, but all I can think of is the awkward misunderstanding about status reports. I don't want to bring that up. "I'm just chugging along. Keeping those engineers on schedule."

There's a pause as everyone waits to see if I have more to add. I take a sip of my cocktail, and an ice cube bumps against my teeth.

"Well, I'm glad you're good." Mom smiles uncertainly.

"Yeah." Dad nods in apparent agreement. "Keep on keepin' on, Mal Gal."

As they return to talking about work, my mind drifts to the

pair of Frye boots I've been dreaming about purchasing after my next paycheck. I recently finished repaying Mom and Dad—a huge weight off my shoulders. Now I might actually have some expendable income.

We gather around the table as Mom leads the blessing over the Shabbat candles. Dinner is a lentil-based faux meat loaf and a salad that's heavy on nuts, seeds, and crumbled blue cheese.

Maeve delicately spears a forkful of lettuce. "How is Gramps doing?"

"You know, it's hard to say." Mom pats her lips with her napkin. "He sounds relatively upbeat on the phone. I've been calling him every couple days, and Trish visits him once a week. But he's never lived alone before."

"No?" I look up, surprised. How is that possible?

"No, he never has. He went from his parents' house to living with college roommates to getting married to my mother. He's never lived alone until now." Mom's voice quivers on the last word.

"Oh, Mom." Maeve reaches out and puts a hand over hers. "It sounds like he's doing as well as can be expected."

"I think he is, yes." She takes a deep breath, straightens her shoulders, and looks around the table. "Who's ready for dessert? I made gluten-free molasses cookies."

At home, I muse over the idea that Gramps never got the chance to live alone. Obviously, he's now living alone for the saddest reason—he's a widower. The idea of it is just foreign to me. I love my alone time so much.

I've tried many low-stakes dating apps over the last year. And by "tried," I mean I created a profile, swiped yes or no on dozens of guys from the comfort of my couch, and failed to keep any conversation alive for more than a day. As for going on a date with any of these guys...it just never seems that appealing. Maybe I'm too comfortable being single.

When I switch over to Bumble BFF and swipe through some would-be best girlfriends, the women on there look so cheerful, so fun, so active. I don't feel that way at all. Most of my photos are from my pre-pandemic life. Somehow it's even more intimidating to try to schedule a meetup with a potential platonic friend than with a romantic partner. It all feels pointless. It's like I'm trying to fill a void that society has told me I need to fill. But I don't mind being alone most of the time. I like it. Is that so wrong?

Anyway, I do have friends. Or if we're only counting non-work friends…at least I have one. And I'm seeing her tomorrow for our semi-regular happy hour. So there.

I get to the restaurant in Belltown at two minutes to five. Carmen texts to say that she's running ten minutes late. I hover on the sidewalk outside. My best friend has known me long enough to know that she shouldn't do this to me.

You can do this, I tell myself. *Nobody cares if you're alone. Nobody is paying attention to you. Go in and sit down.*

Somehow I've reached my ripe old age without learning how to confidently enter a restaurant by myself.

But I can't just stand here blocking the sidewalk. I take a deep breath and go in.

The place is warm and gently lit with red-hued chandeliers. I take a seat at the bar and put my purse on the stool next to me to save it for Carmen.

"What can I get you?" the bartender asks.

"Um…" I laugh nervously, my eyes glued to the cocktail menu in front of me. "I should wait for my friend. She'll be here soon."

She is not here soon. Ten minutes turn to twenty. I've scrolled through everything there is to scroll on my phone when she finally arrives, long hair and long scarf flying as she sweeps breathlessly through the restaurant.

"Sorry, sorry!" She leans in for a hug, smelling like Calvin Klein Euphoria and cold sweat. "Look at you, girl, I love this sweater!"

"Your hair looks gorgeous, did you get a blowout?"

Compliments are our love language. She settles in beside me and we order two Plum Blossom cocktails and a dozen oysters, the tomato and Gorgonzola salad, and the seared ahi tuna.

"How *are* you, what's new?" she asks, sipping her drink. I fill her in on my trip to Florida.

"Ugh, was your cousin Ellie as annoying as ever?"

"I guess so. I don't know. She was fine." I get a prickle of annoyance at the memory of Ellie asking who I was trying to impress.

That's the thing about having a friend for decades. Carmen knows everything about me, and mostly everything about my family, and she has the memory of an elephant. It's almost like trying to be best friends with my sister—we just have too much shared history.

I ask Carmen about herself. One of the many things I love about her is that the girl can *talk*. I cannot express enough how helpful it is for someone like me to be friends with someone like Carmen. She does ninety percent of the talking in our relationship, and we both prefer it that way.

"Oh my God, okay, so you know I said I was thinking about ending things with Peter, right, but I was putting it off because I *do* like the sex. Well, it was totally random, but this guy at the gym actually asked me out a few weeks ago and we've been seeing each other like multiple times a week."

"Wait, Hot Gym Guy asked you out?" I'm intrigued. I've been hearing about Hot Gym Guy for a while now.

"No, not him. This is a new one I hadn't seen before. He's bald but, like, tall and buff. His name's Edgar. He straight up started flirting with me and asked if he could take me out sometime. Who does that?" Carmen flushes happily and pops a tomato slice in her mouth.

It's true, I didn't know people still did that. Getting approached by a man is extremely rare. Heck, making eye contact with a man is extremely rare. Or it is if you're me.

Carmen goes on to update me about her sibling drama and her work drama. She always has drama. I'm familiar with most of her co-workers by name even though I've never met them. Carmen hasn't changed much since we met in gym class in sixth grade. Even at age eleven, she had copious amounts of hair and self-confidence. Becoming friends with her was easy: I mumbled under my breath about how running the mile was cruel and unusual punishment, she laughed and said, "You're funny! I like you." And that was that.

We've had more than our fair share of laughs and adventures together. We were like the stars of our own buddy comedy: her the brash, seductive one, me the snarky, mischievous one. But lately, every time we meet up and I hear about all the funny and fabulous things in Carmen's life, I feel more and more like the sidekick character. It's not necessarily a bad thing, but it sometimes makes me wonder what I'm doing with my life.

"Oh shit." Carmen covers her mouth with one hand, swallowing her mouthful of food, and stares pointedly over my shoulder. "I thought that was Mr. Edelman. Looks like him."

The name has an instantaneous and powerful effect on me. My stomach clenches and my face burns hotter than the tea light candle on the bar in front of us. I'm scared to turn around.

"Calm down, lady, it's not him." She snorts and spoons vinaigrette onto an oyster.

"Then why did you have to say it?" I exhale shakily and glance over my shoulder. There's a man with dark cropped hair and a profile that looks vaguely like—"And don't call him that."

"He'll always be Mr. Edelman to me." She's still smirking, like this is just too funny.

"Call him Alex," I mutter, and even just saying his name sours my stomach.

Carmen bursts into uncontrollable giggles.

"I still can't believe you—"

"Shut. Up."

"And you're so sensitive about it. I would want everyone to know. He was the *hot* teacher."

With a groan, I rest my head on the bar. It's sticky. "Can we please not talk about him?"

"Fine." Carmen slurps down the rest of her cocktail and motions to the bartender for another. "But I will never stop finding it hilarious. Imagine telling your sophomore-year self that you fucked Mr. Edelman."

Like I said: too much shared history. I resist the urge to push her off her stool and instead steal her fresh Plum Blossom for myself.

Chapter 4

It's not what it sounds like.

Unless what it sounds like is that I had sex with my high school teacher. Because technically, that is what happened. But *as an adult*!

This is why I don't like talking about it. People immediately get the wrong idea. I get it, it sounds bad. But it wasn't bad. Or maybe it was, and that's why it had to end.

I was twenty-five, and Alex—Mr. Edelman, our sophomore-year history teacher—was thirty-six. Our paths crossed virtually, on Jdate. It was during the height of dating apps, so it seemed like half the world's population was actively swiping and chatting. Including me. I came across his profile one night and felt a shit-eating grin spread across my face. I had absolutely had a major crush on him in high school (and so had most of my friends). He'd been married for a while but had gotten divorced. And his profile was so endearing, so earnest. Plus he was still smoking hot.

I read and re-read his bio, pacing around my apartment with hot-girl anthems blaring, drinking more Pinot than I'd normally drink at home alone.

"Oh, what the hell," I finally said to myself. "He probably won't respond." So I sent him a "like" and then messaged him: *Fancy seeing you here, Mr. E! Remember me?*

He replied almost immediately.

Of course I remember you, Mallory. How are you?

I had to sit down after that; my limbs had turned to jelly. *Of course* he remembered me? Was there a hint in there? Or was he just being polite?

Things are great! What about you? Still working at North Lake?

I am. Still teaching history. I'm one of the old-timers there now.

You are definitely not old, Mr. E.

There was a pause, and I thought that might be the end of our conversation. But then he wrote: *Call me Alex.*

I did a little silent shimmy-scream. I could not *believe* I was actually flirting with *Alex Edelman*. Holy crap. I took another gulp of wine, my fingers shaking as I tried to think of something suitably cool and funny to say in response.

So you're working in tech? He messaged me before I could reply—showing that he'd read my profile.

Yep. I'm a project manager.

Awesome. I knew you would be successful. You always had potential.

At this, I had to sit down. I curled my legs under me on the couch and read his message four or five times. It did something to me. I felt floaty, like my blood was shimmering. I felt like a teenager again, before my dreams were crushed. I felt proud.

It's just a job, but I'm pretty good at it, I wrote. *So tell me, Alex, have you had any luck on this app so far?*

There was a long, long pause. I wondered if he'd gone to sleep or maybe just decided that this was a bad idea.

Not until tonight.

I threw myself back on the couch and kicked my legs in the air. This was *happening*!

We had long conversations on the app for the next week, and then we moved on to video chats. There was something so intimate about having this virtual tête-à-tête with him, I could feel the sexual tension through the screen. It got to the point where we were texting each other all day and having video calls multiple nights each week. Finally, that summer, we went on our first date. We met at San Fermo, an Italian restaurant in Ballard, where they had set up cozy outdoor tables under strands of string lights. I wore a floral sundress I'd had since college that I worried was too short, subtly tugging at the hem with shaking hands as I walked up to him and said hello.

But what started as something that made me feel good about myself—He saw my potential! He liked me!—devolved into something that made me insecure. We dated for over a year, and it got pretty serious—we stayed over at each other's places frequently, we talked about the future. But we never met each other's families.

At first, it was easy to justify why our relationship was so isolated. People were staying home and social distancing. The world was in and out of quarantine. But after the first vaccines came out, we started running out of excuses. So we just stopped talking about meeting each other's families, about going out with friends. Because deep down we knew that they would think it was wrong. That we shouldn't be together.

One rainy fall night, we ran into a mutual acquaintance at the movie theater. It was a girl from my high school class, Tessa Jordan. We said a quick hello, and the look on her face was like... it was like she was on a gossip-only diet and she'd been starving in the desert for weeks and we were the juiciest gossip steak she'd ever seen. I could practically see a thought bubble over her head with the messages she was about to send to everyone she still knew from school.

That was when I started thinking seriously about ending it. I didn't want to retroactively tarnish my own reputation, but more than that, I didn't want Alex to lose his job. Maybe that wouldn't happen, but how could we be sure? If a single person claimed that we'd had an inappropriate relationship when I was sixteen, he might never work again.

He understood my concerns, but he didn't think it was as big a deal.

"We're both adults. You were twenty-five when we started dating" was his typical argument.

"If it's so fine, then why haven't I met your parents?"

He never had a good answer for that.

I loved the time we spent together. But I didn't love the way being with him made me feel. There was a little voice in my head that kept getting stronger that said I didn't want to hide. I didn't want to be hidden from his family, to have a secret relationship, to never move forward.

So I ended it. Out of the blue, out of nowhere. I took the coward's way out and I texted him that it was over. I didn't even tell him in person. I'm not proud of the way I did it, but I know that ending it was inevitable. We weren't meant to be. No matter how many times I've sobbed alone on my couch, wishing that I could curl up against him and feel the weight of his arm around me as we Netflix-surfed together. But I've been strong enough to resist him whenever he's reached out. I wonder when he'll give up for good. A part of me that simply yearns to feel wanted hopes that he doesn't.

On Wednesday afternoon when I'm fully immersed in a planning meeting with a team of engineers, I'm annoyed by the insistent buzzing of my phone.

Probably a spam call. I glance at it and see the name Eddy Gilberstein flashing on the screen. What? Why is my great-uncle calling me? And why can't boomers learn how to send a text message?

"Mallory, what's the latest on the executive review of the last build?"

Shoot. I have not been paying attention and have no idea what this person just asked me. It takes me a second to refocus, but I manage to stammer out a BS answer. I get caught up in work details for the next few hours and forget about the phone call entirely. It's only when I'm heading out the door for my walk, opening my podcast app, that I realize I have a voicemail.

I play the voicemail and start my trek up the hill, the cool evening air riffling my long hair out behind me.

"Mallory, it's your uncle Eddy here," comes a deep voice tinged with the American Jewish accent all my older relatives seem to have. "Gimme a call back, would you? Been tryin' to reach you. Thanks."

I raise my arms in exasperation. That's it? Honestly, doesn't he know people these days need more information? A phone call is sort of a big commitment. Anyway, it's already past eight P.M. in Florida. I'll call him back tomorrow.

But I don't get the chance. In the morning, when there are five minutes left in my yoga class, my phone rings again. I sigh. The final Savasana is my favorite part of class. Oh well.

"Hello?" I answer the phone, mopping my hairline with a clean towel.

"Mallory, it's Eddy here."

I know. But I'm not going to explain caller ID to him right now.

"Yes, hi, how are you?" I cross the kitchen and start pulling smoothie ingredients out of the fridge. "Sorry I missed your call yesterday."

"Fine, fine."

"What's going on?" I plunk a tub of yogurt and a carton of oat milk on the counter.

"Well, listen." He pauses, somewhat hesitantly. "You probably know I've been handling some of Lottie's affairs. Helping Leonard out."

"That's nice of you." I peel a banana and add it to the blender.

"Yeah, well. So here's the thing. Lottie left you something."

I stop, clutching a handful of spinach leaves. "She did?"

"Mallory, she left you a house. Pebble Cottage. Down in Reina Beach."

I'm silent for so long that Uncle Eddy clears his throat.

"Mallory? You know Pebble Cottage, right? The house your mom and Trish grew up in?"

My brain whirs like an overheated computer. "Uh…yeah? I mean, why—why me? Lottie had five grandkids."

"Well…As I understand it, it's because your sister, Maeve, is married and settled, and the other kids are still in school."

"Ellie's in college, and she already lives in Florida. Why not leave it to her? Or to Mom or Trish?" I take a deep breath and realize I need to sit down, so I do, on the kitchen floor. "Uncle Eddy…are you sure she meant to leave it to me specifically?"

He lets out a booming laugh. "Of course! She left Pebble Cottage to Mallory Rosen. Clear as day."

As I sit cross-legged on the floor, my gaze lingers on the floating shelf above the microwave. That shelf is the extent of my home maintenance experience. It took me a month to decide what to put in that spot, two weeks to commit to buying the shelf, and countless hours of YouTube tutorials before I felt confident enough to drill into the wall. And then I accidentally drilled a hole the size of a quarter and had to call my dad to come and help me fix it. That shelf is currently telling me that I am in no way qualified to be the owner of Pebble Cottage.

"But, Eddy, a house is…" I trail off. A house is a lot of things. A huge responsibility. An even bigger surprise. A windfall. And, now that I'm wrapping my brain around it, it's an honor that Lottie chose *me*. "Well, I'm honored," I say finally.

"Of course, there are some stipulations," Eddy says.

Wait, what?

I'm wary of whatever he's going to say next. Lottie had her own particular way of doing things. It was always her way or the highway.

"In exchange for the house, Lottie has requested that you look after Leonard. And that you not sell the house, uh, while Leonard is still alive."

A ringing silence follows these words. I don't know what to say. This is so Lottie.

"I see," I say slowly. "But...what does that mean exactly, look after Gramps? Doesn't he live in a senior community? Aren't there people to look after him?"

"It's an independent living community. There are staff, like house cleaners and nurses, but I think Lottie wanted to make sure someone would see that he's doing okay. That he's not too lonely, that he's taking care of himself. That kind of thing."

"That makes sense." But what doesn't make sense is, again, *why me*? I'm starting to get heart palpitations. If one single, solitary shelf is the extent of my homeowner qualifications, my qualifications as the caretaker of a grandpa are nonexistent. I don't even own a plant.

I say the first thing that occurs to me next: "But I live in Seattle."

"I know. I'm just the messenger here. Maybe she was hoping you would live in the house."

This is so unexpected, it takes me a second to articulate a response. I settle on "The house has tenants, doesn't it?"

"Well, she had tenants. Their lease is ending next week, and they're not renewing. Maybe they were only staying for Lottie. But the mortgage was paid off ages ago."

I have so many questions, I don't know which ones to ask first.

"Does Gramps know about this arrangement?"

"He knows Lottie left the house to you. That's it. But your folks know about it and all. I'll send over some documents with all the particulars."

"Okay." *Details.* Suddenly my mind floods with all the details I'm going to have to think about. Insurance. Maintenance. Taxes.

"All right, so if you have any questions, call me up. Okay, Mal?"

"Yeah. Thanks, Eddy."

A few minutes later, I sit down with my smoothie and my oat milk latte and read through the documents from Eddy. There are a couple of things I'm supposed to sign. It's all in legalese. I don't understand a word of it.

Luckily, I know some lawyers.

Chapter 5

My dad sits at my parents' kitchen table, reading the house documents. One finger wanders up to scratch the top of his head. I sit across from him, hunched over, biting my thumbnail.

Finally, he tucks his reading glasses into his shirt pocket. "This all looks pretty standard, Mal Gal. After you sign here, we'll send this back to Leonard and Lottie's representation, and it'll be official. You're a homeowner."

I exhale, only just realizing how tense I've been. "And are we sure there's…?" I trail off, jiggling my leg nervously. "I mean, what about… Maeve?"

"Maeve?" my mother asks from the kitchen, where she's making a pot of tea. "Mom left it to *you*."

"Yes, but Maeve is…"

Older, wiser, has caretaking experience? She's a mom, for gosh sakes! a panicked voice in my head squeals.

Hear me out, says another, more rational voice in my brain. *Could this possibly be your little-sister impostor syndrome talking?*

"I guess that's true," I say out loud.

"What?" Mom asks.

Talking to the voices in my head: Add another tally to the column marked "Unfit to Care for a House/Grandpa."

It's been over twenty-four hours now, and I still can't wrap my mind around it. There I was, living my life the same way day in and day out, looking after myself and my apartment, and all of a sudden I've inherited...Pebble Cottage and Leonard Gilberstein.

"Mom," I say slowly. She places a mug of chamomile tea in front of me and sits down. "Do you have any idea why Lottie would do this?"

"Well..." She tilts her head to the side and blinks, staring into the middle distance.

Dad chimes in. "Lottie never explained her reasoning to anyone. As a rule."

"That is true," Mom says, "but she told me enough over the years that I think I can puzzle it out. She saw Gramps in you, Mallory."

"Huh?" I don't know what I expected her to say, but it wasn't that.

"Ever since you were little, she said you were like him. You both have a quietness about you. You both prefer to be on the edge of the action, observing, rather than in the thick of it."

"Oh." I didn't know I shared this with Gramps. It certainly rings true for my own personality. Growing up, though, I always figured Gramps was in his own little world because he was busy and important, thinking brilliant scientific thoughts. It's funny to think that maybe he's actually just an introvert, like me. It sort of makes me smile.

"Well." I bite my lip nervously. "Hand me the pen. Let's do this."

I try to remember the last time I saw the house. My grandparents lived there for decades, raising their two daughters there. They moved into their beachfront retirement community when I was probably twelve or thirteen, so my memories of the house are all from early childhood. I remember the room with the boxy old TV where we watched Cartoon Network—the brown room. Brown carpets and dark-brown, wood-paneled walls. I remember a giant sunroom, enclosed on all sides by screens, with slightly rusty deck chairs and a glass-topped table where Lottie and Mom and Trish would play Scrabble and drink iced tea. I remember stepping down with bare feet onto a cobbled pathway—the stones were always warm from the sun, even at night—and feeling enveloped in the tiny, overgrown backyard, full of lush green bushes, short trees with spiky leaves, and St. Augustine grass. It smelled green. The air was always humid and sweet. And of course, there was the pool. It was small and oblong, shaped like a kidney bean. At night, the water glowed teal from lights under the surface. I liked to watch the water ripple in the evenings as lightning bugs zapped around overhead.

I haven't thought about the place in ages. It became a forgotten memory after Lottie and Gramps moved into Sandy Shores, with its two fancy pools, the endless rooms to explore—the party room, the library, the gym—and, of course, the beach. I'm glad I can remember details about Pebble Cottage now.

I feel like I'm getting a handle on owning the house, so I turn my attention to the other part of the package deal: Gramps.

Midmorning on a Friday, I begin typing an email to him, and then I stop. If I'm going to do this properly, I should put in a little more effort. So I pick up the phone instead.

It rings for a long time before he answers.

"'Lo?"

"Gramps? Hi, it's Mallory. Did I catch you at a bad time?"

"Hello, Mallory. No, no. I was just... resting."

I glance at the time. It's almost two in the afternoon in Florida. Was he sleeping?

"Well, how are you?" I cringe—I have no idea what I'm supposed to be saying or asking.

"Oh, fine. I'm fine, thanks for asking." There's a pause. "How are you?"

"Me? I'm good! Things are great!" *Ugh. Probably not the right thing to say to someone who's grieving.* "I mean. You know."

"Do I?" He sounds thoughtful. "I can't say I do. I don't know much about how you spend your time."

"Uh..." Is he asking me or just commenting? Besides, this was supposed to be about how *he's* doing. "Are you feeling okay? Are you...eating?" *Geez, I am terrible at this.*

He gives a wry chuckle. "Eating, yes, yes. Trish has been bringing me groceries every two days. Apparently she thinks I'm eating for ten."

"Trish is bringing you groceries? That's good." Does that mean Gramps doesn't know how to buy groceries on his own? Was that something Lottie always did? Or is it because he's too depressed to do it himself?

I am in way over my head here.

"All right, well, will you let me know if you need anything?"

"I won't be needing anything, Mallory. But thank you for calling."

"Wait, but—"

He hangs up.

Crap.

I guess Gramps didn't get the memo that he's supposed to *let* me take care of him.

But all I can do is try, right? It's not like Lottie will know if I'm not fully upholding my end of the bargain. That said, it doesn't feel great to shirk on my responsibilities to my dead grandmother. So I promise myself that I'll try again next week. I'll give Gramps a call just to chat, and I'll see if I can glean any insights about how he's really doing.

But next week has a mind of its own. Turns out being a homeowner means I have a whole list of problems I never thought I'd have to deal with.

Chapter 6

My mind should be on work today, but instead I'm mentally calculating how much of my paycheck will go toward the house without tenants paying rent. The mortgage is paid off, but there are still taxes, utilities, and insurance. Basically, it'll be like I'm still repaying my debt to Mom and Dad. The debt I just finished paying off. *Not ideal.*

That evening, I decide to call my parents to discuss what to do. I'm standing on my tiny balcony trying to enjoy the warm evening sun but mostly feeling the chilly spring breeze. My next-door neighbor steps out onto their balcony and lights a joint.

We don't acknowledge each other, though we're so close that we might as well be standing in the same room. We've lived next door to each other for over two years but have never had a conversation. The most contact we've had is when we pass each other in the hallway and they raise their chin in a silent greeting. I would recognize their cropped blue hair and facial piercings anywhere, but I have no idea what their name is.

"It's not ideal that the tenants are leaving, but maybe it's for the best. At least I won't have to be a landlord," I tell Mom. My neighbor's eyes slide toward me.

"Aren't you going to find new tenants?" Mom asks.

"Couldn't I just leave the house empty, and, I don't know, use it as a vacation home?"

My neighbor suddenly chokes and wheezes through a fit of coughs. Damn, that sounded bougie. I angle my body slightly away from them.

"Absolutely not!" Dad's voice sounds distant, like he's yelling from the kitchen. "Leaving a house empty is the best way to ruin it. You'll be dealing with mold, rot, infestations, break-ins, not to mention—"

"Okay, okay. So now I have to find new tenants. How do I even do that?"

I rest my elbows on the balcony railing. I am so not cut out for this. My pulse is racing from the stress of it all. I don't know anyone in Reina Beach aside from my relatives. How on earth am I supposed to find new tenants to live in the house? And what does a landlord do exactly—am I going to have to talk to these people on a regular basis? Like, on the phone?

This is so far outside my comfort zone.

"Trish already gave me the number of a good property manager that everyone uses in Reina Beach. Since the house is across the country, you'll need the help from someone local to find tenants."

"Okay. Good idea." I sigh. "I didn't know owning a house would be so hard." I choose not to mention that I also have no idea what a property manager is. I'm sure my parents—and my neighbor—are questioning my intelligence enough as it is.

My neighbor snuffs out their joint on their balcony railing, staring unblinking at me the whole time. I can read the look plainly enough: They think I'm upper-middle-class scum. I feel my face flush as I avoid eye contact—easier said than done when you're five feet apart. I wait for them to go back inside their apartment before I speak again.

"Speaking of things that aren't easy. Gramps is not very amenable to me taking care of him. He barely wanted to talk to me on the phone. And Trish is already bringing him groceries, so what am I supposed to do for him? I honestly have no idea. I don't know what Lottie wanted me to do. I don't know how to take care of an octogenarian."

"Have regularly scheduled meetings with him. Every day at a certain time. Have an agenda with boxes to check off, like is he eating, exercising, socializing."

My mom is using her attorney voice. Her words are crisp and confident, and for some reason they make me cringe. I may not know how to take care of Gramps, but I have an instinct that he wouldn't like regularly scheduled meetings with an agenda. Maybe it's because of the last phone call I had with him. It was like he couldn't wait to hang up. Do I really want to put us both through that every day?

"I'm not sure if that sounds like something he would like, Mom."

"Oh, Mallory." She sounds irritable now. It also sounds like she's chopping a carrot that has personally offended her. "You'll have to figure it out. You're nearly thirty years old. I'll send you the property manager's number. Call us back when you have solutions instead of just problems."

She hangs up.

I stare at my phone, stung. *Excuse me.* I am only twenty-eight. Rude.

I sit back in my chair and gaze out the window. The day outside is clear and blue. The sun glints off the urban buildings of Lower Queen Anne and flashes off the Space Needle in the distance. The idea of hiring a property manager to help me feels like a huge weight off my shoulders already, but the idea of a phone call fills me with dread.

All I have is this guy's name and phone number. I would really prefer to text him first. But I figure it might be an office landline, so I have no choice. I stall for a few more minutes, placing a DoorDash order for some pad thai for lunch, and then I arrange a notepad and pen on my desk and call the number.

"Hello," comes a man's voice, slightly out of breath.

"Hi, is this—" I double-check the name I'd scrawled at the top of my notepad. "Daniel McKinnon?"

"Yes it is." He pants, and I wonder if he's having a heart attack or something. "And who do I have the pleasure of speaking with?"

"Um. My name is Mallory Rosen?" I'm aware that this comes out like a question, something that happens a lot when I'm flustered.

"What can I do for you, Ms. Rosen?" His breathing is really distracting.

"Look, are you okay? Are you having some sort of cardiac problem? I won't feel bad if you need to hang up and call nine-one-one."

He chuckles, and it's a nice mellow sound. It simultaneously calms me and makes me feel like I've just swallowed some warm vanilla pudding.

"I'm not experiencing an emergency, but thank you for your concern." He sounds normal now, and I hear something like the crunch of gravel. "I was on my bike. Just walking into my office now. So please, tell me what I can help you with."

"Right. Well, I've come into some property." Boy, that sounds pretentious. "And I need some help managing it." Now I'm just repeating his job title at him. *Me have property, you help manage.* I try to sound somewhat intelligent. "It's a single-family home. I asked around and you came highly recommended. I live in Seattle, so I could use the help of someone local."

"Seattle, huh? I was wondering where your area code was from." I hear the squeak of an office chair. I have no idea what he looks like, so I imagine a generic forty-something man, possibly bald, definitely sweaty from biking in the Florida heat. "What kind of help are you looking for, specifically?"

"At the moment, I could use some help finding new tenants. The old ones left."

"Scared them away, did you? What, did you tell them about Seattle politics?" He laughs again, and my stomach squirms. Sweaty and balding he may be, but he has a nice laugh.

"That's definitely something I can help you with," he continues. "Are you aware of any repairs that need to be done on the place, big or small?"

"I'm... not sure. I haven't exactly seen the place. In a while, I mean."

There's a pause. He's surely wondering how someone as incompetent as me became a homeowner.

"In situations like this, I usually send my maintenance guy out for a quick inspection. Would that be okay with you?"

"Yes! Absolutely." I feel a wash of relief. For a moment there, I was afraid he was going to tell me to fly down there.

My phone pings and I glance down to see a message from DoorDash.

"Oh, my lunch is here. I better go grab it before someone else does."

"What do you eat for lunch up there in Seattle?"

"Today? I ordered pad thai. Spicy. With tofu."

"We don't get much Thai food down here. I'd try it, though. Not sure about the tofu, but I could be convinced."

I feel myself grinning and fidgeting with a lock of my hair. Wait. Is this property manager flirting with me about tofu? Or am I delusional? Trish said everyone knows this guy—this is probably why. He's friendly and a good conversationalist. He's the kind of person who can make small talk about lunch feel interesting.

"Don't worry, I won't try to convince you to eat tofu." I'm still grinning. "I really just order it because they charge extra for shrimp and the chicken is usually dry and sad..." I trail off, grin nowhere to be found. Why am I suddenly talking about dry chicken? *Why?*

He doesn't say anything. I managed to stump Mr. Small Talk Expert with my babbling. I wonder if there's an online course I could take about how to win friends and influence people. Or at least how to make normal conversation. Or, heck, how not to ruin a conversation by talking about dry chicken.

"You still there?"

His voice somehow zaps me out of my humiliation. It's just so smooth. I could listen to him talk my ear off about home maintenance, renter's insurance, whatever it is that property managers talk about.

"I am. But my lunch might not be."

"You better run and grab it, then."

"Yes, I should." I don't know what it is about him—I'm usually in a hurry to hang up the phone, but not with him. "I'll email you the address of the house. My aunt should be able to deliver the key to your office if that works for you."

"That all sounds fine." He gives me his email address, which I make him repeat twice because I keep dropping my pen.

"Great. So, I'll email you with the details. And you can let me know when the inspection will be."

"I will. Enjoy your tofu." There's a hint of laughter in his voice.

"Thanks. You too." I hang up just as I realize what I said. My head slowly lowers to meet my desk. I simply can't be trusted with words coming out of my mouth.

Oh no, my lunch.

Mercifully, the plastic bag containing my pad thai is still waiting for me. I've had so many packages stolen here that I've lost count. I don't know what I would do if someone took my food. I get hangry.

Later that night, I can't stop thinking about Gramps, about how to find out how he's actually doing. Finally, I sit at my desk and open my laptop. It takes me a while to think of the words, but soon they come pouring out of me. I let out all my thoughts and questions and frustrations and worries. I re-read it to make sure I don't sound too neurotic or too whiny or too anything. And then I hit SEND on the email to Gramps.

Chapter 7

His reply is waiting for me when I wake up in the morning. I do a double take at the time stamp: He emailed me just after three in the morning his time. *Gramps, what are you doing?*

I read it on my phone, still tucked in bed. It requires a lot of scrolling.

Dear Mallory,

I read your letter with curiosity and delight. You're my second-eldest granddaughter, and I never really got to know you much. When you were growing up, I was still working, and my work was all-consuming. Although I do recall that you had a deep passion for a film called The Lion King. *Your dedication to this film was so apparent that I finally sat down one day and watched it with you and your sister. I cried when the little lion cub's father died. I thought that was too sad for you girls to be watching. Although when I was a young boy, we watched* Bambi, *so who am I to judge?*

This morning, a great blue heron visited me. It perched on the balcony railing just outside my bedroom. We had a lovely chat.

A great blue heron was outside the hospital window when Lottie left me. She loved those birds. I think it was waiting for her. I never believed in souls. There's no scientific proof that they exist and there never will be. But I can't shake my belief in Heaven. It is contradictory, I know. My mother believed in Heaven, and that gave her comfort when my father died. I didn't much care what happened to him. But I like to think that my mother is with him now, and that she is happy. Naturally, I like to imagine Lottie is in paradise now too, with her beloved parents. They'll have a lot to catch up on. Perhaps the heron was her guide.

Your letter reminded me of the things I used to worry about as a young man. How will I pay the mortgage and support my family? Will I be promoted and will I get the grant I need to do my next research project?

Cherish it, Mallory. Cherish your youth and this time in your life. It seems endless now, but it's fleeting.

Here I'll remain, in God's waiting room,
Affectionately yours,
Dr. Gramps

I read it a second time, impatiently wiping away the tears leaking from my eyes.

I don't have a response. What is there to say to an email like that? But I can't stop thinking about it as I go about my day. The part about the heron makes me want to sob. Lottie had loved those birds, just like Gramps said. So what if the heron was her visiting him or sending him a message? Did he think of it that way? Did it bring him comfort, or just make him sad?

As the day wears on, I fixate on the deep sadness behind his words, and on the phrase "God's waiting room." I think I know what I have to do. I need to get Gramps a therapist.

It takes a lot of googling but I find one: Shauna Mellors. Her office is in St. Pete, not too far from where Gramps lives. I email Trish, asking for Gramps's insurance information so I can schedule him an appointment. Trish calls me instead. I'm in a meeting where

I'm mostly just there to take notes, so I turn off my camera and make sure I'm muted before answering.

"Hi, Trish," I say.

"Why are you trying to make him a therapy appointment, anyway?" Trish cuts straight to the point. She crunches on something, and I guess that it's her lunch break.

"He sounded so sad in his email. I mean, he signed off saying he's in God's waiting room. Like he's waiting to die."

Trish lets out a sharp laugh. "That's what they call Florida! God's waiting room."

"Oh. I didn't know that." I chew on my cuticle, my resolve flagging for a moment. But then it strengthens again. I am supposed to look after Gramps, and he's clearly grieving. Therapy is the right move. "Still, he should talk to someone to process his feelings about losing Lottie."

"Spoken like a true millennial," Trish snorts. "You're not wrong, Mal, but I don't see him agreeing to this."

"So can you help me? Can you ask him if he'll try it?"

Trish pauses and I hear the rustle of paper and the slurp of a drink. "Yeah, sure, I can mention it when I drop off his groceries tomorrow."

"Thank you! That'll be a huge help."

Trish's agreement helps me feel like I'm doing the right thing. I call Shauna Mellors and explain the situation and get Gramps scheduled for his first appointment this Thursday.

The next day, my boss sends me a message.

Kat White: *Hey, Mallory, how are things going with you?*

This is so vague and out of the blue, I stare at the message for a full minute. Why is she asking? We don't make small talk like this.

Mallory Rosen: *Things are good, thanks. Not too busy yet this week, but that'll change in a few days with the V2 console beta launch.*

Kat White: *Great. You seemed a little distracted this morning at the EngPlat meeting, so I wanted to check in. Is there anything you want to talk about?*

My armpits start to sweat. Maybe I should just tell her. Tell her what's going on with the house and my family obligations. But it feels wrong on so many levels: Kat is not my friend. She's my boss. And on top of that, I don't want to tell her anything that might make her doubt my capability at work.

Mallory Rosen: *No, everything's fine. I probably just need another cup of coffee. Just one of those days! I'll make sure to caffeinate better tomorrow!*

She types, then stops, then types again.

Kat White: *Sounds good and no worries.*

I exhale hard. I'm going to have to put in some extra work this week to prove to Kat that I'm just as competent as ever.

Before I can forget, I send a quick email to Gramps telling him about the appointment I scheduled for him. After the confessional emails we'd exchanged, I feel a twinge of awkwardness now, sending him this brief, business-like message. But two people have pinged me in the sixty seconds it took to write the email; I really need to refocus on work. I brush away the awkward feelings and tell myself I'm doing the right thing. *Taking care of Gramps: check.*

It's only at the end of the day when I come up for air that I realize Gramps never responded.

I also got a call from the property manager, Daniel McKinnon, who left a voicemail. I listen to his message. He says that his inspection person found a few problems that need to be addressed—some plumbing issues and a minor structural problem. As I listen to this, I feel my blood pressure rise, especially when Daniel utters the words "maybe up to ten grand." I'm going to need a second opinion. I start typing a text to Trish to ask if she knows of anyone else who can take a look at the house, but before I finish the message, she sends one to me.

Listen, Dad didn't seem crazy about the therapy idea. Maybe you should cancel it and try again some other time.

Great. On top of everything else, Gramps will probably be mad at me now. I should have just talked to him about it directly. What was I thinking?

My heart pounds and I realize that I'm gnashing my back teeth together. I try to relax my jaw and take a deep breath. *Compartmentalize, Mal.* I'll think about the house and Gramps later. Right now, I need to meet Carmen at Green Lake. I suggested it in place of our usual happy hour, because I'm hoping a long walk will clear my head.

Carmen gives me a tight hug, her floral-scented hair pressing into my face. We're both wearing black leggings and Patagonia fleece jackets. It had been a sunny day and there's still a thread of spring warmth in the air.

"Everything with Edgar exploded in my face." We're walking at a quick pace. Ducks splash in the shallows of the lake, the surface of which is dotted with a few kayaks and one lone paddleboard.

"Oh no, what happened?"

"He was *married*."

I grimace. "Seriously?"

"Separated from his wife, but yes. One day she just showed up at his place. Just straight up let herself in with her own key."

"That's awful. Did she know about you?"

"Not specifically." Carmen glowers and picks up the pace so we're basically power walking. "She saw me sitting on the couch and said something to Edgar about having another one already."

I groan.

"Yeah. But this was the first I'd heard of *her*. So I was like, What the hell is going on? But they went and started bickering like an old married couple—which they are!"

"Forget him," I say. "You can do so much better."

"I'm never uttering the name Edgar again." Carmen tosses her hair and asks what's new with me.

You know, just inherited a cottage and a fully grown grandpa from my dead grandma... same old, same old...

"Well..." I say. My phone pings in my pocket, and I check it automatically. It's an email from the therapist, Shauna.

Hi Mallory,

Unfortunately, cancellation within 24 hours of the appointment time incurs a $100 fee. And from everything you told me during our call, it's my professional opinion that Leonard would benefit greatly from counseling, if only a few sessions. If you can encourage him to attend the appointment, it would be a win-win. If not, you can send the money via check or PayPal.

All the best,
Dr. Mellors

"Seriously?" I mutter. Reluctantly, I open Paypal and send her the money.

Carmen glances at me. "What's wrong?"

I pick up the pace, pumping my arms. It feels good to get the blood flowing. "Some stuff has happened..."

I fill her in on all of it.

"Let me get this straight." Carmen pants as we zoom past a group of moms pushing strollers. "You're attempting to do welfare checks on your grandpa from across the country. Don't even get me started on scheduling him an appointment without asking him first. And you have this house that needs tenants *and* repairs? And you're just going to take this Daniel guy's word for it without laying eyes on him *or* the house?"

She raises an eyebrow at me. She's gorgeously flushed with a glowy sheen of sweat on her cheeks. Meanwhile, I have reason to suspect that I look like an overripe tomato with frizzles of hair framing my face.

"Well, it sounds bad when you say it like that."

Of course she's right. I had no business making that appointment for Gramps, but I don't know how else to help him from afar. And the house situation is a mess. I can't spend ten grand that I don't have to fix up a house that I haven't even seen in years.

"You should *be* there," Carmen says.

"Excuse me?" I say, even though my brain was clunking toward the same realization.

"See what's wrong with the house. Spend time with your grandpa. Get to know him, otherwise you won't be able to do shit."

"You're eloquent, as always."

"I'm right, as always."

I slow to a stop, breathing hard with my hands on my hips. I gaze out at the murky depths of the lake.

I can see how it will unfold: Gramps will be annoyed that I'm intruding in his life, he'll be surly because of the therapy appointment debacle, and I'll feel like a useless lump. I'll meet with the property manager, he'll explain what's wrong with Pebble Cottage, and I'll just nod and accept it, because I won't understand anything he's saying. And then I'll shell out money I don't have to pay for the repairs, because what choice do I have? I can't let the house fall apart.

But despite this uninviting prospect, I know, deep down, that

Carmen's right. I'm no use to anyone being all the way across the country. The problem is, Kat won't be thrilled about me requesting to take PTO on short notice—so I'll have to work from Florida. Which Kat also wouldn't be thrilled about. So hopefully she won't find out.

"Well, crap," I say. "I guess I'm going to Florida."

Chapter 8

Two days later, I'm rolling my carry-on suitcase down the hall when I stop in front of my blue-haired neighbor's door. I listen for a moment and hear them bustling around in the kitchen, probably making breakfast. I hesitate, gather all my courage, and knock.

They answer the door without a word, their face scrunched in confusion.

"Hi." I give a wave that's too big, considering that we're standing a foot apart. "I live next door."

"Yeah." Their mouth twitches in amusement. "The reluctant landlord."

"Uh... Right. Anyway, I'm going to be out of town for a couple days, and I was wondering, if you see any packages by my door, could you grab them? And I'll get them from you when I'm back."

"Sure. How many are you expecting?"

"I... I'm not sure."

They stare.

"I shop a lot." I laugh weakly and shift my tote bag higher up on my shoulder. "I lose track."

"Okay... Do you have any, like, plants that need to be watered?"

"No, no plants."

Their face drops just enough for me to notice. Great, now they're judging me for not being a plant person.

"Got it. Will do."

"Thank you so much."

"What's your name?" It feels painfully awkward for them to ask this question now, after a full conversation, not to mention after living next door for two years. And it feels even more awkward that it didn't occur to *me* to ask *their* name first.

"Mallory. You?"

"Sam."

"Okay, thanks, Sam, I really appreciate it. I owe you one."

I start to walk away when Sam says, "What's your number? Just in case."

"Oh, right. Why didn't I think of that?" I give a little snort laugh that makes me wonder, for the thousandth time, why I am the way that I am.

We exchange numbers, and I silently hope that Sam won't actually text or call me. And then I feel bad, because they are doing me a favor. I thank them again before heading to the bus stop.

Arriving in Tampa at four P.M. was a mistake. Both the sun and the snarling traffic are giving me an inhospitable welcome. Even with the rental car's AC blasting, I'm sweating by the time I get to Sandy Shores Retirement Village an hour later. I find the visitor parking, and start hoofing toward Gramps's building. This place is a compound with multiple buildings sprawled across a campus dotted with palm trees. I know the way by heart. The sticky heat is oh so familiar to me, and it's kind of nice after a long Seattle winter. It sinks into my bones in a comforting way, although I know I'll be sick of it soon enough.

In the center of the campus is a grassy area with a large white gazebo. A bunch of seniors are milling around in workout clothes, chatting and mopping their faces with white towels. They probably just finished tai chi or something.

"Maeve?"

I do a double take. One of the women is approaching me, beaming.

"Uh, no, I'm Mallory. Her younger sister. Hi…" I know I should know her name. She's petite with a cloud of blondish hair, light-blue eyes rimmed with black mascara, and an incredibly white smile. She's also kind of hot for an octogenarian. Underneath her lilac Lycra, she looks strong.

"Angela!" She spreads her hands. "I was friends with your grandmother." She has a lyrical Southern accent.

"Yes, of course. Hi, Angela." I feel disheveled, and I probably smell like airplane. I plunk my tote bag down on my suitcase.

"Here to visit Leonard?" she asks, her voice sympathetic.

"Yeah, I am. Just for a few days."

"It's good that you're here." The way she says it makes me pause.

"Have you seen him lately? How's he doing?" I ask.

"Oh yes, I see him at meals here and there. And at the pool."

"He's been swimming?"

"No, no, he brings his newspaper down in the mornings." Angela bites her lip and looks away for a second. "Lottie used to swim laps, you know. In the mornings."

"Oh…" My breath catches at the sadness of this revelation. Gramps still goes down to the pool like he used to with Lottie. Only now he does it alone.

"He hasn't been coming to poker night or the weekly breakfast with the guys. You know, he used to always join those. The men have been wondering where he's gotten to."

"He's still grieving," I say uncertainly.

"Of course, of course." Angela flips her towel over one shoulder. "But you know, Mallory, Patrick Zhang lost his wife last month and he's been coming to everything. Every breakfast, every bingo night, every event."

"Has he?" This information is the opposite of comforting. If Patrick Zhang is throwing himself into social activities in the wake of his grief, does that mean Gramps should be doing that, too? It's one thing to be an introvert, a trait Gramps and I apparently share, but what's the right way to get over losing your spouse? Is that even something you *can* get over?

I am so very unqualified. I should go home immediately. Gramps doesn't need someone like me bumbling around, asking awkward questions. He needs someone with more life experience, someone who can understand him.

"Angela," I begin haltingly, "I'm supposed to help Gramps, somehow, like make him feel better, I think. It's what Lottie wanted. But I have no idea how I'm supposed to do that."

She blinks her bright eyes at me, and I fear I've just completely overshared. But then she laughs.

"Sweetheart. When it comes to grandchildren, your mere presence is what lifts us up. You don't have to *do* anything. Being around young folks invigorates us." She gives my shoulder a firm squeeze, and I catch a waft of a powdery perfume smell. "You have a good heart, coming here to be with Leonard. Just be yourself."

Wow. Embarrassingly, tears spring to my eyes.

"Okay. Thanks. I guess I needed a pep talk."

She makes a *shoo* motion with her hands. "Get on up there. I'll see you and Leonard around, I'm sure."

I give a little wave, and she trots back to her friends.

Gramps's condo is on the sixth floor of building C. I knock and hitch a smile onto my face.

"Hi, Gramps!"

"Mallory, hello, welcome." He grins back and reaches for my bags.

"Don't worry, I got these," I say, trying to scoot past him through the doorway. He wrests the bags from me anyway and shuffles down the hall toward the guest room. I kick off my Birkenstocks and pause, the white tile floor cool under my feet. It's a little dark in here; he has half of the blinds drawn, shutting out the gulf view. I feel the lack of Lottie so distinctly. When she was alive, their home was bright and full of energy, with fresh flowers in a blue vase on the table, and jars full of pretzel sticks and Fig Newtons. With a jolt, I notice that the snack jars are still on the counter. The pretzel jar is a quarter full. The Fig Newton jar is empty apart from crumbs.

"Did you get lost?" Gramps calls.

I follow him toward the room I'll be staying in. Impulsively, I throw my arms around him. He chuckles and pats both of my shoulders lightly. He smells like the shaving cream they used to let us play with when I was three or four. I take that as a good sign—he's been shaving and, I assume, showering. Keeping up his personal hygiene.

"Thank you," he says.

"You're welcome," I say stoutly, my arms swinging back to my sides. I feel like I'm four again.

"So, here's your room." He gestures to the bed—a queen with the same seashell-patterned comforter that's been there my entire life. There's also a beachy white dresser, decorated with a bowl of sand dollars and an oval-shaped wicker picture frame. It contains a picture of a young Lottie, pregnant with Trish, sitting on the beach with my mom as a toddler. They're both beaming and squinting their eyes against the sun.

"You can put your things away in these drawers, if you like. I know you're only here for a few days, but best to be comfortable, isn't it?"

I nod. I should ask him how he's feeling or something. But it doesn't feel like the right time. We look at each other for a long moment, both of us smiling placidly. It is an exceedingly awkward moment. That's when I realize I've never really been alone with Gramps. Usually, we're surrounded by family. What have I gotten myself into?

I blurt out, "Gramps, I'm really sorry about that therapy appointment. I should have asked you first, I…"

He gives a tiny shrug. "Pfft. No need to apologize."

"But…"

"You probably want something to eat," he says.

"Uh. Sure." *That went well. Not.* "Do you want to go have dinner downstairs with Angela and the others?"

"No, no," he says. "I usually just eat here."

"Oh. Okay. Do you want me to cook something?"

"Please, don't trouble yourself. I have a beef casserole in the freezer. People keep bringing me food. I'll heat that up."

"Right."

I sit at the kitchen table, feeling useless, as he slowly turns on the oven, sets the table, puts the casserole dish in the oven, and sets the kitchen timer.

"It'll be about half an hour." Gramps sits across from me and picks up his newspaper. The timer ticks loudly.

I hesitate, then grab my book and take it outside to the balcony. I stand at the railing for a moment, closing my eyes and drinking in the sultry air. The gulf sparkles under the clear blue sky, crashing gently against the white sand. I plop onto a lounge chair, stretch out my legs, and read.

After dinner—beef casserole served with Lipton iced tea with lemon—I ask Gramps what he wants to do next.

"I usually watch the news, then read for a while before I turn in."

I glance at the microwave clock. It's seven P.M.

"Okay."

"You're welcome to watch the news with me. I probably have some ice cream in the freezer I could dig up for you."

"That's nice of you." I consider it for half a second, but I'm filled with restless energy. I don't want to stay cooped up here all night. "But I think I'll go see my house." *That sounded weird.* "The house, you know, Pebble Cottage."

Gramps nods. "That's a good idea. Go take stock of the place. Take the key from the hook there—it's yours now." He clicks on the TV—the volume blares. "I'll be in bed by the time you get back. The door will be open. Good night, Mallory."

I watch him, his face illuminated by the glow of MSNBC.

"Night, Gramps."

I take the house key, which is connected to a key chain that looks like Barack Obama on a surfboard, grab my bag, and shut the door quietly behind me.

Chapter 9

I drive up the peninsula along Gulf Boulevard, a long, two-lane road that stretches from the southern tip of St. Pete Beach all the way up to Clearwater Beach. Pebble Cottage is in Reina Beach, a few miles north of where Gramps lives. I keep the radio off and open the windows to the balmy evening air.

When I reach Reina Beach, I turn right, away from the beach, and slowly wind my way through residential streets. Like the houses, the streets here are small and quiet, lined with lush green trees draped with Spanish moss.

I turn into a cul-de-sac and find Pebble Cottage. Carefully, I pull into the carport on the right side of the house. The front yard is small and tidy, nothing more than a patch of overgrown grass and a single tree. I climb the two front steps—no front porch here, just the giant sunporch in the back—and hesitate before I let myself in.

It's dark inside. Inside the front door is a narrow entryway with a row of peg hooks on the wall. There used to be a shoe rack here, overflowing with my family's sandals and Lottie's gardening clogs. Now the house is empty. It shouldn't surprise me, but it does, because I haven't been here since it was Gramps and Lottie's home. Back then, it was full of their things: well-cared-for furniture from the 1960s and '70s—most memorably, an angular sofa in brown-and-orange plaid—paintings and decorative sculptures from their travels, and a glass cabinet full of crystal teacups and candlesticks that had been passed down from Lottie's mother.

The hallway floor is still a brown-and-orange floral tile that screams 1970s. The living room is still brown: brown shag carpet and brown, wood-paneled walls.

First, I stop in the kitchen. The force of nostalgia almost takes my breath away. I spent so much time here: countless Thanksgivings, standing on a step stool to help stir mashed potatoes and gravy; lazy summer mornings asking Lottie for a glass of lemonade; late nights with my sister and cousins, pilfering chocolate cake from the fridge.

It looks exactly the same. Same yellow laminate counters and brown wooden cabinets. Same pale-green curtains framing the window over the sink. Same retro booth that served as the breakfast table. It's alarmingly old-fashioned, but at the same time I'm glad it hasn't been remodeled. My family had a lot of happy times in this kitchen.

I wander down the hallway and peek into the two smaller bedrooms. They all have the same closets with brown sliding doors and beige carpeting that was probably white once upon a time. The larger bedroom, the one that used to be Gramps and Lottie's, has a walk-in closet and a small bathroom with a stall shower. The bedroom also has a full wall of windows facing the backyard, and a door that Lottie used to say led to her secret garden.

I open the door and the warm, humid air hugs me immediately. This door opens onto the left side of the backyard; the pool and the screened-in porch are to my right. Although it's overgrown and has an abandoned feeling to it now, I can still see the remnants of Lottie's secret garden. There's a winding path made of cobblestones and pebbles, lined with flower bushes, leading to a stone bench. Among the weeds are garden lanterns. I used to think they were magic, the way they turned on as soon as it got dark outside.

The light outside is magical right now. The sky overhead spans from pale pink in the west to dark blue in the east, streaked with long, pale clouds. I step carefully over the pebbles toward the pool. My chest feels heavy and achy, and I stare at the gently rippling water, trying to figure out what I'm feeling. Sadness that Lottie is gone. Longing for the times of happy togetherness we spent here. Overwhelm and gratitude that this place is mine now.

After locking up the house, I stop at the tree in the front yard. It's a little taller than me, and it has tightly furled buds among its green leaves. It's beautiful, and it doesn't have any other trees to keep it company, and it's mine now, so I feel some responsibility toward it.

After a long moment, I realize I'm standing and staring at a tree. *Trees don't get lonely, Mallory. Trees are trees.*

Quickly, I get back in the car and drive a slow loop around Reina Beach, checking out the neighborhood. There's an ice cream parlor and a coffee shop, a local grocery store, a Mexican restaurant, a seafood restaurant, some tourist-trap shops. The shops are mostly closed now, but the restaurants seem fairly busy. Of course, it is Saturday night. There's a tiki bar on the beach, with flaming torches and outdoor tables crowded with people laughing loudly. Another is a cheerful yellow building with a blue awning next to a boardwalk. It has a mermaid on the sign. Impulsively, despite my abhorrence of going to restaurants by myself, I decide to stop for a drink.

As soon as I walk in, I feel like I made the right choice. The walls are painted teal, and I swear I can smell the fresh paint, which tells me it must be a new establishment. The walls are adorned with a ridiculously large collection of mermaid-themed art, with vintage-looking mirrors scattered here and there. I hesitate, scanning the tables for a seat. The place is a little less than half full, but it feels awkward to take a whole table to myself. The mostly empty bar, which looks like a huge slab of shiny driftwood, seems more my speed.

I slide onto a barstool, smile at the bartender, and scan the chalkboard list of drink specials above the bar.

"What can I get you?" The bartender is a woman around my age, with glowing skin and a tiny Afro pulled back with a purple headband.

"I'll have the Andrina, please." I name one of the signature cocktails, something with gin, cava, and lavender.

"Good choice!" She mixes my drink and then says, as if she can't help herself, "Did you notice?"

I laugh nervously. "Notice what?"

"The menu." She lifts her eyebrows and grins. "The drinks."

"Uh..." I read the menu again. Arista, Attina, Adella... Something stirs deep, deep in my memory. Something set to a tune I heard a million times as a kid. "The mermaids!" I shout a little in my excitement. "Ariel's sisters!"

"Yes!" Her shout is even louder than mine. "She got it! Hey," she calls to the server, a twenty-something guy with blond hair, "she got that it was the daughters of Triton!"

"Congratulations, man," the server calls, possibly sarcastically.

"You're the first," the bartender says, sliding me my drink. It's in a coupe glass, and it has a little purple flower floating in it. "No one gets it."

"Well, I think it's genius." I take a sip of my drink. "And this is amazing. Seriously."

"Thanks. That's one of my favorites." She reaches down under the bar and then passes me a small bowl of potato chips. "We just opened last month."

"Is this your place?" I crunch gratefully into a chip. *Free potato chips, nice touch.*

"Yep!" Her face glows with pride. "I'm Amanda. Are you local?"

"Mal. And no, just visiting."

"Bummer. Hey, write us a good review on Yelp!"

I start to promise that I will when we're interrupted by a raucous laugh. A group of men has walked in the door, all talking over one another about some sports game.

They settle near the other end of the bar, and Amanda meets them there.

"You really should've been watching the game. Three runs in the fifth? I mean," one of the guys tells her, and then mimes his head exploding.

"You know my policy. No TVs. Although I'm sure I missed out on a fascinating game of—what sport are we talking about?" Amanda laughs as they all groan.

She takes their drink orders, and they carry on their conversation. I'm actually impressed by how long they can talk about this baseball game. After commenting on the score and a couple of notable moments, I'd be tapped out.

I listen in, enjoying my chips in solitude. I'll admit, part of me kind of wishes they would, I don't know, acknowledge my existence. But I think that's just a fantasy of what small-town life might be like. In reality, I'm the same Mal here as I am back home. It's all too easy for me to fade into the wallpaper.

Their conversation finally veers away from baseball as they sip their beers. My ears perk up when one of them mentions that his girlfriend is mad at him.

"Is this still about the gift card?" one of the others asks.

I don't hear an answer, so I glance up surreptitiously. The guy with the angry girlfriend is nodding. He runs a hand over his fade haircut, his face morose.

"Why did you think an Amazon gift card was a good birthday gift, man?"

I snort with laughter and then cover my mouth with one hand.

None of them seems to notice, except one. He's directly across from me and glances up sharply. His mouth quirks in a questioning way. I look down, but not before noticing his freckly arms, square jaw, and slightly overgrown red hair. I almost slip off my barstool at the sudden unexpected hotness.

"I just didn't know what to get her. For Christmas, I got her this cute outfit, and she's never worn it once. I think she hated it. I just wanted to get it right this time. I'm surprised she hasn't broken up with me. Shit is hard, man."

I press my knuckles against my lips to stifle another laugh.

"Any tips?" I hear a different voice ask. "Miss?"

I look around, swiveling on my barstool.

"Yes, you." The redhead is looking at me again. My mouth pops open in a startled O as the group of men all stare at me. Turns out I'm much more comfortable fading into the wallpaper.

"What would you recommend this young man buy for his lady next time?" the redhead persists.

"Um. Let me think." I give a nervous laugh, and then count off on my fingers, "Expensive perfume. A necklace with her initial. A huge candle. Even a home-cooked dinner with a bouquet of roses would be nice."

The redhead nods at his friend, gesturing at me like, *See?*

"I hope you're writing this down," another guy jokes.

Angry Girlfriend Guy raises his drink to me in a mock toast, and they go back to talking about sports.

I glance up and see with a start that the redhead is still looking at me. This time he smirks and shakes his head ever so slightly.

What? I mouth.

Naughty, he mouths back.

Me? I point at my chest.

He slips away from his friends and perches easily on the stool next to mine.

"Did your mama not teach you that it's not polite to eavesdrop?"

I let out a surprised laugh. "I couldn't help hearing."

"Sure, sure." He crosses his arms—biceps, dear Lord, *biceps*. I shove a handful of chips in my mouth to make myself stop looking at his arms. He seems to enjoy watching me crunch, because his grin broadens.

"Saw you talking to Amanda earlier. Are you two—?" He points from me to Amanda in a suggestive way.

"What?" I brush my mouth with the back of my hand. "You mean—is Amanda…? *I'm* not…I mean, in college, yes, sometimes, but now, I mean I've mostly settled on—actually I am very much settled on—" Helpfully, I gesture up and down his torso. "But single, yes, I am."

He stares at me for a very long moment. I would think that he was questioning my sanity, except his nostrils are flared with amusement.

"Great. Fantastic. Thank you for sharing—all that."

If there was ever a good time for a tsunami to strike and carry me away, this would be it.

But then his face relaxes into a friendly, neighborly smile. "I was just checking. Amanda and I go way back, we both grew up here, so if you were dating her, I wanted to make sure I said hi."

"That's so nice of you," I say, genuinely. "This must have been a fun place to grow up." I feel a twinge of nostalgic longing at the thought. When I was a kid, I used to fantasize about living here full-time. I loved visiting Lottie and Gramps so much. But my parents never considered leaving Seattle. And besides, living here wouldn't have been the same as visiting, when I was always surrounded by cousins and aunts and uncles visiting at the same time.

"You bet." He waves toward the window, where the dark beach is visible, the first stars dotting the purplish sky. "Where else could a boy grow up half feral, catching snakes for pets and shooting Coke cans off the fence with a BB gun after school?" His smile is lopsided and a tad sardonic. "Only in Florida."

"Is that really what you were like as a kid?"

"One hundred percent. Two older brothers. They showed me how to climb trees, how to fish for mackerel, how to find shark's teeth and arrowheads in the woods. 'Course, now they're both dads who won't even let their kids walk home from school alone. And if they try to walk in the house with dirty shoes on…" He fakes a horrified shudder.

I smile and sip my drink. I'm completely charmed by his lack of small talk. Normally, if I found myself on a barstool next to a handsome stranger, he'd be asking me where I'm from and what I do for work. After a few questions, the conversation would hit a dead end and we'd avoid eye contact in the ensuing awkward silence.

This guy is not avoiding eye contact. I feel color rise to my cheeks, because he's looking at me intently. I flick my eyes up to meet his.

"Let me guess what you were like as a kid."

"You literally just met me, but okay," I say.

His eyes, I notice, are light brown. He doesn't look the least embarrassed as he carefully examines my face and hair and then my outfit. In the few seconds it takes for him to size me up, I experience a number of things. First, relief that I put makeup on. Second, wishing I'd worn my hair down—my long dark-brown hair is a point of pride for me. Third, feeling silly for wishing this. And fourth, a full-body surge, something like what I imagine the gulf feels as the tide flows inexorably toward the moon. It's lust. I haven't felt this way in years, since I was first dating Alex.

I decide in that instant that I'm entitled to a little lust, a little flirtation. I'm alone at the beach on a balmy evening, and I haven't had sex in almost two years.

Not that I'm going to have sex with this stranger, but hey, I'm a human woman. And I know all too well how rare it is to strike up this kind of conversation with this kind of stranger.

"You were a reader," he says. It takes me a split second to remember that he's deciding what kind of kid I was. "You were the one who took a book everywhere and sat under a tree at recess reading instead of playing."

I can't help the loud laugh that escapes me. "Archie comics, maybe. Or the American Girl doll catalog," I tell him. Secretly, though, I'm flattered that this is his impression of me. "I definitely played during recess, though. Kickball was my favorite. And badminton."

"Badminton? We didn't have that here. Kickball, though, was definitely a thing. I'm sorry, I didn't realize I was talking to a multi-talented athlete."

"And I haven't even mentioned my four-square career."

"Four-square, huh?"

"I was the fourth-grade champion." I examine my nails nonchalantly. This makes him laugh, which, in turn, makes me feel ridiculously pleased with myself.

"Fourth-grade me would've been intimidated by fourth-grade you." He turns slightly on his stool so that his knees are pointing directly at me. Something shivers deep in my belly. I toss back the last of my purple drink.

"Are you in town for long?" he asks.

"No, just a couple days."

"Too bad." Again with the eye contact. The dating apps back home have got nothing on the small-town bars in Florida.

I swallow and feel like I have to end the tension somehow. "Yeah, it is too bad." Saying this acts as a reminder that this conversation, albeit fun and distracting, is not actually going to lead anywhere. I'm going home in two days.

I leave some money on the bar for Amanda, then stand and shift my purse onto my shoulder.

"On that note, I guess I should get going. It was nice talking to you."

"The pleasure was all mine." He stands, too. "Why don't I walk you out." He looks back over his shoulder and calls, "Be back in a sec." His friends hoot and holler him out, which makes my face flame, but luckily he's walking behind me and can't see my embarrassment.

Outside, I gesture to my little red car. "This is me." We stop beside the driver's-side door. "Have a good night." It comes out uncertainly, almost like a question.

He stands directly in front of me, smiling politely with his hands in his pockets. "You too. Drive safe."

This is the part where I'm supposed to get in the car and drive away. But there's some kind of magnetic thing happening between us, and I really don't want to say goodbye, knowing I'll never see him again. Standing this close, I can smell his unfamiliar, woodsy deodorant or cologne, mingled with the potent tang of salty skin. I haven't hooked up with a random stranger in years, but that doesn't stop me from wanting something to happen in this moment. If anything, it makes me want it more. I haven't felt chemistry like this in so long, and the stakes are low since I know it can't lead anywhere. Why not have a little fun before I go back home to normal life?

His hands are still in his pockets, and I get the sense that he has some sort of gentlemanly propriety about him. So I take a tiny step forward, leaving only an inch between us. He must have been waiting for a signal, because the next thing I know his hands are on either side of my jaw and his mouth is on mine. It's the kind of kiss where I lose myself completely in the sensations, the warmth of his mouth and tongue and our bodies pressing together. Our hands feverishly move from face to neck to back, pulling each other closer. We can't get enough, we can't taste enough of each other, we can't get close enough. I'm distantly aware that this is the kind of make-out session that should be embarrassing to have in public, but I can't make myself stop.

After a minute or maybe five, we pull apart. We're both dazed. We look at each other for a long moment and I can see the question on his face. We're each waiting for the other person to ask some form of *Your place or mine?* But "mine" is actually "my grandpa's place." So that's not an option. And the thought of creeping back into Gramps's in the wee hours after a one-night stand kind of takes the shine off the situation.

So I reach out and squeeze his hand.

"Good night," I say. "It was really, *really* nice to meet you."

He looks down at his shoes for a brief moment—to hide his disappointment?—and then smiles up at me. "Night." He pauses to look at me again, apparently hesitating. Then, finally, he says, "Safe travels, you hear?"

And he stands back as I drive off, wondering what on earth just happened.

Chapter 10

The next morning, I wake up more refreshed than I've felt in a long time. The guest room here is perfectly dark and quiet, chilled to perfection by the strong but silent AC. Part of me also wonders if the kiss incident last night released some kind of relaxation hormones in my brain. I laugh at myself, remembering it. I don't know what got into me, but I don't regret it. I deserve to kiss a hot redhead now and then. Whatever the reason, I am bright-eyed and bushy-tailed this morning and have no desire to sit around the condo all day.

Gramps has already eaten a bowl of Grape-Nuts, but he agrees to accompany me to the dining room for breakfast.

I know at once that this was a good decision: There's a buffet of fresh fruit, scrambled eggs, sausages, and potatoes. There's even a self-serve waffle maker.

I fill my plate, drop it off at the table where Gramps is reading his newspaper, then make a second trip for a glass of cranberry juice and a mug of coffee.

"See, I don't know why you don't come here every morning," I say around a mouthful of eggs.

Gramps sips his black coffee and shrugs. "I have everything I need upstairs."

I take in the room: It's pretty empty—it is after nine, which is probably way later than most of the people here have breakfast. But there's enough gentle chatter in the background to add to the pleasant ambience. It's also huge, with a soaring ceiling and floor-to-ceiling windows facing the gulf. Then again, Gramps has a gulf view from his kitchen, too.

"Okay, well." I cut into a piece of cantaloupe. "It's Sunday today. What would you normally do all day?"

He looks amused at the question. He scratches his head, ruffling his thick white hair.

"Let's see. Breakfast, check. Coffee, check. I guess I might take my paper down to the pool to finish reading it. I like to do the crossword on Sundays. Lunch—maybe a sandwich. Then, I don't know, I like an afternoon nap. After that, while away the time until dinner, I suppose."

There's a long pause. I stare into my creamy coffee, feeling unexpectedly crushed by how sad this sounds. I mean, isn't he bored? Lonely? He must be, right?

"But we can do whatever you like," he says. "What tickles your fancy?"

How about if you show me beyond a doubt that you're doing just fine? How about if you hang out with Angela and your other friends, so I know you have a social life? That would all tickle my fancy, for sure.

Of course, I don't say any of that. Instead, I say, "Let's start with the pool."

I step out of my white cover-up, revealing a black halter one-piece. Then I slather SPF 50 on all my exposed skin as Gramps settles himself in a chair under an umbrella.

"Don't you want to get a suntan?" His face is mildly amused.

"I mean, that would be great, but not at the risk of skin cancer." I rub vigorously at my arms.

"Oh, that? They just cut those spots off. No big deal." He's openly laughing now. "I've had two cut off my nose."

"Ew." I pause to rummage in my bag, pulling out the tinted SPF I use on my face. "And also, no. You can die from skin cancer. The bad kind."

"Yes, well." He looks out across the beach, still smiling. "You have to go some way or other. Might as well be from sitting in the sun."

I stare at him. I don't know if he's joking or not, but even if he's not joking, how would I respond to that?

He turns back to me and remarks, "Now you look like Casper the friendly ghost."

I look down at my legs and try rubbing the cream in more, but it's no use. The sunscreen is merely highlighting my natural pallor.

"I think that crossword puzzle is calling your name."

"Ah, yes." He takes a pencil out of his pocket and focuses on the paper.

I slip into the pool, which feels like bathwater. When I was a kid, I didn't really like swimming, other than to flip my hair upside down and pretend to be George Washington. But this feels amazing, almost as warm as the hot tub. I swim a few lazy laps.

I hear Gramps greeting someone and pause, hanging on to the far wall of the pool. Two women are crossing the pool deck. It's Angela, dressed in a pale-pink tennis skirt and polo shirt, and another woman dressed similarly, though not entirely to the same effect.

"Hello there," he says.

"So nice to see you with your granddaughter," Angela says.

"Oh yes. We're having a nice weekend together." All three seniors turn to look at me, treading water in the deep end. I wave my fingers at them.

"Is he showing you a good time?" Angela calls.

"Almost too much," I say. "Can't keep up with him. Never knew he was such a firecracker."

The ladies laugh like I've said something truly hilarious. Gramps smiles, too. I realize, watching him, that I get a heady sense of accomplishment when he does that. He doesn't laugh loudly, like Angela and her friend, but he smiles with all his teeth when he's amused. I suppose, now that I'm thinking about it, I always wanted to impress him when I was a kid, knowing that he was a brainy academic, a scientist. I realize now that he probably just has a different sense of humor, and it's nothing to do with his intelligence. But still, I enjoy making him laugh.

They exchange a few more words, and then the ladies wave goodbye and head for the tennis court.

"What did she say?" I ask, swimming closer to where Gramps is sitting.

"Nothing, nothing. They asked if I wanted to join their cinema thing tonight."

"Cinema thing?"

"It's movie night. Sunday. They're showing a Wes Anderson film."

"That sounds like fun!"

"I don't care much for Wes Anderson." He pauses to pencil in a crossword answer. "Or is that Woody Allen? Anyway, I can watch whatever movie I want right in my living room."

"Right." I consider pressing the point—after all, I am here to help him, aren't I?—but I can tell he's made up his mind. So I climb out of the pool, spread my towel on a lounge chair, and lay out with a book in hand. If nothing else, at least I can work on this Casper situation.

"Did you know this vinegar expired in 2011?" I'm pulling things out of the pantry, slightly distracted from my mission to make dinner for Gramps.

"Vinegar doesn't go bad," he says. He's on the couch, scrolling through the TV guide with one hand and holding a glass with the other. I'd asked if I could make him a cocktail, to which he'd replied, "I'd love one. Seltzer with lime."

I made the same for myself and decided I would make a pasta dish. I found an unopened box of spaghetti, a jar of minced garlic in the fridge, and a shallot. Now I'm sitting on the kitchen floor surrounded by dry goods that expired anywhere from two to twenty-two years ago.

"This cardamom is older than I am." I'm only slightly exaggerating.

"I use that in curries," Gramps calls back.

"When's the last time you made curry?"

He pauses. "Nineteen ninety-seven."

This makes me chuckle. I decide I've done enough for now, toss the expired things in the trash, and tie up the bag.

"Be right back."

I take the garbage bag outside to the trash chute in the hall. The open-air hallway looks out over the grounds, and the sound of laughter drifts up. I peek over the railing and see a group of seniors walking up the path from the beach, talking loudly. The sound reminds me of college, when students traveled in packs and felt like whatever was going on between them and their friends was the pinnacle of sophistication and importance. It makes me nostalgic for that kind of camaraderie. It also makes me sad for Gramps. These are his peers, his neighbors, his would-be, should-be friends. I want him to be part of a laughing group. Not holed up in his condo, alone.

After dinner, during which Gramps gamely eats my concoction

of spaghetti tossed with garlic, lemon, and some buttered peas I'd found in the freezer, I broach the topic.

"I was thinking, maybe we should go to that movie night."

"Why?" He rifles in a kitchen drawer and pulls out a peppermint candy. "We can watch a movie here. What do you want to see? I have all the channels."

"It's not about the movie exactly. I was thinking…"

He crunches into the peppermint immediately. My mom eats hard candy the same way. It's hedonistic.

"What I'm trying to say is, don't you want to make some friends?"

He finishes chomping on the peppermint and then says thoughtfully, "I've lived here for over fifteen years. I'm not the new kid in town, Mallory. I have friends. Or Lottie did."

His last words hang in the air.

"So, do you feel like they were all Lottie's friends? Is that why you've been…" I gesture around his kitchen and living room.

"Compared with her, who would want to see me?" He shrugs and grins, like it's a throwaway comment.

Lottie did have a habit of stealing the show. She wore bright colors and had a megawatt smile. She also had this way of making each person she talked to feel *seen*. I always admired that.

"Angela seemed like she wanted to see you." I raise my eyebrows suggestively. Gramps just looks at me, his face blank. Perhaps it was insensitive of me to suggest a flirtation with another woman mere weeks after the death of his wife of sixty years.

"Sorry," I add quickly.

He's quiet for a while, returns to the living room to fetch his empty cocktail glass, and comes back to the kitchen. He opens the fridge and pours some more seltzer into his glass.

"Lottie was a social butterfly. We met at a party—a dance—in

Columbus. She was a sophomore coed and I was a graduate student." He twirls the ice around in his drink. "I noticed her right away. She was wearing a purple dress and matching purple shoes. She had a magnetic energy around her that made everyone in the vicinity drift toward her. Including me. I didn't usually ask girls to dance. Maybe one at each dance, to get my friends off my back. But Lottie, I had to ask her. And she said—"

"On the condition that we do the mashed potato." I've heard this part of the story a few (hundred) times before.

"I think she thought I wouldn't know how. Maybe she wanted to get out of dancing with me," he laughs.

"Not true. She told me that she'd noticed you on the quad and had been stalking you for weeks."

He seems pleased by this, although he's heard Lottie's version plenty of times before. "Yes, she did say that. Maybe it's true, I don't know. Personally, I think I won her over with my mashed potato."

And to my sheer delight, he sets his drink down on the counter and does a slow-motion, old-man version of the dance, shimmying his knees together with his elbows tucked at his sides. I burst into giggles.

"Like this?" I mimic his dance moves.

"Not even close," he says. "Anyway, it's better with the song."

"Okay, wait." I grab my phone and pull up the song "Mashed Potato Time" by Dee Dee Sharp.

"This is it," Gramps marvels. "How did you know?"

"I didn't. The internet did. Okay, now show me."

He does the moves again, this time picking up the pace until his feet become a blur. I'm stunned. I've never seen anybody move their feet so fast.

"Holy... how do you... *what*?"

He's beaming, wagging his head to the beat as his limbs do their own thing, like he's possessed by the spirit of the 1960s.

"I practiced in my room every night after that dance." He's out of breath now. "Just in case Lottie ever asked me to do it again. The first time I just copied what she was doing."

I try to keep up with him but I end up tripping over my feet and crashing into the counter, which makes us both laugh so hard we have to sit down. We migrate to the couch with our seltzer mocktails. Gramps flips through the channels.

"You leave on Tuesday?"

"Yeah. I have a meeting tomorrow morning with the property manager. Need to figure out the next steps with the house. And then—" I pause. "And then, yeah, I fly out on Tuesday."

Gramps nods, his eyes on the TV.

"*The Music Man*. Lottie and I saw this on our second date."

"I'll make some popcorn," I say.

"Don't bother. It expired in 2015."

My appointment with the property manager, Daniel McKinnon, is at nine A.M. Over coffee, Gramps had given me a Pebble Cottage primer of sorts. I drive up Gulf Boulevard, mentally repeating what he'd told me about the house.

New roof, 2006. Exterior painted, 2015. Needs gutters cleaned. Sump pump is—shoot, what did he say about the sump pump?

As I drive up to the house, I'm nervous, like there's going to be a test. Really, I'm just worried about exposing how little I know about home maintenance.

There's a white van parked in front of the lawn. An older man wearing coveralls is leaning against it, talking on the phone. He gives me a wave. I'm unsure if he's the contractor or Daniel, the property manager.

As I pull into the carport, another man rides up on a bike. That's right, Daniel was riding a bike during my first phone call with him. I notice with mild amusement that he's wearing a skintight cycling outfit, black with neon-yellow accents. I guess that passes as professional when it's eighty degrees out and you commute on your bike.

I give him a friendly and, I hope, confident wave as I turn off the car.

"Hey, Daniel," the contractor calls, walking over to him and pocketing his phone. "Morning, Ms. Rosen."

"Good morning," I call back.

But the property manager hasn't said anything. He's just standing there, staring at my red Toyota Yaris.

"Morning," he finally says, and his voice doesn't sound confident at all. As I start across the yard toward the two men, it's just dawning on me that Daniel's face looks familiar. And then he takes off his bike helmet, revealing a head full of tousled hair. Tousled *red* hair. I stop in my tracks.

Okay, so small towns have their downsides.

Chapter 11

"Hi. Hello, Mr. McKinnon." Before I know what I'm doing, I stick out my hand to shake his.

"Morning, Ms. Rosen." He speaks slowly, like he thinks he might be in a nightmare, or on *Punk'd*. The contractor doesn't seem to notice a thing.

"Nice to meet you." The man shakes my hand, too. "Alan Gregson."

I mumble a polite greeting, unable to tear my gaze away from Daniel, whose face is flaming red. He's fumbling in the pannier bag on his bike, searching for something.

I'm feeling a combination of stunned embarrassment and a mad desire to laugh. So I made out with the property manager. The person who's supposed to manage my property for me. Maybe he makes out with all his clients. Maybe that's why he's so highly recommended.

At this thought, a snort escapes me.

"What?" Daniel says, a touch sharply. He's found what he was looking for, a small iPad that he's now clutching like his life depends on it.

I glance from his miserable, strained face, to the obliviously polite face of Alan Gregson. "Nothing. Nothing at all." I flash my most winning smile. "Shall we get started?"

I unlock the front door, and then Alan leads the way. I gather that he was the person who had done the initial inspection, using Trish's spare key. He points out the areas that need structural reinforcements and the plumbing problems in the spare bathroom. As we walk, Daniel scrawls notes and snaps photos with his iPad. He doesn't look at me once.

"Of course, the pool needs to be treated and most likely needs new filters. From what I saw last time, the HVAC is in good shape," Alan concludes as we finish our loop and end up back in the kitchen.

All the unfamiliar terms tumble around in my brain. That, and sheer terror at the idea of how much all this will cost. But before I can say anything, Daniel dives in with his own spiel.

"Alan covered all the necessary repairs. But there are a lot of optional, aesthetic things to consider as well. The living room, for example."

"The brown room," I say.

"Right. It's brown. If you make it less brown—paint the walls and pull up the carpet, maybe replace it with a light, bright flooring, maybe a bamboo—it would make a huge difference. Now, if you were to repaint and refloor the bedrooms as well, you could significantly raise the rent. And this kitchen."

"What about it?" I'm feeling defensive. I know the kitchen is hideously outdated. I know people want updated kitchens. But it's always been like this, and the idea of ripping it all out makes me sad.

"It's…" Daniel glances around the room. I can tell he's trying to be diplomatic, which I appreciate. "It could use new appliances, for a start. Maybe a coat of paint."

"It's old-fashioned," Alan pipes up.

"It's vintage," I argue.

"Well." Daniel shrugs and glances back down at his tablet, probably so he doesn't have to look at me. "Anyway. The more updates you make to the house, the more you can charge for rent."

"Okay." The idea of upping the rent mollifies me somewhat. The more I can charge each month, the less stressed I'll be about going into debt for all the repairs and updates.

We head out to the front lawn. Alan promises to send us an updated estimate this afternoon, and then he drives off in his white van. Daniel and I stand there, side by side, watching him drive away.

"Thanks for your help," I say, just as he says, "Look, about the other night."

Oh, this should be good. I turn to face him expectantly. I can tell this makes him nervous. His ginger eyebrows twitch. I'm not used to being the one who makes other people nervous.

"That was pretty out of character for me," he says. "If I had known who you were—if I had known you were a client—I never would have..."

My face flames. But honestly, I'm glad he didn't know I was a client. That kiss was worth this embarrassment. He's clearly distressed, though, his eyes as worried as those of a Labrador who's been yelled at, so I want to end his misery. I slap his arm in an attempt at a friendly gesture. (Damn, forgot how hard his biceps are.)

"I wouldn't have kissed you if I knew who you were, either."

He exhales in relief and runs a hand through his hair. It sticks straight up with the humidity.

"Don't worry about it," I continue. "I'm serious. And I really am leaving tomorrow, so. We won't see each other again. It'll just be emails and phone calls from here out. Please don't drop me as a client because, clearly, I need your help."

"I won't drop you." He slaps my arm back playfully, but he's so strong that I wobble sideways. "I'll find you the perfect tenants. It'll be good."

"Yes, great! Perfect." I twirl my keys around my finger. "Well then..."

"Glad we cleared that up." He laughs, and I can tell he is truly very relieved. It's a little annoying, actually. I would prefer for him to pine after me, but I guess that wouldn't be professional.

"Of course. Me too."

"Won't happen again." He cocks his fingers at me, winking, as he heads back to his bicycle.

"Bye!" I give a mock-friendly wave as I climb into my car.

As I drive away, my mood melts from amusement to mortification. Until an hour ago, the memory of that kiss was funny and sexy. It made me giggle, that I would do something like that, and that it was surprisingly hot despite the guy being a total stranger. But now? Now it's like remembering saying something embarrassing in front of a group of people. I kissed Daniel McKinnon. Now he thinks I'm the type of person who kisses random strangers in bars. And there's nothing wrong with that, but it's not who I am. I mean, not usually. I wanted him to think I was a levelheaded homeowner who knows what a sump pump is.

I drive down palm-tree-lined streets and tell myself to take a deep breath. It doesn't matter what he thinks of me. I'm leaving tomorrow, and I won't have to see him again. Our conversations will be brief and professional and won't veer too far from the topics of tenants and home repairs.

See, this is why I'm better off being a hermit. When I'm out in the world, interacting with people, I embarrass myself. It's just what I do. I say the wrong thing, make the wrong face, kiss the wrong person. This trip has been a—not fun, exactly—an interesting interlude, but I'll be glad to get home. Back to my normal routine and my solitude.

"Hey, Gramps," I call, letting myself into the condo.

There's no answer. I duck my head into the kitchen, expecting to see him at the table with his newspaper, but he's not there.

"Hello?" I check the living room, but he's not in his armchair. Maybe he's taking a nap? It's only eleven A.M., several hours earlier than his usual afternoon nap time.

"Gramps?" I whisper, poking his bedroom door open with one finger.

His bed is empty. The sight of his crisply made bed fills me with a sudden panic. A second later, I remind myself that he's a fully grown man, not a lost toddler. He's probably down at the pool or taking a walk.

I clomp down the stairs instead of waiting for the elevator. At the pool, there's one woman swimming laps and a few other people sunning themselves in lounge chairs, but no Gramps. I definitely thought he would be at the pool. He doesn't even *take* walks. Just to check, I stand at the gate to the beach path and scan the beach, one hand shielding my eyes. There are a couple of families lounging under umbrellas, one jogger, and a few people walking slowly in the surf. No sign of Gramps.

So maybe he's in the breakfast room, or... I mean, obviously he wouldn't be at the gym or the tennis court. I walk back toward the building, anxiety fluttering in my chest. Where could he have gone?

I could ask someone if they've seen him this morning. Maybe the next-door neighbor or—*Angela*. Angela seemed like the kind of person who would know these things.

I speed walk from the pool to the gazebo, where I'd seen Angela with that exercise class when I first arrived, but there's no one there. I decide to try the tennis court. By the time I get there, sweat is dripping down my back. The sun beats down unforgivingly from straight overhead.

"Angela!" I call. She's on the court, wearing a mint-green outfit today. She thwacks the ball toward her partner and then looks around.

"Mallory?" She squints at me from underneath her visor.

I half jog over to her, panting and flushed. "Have you seen Gramps this morning?"

"Leonard? No, I haven't seen him today. Why, what's wrong?" She rests her racket against one shoulder.

"He's not at home and I can't find him anywhere." I try to sound calm, but some of my worry seeps into my voice.

"He didn't leave a note?"

"No, no note."

"I haven't seen him, doll. Is his car here?"

"His car! Good idea. I'll check. Thanks, Angela." I take off toward the parking lot, leaving Angela looking after me with her mouth puckered in concern.

I jog through the garage and find Gramps's parking space. His white Mazda Miata is gone.

Chapter 12

So he took off in his car. It shouldn't necessarily be alarming for a man in his eighties to drive somewhere by himself. But it feels off to me. He hasn't driven anywhere the whole time I've been here, and I know he doesn't do his own grocery shopping. Where could he have gone?

Should I call him? Even if he has his phone, I don't like the thought of him trying to answer the call while driving. The man can barely use his phone while standing still. Sounds like a recipe for disaster.

Before I drive all around Pinellas County looking for him, I try one last thing.

"Hey, Trish," I say when my aunt answers on the second ring.

"What's up?"

"Gramps isn't with you, is he?"

"What? No. I'm at the office. What's going on?"

"Do you know of anywhere he might have gone today? An appointment or... the library?" I guess wildly.

"No. Mallory, what is it? Have you lost my dad?" She says it in a kind of joking way, but I'm not finding this very funny at the moment.

"No. Sort of. Maybe. I should go. I'll talk to you later." I hang up before she can say anything. And then I get in my rental car and drive into town.

I drive slowly past the shops and restaurants of Reina Beach. I don't see a Mazda Miata in front of Ken's Market or the Crab Shack. This feels increasingly pointless. What if he's driving down the highway, making a bid for freedom? I'll never find him. And I need to log into my work computer soon—it's almost nine on the West Coast. Maybe there's some sort of shop for nerds around here, someplace that sells scientific textbooks and chess sets. That's where he would go if he were in need of retail therapy.

I'm driving so slowly, scanning the public beach on my left and the shop parking lots on my right, that the truck behind me honks and swerves. I'm wondering at what point I should give up, or call in a silver alert to 911, when I see it. A little white sports car parked in front of a strip mall that's home to a nail salon, a liquor store, and a couple of tourist shops.

I park in the first open spot and hurry over to Gramps's car. He's sitting in the driver's seat, and from behind, it looks like he's laughing lightly, maybe to something on the radio. Trying not to startle him, I approach the driver's side. I'm about to tap on the window when I see that he's not laughing at all. His posture is rigid and straight, his eyes are closed, and tears are coursing silently down his cheeks.

Oh no. I freeze. Part of me wishes I could run back to my car and pretend not to have seen him. I'm standing there like a moron when Gramps opens his eyes and sees me.

Hi, I mouth. *I'll just...* I point to the passenger side, walk around the car, and climb in.

"Hi," I say again.

Gramps looks straight ahead. His shoulders have stopped shaking, but the tears are still flowing. I don't think I've ever seen a grown man cry before, except for my dad when the Seahawks won the Super Bowl. And my brother-in-law many times, but he doesn't count.

I consider reaching for Gramps's hand, or saying something, but finally I just fish around in my purse for a pack of tissues and hand one to him. He dabs at his cheeks and then blows his nose with a sound like a ferry horn.

"You found me," he says with a wry chuckle.

"Yeah." I consider telling him the whole saga but settle on "I saw your car."

"It sticks out, doesn't it? I considered getting a Honda Accord. I would've blended in, then. But Lottie liked riding with the top down." He gestures to the roof of the car. "I haven't bothered opening it since..." He chokes on the last word and grits his teeth over renewed, silent sobs. Something about the silence makes it so much worse. I would rather he keen like a wounded animal than keep it all bottled inside.

Without overthinking it, I reach over and grab his hand. He grips back, hard. The pressure of my tight squeeze seems to help him calm down again.

"Gramps? What are you doing here? You didn't leave a note, and..." It feels a bit out of line to say *And you never leave your condo, as far as I know.* "And I was kind of worried."

He takes a couple of deep, shuddering breaths.

"I wanted to get you something."

"Me?"

He looks at me sideways. "Yes, you. You're leaving tomorrow and I wanted to get you a gift."

"A gift?"

We both stare straight ahead, and I realize we're parked in front of a shop called Bettina's Beach Boutique. In the window are floral cover-ups, bejeweled sandals, and one very glittery caftan.

"Oh," I say softly. I bite the inside of my cheek to stop the tears that spring to my eyes. "I don't need anything, Gramps."

"A gift is not something you need. A gift is to say that I appreciate you."

Even though he didn't actually make it inside the store, even though I have no need for glittery caftans, I suddenly feel that this whole trip was worth it for this moment. Gramps and I have never been close. To hear him say that he appreciates me...it means something. It means a lot.

"It's nice to be appreciated," I say lightly.

He pats my knee twice. I think the crisis is over now, although he still looks shaken.

"What happened?" I ask. "I mean, did something happen?"

He answers slowly, thoughtfully. "I couldn't go in. I never set foot in a place like this without Lottie. She loved to shop. I didn't mind going in stores with her. I liked to buy her things. Going in without her...I couldn't. I couldn't get out of the car."

I nod. "That makes sense."

"I'm not a solitary person. I don't work well on my own. And now that you're leaving tomorrow, well, it hit me all over again, I think."

"Oh," I whisper again. His tone wasn't accusatory, but his words hurt. I came here to help him, not to make him feel even worse. I can't think of one helpful thing to say.

"I just miss her is all," he says. It seems like the understatement of the year.

A long moment passes, and I'm about to suggest that we head back home, when Gramps says, "So, can I buy you something?"

"Uh." I glance again at the storefront. I doubt there's a single thing in there that I would wear. And yet there's no way I can say no. "Okay, Gramps. Let's check out Bettina's."

Inside, we greet the saleslady, and Gramps ambles slowly, taking in the displays with his hands behind his back.

"See anything you like?" he asks.

I tear my gaze away from a white crocheted bikini that costs $150. "My suitcase is so small, I don't have much room for…" I gesture to a lavender polo shirt that reads BEACH BABE.

He nods, and then his eyes light up and he walks a little faster toward a jewelry display. It's home to seashell earrings and dolphin necklaces that I would have loved when I was twelve. There are a few dainty gold earrings that might be okay.

But then Gramps says, his voice excited, "How about one of these?" He's pointing to a row of beaded bracelets. They're made with round stone-like beads of different colors. Gramps gently removes one and holds it up, gesturing for my wrist.

I hold out my left hand and he slides it on, his hand shaking slightly. It's made of marbled white beads, with a small gold charm shaped like a heart. I look from the bracelet to Gramps's face, which is grinning with encouragement. Well, at least he didn't choose the turquoise one with the dolphin charm.

Back at the car, I admire the way my new bracelet catches the sunlight.

"Thanks again," I say.

"My pleasure."

"I'll meet you at home? You won't take off anywhere else?" I tease.

"I'll see you there."

"By the way." I pat the roof of the Mazda. "I wouldn't mind driving with the top down sometime."

"Yeah? You would like that?"

"I would love it."

Over a lunch of turkey and lettuce sandwiches, with my laptop open on the table next to me in case someone pings me, we mostly discuss the weather. We're expecting a thunderstorm this afternoon. I can tell that Gramps doesn't want to talk about the emotional scene in the car, and neither do I. We've had enough drama for one day. But there is one more non-weather-related thing that I need to talk to him about.

Gramps carries our plates to the sink. I follow him and load them into the dishwasher. As he wipes the crumbs from the table, I broach the topic I've been avoiding for the last two days.

"So, Gramps." I lean against the sink. "I know I was out of line when I tried to schedule you for therapy before. But I was wondering if you might consider it. I think it might be helpful for you to talk to someone."

"What, now that you've seen me cry you think I'm a whack job?" He steps around me to toss the crumbs into the sink.

"That's not—technically, we don't call people whack jobs anymore, and no. It's because I think a grief counselor might be able to help you process your feelings."

He stops on his way to the fridge, turns, and looks at me. "Mallory, in my day, the only people who went in for psychotherapy were serial killers and people with an Oedipus complex. As far as I can tell, I am neither of those things."

There are so many things wrong with this statement, I'm stunned for a second.

"That may have been true," I say slowly, "but now, in the twenty-first century, it's very common to see a therapist. People with all kinds of mental health issues benefit from having someone to talk to. Even people without issues—like yourself."

He snorts. "Nice try." He opens the fridge and grabs a can of seltzer.

"The doctor I found sounds like a great fit for you, Gramps. She specializes in grief." *And old people*, I add privately.

"Grief." He shakes his head, like such a tidy word could never encompass everything he's feeling.

"Talking to her might make you feel better. At the very least, it might make you feel less alone. Can I make the appointment for you?"

"I think today has demonstrated that I can't be trusted to take myself anywhere." He laughs lightly.

He has a point there.

"What about a virtual appointment? She sees patients over Zoom, too."

Gramps just looks at me, one side of his mouth hitched up in amusement.

"Mallory, if my computer disconnects from the Wi-Fi, I have to call someone to fix it. I wouldn't know where to start with a Zoom appointment."

Right. Did not think of that.

"I could show you?"

"Sure, you could show me today. But what about next time, when some unexpected problem occurs? How will you show me when you're not here?"

I blink.

"And I guess Trish is usually pretty busy..."

"Trish?" Gramps gives me a strange look. "Trish won't be here to help."

"Huh?" I have absolutely no idea what he's talking about. He appears surprised at my confusion.

"Did no one tell you that Trish and Ron are moving to North Carolina?"

"North Carolina?"

"They've been building their so-called dream home up there in the mountains. They'll be gone by the end of the summer."

It is so like my mom to forget to tell me important family updates like this. And it's hard to believe that Trish would up and leave when her dad is all alone and only going to need more help as he gets older. But I guess you can't plan for everything in life, and if it's her dream house... I'll have to think about all this later. I try to return to the thread of our conversation.

"Maybe you could Uber to your appointment? Or take a taxi?" I can hear the pointlessness before the words even leave my mouth.

"I appreciate the thought, but I don't think it'll work for me. Now, I'm going to take a nap. Enjoy your afternoon. Maybe work on your tan before you go back to the city of clouds."

"Have a good nap."

I decide to do as he says and hit the pool. After all, I don't have any more meetings this afternoon, and I'm only here for one more day—might as well enjoy it. As I'm changing into my bathing suit, I rehash our conversation. As much as I would like Gramps to go to therapy for his mental health, something else is bugging me. And then I realize: He's saying he can't take himself anywhere. Anywhere? What if he needed to see a doctor? What if he needed some kind of urgent appointment, let alone regular checkups? Is there some kind of shuttle service here to help the elderly residents with things like that? They have medical assistants on staff, but I think they're mostly here to distribute medications.

Downstairs at the pool, I spread my towel on a lounge chair. Maybe he doesn't *need* therapy. Maybe I can be the person he talks to. Obviously, I can't provide real, professional counseling, but talking to me is better than nothing, right?

I lay out with my book and can't ignore a nagging worry. The man had a panic attack in front of Bettina's Beach Boutique. Do I really think he'll be fine with a few extra emails and phone calls from me? I'll just have to keep in close contact with Trish—while she's still here—and do the best I can from home.

Chapter 13

I've gotten a couple of chapters into my book when my phone pings with two new emails. Squinting against the sun even with my sunglasses on, I see that they're both from Daniel McKinnon. One is a forwarded message from Alan Gregson. I scan that one first. It's an estimate of what Alan and his team would charge for the work we discussed this morning: reinforcements at the back of the house and in the attic, plumbing repairs in the bathroom. The estimate is just over eleven thousand dollars.

Feeling numb, I open the other email from Daniel. He's helpfully provided the names of some paint suppliers and painters, a flooring supplier, and his "floor guy." My eyes jump down to the end of the second paragraph.

If you use the folks I recommend, based on some of my past projects, my estimate would be about five grand.

I have such a visceral reaction to this number that I almost chuck my phone into the pool.

It's an investment, he continues, *but like I mentioned this morning, with a little polish you'd get a lot more interest from potential renters and could charge slightly above market. If you're interested, I can also send over some ideas for new kitchen appliances.*

"No, Daniel, I am not interested!"

I glance around to see if anyone noticed me yelling at my phone. Indeed, two white-haired women are looking at me from their lounge chairs a few feet away.

"Hi," I say to them. They just stare. "It's my property manager." I attempt a nonchalant shake of the head, like getting frustrated with people who work for me is a normal part of life. The women exchange a smirking glance that clearly says, *Young people*.

I feel nauseous. I lie back and cover my face with my hands, thinking. I know homeowners have to go into debt sometimes—or as Maeve said when they remodeled their basement, they "pay it off monthly." But I just finished paying off my parents monthly. I was looking forward to having some expendable income.

I sit up again and send a quick email back.

How much could I charge if I don't do any of these things?

I lie down again, not expecting him to reply anytime soon. Inheriting Pebble Cottage was supposed to be a windfall. Instead, it's a money pit. Even aside from the terrifying thought of spending so much money on the house, the thought of ripping up floors and all that makes my skin crawl. I just want to be back in my clean, orderly apartment, surrounded by curated objects that bring me joy. That's what I want to spend my hard-earned money on: stuff. Pretty, comforting stuff. Not paint and dishwashers and structural reinforcements, whatever that means.

Ping.

Oh no. He can't have responded already. I don't want to think about this anymore. I want to think about being on the flight home tomorrow, drinking a crisp Chardonnay and watching a movie that'll make me forget about real life for two hours.

I flip over onto my stomach and reluctantly tap open the email.

Ok if I call?

I frown at my phone. Daniel can't be more than a few years older than me; shouldn't he have the same millennial loathing of phone calls? I guess his line of work requires a lot of... communication.

I could tell him that I can't talk right now. Or I could not respond. But I'm a *grown-up*, and a *homeowner*. I heave a sigh and force myself to respond with two letters: *Ok*.

He calls a second later.

"Hey, hey, enjoying our sunshine?"

Goodness, his voice sounds like sunshine itself. It's... jarring.

"Are you always this perky?" I ask before I can stop myself.

"What's not to be perky about?"

I say nothing. This seems to remind him that he just emailed me asking me to part with an ungodly sum of money.

He clears his throat. "Well. I thought it'd be easier to address your question over the phone. Look, without the aesthetic improvements, you're looking at nearly half the monthly rent you could otherwise charge. Ethically, you really can't rent the place without the maintenance Alan recommended. Since you have to do that, in my professional opinion, you might as well do the whole shebang."

"How much more could I charge with the improvements?"

He names a number that's almost double what the last tenant paid. I do some quick mental math. Even with the higher rent, it would take me at least a couple years to pay off this investment.

I bury my face in my arms to stifle a groan. The sun burns into my shoulders. I never signed up for this much responsibility. I've only ever had to take care of myself, and I just recently started doing an okay job at it.

"You still there?" Daniel asks.

"Yep." My voice is muffled with my face still squished against my forearms.

"If it helps, Alan offers a monthly payment plan to clients who meet the credit threshold. And I've had clients opt to do home improvements themselves to save a chunk. So that's something to consider."

A shrill laugh escapes me.

"Daniel. I don't even know how to hang a picture on the wall. I can't do home improvements myself."

"You don't know until you try." He sounds like he's bouncing on the balls of his feet as he talks. What does he put in his coffee?

"I do know. I had to call my dad for help with one measly floating shelf. I did put together an IKEA bookshelf by myself once, but I put the shelves on backward. I cried for half an hour and then just left it like that."

"You—you left the shelves on backward?" Now he sounds like he's trying very hard not to laugh.

"It's a sore subject."

"I get it." There's a pause, and then he continues, "My mom was a chemistry teacher, and when I was a kid she used to say she didn't have a creative bone in her body. But when she retired, she decided she wanted to change that. She watched a YouTube video about needlework—like embroidery and stuff—and decided to teach herself. Boom. Now she's an expert in all things needle and thread. She has an Etsy shop and everything."

"I—wow."

"So..." Daniel's tone implies that I'm missing the obvious. "If my mom can teach herself how to embroider and crochet and quilt after the age of sixty, what's stopping you from learning how to paint a bedroom?"

Okay, when he says it like that, I'm almost offended. It does sound simple.

And... "to save a chunk." How much is that? I look back at his first email to see his estimate for paint and floors. If I keep the cost of the paint and floors but subtract the cost of labor…It is a big difference.

"And I could save a chunk," I say.

"A chunk," he confirms.

I wouldn't even know where to begin doing that stuff myself. But it is interesting.

Ugh, what am I thinking? I have to go back home, to my apartment and my job. Maybe I'll just do the necessary improvements and rent it out cheap. Daniel clearly doesn't like that option, but hey, it's my house.

"I don't know. I'll think about it. It's complicated, because I have to go home. Tomorrow."

"That does complicate things, doesn't it?"

Am I imagining it, or is he implying that it complicates things with the house and…with us? No, I'm definitely imagining it. Because there is no us. Obviously.

"Well, let me know what you decide," he says. "There's no rush, of course."

No rush for him. But for me? I could definitely use the rental income to start covering these costs. The numbers and the impossibility of the situation make my head spin.

"Okay."

"Lucky planes," he says.

"What?"

"It's what we say in my family before someone boards a flight. You know, safe travels and all that."

"Oh. Thank you."

I want to ask where this saying came from, and whether he traveled a lot as a kid, or whether he does now—because I don't want to hang up the phone. Again. What is this power his voice has over me?

But I don't ask any of those things, because that wouldn't be professional.

Instead, I say, "I'll be in touch after I've made a decision," which comes out sounding like I have a stick where the sun don't shine. Why can't I just sound normal for once in my life?

"Looking forward to hearing from you," he says smoothly. "Bye, Mallory."

Back at the condo, Gramps is still asleep. I curl up on the couch and watch out the sliding glass balcony doors as the promised thunderstorm moves in. The clouds churn, darkening to a purplish gray. The gulf roils up to match the sky, dotted with white peaks. I grab my beach towel and tuck it over my knees like a blanket. That's one thing about Florida: People never have enough blankets.

The rain rolls in, and it's a true summer downpour. It's so loud that it drowns out the sound of Gramps snoring in the other room. Nature's white-noise machine. I tap my phone and check my calendar. Tomorrow's a full day of travel—I might need to lie to Kat and tell her I'm taking a sick day. The next day, Wednesday, is packed with meetings from nine to four. Skimming the meeting titles with words like "OP planning" and "milestone check-in" fills me with a faint sense of dread. Faint, because I'm used to it, and because I really, really need the paycheck. Dread, because it's all mind-numbingly boring, and because my mind has been so far from work the last few days that it might take some effort to get back into it.

There's a sudden bright flash, followed immediately by a *crack* of thunder. It makes me drop my phone. Heart pounding, I retrieve my phone from the plush rug, and then tiptoe to the door of Gramps's bedroom.

I crack the door open slightly and peer inside. He's sleeping on his side with his hands tucked under his cheek. The thunder doesn't seem to have woken him. As I watch his chest rise and fall with each breath, I'm filled with some kind of feeling that I've never felt before. It's tender and achy and peaceful and nostalgic all at once. I guess that it might be similar to how Maeve feels watching her son sleep. And then I picture myself driving off to the airport tomorrow morning, waving goodbye as Gramps stands back and watches me go. I imagine him coming back upstairs, alone. Looking around the empty kitchen, pulling out his newspaper, putting it back down, climbing into bed to sleep the day away.

Crack. This time I feel the thunder in my chest. Gramps doesn't stir, so I close the door and return to the couch. I check my calendar again, and something clicks. These meetings are virtual. I do them all from my living room at home. Why couldn't I do them from Gramps's living room instead? Kat wouldn't even need to know.

As much as this idea terrifies me—I learned my lesson the hard way, back in my wannabe-digital-nomad days—it also fills me with relief. I *don't* have to leave. My apartment will be fine without me for a few more days, but Gramps needs me. Sure, I miss the comforts of home. But this condo isn't so bad. Plus, I have my laptop, meaning I can still watch *Outlander* before bed.

I grab my phone again, open the Pottery Barn website, find the fluffiest blanket they have, and order it to be shipped here. And then I cancel my flight.

This was the right decision. Everything will be fine. There's no way Kat will find out I'm not where I'm supposed to be.

Chapter 14

At dinner that night, Gramps and I silently pick at our casserole (this time it's tater tot, something I'd never heard of that is surprisingly delicious).

I clear my throat. "So, I was thinking."

"Hmm?" he says without looking up from his plate.

"I don't think I'll leave tomorrow after all. I was thinking I'll stay for another week or so. If that's okay with you."

His light-blue eyes flash up at me, and the side of his mouth lifts in the barest hint of a smile.

"Whatever you like," he says.

His words were casual, but I saw that look in his eyes. I can tell he's happy. It fills me with a warm flush, and it reinforces that I made the right decision.

I nod and return his almost smile. We return to eating in silence. After a few more bites, I can't take it anymore.

"Okay, who made you this casserole? It might be the best thing I've ever tasted."

"Angela. Must be a Texas dish."

"Is that where she's from?"

"Can't you tell by the accent?"

"I guess so."

From there, Gramps goes on to tell me about various Texans he'd met in his life. The tale begins with a cattle rancher he'd met in the Ontario airport in 1971 who'd tried to get him involved in his Ponzi scheme, and ends with the police officer who'd chased Gramps through the Houston suburbs in an attempt to give him a parking ticket. When the officer finally caught him, Gramps pretended he only understood Polish.

"So you got out of the ticket?" I prompt. *Talking his way out of a ticket* has always been Gramps's favorite type of anecdote.

"I got out of the ticket." He chuckles and wipes his mouth with his napkin. "*Przepraszam, Oficerze, nie rozumiem.*"

I wake up early so that I have time to take care of all the logistical stuff on my to-do list before my workday starts. To start with, I need to return my rental car. It physically pains me to think of how much EZCar would charge me if I kept the little red Yaris for another day, let alone another week. Other items on my list include stocking up on essentials and notifying my parents and my neighbor, Sam, that I'm not coming home yet.

Gramps offers to follow me to EZCar so he can drive me home afterward, but I decline.

"It's right in the middle of Reina Beach. I'm going to run some errands up there and then I think I can take the bus back here." I peer at the maps app on my phone. The bus option seems straightforward enough. Gramps gives me a weird look, probably because he hasn't been on a bus since the 1960s.

I return the car with little fanfare. The teenage employee couldn't care less that I'm returning it here instead of at the Tampa airport like I'd planned.

I step out of the air-conditioned lobby and into the midmorning heat. Next up, errands. I squint through my sunglasses at the list I'd typed on my phone.

> *Shampoo and conditioner (full size)*
> *Hair cream*
> *Face wash*
> *Face lotion*
> *Smoothie ingredients*
> *Work snacks*
> *Frozen pizzas*
> *Wine*

I would also love new bedding, but I'm doubtful they have a suitable home goods store around here. I could order some online, but I should probably stop spending money since I'm about to spend all of mine on Pebble Cottage.

I scan my surroundings: an ABC liquor store, a high-end seafood restaurant, a gas station. The downtown core of the town, such as it is, is a few blocks south. There are plenty of stores there.

Hopefully, I use my phone to search for the nearest Target. No luck. The closest one is ten miles away. Why did I return the car before running errands? Okay, what about Ulta? There is one slightly closer, but according to my phone, it would be a two-hour walk. *Great.* I'm not even going to bother searching for a Sephora.

Cursing my foolishly laid plans, I walk toward the cluster of downtown shops. The atmosphere is pleasant enough—there's a sidewalk lined with shrubs and the beach is right across the street, giving me a perfect view of sparkling blue water and white sands—but I can barely enjoy it because of the heat pounding down on me. I'm wearing a Seahawks cap and a white linen top over denim shorts, yet the sun is relentless. I wipe sweat from my upper lip and grimace as it drips between my breasts and shoulder blades. After a five-minute walk, I'm in a bustling part of town—as bustling as this town gets, anyway. Families troop down the path toward the beach, pulling wagons full of towels, floats, and coolers. Tourists buzz from one shop to another. There's even a cute café with people sipping cappuccinos at rickety sidewalk tables.

I pause and gaze around from one side of the street to the other, trying to figure out where to go. Shouldn't there be some kind of local beauty store? Like a Bethany's Beauty Corner or a Helen's Hair Haven?

"Can I help you find somethin', hon?" A woman wearing a bedazzled Mickey Mouse shirt has paused beside me. She peers at me over the top of her oversize sunglasses.

"Oh!" I startle, not expecting a stranger to talk to me, and then feel bad for being startled. She's just being polite. "Do you know if there's a beauty store or something nearby?"

"Like a hair salon?"

"No, a store for buying skin-care products and hair products?"

She stares at me for half a beat, smacking the chewing gum in her mouth. "Hon, there's a CVS right there." She points a manicured finger to the drugstore across the street.

"Of course. Right. Thanks!"

Not exactly what I had in mind, but what can I expect from a small town? I hurry through the aggressively air-conditioned drugstore, making do with the brands they have. No Kiehl's or DevaCurl here. Oh well, I'll survive, and it's better for my wallet anyway.

Next up, I need to find a grocery store. Should be easy enough. I scan my surroundings for a Publix. I hoof up and down a couple of blocks, and it quickly becomes apparent that there's no big-box grocery store with a bright-green sign. I stop and type "groceries" in my maps app. There *is* a Publix... ten miles away in St. Pete. Farther north, there's a Walmart Supercenter. Closer to me, there's something called Paddy's Fisherman's Supply—I'm guessing that's not the store I'm looking for—and a place called Foxy's Market. I guess I'm going to Foxy's.

By the time I get there, my sandals are rubbing painfully on my heat-swollen feet. How do people *live* here?

I just need to get a few things, and then I'll be on my way back to the comfort of Gramps's condo. I fully intend to spend the rest of the day in the AC with my feet up.

"Welcome in!" a chirpy voice greets me as I step through the sliding doors. Ugh, I'm in no condition to make small talk, what with my sweaty tomato face. I give a tight smile and nod. "What can I help you with?"

"Uh..." I look from the beaming smile of this middle-aged woman with dyed brown hair, to the list on my phone, to the well-labeled grocery aisles. "I think I'll be okay."

She looks disappointed, but I mean really, I have a short list, and it's a grocery store—a small one. I truly don't need help. The introvert in me is chafing at the overt friendliness around here.

I grab my wine, snacks, smoothie ingredients, and frozen pizza, and head to the checkout. I was crossing my fingers for a self-checkout, but no luck. There's one staffed checkout lane, and it's staffed by Foxy herself. I might be imagining it, but it feels like she's scowling at me.

"Thank you," I say as she bags my groceries. "Foxy." I add her name in an attempt to be small-town polite. I'm rather proud of myself.

She glances up at me and for a second I think she's going to say something rude or not say anything at all. But then she says, "You're welcome. Have a nice day."

Ha! Small-town manners win the day.

Outside, I shuffle the plastic CVS bag and the plastic grocery bags from one hand to another, trying to find the right balance. I wish I'd thought to bring tote bags, but Gramps probably doesn't even have any. He would be aghast if I told him Seattle has outlawed plastic bags. Or maybe he wouldn't actually have an opinion, given that he doesn't grocery shop.

I should probably teach him how.

It takes me a full ten minutes to find the bus stop, by which point I'm certain I have contracted heatstroke. It takes me another five minutes to figure out if this is, in fact, the stop for the bus that will take me back to Gramps's. It is, but I'm on the wrong side of the street. I figure it out just in time; this bus only comes every half hour. Clearly, people here don't rely on the bus for everyday transportation the way we do back home.

When the bus finally comes, I'm wilting. The sun has been beating down on me for so long, I can barely remember my own name. So I think I'm hallucinating when a bright-red, open-air trolley playing jingly music stops in front of me.

"Uh..." I say eloquently when the driver looks at me expectantly. "Is this...the bus?"

"It's the trolley." The driver's deadpan voice does not match the jingly trolley vibe.

"And the trolley is...the bus?" I realize on some level that I sound like an alien, but I can barely think straight, and this situation isn't helping.

"Only bus around these parts, unless you want a Greyhound, and that's only from the depot in Tampa."

Dazed, I step up onto the touristy contraption and drop the fare in the coin slot. Rather than normal bus seats, there are two long wooden benches on either side. I take a seat and try to balance all my bags on my lap. There are a few other passengers on board, hanging their heads out the open windows like happy dogs. Despite the old-fashioned look and the ice-cream-truck-esque music, it does appear to function like a normal bus. It stops by the boardwalk and then again by a public beach, each time after a passenger has pulled the pulley with a cheerful *ding*.

The driver lets me out outside of Sandy Shores and I thank her and stumble down the steps. By the time I cross the green lawn and hoof it all the way to building C, I'm ready to collapse. I let myself into the condo and drop my bags in the entryway, gasping in the sweet, cold AC. My hair is matted to my face, and my clothes are soaked through with sweat. I limp to the kitchen to stash my groceries in the fridge and freezer. I'm kind of hoping Gramps is napping so he won't see me like this, but he is sitting right there at the kitchen table.

"Wow," he says, and I await some sardonic comment about my appearance. He swims slightly in my vision, and I think I might actually faint.

"You finally got some color," he says.

Chapter 15

That afternoon, I send my neighbor Sam a text saying I'm extending my trip by a few days. They respond with: *You got eleven packages. They're clogging up my living room.*

Really? I ask.

No, you got four. But they are clogging up my apartment.

I really, really appreciate it! I'll be home in a week, max. I'll bring you something from Florida.

Sam responds simply, *K.*

My parents are another story. After my final meeting wraps up, I step out onto Gramps's balcony and give my mom a call to let her know about my change of plans.

"You're staying there? Is everything okay?" My mom's voice is shrill with worry.

"Yeah, everything is fine. I just need to figure out some stuff with the house, and, I don't know, I think Gramps likes my company." I perch on the edge of a deck chair, which squeaks with age.

"Of course he does. Who wouldn't enjoy your company?" she says with the certainty only a mom can have. "How's he doing?"

"He seems okay. He seems like Gramps." I hesitate, wondering if I should tell her about his panic attack outside Bettina's Beach Boutique. Normally, that is the type of thing I would tell my mom without a second thought. But for some reason, it feels like a secret between Gramps and me.

"Okay. But you can't stay there forever, you know."

"What? Who said anything about staying here forever?"

"You have your life here, your home, your *parents*."

"Mom, I am not staying here forever."

"Because Florida sunshine is not all it's cracked up to be. It can really age you. Plus, their politics there are just…" Mom makes a noise of disgust. "You haven't talked to anyone about politics, have you? Because those people can turn on you like that." She snaps her fingers.

"No, I haven't talked to anyone here about politics. It's not like I'm going to dinner parties. I've made small talk with, like, three people." *And made out with one*, my brain interjects rudely.

"Good."

"But you know Gramps watches MSNBC. What's the big deal?"

"Yes, but he lets his friends think he watches Fox News."

"That cannot possibly be true."

"Anyway. You are *much* better off at home in Seattle."

I gaze over the balcony railing at the Gulf of Mexico shimmering lazily under the bright sun. I suddenly have a very strong urge to be sprawled out in the hot white sand.

"Whatever you say, Mom."

We say our goodbyes and I tell Gramps I'm heading to the beach.

"Do you want to join me?" I ask.

"No, no, it's time for my nap. You have fun."

I realize, with a heavy feeling in my chest, that although Gramps lives on one of the most beautiful beaches in the world, he never ventures beyond the pool deck.

The next morning, it's back to my workday routine...Florida-style. With the time difference, I don't have to start work until noon here. I sleep in until a luxurious nine forty-five.

"The dining room closes at ten," Gramps tells me, sitting at the kitchen table as I enter the kitchen, rubbing my eyes.

"I know. I usually just have a smoothie before work."

"Work, yes. I'm very interested to see this so-called remote work in action."

I side-eye him as I gather my yogurt, spinach, and frozen peaches. "It's not all that interesting. It's literally just me sitting at my laptop."

He shakes his head and flips a page of his newspaper. "In my day, it was a lot of bustling from lab to lab, holding twenty-person meetings in windowless conference rooms, and chatting with colleagues in the office kitchen."

"Well," I say, ducking down to look in a cabinet, "I guess scientists can't really do all their work from home. So if you'd still been working in the 2020s, you would have been spared the dreaded remote work."

"You think so?" Gramps says thoughtfully. "I didn't care for the office environment all that much. The kitchen always smelled like tuna fish. Do people still eat tuna fish sandwiches?"

"I wouldn't know." I stand on my tiptoes to check another cabinet, a sliver of panic creeping in. "Gramps, do you have a blender?"

"A blender? Of course!" He heaves himself out of his chair and opens the cabinet beneath the toaster, from which he extracts a boxy, yellowing blender with square buttons. He hands it to me with a proud smile.

"Osterizer," I say. "Hey, didn't we used to use this to make milkshakes when I was a kid?"

"Indeed! I bought this for Lottie for our tenth anniversary. Ordered it from the Sears catalog."

"The Sears catalog? Wait, so have you had this blender since the 1970s?"

"Sure!"

I peer skeptically into the pitcher, half expecting to see a thick layer of dust.

"Okay...thanks."

I load it up with my usual smoothie ingredients, plug it in, and press the BLEND button, which gives a satisfying click. The blender does not erupt into flames. It is, however, extremely loud, and after thirty seconds or so, it gives off a pungent odor of burning plastic.

"Oh my God," I choke, pressing the OFF button. "When is the last time you used this thing?"

Gramps looks up from his paper unconcernedly. "Hmm? Oh, I don't know. When was the last time we made you kids milkshakes?"

"What?"

"Or, no, wait, Lottie used it to make daiquiris once. That must have been around 2006, because it was when the Wilsons had their going-away party. So, 2006."

I gaze sadly at my plastic-ified smoothie. "That was, like, almost twenty years ago."

"Well, at least we haven't worn it out."

With the smell of burnt plastic in my nostrils, I can't even bring myself to taste my smoothie. I pour it down the drain. My stomach rumbles.

I root around in the freezer, extract a loaf of bread, and pop two slices in the toaster. This feels like a negative omen of sorts. I never have toast before work. I always have a smoothie.

As I scrape some butter onto my toast, I glance at the microwave clock and let out a squeak. It's almost ten thirty already. Time for my virtual yoga class. I cram the toast in my mouth, gulp down a small glass of orange juice—it's heavy on the pulp—and try to find the optimal place to set up. I don't have my yoga mat with me, but a blanket will work in a pinch.

I scoot the coffee table out of the way and spread a blanket in the middle of the living room. A sense of peace settles over me as my usual yoga instructor greets the class and starts moving through the flow. When I stretch into the first downward dog, I look between my legs and see Gramps standing there, watching me.

"Ah!" I yelp and crash down onto one elbow.

"Don't stop on my account." Gramps grins and settles onto the sofa with a mug of coffee.

"What are you—Gramps, I'm trying to—" I splutter.

"Is this yoga?"

"What—of course this is yoga. What else would it be?"

"Please, continue. I'm here to watch and learn."

I look from him to the instructor on my screen. I've completely lost the flow. A part of me would very much like to tell him to give me some space, to go to another room for the next forty-five minutes, but I rein it in. After all, I am in his living room.

"Do you want to try?" I ask brightly, patting the blanket next to me.

"Me? Goodness, no."

"It'll be good for you. A nice stretch. Get the blood flowing."

"No, no. Please." He waves a hand, telling me to carry on.

With a sigh, I try to get back into it. The teacher has already moved on to the second flow, so I've completely missed the first one.

And let me tell you, if you have never tried to do a one-woman yoga class in front of a watching grandpa, it is uncomfortable. No, it is impossible. I can't get back into the right headspace. I fumble the moves. I don't feel relaxed or stretched or anything. During the final Savasana, as I try to relax into a naplike state, I can't take it anymore. Gramps doesn't even have the courtesy to read a book or something. He's just watching, like I'm six and putting on a play for his entertainment.

I stand, roll up the blanket, and close my laptop.

"Finished already?" he asks.

"Yep!" I try to bite back the aggression in my tone.

"Looks like a lovely workout."

"Mm-hmm. Lovely." I head toward the bathroom.

"Angela does an exercise class, too. Down on the lawn. She's very passionate about it. Maybe you could join her sometime."

I stop at the bathroom door. The thought of joining a senior citizens' workout class in the sticky heat is deeply unappealing, but not as much as the thought of repeating the yoga fiasco I've just experienced. "Maybe I will."

"Wonderful. Enjoy your shower!"

Freshly bathed and dressed, I hunker down in my bedroom, door closed. I've pulled a kitchen chair up to my nightstand, which is cleared of everything except my laptop and a mug of Gramps's bitter coffee. I miss my Nespresso machine.

As soon as I log on, Kat pings me.

Good morning! Sending everyone on the team a friendly reminder to submit your reports by the end of the day.

Oh boy. I choke down a gulp of coffee, then send her a thumbs-up emoji. I've definitely been slacking since I've been in Florida. I need to get it together today.

The hours pass slowly as I sift through dozens of unread emails, pausing here and there to add notes to my status reports for each project.

Around three—lunchtime in Seattle—I head to the kitchen to heat up my frozen pizza. I'm in a meeting—camera off—which I listen to with my noise-canceling headphones as I bustle around the kitchen. I pop the pizza in the oven and start the timer, then grab a bag of baby carrots from the fridge.

Gramps has materialized, and he's leaning over the kitchen table peering at the faces on my laptop screen.

"Gramps!" I whip the headphones off one ear.

"Zoom meeting?" He sounds pleased with himself for knowing the terminology.

"Yes. And it's, you know, my job. You didn't touch anything, did you?" I scan the screen to make sure he didn't turn on the camera or type anything in the chat box.

"Of course not." He sounds slightly injured now.

"Sorry. Just—" I stop, because Kat is asking me a question. I jab the UNMUTE button. "No, Antonio's team is behind by at least a week. They've already let Ben know, so he's aware of the situation."

From the other side of the table, Gramps mouths, *Wow. Nice.*

I don't know whether to laugh or cry. Before I can say anything, he meanders over to the oven and cracks it open to peek at my pizza.

"Did you make this?" he asks.

"It's a frozen pizza from Foxy's," I whisper. "You can have some. When it's done." With one finger, I push the oven door closed.

"I couldn't; it's too close to dinnertime. Well, I'll let you get back to work." He goes to his bedroom and closes the door behind him.

I sigh with relief, and then feel guilty. Gramps isn't really *annoying* me, it's just that I don't like to be interrupted while I'm working.

The timer pings, and I carefully transfer my pizza to a cutting board. Half listening to the meeting, I search every drawer in the kitchen before accepting the fact that Gramps does not own a pizza cutter. Grumpily, I cut the pizza with a knife instead, then eat it and a handful of baby carrots at the kitchen table.

By eight o'clock, I've managed to submit all my reports to Kat. I could hear Gramps snoring after lunch, but I clamped my headphones back on and it successfully drowned out the noise. By the time my workday is over, I'm angsty to get outside and feel the sun on my skin. But standing on the balcony, I realize that the day is over. It's almost sunset, and it's not a pretty one today, either. The sky is full of rain-soaked clouds, threatening to overflow. The air is still, humid, and crackling with the anticipation of a storm. The pool deck and beach below are both empty.

I guess I might have to spend some time outdoors tomorrow morning, before my workday starts. I don't like it. It's not my normal routine. But I can't be at the beach and not spend any time in the sun. For now, I'm going to take my usual after-work walk, even if it means getting caught in a thunderstorm.

Chapter 16

The threatened storm doesn't materialize, although the sky continues to bulge with dark-gray clouds as night falls. I'm refreshed and sweaty after a long walk on the beach, catching up on the latest episode of *Elementary*. As I walk back to the condo, the shimmering blue light of the hot tub catches my eye. A dunk in the Jacuzzi sounds lovely, and I still have a few minutes left of my episode to listen to.

The only problem is I'm not wearing a bathing suit. I glance around the deserted pool deck and give a cursory glance at the balconies up above. There's no one around, so I strip down to my bra and underwear and step down into the hot tub. The warm, gently bubbling water feels so good that I let out a sigh of contentment. I'm about to slip my headphones back on, but then I notice the sounds: the ambient noises of the beach at night. The waves whisper softly as they rush back and forth, and the palm trees overhead rustle in the warm breeze. There are other sounds, too, like the musical chirping of something that might be a cricket, and the unmistakable deep croak of a frog.

"—and I told her, 'Not with my money, sugar!'"

I startle at the sudden peal of laughter nearby. *Crap.* I go for my clothes, but they're just out of reach, and before I can hop out, I have company.

"Mallory, is that you?"

Angela appears, wrapped in a white bathrobe, accompanied by a man and a woman I haven't met.

"Hi, Angela." I sink further into the water, hoping she doesn't look too closely at my skimpy pink bralette.

"Isn't a late-night soak just heavenly?" She gracefully removes her robe and drapes it across a chair, revealing a bright-purple one-piece. "It's a ritual of ours. This is Pam and Simon." The two strangers wave hello. "Mallory is Leonard's granddaughter."

"Ohh, poor Leonard," Pam says, climbing down into the Jacuzzi.

Simon makes a sympathetic noise in agreement as he sits across from me.

"We're sorry about your grandmother," he says with a heavy Brooklyn accent. "She was a delight."

"Thank you."

"When do you fly home, Mallory?" Angela asks, settling into the water between Pam and me.

"In a few days," I say vaguely.

"And have you had a nice trip so far? Is it what you were hoping?"

"Yeah. It's been...nice." The question makes me think about the reasons I'm here, and it occurs to me that I made absolutely zero progress today on the house stuff. I'm supposed to be making decisions about renovations. Instead, I let the entire day be consumed with work. I didn't extend my trip just to work from Gramps's living room. Tomorrow, I need to wake up earlier and actually get things done.

"Young people today," Simon booms. "So virtuous. When I was your age—what are you, twenty?—I was hiking and drinking my way through Mexico with my buddies. Ha! Visiting grandparents? That was only if my parents dragged me along."

I smile slightly. When I was twenty-two, I was sipping espressos at sidewalk cafés in Paris, snorkeling off the beach in Kantiang Bay. More recently, Alex and I had daydreamed about taking trips to Japan or Peru. Of course, that never happened, and it never will.

"I did some traveling in my early twenties," I say. "Thanks for thinking I'm twenty, by the way. But it's been years since I've traveled anywhere, other than here."

"*Years?* What've you been doing?" Simon sounds scandalized.

"The pandemic, dear." Pam slaps her hand lightly on top of the bubbling water.

"Oh, that. Well, it's time to shake it off, all right? That's behind us now. You grab some friends and go see the world."

I bite back a laugh. *I wish it were that easy.* I glance at Angela and see that she's giving me a soft, empathetic look.

"Actually, I'm also here because I inherited Lottie and Gramps's old house. So I'm figuring out what it needs. And how to pay for it."

Angela shakes her head with a click of her tongue. "If only you could've talked to Lottie about this. What a shame. Do you know, she was so talented at getting things done for free. She would call in personal favors with no shame. And if she couldn't get someone to help her, she'd find a way to do it herself. I remember the time she single-handedly replaced her Toyota's muffler. Didn't know a thing about cars."

"How did she do that?" I ask.

Angela lifts both hands in a shrug. "Checked out a book from the library!"

Of course, the library. Pre-internet. With a sudden painful longing, I wish I could talk to Lottie about Pebble Cottage to get her advice. I wonder what she would say.

"Well, I better get going." I point to the clock on the wall, above the sign listing out the "Spa Rules." "I've been in here for more than fifteen minutes."

Simon roars with laughter, and Pam leans over and says, "Darlin', you want to loosen your grip on the rule book of life. Trust me, it'll be more fun that way."

I stare back at her for a moment. And then, head held high, I climb out of the hot tub with my Victoria's Secret cheekies riding all the way up my ass.

As I walk away, clutching my clothes against my dripping-wet chest, I hear Angela say quietly, "I don't know where these young people buy their bathing suits."

"Brazil?" Pam suggests. The sound of their laughter rings through the sticky night air.

In bed, freshly showered and wearing buttery-soft shorty pajamas, I curl up underneath the seashell comforter with my laptop balanced on my legs. The sky finally breaks open as I'm watching *Outlander*, thunderclaps booming every other minute. It's very cozy. Still, I can hardly focus on the episode. What am I going to do about Pebble Cottage? I suppose I should give Alan the green light to do the work he needs to do. I wonder how long that will take. Maybe I should schedule another trip after he's finished so that I can make a decision about the cosmetic updates. But how long can I afford to wait before finding new tenants? I guess I should go over the numbers again in the morning.

What would Lottie do? I wish, again, that I could ask her.

I wake up at seven forty-five. (I was aiming for seven thirty, but I hit the SNOOZE button in my sleep.) Gramps has already been up for an hour and says he's content with his bowl of Grape-Nuts, so I head to the dining room alone. I pile my plate with scrambled eggs, pancakes, and melon, and wolf it all down with a glass of cranberry juice and a mug of creamy coffee. It's better than the coffee Gramps makes, but I miss my oat milk lattes. No one tries to talk to me, and I have a little table to myself next to an enormous window overlooking the gulf.

As I walk back to Gramps's through the grassy lawn, the morning sun warms my face. The humidity at this hour is not only bearable but downright pleasant. Maybe the key to living in Florida is waking up early.

Under the white gazebo, Angela's exercise class is in full flow, a dozen sweating seniors in formfitting outfits. I don't know what the class is, but they're moving fast and making a lot of grunting noises. It looks a bit intimidating, to be honest.

I spend the next hour going over everything about Pebble Cottage: the estimates for Alan's work, for the cosmetic work, and the costs of property tax and insurance. I'm not really a numbers person, so I have to triple-check my work.

If I pay off Alan in monthly installments, I could go maybe three months without tenants. Any longer than that, and I'd be too far in debt for my liking. That should be enough time to figure out the aesthetic updates. I feel somewhat divided on that issue, and I'm not sure why. It's as if part of me doesn't want to disappoint Daniel McKinnon, even though *all* of me doesn't want to shell out a premium for his so-called paint and floor guys. But I don't exactly feel like picking apart these feelings right now. I need to stay focused on the numbers; I absolutely cannot let my financial judgment be clouded by the fact that I made out with my property manager—hot redhead or not.

And he is hot, a sly voice in my head reminds me.

Calm down, I tell her.

Before I devolve into having a full conversation with the voices in my head, I decide to take a walk. I'm not about to attempt yoga again with Gramps around, but I need to move my body before sitting at my laptop for eight hours.

Forty-five minutes later, my limbs feel pleasantly warm and loose from my beach walk. I make myself a turkey sandwich and bring it to my room to start my workday.

Before I get sucked into Slack messages and Zoom meetings, I send a quick email to Daniel and Alan letting them know I want to get started with the maintenance. This makes me feel like a responsible, accomplished adult, which launches me into work on a high note.

That note quickly sours, though, thanks to Gramps's Wi-Fi. It worked well enough yesterday, so I can't understand why it keeps flickering in and out today. In a team meeting, I can barely understand what my co-worker is saying, because she sounds and looks like a pixel-y robot.

Walking from my room to the kitchen to the living room, I say loudly, "Can you say that one more time? Sorry, my internet!"

A few more warbled words, and then, "—think we've lost Mallory."

"No! I'm here!" I yell into my laptop. "Can you hear me?"

"Loud and clear," comes Gramps's voice.

"Ah!" I yelp and spin around to face him, simultaneously jabbing the MUTE button, which makes me drop my laptop. "Crap!" I shout-whisper, scrabbling to pick it up, trying to make sure I'm still in the meeting and also muted.

"Sorry, Gramps," I whisper. He stands there holding a book, his face unusually stern.

"I'm trying to read." He brandishes the book. As he waves it through the air, I catch sight of a red cover that includes the words *Modern Physics*.

"I'm sorry! I'm having trouble getting a good signal, and I'm in a meeting."

"And is this meeting more or less important than the discovery that nebulae can act as both source and lens in the gravitational lens effect? Because that is the chapter I am reading."

"I…"

"Is your meeting going to change the path of scientific discourse?"

I stare at him like a goldfish. "Definitely not. It's about a project to test out a new time management tool."

"Time management?" Gramps sounds, for a moment, like this might pique his interest.

"You know, tracking how we spend our time during the workday. Logging the minutes spent on emails, meetings, spreadsheets…"

His face droops down again in disappointment.

"Can you find somewhere else to have your meeting?"

I bite my lip, my heart pounding in uncomfortable frustration. I *hate* the feeling of a meeting going on without me, the idea that my co-workers might think I'm slacking. It gives me a panicky, fight-or-flight feeling. But I have no choice but to agree with Gramps. This is his home, after all.

"Okay. Sure."

He nods briskly and returns to his room.

Sweating slightly, I type a quick message into the meeting and update my Slack status. "Internet troubles. BRB."

I hurtle downstairs to the communal library. It's a small room with plush chairs and couches, and a couple of bookshelves lined with tattered paperbacks. I try the Wi-Fi here, but it requires a password. *Come on!* I scan the room looking for a sign or poster of some kind with instructions on how to connect, but no. And of course, there's no one around to ask.

There was a coffee shop in town. I'll try there.

By the time I climb out of my Uber in front of the café—quaintly named Paradise Coffee—I'm extremely disgruntled. My meeting has ended, and I have another one starting in twenty minutes. No offense to Florida, but my hopes for this coffee shop are not high. In Seattle, we have a coffee shop on every corner with free Wi-Fi and all the alternative milks you can dream of. If there's no internet here, I might have to take an unplanned day of PTO. Kat would not be pleased.

I weave through the sidewalk tables, where clusters of people are enjoying their coffees in the sun, and push the door open. A bell tinkles to announce my arrival. Inside, the space is small and warm, but there are plenty of tables, about half of them occupied, so there's a pleasant ambient buzz of chatter.

"How can I help you?" The middle-aged woman behind the counter has smooth, tan skin, an impeccably chic curly bob, and, surprisingly, a French accent.

"Hi," I say, quickly scanning the menu on the wall. "Oh my God, you have oat milk?"

Her mouth forms a moue in amusement. "Yes. As well as almond and coconut."

"Can I have an iced oat milk latte, please?"

As I pull out my wallet, I notice a sign on the counter that reads:

Wi-Fi: ParadiseCoffee
Password: joiedevivre

Yes! Now, this is civilized. I love a place that doesn't make you ask for the password. I'm beaming as the man behind the counter hands me my iced coffee.

"Enjoy," he says, and I detect a hint of a French accent behind the word.

I'm so happy and relieved—an oat milk latte *and* free Wi-Fi!—that I find myself making small talk. "Are you two from France?"

"*Oui*," the woman says, rubbing hand sanitizer into her hands and smiling. She really does have amazing skin, with just a few lines around her dark eyes. "But we 'ave lived here for almost twenty years now."

"What made you move here? I mean, I would never leave France!"

The man laughs heartily. "Have you looked outside?" He points out the window, where the gulf is visible across the street.

"We came here on holiday with our children, and we never wanted to leave," the woman adds. "So we didn't!"

"I mean, I guess it is paradise, right?" I take a sip of my latte. It's impeccable. "How many children do you have?"

"One daughter," the woman says. "She moved back to France after she married a Frenchman. And one son."

"Who will never leave us, no matter how we ask him to," the man jokes.

"And why would I, when I have the world's greatest parents?" A guy in his late twenties emerges from the back room, tying a dark-green apron around his waist. He has a deep, fully American voice, and his parents' dark-brunette coloring. He is also tall, broad, and extremely cute.

"I mean, I get it," I say, unable to wipe the grin off my face. "I'm Mallory, by the way."

"Jeanette," the woman says. "And my husband, Antoine, and our son, Leo."

"Nice to meet you! I'm so glad I found this place. I really needed this latte. I have some work to do, I hope it's okay if I…" I point to an empty table by the window.

"Of course," Jeanette says with a sweep of her hand. "Please, feel free."

With a grateful wave, I settle in at the table. Within ten seconds, I'm connected and checking in on the messages I've missed. I apologize to the people who were in the meeting I dropped, and then notice that I have a new email in my personal inbox.

It's from Daniel.

Excellent! I'll discuss logistics with Alan and CC you on everything. Let me know when you've made a decision about paint and floors.

Great. I feel a rush of relief that I handled the main hurdle, combined with a tinge of guilt about keeping Daniel waiting about the other stuff. But, I mean, he works for me, right? I shouldn't feel guilty.

Unexpectedly, another new email flashes up on my screen. It's from Daniel again, with a new subject: *Hope you had a good trip.*

The body reads: *How's Seattle?*

What? Umm, this is weird. But also possibly flattering? Starting up a new email thread just to ask about my trip? I feel heat in my cheeks as I type a reply.

It's—I look out the window at the impossibly blue sky—*gray and drizzly, as usual. Flight was good, thanks!*

And send. I don't want to misinterpret the vibe and send anything too flirty. And it's a little awkward to be straight-up lying about my whereabouts like this. But things were so awkward with him the other day, and I told him he wouldn't have to worry about seeing me in person again.

I give my head a little shake to clear it, and then switch over to my work inbox.

But Daniel writes back immediately.

Drizzly, huh? I could've sworn the weather forecast said something about...Paradise.

What the heck? My heart jumps into my throat as I re-read the email twice, my face scrunched in confusion. Paradise? Like Paradise Coffee? Or is it a reference to something I don't understand?

Before I can start typing back—not that I know what I would even say—he emails again.

Enjoy any oat milk lattes recently?

Okay, what is going on? I crane my neck around to scan the other coffee shop patrons. Sure enough, a redheaded man is sitting in the opposite corner, waving at me over his laptop.

I let out a long, deep, humiliated breath, and then raise one hand in a weak wave.

He strides over to me, beaming in clear amusement.

"Hi," he says, taking the chair opposite me.

"Have you been here this whole time?"

"*Mais oui*. Imagine my surprise when you waltzed in. I thought I must be mistaken, until, well." He makes a vague up-and-down gesture with his hand, and then his face instantly flames red.

"Until what?" I'm weirdly certain that he was going to say something about recognizing me from behind. My butt? My legs? I mean, they do look amazing in these shorts.

"Until I heard you jonesing for your oat milk latte. I recognized your Seattle voice."

"My *Seattle* voice?"

He taps one finger on the table. The back of his hand is freckled. "You talk fast. Real fast." As he says it, his voice drawls, sounding more Southern than usual.

I grin at him. "I have heard that before."

"So what happened? I thought you were headed home." He raises his arms and folds them behind his head, leaning back in his chair. I have a strong suspicion he is doing this to draw attention to his biceps, which bulge out of the sleeves of his white T-shirt. Not that I'm looking at them. Not at all. That would be entirely unprofessional.

I flick my gaze upward as though I'm lost in thought. "Well, the stuff with Pebble Cottage felt unfinished. It felt a bit premature to fly back home. And my grandpa seems..." I trail off. I was going to say he seems like he needs me, but I don't even know if that's true. He did chase me out of the condo this morning, after all. But then there was his panic attack. He might not show it, but I know he doesn't want to be alone.

"I'm helping my grandpa out," I conclude.

"I see." Daniel leans forward again, his face more serious. "Is he in poor health?"

"Not exactly, but he recently lost his wife—my grandma."

"Aw, no, I'm sorry to hear that." He reaches across the table and gives my arm a gentle squeeze. The gesture doesn't feel forced or flirtatious, it just feels natural, like it's just the kind of person he is.

"Thanks." I pat his hand before he pulls it away, and that—my hand pat—definitely feels awkward. Because that's just the kind of person I am.

"How long will you be staying?" he asks.

A week, tops, my panicky, rule-abiding brain shouts. But I say, "I'm not sure. I can work remotely, so." *You are illegally working remotely*, my brain reminds me. *And it's not going so well, by the way!*

"Oh, shoot," I say, glancing at the time. "Speaking of which, I have a meeting starting in a minute."

He slaps the table and stands up quickly.

"I'll let you get to it. We'll be in touch. Have a good one, Mallory." And with a little salute-like wave, he heads back to his table, packs up his laptop, and leaves.

I watch him ride away on his bike, and I'm so distracted by the broad muscles in his shoulders and the view of his thighs peeking out from his shorts that I end up being three minutes late to my meeting.

Oops.

Luckily, I remember to turn off my video. I'm not sure how I would explain the blue sky and water visible behind me.

And I'm not sure if it's the proximity of the beach or the encounter with Daniel, but I find it nearly impossible to focus on work for the rest of the day.

Chapter 17

Over the next couple days, Alan begins his work on the house, saying he'll call me for a walk-through later this week, and I manage to work something close to eight-hour days, between working from my bedroom and Paradise Coffee.

I am not loving being out of my routine. My body feels discombobulated from eating heavy food for breakfast and then not starting work until noon—not to mention the lack of yoga and the working until eight P.M. But I know I can't go home until I've accomplished certain things—and one of those things is getting Gramps to see Dr. Shauna Mellors.

"I am in full possession of all of my faculties," Gramps says stubbornly. We're sitting at the kitchen table in front of steaming bowls of minestrone soup. I'd found the recipe on Pinterest—veggies, beans, and pasta all in one pot. (Unfortunately, in order to have dinner before Gramps's bedtime, I have my laptop on the chair next to me just in case someone pings me.)

"I know you are." I try to make my voice soothing. "The doctor would be someone for you to talk to about Lottie."

"I talk to you about Lottie."

"About losing Lottie."

Gramps is silent. His furry white eyebrows come together, like he's angry about the idea of discussing his grief.

"What is this, something Italian?"

I sprinkle our soup with grated Parmesan cheese.

"Yes, it's minestrone."

He blows on a spoonful, gulps it down, and smacks his lips. "Mm."

"Good?" I ask. The veggies came out a bit, well, mushier than I'd expected, and the pasta looks a tad bloated and overcooked.

"Mm," he repeats. "Tasty."

Something in his tone makes me think he's just being polite. I take a bite. It's...not the best. Gramps beckons wordlessly for more Parmesan.

"Anyway," he says, after another brave mouthful. "It's not necessary."

"Maybe not." I sip my iced tea with lemon. "But I think it would help, and that's what I'm trying to do. Help you."

"Why?"

I squint at him. "Because you're my grandpa?"

"Exactly. Children shouldn't have to care for their parents. Grandchildren especially shouldn't have to care for their grandparents."

"Well, sometimes that's life." I swallow a bite, and then add, "People care for their elders. It happens."

A look of incredulity and amusement flashes across his face. "Elders? I'm not blithering and blathering, you know. I can still recite the periodic table *and* fifty digits of pi."

"I never said you were blathering."

"So why? Why are you so insistent on helping me?" He doesn't use air quotes, but he might as well have.

"Because..." I take a deep breath. I'll just tell him. No one ever told me it was supposed to be a secret. "Because Lottie wanted me to."

He stares.

"Lottie? Did she tell you this?"

"Not directly, but it was in her will, I guess. The part where she left Pebble Cottage to me. She also said I should look after you."

"But why? Why did she think I needed looking after?" Gramps sets down his spoon, his light-blue eyes crinkling with confusion.

"I don't know exactly," I say slowly, "but I think she didn't want you to be alone."

At this, he sits heavily back in his chair and turns his head to gaze out at the gulf. The sky blazes bright and blue and the sea glimmers, not a wave in sight.

"Of course." He laughs gently. "Of course she would tell you to look after me. She always took care of me. She was so good at it."

He looks down at his bowl of half-eaten soup.

I'm trying, I want to say. *I know I can't cook the way she did, but I'm trying to take care of you the way she would have wanted.*

"Yeah," I say instead. "So would you visit this Dr. Mellors just once? For me? And for Lottie?"

He shrugs as though, suddenly, it's all the same to him. "Fine. Of course, you'll have to drive me."

I manage to get him an appointment the very next day. Dr. Mellors had a cancellation, and she said she'd been keeping an eye out for an email from me.

After lunch, I drive Gramps to a quaint, one-story office building halfway to Reina Beach. It's right off Gulf Boulevard, and it has three round rhododendron bushes in front. I park and unbuckle my seat belt, but Gramps gives me a look.

"I do know how to check myself in for an appointment."

I pause awkwardly, holding my seat belt with one hand. "So you don't want me to come in?"

"I don't think so." He climbs out of his car, then ducks his head back down to add, "I would, however, like a ride home. Please."

"Of course I'll give you a ride home. I'll find somewhere to work and I'll be back in an hour."

"The appointment is only fifty minutes."

"Fifty minutes, then." I wave from the driver's seat, feeling absurdly like a parent dropping her kid off at school. "Good luck!" I call, but he's already across the parking lot.

I use my maps app to search for a nearby coffee shop. There's one two blocks away called Jitters. Inside, it's a bit cold and dingy. It's also severely lacking in attractive Frenchmen. But it serves as a place for me to bang out some work for forty-five minutes. I'm supposed to attend a meeting at two o'clock, but fortunately it's not super important for me, so I send a quick message saying that I can't join today. So far this week, I've been able to attend almost all my meetings without any hiccups, despite being across the country and three hours off schedule. I don't think anyone will notice that I have to miss one.

I'm parked outside the office building when Gramps comes out.

"How did it go?" I ask encouragingly as he drops into the passenger seat. His face looks oddly blank and colorless. But maybe I imagined it, because he turns to me with a big grin.

"Fine. Just fine! The doctor must have received top marks at shrink school."

"What did you talk about?"

"You know, Mallory, before the appointment they had me sign some forms. One of them mentioned doctor-patient confidentiality."

"Of course, I was just..." My laugh trails off at the barely disguised shell-shocked look on his face. "...curious."

After a minute, he says, "We didn't talk about Lottie much at all. Mostly about—well, about me."

I nod, glancing sideways at him as I drive.

"I wasn't expecting that. She asked about my mother."

I can't help the quick laugh that escapes me. He gives me a sharp look.

"It's kind of a cliché to talk about your mother at therapy," I explain.

"I hadn't given my mother that much thought in—ever. I've never done that."

"Uncomfortable?" I ask.

"Extremely."

"Did it help?"

He gives a bewildered shake of his head. "I've no idea."

He doesn't say anything more, so I drop it. Maybe he'll tell me more later, but maybe not. As snippets of beach interspersed with ostentatious mansions flash past us, I try to convince myself to let it go. Let go of trying to control everything, trying to know everything. I got Gramps to attend one therapy session—I did my best. I'm not going to be able to transform him into a happy, active version of himself who goes to therapy weekly and plays tennis and attends social hours with his friends. But I've spent enough time with him to see that he's going to be all right. I've done what I came here to do.

In my room, I'm about to close my laptop for the night when I get a new email from Alan. He says that he expects to finish up tomorrow and would I like to come take a look at the house tomorrow evening.

I reply in the affirmative, toss my laptop onto the bed, and stretch my arms overhead. It looks like all my loose ends are tying up neatly. Maybe tomorrow I'll search for flights back to Seattle.

There's a knock on my door. Gramps pokes his head in.

"I thought you were asleep," I say.

"Heading that way. I just wanted to let you know, my next appointment with the good doctor is Tuesday morning. Sweet dreams!"

So Gramps liked his therapy session enough to schedule another one. That's a good thing. It's actually beyond my wildest expectations. I never expected him to humor me twice.

Of course, he'll probably expect me to be his taxi driver again. But maybe I can fix that before I leave. Maybe I can have him do a trial run driving somewhere on his own, to pick up groceries or something.

Then I would need to teach him how to grocery shop. That's doable, I guess.

I'm at Paradise Coffee, and I should be head-down focused on work right now, but I'm distracted by the new development. I really thought I'd be booking a ticket home today. But I don't want to risk Gramps changing his mind about therapy just because I'm not here. Maybe I could stay for one more session. No, no, first I'll attempt the grocery store trial run. He does know how to drive, after all. It's just his pesky panic attacks. I should make sure he mentions those to Dr. Mellors.

"Your job looks complicated," a voice says behind me.

I whip my head around to see Leo carrying a bin of dirty dishes, smirking in a way that makes his cheek dimple. I look back at my laptop to see what he sees: a gnarly spreadsheet full of graphs and projections.

"It is kind of awful sometimes," I agree.

He grabs my empty plate that held a chocolate chip cookie ten minutes ago.

"You should try working at a coffee shop," he says, putting my plate in his bin.

"Also awful?" I ask.

"No!" He seems momentarily horrified by the misunderstanding. "It's the best. I get to chat with people, neighbors and regulars—like yourself. I'm on my feet and working with my hands—no time to get bored or gloomy."

"Ha! It sounds like you know what that's like."

He nods. "After college, I worked at a consulting firm for a year. Most boring, gloomy year of my life."

I look around the cheerful, sun-filled café and back at Leo. He is alarmingly handsome, tanned from the roots of his dark hair all the way to his fingers, and he has veins running down his arms and hands. I bet he works out. A lot.

"You've convinced me. When's my first shift?"

He laughs, a rich sound that betrays his French background. I wonder if he whitens his teeth.

"Hey, would you like to get dinner sometime?" He asks it without a hint of self-consciousness, shifting the bin from one arm to the other.

I feel my mouth drop open, and then close it at once. So what if it has been literal years since anyone has asked me out? I straighten my shoulders and try to act like someone who is used to this type of attention, even as one of the voices in my head cackles maniacally.

"I wish I could say yes," I say truthfully. (I mean, look at him!) "But I'm heading back to Seattle in a few days."

The cackling voice stops laughing and adds, *Plus we're holding out for a certain redhead.*

We are not, I chide her.

"Ah well." Leo shrugs with a friendly wink. "Hope you enjoy the rest of your vacation. Say goodbye before you leave, yeah?"

I nod and wave as he returns to the other side of the counter.

We are, too, the voice in my head says. I ignore her.

At four P.M., I decline a meeting and put an away message on Slack saying that I have an appointment. Which is true: I have an appointment with Alan at Pebble Cottage. I just hope Kat doesn't notice that I'm offline in the middle of the afternoon, Seattle time.

I pull up to the house in Gramps's car and immediately notice the familiar red bike parked in the grass. I have a sudden urge to check my hair and teeth in the car mirror. Of course Daniel is here, too. As my property manager, he's supposed to be involved in all things Pebble Cottage. I just wasn't expecting him. Although, now that I think of it, he did reply to Alan's latest email with *Great!!* So maybe it was implied that he would join us. I just wish I could act normal around him. But I'm a spaz on the best of days, so when it comes to a property manager I shared a hot make-out session with that I now have to pretend never happened, there's no hope for me.

I hop out of the car and greet them both in what I'm pretty sure is a normal way. Strong start.

Alan gives me a nod, sliding his phone into the front pocket of his overalls. Daniel, wearing skintight black bike shorts and a white T-shirt, smiles and bounces on the balls of his feet as he says hello. Is he always this happy? Maybe it's the bike-riding endorphins.

"I still don't know how you ride a bike everywhere in this heat," I say, wiping sweat from my hairline as we step inside. He glances at me, like he wants very much to launch into a lecture on the benefits of biking, but then Alan starts to talk.

He guides us from the small bathroom to the boiler room, explaining what he's fixed and pointing out the improvements. I'm filled with a gut-sinking sense of impostor syndrome. I have literally no idea what any of this means. He could be completely screwing me over, and I wouldn't know it. I would just nod and smile and give him my money. I'm familiar with this just-smile-and-nod feeling, because I've felt this way at work many times. But now that it's about Pebble Cottage—my house—the feeling is more troubling, because my ignorance could cost me huge sums of money. On the one hand, I'm relieved to have Daniel here, because he actually does know what Alan is talking about, and his interests are aligned with mine now that he's my property manager. On the other hand, I really, *really* need to learn about all this house stuff. I don't want to feel like it's just a matter of time before I become the victim of a con artist.

Back in the entryway, Alan claps his hands together and says, "So, that's everything. Daniel's already set up the payment plan. Give me a holler if y'all need anything else."

"Thanks, Alan. Talk soon," Daniel says, walking him to the door.

"Thank you!" I call after him.

"So." Daniel's tone is businesslike. I startle, realizing that we are now alone in my empty house. "Have you given any more thought to the…" He gestures from the retro carpet to the brown walls.

"Um." I take it all in: the dark living room, the carpeted hallway. What's some carpet and paint, really, when it comes down to it? "Yeah, I'm thinking I'll just take care of it."

The words have left my mouth before I can stop them.

"You mean…" Daniel presses his lips together, looking not so much puzzled as amused. "As in, you're going to do it yourself?" I see his bright-hazel eyes flick from my face down to my (puny) arms. I cross them defensively, and he looks back up at me, now trying and failing to hold back a snort of laughter.

"Size is no indication of strength," I say.

Laughter bursts out of him like he just can't hold it anymore.

"I never said—" He takes a deep breath to calm himself. "I mean, I'm sure you are—have you ever pulled up carpet before?"

I would very much like to lie and say yes, but instead I say, "No, I have not." This only makes him laugh again.

"Is this a point-of-pride thing or a money thing?" he asks.

I stare at him, my face stone-cold. I am obviously not going to tell him it's a money thing.

"Right," he says. "Pride. Got it." He glances around the room, and I follow his gaze, realizing how much work I just signed up for. There's carpet *everywhere*. What is wrong with me? Why did I say it?

"Weren't you planning to go home soon?"

"I was. I mean, I still am. But a few things came up. Including... all this."

"Oh, this? If you know what you're doing, you can change out the flooring and paint the place in a week or two."

And if I don't know what I'm doing? And if I'm doing the work in addition to my full-time job? How long will that take, six months?

"What are the other things?" he asks curiously before I can reply.

"Some stuff with my grandpa." I tap my keys anxiously against my thigh. "I need to help him with a few things. Actually, he took my advice and went to therapy, so that was a win."

"That's great!" Daniel taps my shoulder in a manly way-to-go kind of way. He checks his watch. "I should get going. Keep me updated on your progress, all right? I'll have my photographer buddy on standby to take photos when you're done."

"Photos?" I follow him to the door and stop short when he turns around.

"Yeah, for the listing. The rental listing."

"Oh. Okay. Makes sense." I'm clutching the doorknob and squeezing my belly in to make more space between us. He doesn't seem to notice that we're two inches apart.

"We won't bother staging it. With the touch-ups and the right price, it'll rent quickly, even with empty room photos."

"Great." We descend the two front steps and turn right toward his bike, into the sweet-smelling St. Augustine grass. The idea of some strangers moving into the house and filling it with their own furniture, their strange belongings, makes my stomach clench. Obviously, this is the goal. So that I can collect rent and return to my own place across the country. But walking through the empty house and then picturing it filled with other people's stuff—I don't like it.

Of course, I can't tell Daniel this. He wants to find new tenants as soon as we can, so he can take his cut of the rent. That's his job.

He buckles his helmet and swings a leg over his bike.

"How *do* you do it?" I ask. "Bike, I mean."

His mouth quirks to one side as he gives me an appraising look. "I drink a lot of water, for starters. And also..." He stops, apparently trying to think of the right words.

"What?" I prompt.

"Once you start, you can't stop." I feel my forehead scrunch with skepticism. He laughs and continues, "I mean, the feeling of fresh air whipping you in the face, compared with the cramped feeling of being in a car with the AC blowing at you—there's no going back."

"Okay..." I'll keep the comfort of a climate-controlled car any day.

He lifts his chin and gives me a knowing sort of smile. "You'll see."

"I will?"

"I'll get you on a bike someday."

"Sure. Good luck with that."

He laughs again, then kicks off and glides away into the quiet cul-de-sac. "Have a good one, Mallory."

"You too, Daniel," I mutter, but he's already gone.

I stop by Foxy's Market on my way back to the condo. I grab a rotisserie chicken, a baguette, and a Caesar salad kit to share with Gramps for dinner. On a whim, I also buy a package of Fig Newtons. When I get home, Gramps is reading out on the balcony, and I stealthily empty the package into the cookie jar on the counter. The one that Lottie always kept full. I can't wait to see Gramps's reaction.

I put the chicken and salad in the fridge and check the microwave clock to see how close it is to six o'clock, Gramps's preferred dinnertime. It's a quarter till, so I start to set the table, when all of a sudden, my heart freezes.

Shit.

I've been offline for two hours. *No, no, no.* What was I thinking? How could I just forget about work?

Hurtling across the room to where I dropped my bag on the floor, I check my phone with one hand and pull out my laptop with the other. Slack is blowing up. I feel fizzy with panic, my armpits prickling with sweat. I log into my computer and see that most of the messages are garden variety: team chatter, and some questions from stakeholders that aren't necessarily urgent for me to answer right away. But the name Kat White is flashing, with the number 5 next to it. Five unread messages from my boss.

Chapter 18

I take a deep, shaky breath, and click on Kat's name.

Kat White: *Hi Mallory. Dominic let me know that you couldn't make it to the retrospective for his project. Would have been nice to have you there for the key takeaways.*

Kat White: *Looks like you're at an appointment, and that's fine. Just let me know next time.*

Kat White: *And preferably schedule future appointments during lunch.*

The next two messages are from an hour later.

Kat White: *Ping me when you get back.*

Kat White: *Just want to make sure everything's ok.*

Oh no, *oh no.*

My fingers tremble violently as I type back.

Hey Kat, I'm so sorry about all this! I had no idea my appointment would run so long. It was a dentist appointment that I think I told you about last week. So sorry for any confusion! I will ask Dominic for the notes from his retro.

I bite my tongue at the lie. But I really, *really* don't want the wrath of Kat turned on me. It did occur to me for half a second to tell her the truth about where I am and what I'm doing, but I don't want to open a whole other can of worms.

She types back at once.

Kat White: *I don't have a record of that, but it's possible I forgot. I know how dentist appointments can be. No worries. Thanks for letting me know.*

I exhale in relief. I skated this time, but Kat is a stickler for attendance and has a flawless memory. I know that she knows I didn't tell her about my so-called dentist appointment. I really need to be more careful from now on.

I reply to all the other messages I've missed, until it's six forty-five and Gramps comes wandering in, no doubt guided by his rumbling stomach.

"Hello," he says cheerfully, opening the fridge. "Think I'll just make a sandwich."

"Wait, Gramps, I bought dinner for us," I say, typing furiously at the same time. "See the chicken and the Caesar salad kit in there? Can you grab them? I'll get everything ready in one sec."

"Hmm?" He straightens up and looks at me like he's never heard the words "salad kit" before.

"Never mind, just one second." I finish typing my last message so fast it makes my knuckles hurt. Keeping my laptop open, I set it carefully on the counter in front of the Fig Newtons.

Five minutes later, we're sitting at the table enjoying our Foxy's Market supper. Gramps happily slathers butter on a hunk of baguette and plops a bite of chicken on top before he eats it. I take small nibbles of the salad. My stomach is still in knots from the work stuff. Missing so many messages, coming so close to a reprimand from Kat: It feels like someone has taken a cheese grater to my nerves. I can't believe I actually forgot about work for two whole hours on a Thursday. The possibility of getting fired flashes before my eyes: no more cushy paycheck. Having to interview again. Oh God, interviewing is horrible. I would stay at this job for fifteen years to avoid having to interview again.

I set down my fork, my appetite vanished.

"Everything okay?" Gramps asks, reaching for his glass of iced tea.

"Just thinking about work stuff." I hear how shaky my voice is, so I clear my throat and try to snap out of it.

He shakes his head. "Preoccupied about work. You know, if you wanted to, a girl your age could be a stay-at-home mother. Find a husband, have a baby, and tend to the house all day."

I give him a look.

"Old-fashioned?" he asks.

"Uh, yeah." I pull off a piece of chicken with my fingers. "People still do that, but like, I think it's because of the cost of child care. Besides, why would you suggest that when your own wife had a career?"

He grins. "Just trying to help."

"It would be more helpful to tell me how to deal with a boss who's all up in my business," I mumble.

"Hmm." He gestures thoughtfully with his fork as he swallows a mouthful of bread. "This I have experience with."

"Really?"

Gramps nods. "I had a supervisor once—this was when I was in my early thirties—who was fastidious about confirming the results of our experiments. Checking our lab notes, reading our reports, that was all normal. But this guy—Chester Crevasse—he was something else. More often than not, he would have us repeat our tests while he watched, so he could confirm the results with his own eyes."

"That sounds really annoying. And time consuming."

"It was. And it didn't win him many friends, either. We called him Chester Stick-Up-His—you know what." He laughs like this is a fond memory.

"So how did you deal?"

"Aside from talking about him behind his back? We just had to go along with it. Academia is full of inconveniences, from lack of funding, to bureaucratic red tape, to Crevasse-holes." He pops another bite of chicken into his mouth. "Actually, though, we got him fired."

"What?"

"It turned out he was stealing some of our experiments to use in his own research papers."

"No way."

"Yes way. In our field, the number of research papers you published was the most important number on your CV. Anyway, that explained why he wanted to watch us replicate our results."

"Unbelievable." This story has made me feel better about my own situation, and I find I'm hungry again.

He watches me eat for a moment, then asks, "What's so terrible about your boss?"

"Well." I pat my mouth with my napkin. "She's always checking in on me, micromanaging my time, making sure I'm attending meetings. It doesn't sound like much, I guess, but it's kind of suffocating."

"If you work remotely"—Gramps says the word slowly, like he's trying it out—"what else is she supposed to do? What kind of manager would she be if she wasn't checking in on her employees?"

"I guess, it's just...she should treat us like adults, you know? Just trust that we're doing our jobs."

He gives a little shrug. "I don't know. Sounds like the nature of work to me."

I fight the urge to roll my eyes. This feels sort of lecture-y, which makes me feel like a petulant teenager. I carry my plate to the sink.

"What do you like about your job, anyway?"

"Um." It's a thoughtful question, so I try to give my answer some actual thought, too. I picture a typical workday: the easy routine of sitting at my computer; the structure of following my calendar from one meeting to the next; knowing that I'll be prepared if I take enough notes. "It's...comfortable, but challenging. I have to use my brain, and I'm kept busy all day, so the hours pass by quickly."

"What do you use your brain doing?" Gramps leans back in his chair, hands behind his head.

"I guess...trying to follow all the technical jargon to make sure I'm not missing anything. Piecing together everyone's projected schedules to make sure teams hit their target dates."

"Ah." He leans forward again and clears his own dishes. "Well, if you find it interesting."

This comes off a bit dismissive. For a second, I was enjoying being the focus of his attention and curiosity. Now I feel like he's deemed me and my job boring. And it *is*. I want him to keep asking questions so I can tell him the truth: It's soul-crushingly boring, and I only do it for the paycheck, and if you ask me where I see myself in five years, I will say, *Please, anywhere but here,* except I'm too scared of failure to try anything else.

Gramps closes the dishwasher and looks around at me.

"When you were little, you said you wanted to be an artist."

"Too bad I never advanced beyond drawing sunflowers with oil pastels."

And then, as though he read my mind, he asks, "What do you need the paycheck for?"

"Umm...life?"

"Mallory." His eyes drill into mine, and I can tell he's trying to tell me something, but I don't know what. "You're young. You don't have a spouse or children. You can do anything."

"Right, but." I take a deep, frustrated breath. What is it with old people not understanding today's economy? "I have to pay rent. Which is really expensive."

"Mallory," he says again. "You just inherited a house."

"Yeah, and it's causing me nothing but problems," I snap. My laptop pings and I snatch it irritably from the counter.

Gramps stares.

"What are those?"

I follow his gaze to the full jar of cookies. "Fig Newtons."

He doesn't say anything, and his face isn't lighting up with joy, either.

"Lottie always used to—" I start.

He cuts me off. "Please. Take those away and don't ever do that again."

"What? But I thought you'd like—"

"Well, I don't." He turns a brittle gaze at me. "I've passed anger and bargaining, and I've moved on to acceptance. I know Lottie is gone. And filling her cookie jar is not going to bring her back."

I don't point out that he missed a few stages of grief there. I don't say anything at all, because my throat aches, full of tears.

"Sorry," I whisper, but he's already crossed the kitchen and shut himself in his room.

Around nine that night, when I've finally shut my laptop, my phone rings. I expect it to be my mom calling, my mind already racing ahead to how I'll fill her in on the Fig Newton debacle and how she'll know just the right thing to say.

But it's not my mom. The name DANIEL MCKINNON flashes across the screen. Why is he calling so late?

"Hello?"

"Hi, Mallory. Daniel McKinnon here."

"Hello, Daniel," I say, lightly teasing his formal tone.

"Sorry to call so late, but I figured you might be on West Coast time anyway."

"I am. Sort of." I sit cross-legged on the bed and pull a seashell pillow into my lap. I wonder where he's sitting. In his apartment? Does he have roommates? Is his place a monochromatic bachelor pad, decorated in shades of chrome and black, with an oversize painting of a galloping horse above the couch?

"Listen, I wanted to apologize."

I almost think I've misheard him. "For what?"

"I laughed. When you said you were going to pull up the carpets on your own."

"Oh." I'm so surprised by this, I don't know what to say. Looking back, I guess it was a bit rude. But I'd also thought it was sort of flirtatious ribbing. So maybe it wasn't flirting at all, but genuine hilarity at the thought of me doing house renovations by myself.

"What I should have said," Daniel continues, "was that I'd be happy to help."

Okay, now I'm more confused than ever. He wants to help me? Is *this* flirting?

"I've done this sort of project half a dozen times," he continues. "I'm not an expert by any means, but with another pair of hands you'd be finished twice as fast."

I must still be on edge because of the work fiasco and the Fig Newton argument, because this rubs me the wrong way.

"What, you think I can't do it myself?"

"Whoa," he says, half laughing. "I would never suggest such a thing."

"Good, because—" I start, my voice rising aggressively.

"Hey, now." He's not laughing anymore, his voice like warm honey. "What's going on? Is everything okay on your end?"

A little fighting part of me wants to keep arguing with him, to vent some of my frustration about, well, everything. But instead, I melt.

"Not really." My voice cracks embarrassingly. I clutch the seashell pillow to my chest. "I'm having a...hard time." The introvert in me is extremely uncomfortable sharing my feelings like this with Daniel, someone I'm supposed to be on professional terms with. But talking to him on the phone like this, late at night, it feels okay. Comfortable, even. And I *did* kiss him, so.

"Tell me what's going on."

The way he says it is so inviting, everything pours out of me. My worries about working remotely, the argument with Gramps, how I just want to help him but I don't know if I'm actually helping.

After I come up for air, he doesn't say anything for a moment. That's it, I've scared him off. I knew I should have kept it professional.

But then he says, "I know what will help."

"You do?"

"Mm-hmm. My buddy Jones is having a party tomorrow night. You're welcome to join me. Get your mind off your troubles for the evening."

When I don't say anything for a moment, he adds, "Amanda will be there."

I have a lot to do, but it's not like I'm going to accomplish all of it tomorrow night. The idea of having some fun is extremely tempting.

"I would love to."

"Wonderful. I'll text you the details. Actually, I can pick you up if you like."

"On your bike?"

He laughs. "No, ma'am. I do own a car."

"Deal. And, Daniel, there is one more thing that's bothering me."

"What's that?"

I hesitate. "I have no idea how to install new floors."

He rumbles with laughter. "Are you accepting my offer of help?"

I bite my lip, smiling to myself, my heart racing with giddy nerves. The idea of him helping me with the house—well, it's a lot. It would be a big commitment from him, and a big expectation for me to spend so much time with him. One-on-one.

"Mallory?" he prompts.

Put on your big-girl pants, I chide myself.

"I could really use some help. Yes."

Chapter 19

The next evening, I'm barely recognizable, which is exactly what I wanted. I want to feel like someone else for a minute, or at least like the best version of me. I've blow-dried my hair, so it flows long and sleek almost to my elbows. I've applied every type of makeup I brought with me. And I'm wearing a new outfit purchased from Bettina's Beach Boutique: strappy nude sandals and a short, black wrap dress.

Gramps and I barely spoke to each other all day. I've been nursing an emotional hangover from everything that happened with him and with my job. I'm one hundred percent ready to enjoy the party tonight and to not think about any of these things for a few hours at least.

"Enjoy your evening," Gramps says as I hover in the entryway, watching him watch TV.

"Thanks." I fidget with my keys, unsure what to say but feeling like I have to say something. "By the way, Gramps, I'm really—"

He looks over at me, his blue eyes intent on mine. "There's no need."

"But I'm sorry about the—"

"There is no need," he says again, "to apologize for a kind gesture. That's what it was."

He turns back to the TV. After a moment, when I'm still standing there unsure of what to say, he waves a hand at me without taking his eyes off the news anchor.

"Go on, go see some people your own age."

"Okay. Night, Gramps."

"G'night."

Outside, the sweet, warm air sinks into my skin. I'll never get over how warm it is at night here. I cross the grassy lawn toward the entrance and find Daniel already waiting for me. He leans against a little white Hyundai, wearing a black polo shirt and khaki shorts. In the golden-hour light, his hair looks particularly fiery. I can't help the smile that springs to my face when I see him.

"Wow, you look beautiful."

I hear the words, but I snag on the look on his face. He looks... startled? I'd like to be flattered, to think that he's caught off guard by how gorgeous I look, but I'm pretty sure he's startled for a different reason.

"Uh." I pull at my dress nervously as he opens the passenger-side door. "You never said where the party is, so I..."

"You look perfect." He ushers me into the car and then hops in on the driver's side. "I mean it."

I stare at him. "I way overdressed, didn't I?"

His face twitches in an effort to hold back a grin.

"Oh my God." I hide my face in my hands.

"No! Mallory, no. I mean." He turns the key in the ignition. "We're going to play shuffleboard. I should have told you."

"What's shuffleboard?"

This only makes him laugh.

"I'll go change. Just tell me what shuffleboard is so I know what to wear."

He laughs for another eternity. Finally, he shakes his head and places a firm hand on my knee. "You're perfect. Like I said. Don't worry, all right? You'll fit right in."

I shrug, willing the heat to leave my face as we drive. Daniel leaves his hand on my knee longer than is strictly necessary. I grin to myself, watching the palm trees flash by.

We pull up to a squat, brightly painted building with a large sign outside that reads, simply, SHUFFLE. The sound of live music wafts toward us from the back of the building, some kind of indie rock with a Latin vibe.

Daniel leads me through the inside, a cute bar full of kitschy signs, to the outdoor area in the back. It's a small garden with string lights overhead and a stage where the musicians are illuminated by a purple glow, the whole scene dominated by a huge shuffleboard court.

A group of people hails Daniel and waves us over.

"Happy birthday, buddy," Daniel says to one of them, giving the man a one-armed hug. "Your gift is in your inbox."

Jones, the birthday boy, gives Daniel a quizzical look. I recognize him as the guy from the first night I met Daniel, the one who was terrible at buying gifts for his girlfriend.

"It's an Amazon gift card," Daniel says. Jones and the other guys roar with laughter. Jones shakes his head in a morose way that makes me think the girlfriend might now be an ex.

Daniel introduces me. "This is Mallory."

"Pleasure to meet you." Jones shakes my hand while giving Daniel a raised eyebrow.

"Mallory is in town for a while so I invited her along," Daniel says. You can practically hear the *as friends* that he didn't tack onto the end of that sentence.

"Ah," Jones says.

"Happy birthday," I say. "I can't wait to find out what shuffleboard is."

Everyone roars with laughter a second time. I decide to pretend that I was, indeed, joking. They'll find out soon enough when they see me play.

The group disperses, some to order drinks, some to start a game. Daniel asks for my drink order, and I request a gin and tonic and start to awkwardly follow him toward the bar when I see Amanda, the owner of the mermaid bar. She's at a patio table with a couple of people I haven't met yet.

"Hey!" I stop by her chair. Even though we met only a few days ago, I'm convinced that she won't remember who I am. Why am I like this? "Amanda, right? I'm—"

"Hi, Mallory." Amanda's answering smile is so genuine and friendly, I feel a rush of relief.

"You remember!" I'm shocked. Does she remember the name of every customer she talks to? A bartender—or bar owner—in Seattle would never remember your name, or if they did, they wouldn't admit to it.

"Yeah." She gives me a slightly puzzled look but glosses over the moment by asking, "You're still in town?"

I nod. "For a few more days."

"You came here with Daniel?" At my flustered splutter in response, a huge grin overtakes Amanda's face. "Just teasing you. It's nice to see him with a date. It's been long enough."

I'm dying to ask for more details, but Amanda gestures to the couple sitting with her and makes introductions. Daniel returns with my drink and asks Amanda how business is going. I'm half listening and half soaking up the cozy party atmosphere: laughter and voices and music mingling in the sultry evening air, punctuated by the occasional thwack of the shuffleboard... ball? Puck?

Daniel sees me glancing at the court over my shoulder. He plucks the plastic cup from my hand, sets it on the table, and says, "All right, let's go. Time to teach you a thing or two."

Amanda waves. "Have fun!"

"Want to join us?" My voice has a plaintive tone. I would rather make a fool out of myself in front of a friend than strangers.

"I'm more of a sit-on-the-sidelines gal."

"But wait, me too!" I'm not joking, but Daniel's grip on my hand is firm, pulling me onward.

"Unfortunately that's not an option for you tonight. You're with me."

We stop at the far end of one of the courts. All I see are a bunch of triangles on the ground, and some very long sticks.

Daniel's grabbing two of the sticks and shouting something across the court at two guys who are, apparently, playing with us. They exchange some ribbing about a previous match. Match? Game?

"Am I sensing a competitive streak?" I ask Daniel.

"Competitive? Me? Nah." The way he rolls his shoulders and then stretches his neck belies the casual tone.

"Okay, well, just so you know, I'm not the best partner to help you win. I still don't know what shuffle ball is."

"Shuffle*board*," about five voices yell at me from every direction.

Daniel gives me a devilish look. "Oh, we're not playing together. You're on his team." He points across the court to the guy standing opposite me. The guy is giving me a doubtful once-over, probably taking in my ridiculously misguided mini dress. "Billy, this is Mallory. She's a world-class player."

I stare between the two men, sweat prickling the nape of my neck. Jones stands next to Billy. "So you're on Jones's team? I'm playing against you?"

Daniel hoists his stick up, holding it like a pool cue. "I'll help you along. A bit."

What follows is a series of embarrassing attempts to push the puck into certain triangles while making sure I don't bend over too far and moon everyone. It's easy enough to make contact with the puck, but impossible to aim. For me, at least. The other guys rack up the points like it's nothing. Especially Daniel.

"Seven!" Jones calls as Daniel scores them yet more points.

"How is that seven points, but mine was zero?" I ask, pointing to one of my pucks that landed in the same area.

"Yours is touching the line," Daniel says somewhat smugly as he leans on his stick.

"Sounds made up," I mutter, lining up my next shot. Across from me, Billy looks despondent, like he can't wait for this game to end. *Right there with you, Billy.*

I hit the puck, disk, whatever, as hard as I can. It gives a satisfying thwack as it careens off one of Daniel's disks. His flies off into no-man's-land—they explained it to me, but I forget what it's called—and mine glides smoothly into an area marked with an eight.

"Yes!" Billy punches the air.

Daniel turns a genuinely shocked face to me.

"What does that mean?" I widen my eyes innocently.

"It means you get, uh—" He reaches up and scratches his head, leaving his hair ruffled in the back. "You get eight and I, well, we lose seven."

"Aw." I pout, tucking my stick under one arm. "Sorry!"

He stares me down, and then his mouth quirks with a slight smile. "Oh, it's like that? Okay then."

I turn to watch Billy and Jones take their turns, but I'm not paying attention. I get a shiver of secret delight every time Daniel glances at me from the corner of his eye. I never would have guessed he had such a competitive side. The desire to keep pushing his buttons fuels the rest of the game, and I manage to rack up another dozen points. At the very end, it's not even close—they're kicking our butts—but Daniel knocks one of my disks out of the way, losing half my hard-won points.

"Hey!" I whip toward him, my stick flailing dangerously close to him.

"Whoa, whoa!" He grabs the stick firmly. "We don't wave these around. You could bonk someone."

"Like the person who just lost me my points?" I try to pull it away from him, but he is surprisingly strong, the stick barely moving in his grasp. He gives a yank and I stumble toward him.

"Consider it payback."

"Is there a rule book somewhere? I want to consult the rule book."

"You are a rule follower, aren't you? I see that about you." At this point, my shuffleboard cue is resting on Daniel's shoulder and I'm still holding the end of it, a mere foot away from him. As he regards me, I feel that tingle again. *Okay, Mallory, time to get some air.*

I clear my throat pointedly, and he releases my stick. Jones plays his turn and then cheers.

"That's game!" he calls.

He and Billy high-five, and Daniel and I do the same. The competitive tension fizzles away.

"Good game," he says.

"You too! That was fun." It was not. Other than the close proximity to Daniel. I need another drink.

I pass Billy and Jones on my way to the bar, giving them both a high five. With a fresh G&T in hand, I rejoin Amanda, where she's engaged in a spirited conversation with a small group, something about Marvel fan theories. After a minute, I sense Daniel's presence at my elbow.

"There's just no way Tony Stark could be Dr. Doom. It makes

no sense." He stands unnecessarily close to me, his abdomen grazing my arm. I pretend not to notice, and we stay that way for five minutes or more, chatting with the group without so much as looking at each other. Finally, the group disperses to start a new game of shuffleboard. As the others mill about in different directions, I turn to Daniel. Should I order an Uber back to Gramps's? I don't know how much longer Daniel plans to stay, and I'd rather quit while I'm ahead. Before I have a chance to say or do anything too awkward.

But Daniel gently nudges me and tilts his head toward a nearby bench. I follow and sit beside him. My drink sends beads of condensation between my fingers.

"Enjoying your first shuffleboard experience?"

I nod. *Other than the shuffleboard part, it's great.* "Thanks for bringing me."

"Has it helped you take your mind off things?"

"You know what? It has."

"Good." He stretches both arms along the back of the bench. I instinctively straighten so I don't accidentally rest my shoulders against his arm.

"So." As the words leave my mouth, my brain begs, *Don't say it.* "Amanda mentioned that it's been a while since you've dated." *Annnnd I said it.* I fumble to recover, adding, "Me too. So, not that it's weird or anything. And not that this is a date."

My words hang in the air. I wish, how I wish, I could shove them back in my mouth. The silence between us lingers for so long that I consider standing up and walking away. It wasn't even a question, it was just a statement that somehow managed to be nosy and inappropriate. I slurp the rest of my watered-down drink.

"Well," Daniel begins thoughtfully, "I s'pose that is true. My ex and I broke up about a year ago, and I haven't exactly been out there, if you know what I mean." His gaze slides toward me.

"I do know. How did it end between you two? If you don't mind me asking."

He tilts his head back and exhales a little puff of air. "Nothing dramatic. Kelly moved to New York for a job. We'd been together for a couple years at that point, so we tried to keep it going. Didn't work, though."

"Long distance." I nod sympathetically, though I haven't actually been in a long-distance relationship myself. "Sounds hard."

"Yeah. Hard to keep the spark going over FaceTime. We tried to fly out to see each other every month or so, but." He shrugs. "It wasn't working out."

I wonder if there's something more in his nonchalant tone, some bitterness or hurt. But I suppose when it comes to breakups, there's always something more there. We all have our secret aches.

And then, as I gaze down into the ice in my cup, another meaning to his words creeps up on me. He's been burned by a long-distance relationship. He's not going to want to try that again.

Not that we're doing anything here. But now I know for sure that there is no *there* there. It would be impossible.

He doesn't return the line of questioning, and I'm glad. I don't want to talk to him about Alex. I wish I hadn't asked about his past.

We talk about light topics for the next ten minutes, mostly about how he knows Jones and some of the other friends here, and then I decide to make my exit.

"Thanks again for the invite," I say after summoning an Uber.

"Sure I can't drive you home?" Daniel asks, hands in his pockets. The party is still in full swing around him, the band cranking it up as the hour grows later.

"It's okay, you stay and enjoy. I have a lot to do tomorrow, so." I feel like the spark I'd felt an hour ago has disappeared completely. I doused it out by asking about his ex. Now we both know nothing can happen between us, and the air feels flat. I wonder if he feels it too.

"Well, hey, remember to let me know about the floors. We can set a date for me to come by and help you out."

Oh, right. I'd almost forgotten about that. I feel a tiny flare of something again, if only because I'll be spending more time with him. Silly, but I can't help it.

"I will."

I say a quick goodbye to Amanda and the birthday boy, and then slip into the waiting car.

Chapter 20

"We're going to Foxy's." I burst into Gramps's room. He doesn't even startle, just looks up from his physics book in mild surprise.

"Good morning," he says. "Don't you want to have breakfast first?"

I'm a little insulted by this, given that it's past nine in the morning. Has he not noticed that I've been waking up early for the past week?

"I already had breakfast downstairs."

"What do you need at the market?" he asks.

"I need to teach *you* how to grocery shop."

He slowly marks his page with a bookmark, places the book on his cluttered secretary desk, and says, "May I ask where this idea came from?"

"It came from the fact that you need to be able to take care of yourself. Starting with driving to Foxy's and buying your own groceries. And ending with driving yourself to your therapy appointments."

He cocks his head and stares at me like a dog trying to understand human language.

"Ah," he says finally. "You want to go home."

"No, I—" I glance around the room, taking in the photos of Lottie and Gramps and their children and grandchildren. "I *am* going to go home, and I need to make sure you can take care of yourself before I go."

"I see." Gramps picks up a fountain pen and examines the end of it as though it might tell him something. "And when is your flight?"

"I don't have a flight booked yet." It occurs to me that it's been a full week since I canceled my original flight home. A full week, and I'm not even close to finished with the things I need to do.

"No?" Gramps looks up at me, suddenly cheerful. "Well, you should probably get on that." He heaves himself to his feet and sighs. "Lead the way to Foxy's."

"You're driving," I remind him, handing him his keys.

At the store, I confidently steer a shopping cart through the automatic doors.

I wave hello to the owner, in her usual spot by the first register. "Morning, Foxy!" She waves back, slightly bemused; clearly, she still hasn't forgiven me for not letting her help me that one day.

"Now, let's think about your staples," I say to Gramps.

"Staples?"

"The things you buy regularly. Grape-Nuts, milk, orange juice."

He looks around the small grocery store appreciatively. "I suppose some others might be apples, bread, tomatoes, and turkey."

"Great! You're getting it already." I turn the cart toward the produce section and point at the signs above the aisles. "See, each aisle has a sign above it telling you what you'll find there. That's how you find what you're looking for. And if you still need help, you can ask someone who works here." I pause, not sure how much detail to include. "They're the ones wearing green vests."

"Hmm." Gramps nods seriously. "And how do I address them?"

I stop short next to the bananas. "What do you mean?"

"Should I refer to them all as Foxy? Or perhaps Mr. Foxy or Miss Foxy?"

"What? No. Are you—" I peer up at him, wondering if he could truly be this confused. But then I see the twinkle in his eye. "Very funny."

"After all, you called Elaine Foxy. When we came in."

"Huh?"

"Elaine. The manager. You called her Foxy."

"But..." Heat rushes to my cheeks. "Isn't her name Foxy? I thought she was the owner."

Gramps grits his teeth together, biting down on a laugh that nonetheless escapes through his nose.

"Stop laughing!" I hiss. "Is her name not Foxy?"

"Her name is Elaine," he whispers. "She's the manager."

"Then who is Foxy? And how do you know this?"

"Lottie knew everyone in this town. She would always greet them by name and ask after various family members and medical ailments. Elaine's was shoulder bursitis."

"Of course Lottie would do that." I touch my hand to my cheek, willing it to cool down. "I've been calling her Foxy every time I come in here."

"Well, perhaps she took it as a compliment." Gramps commandeers the cart and tosses in a bag of apples.

Because it's Sunday, I don't have to be chained to my computer all day. The pool is calling my name, but I resist; I need to make some progress on the house. After a quick lunch with Gramps from our Foxy's haul—I can never show my face there again—I borrow his car and drive to Pebble Cottage.

I let myself in, the slightly musty smell of the empty house somehow comforting. The AC hums gently—I've been keeping it set to seventy-nine degrees to prevent mildew growth, based on the advice I found on the Florida Power and Light website. It feels comfortable in my shorts and tank top. I feel an unfamiliar sense of ownership here, like I can do whatever I want, with even more freedom than I have in my rented apartment: I can set the thermostat to the perfect temperature; paint the walls whatever color my heart desires; plant flowers and tomatoes and spicy peppers in the yard if I feel like it. For now, though, it's the floors that I have to focus on.

Remembering what Daniel said last night, I look skeptically at my phone. He'd said we could set up a date for him to help me. Not that he could drop everything and come over right away. But I don't have time to spare. Maybe I should just not ask him. He was probably just being polite, anyway, offering to help.

But... there is a lot of work to be done, and I don't know where to begin. That and the fact that I would be lying if I said I wasn't excited to see him again. He just makes things more fun.

Before I can talk myself out of it, I text him.

Hey! I know this is last minute, but I'm planning to work on the house today. Feel free to join me if your offer still stands!

Heart thumping uncomfortably, I wait for a moment, but no typing bubbles appear.

I'm full of regret. And embarrassment. I shouldn't have texted him, but whatever. I can't undo it. I try to ignore the humiliated knot in my stomach and focus on the house.

In the middle of the living room, I stare around at the carpet. It looks very... permanent. I walk to one corner, crouch down, and tug experimentally at the brown fibers. The carpet doesn't budge. I should have watched more HGTV to prepare me for this moment. My confidence deflated, I go out to the sunroom, where I sit at the Scrabble table and look up videos of people ripping up carpet.

My first thought is: *I need tools*. I didn't think I would need any tools. My second thought is: *I can't do this*.

Sure, actually ripping up the carpet seems doable, if I'm even strong enough. But then I have to cut it up and roll it and haul it out to the curb. And there's a part about prying up some narrow wood boards that I don't even want to think about right now. Oh, and I have to, apparently, peel up the padding underneath the carpet and scrape up a thousand tiny staples. And then what do I do with little staples littering the floor-that's-not-even-a-floor? I should get a broom.

I grumble to myself and start a shopping list on my Notes app.

Broom
Gloves
X-Acto knife
Duct tape
Hammer
Nails
Staple scraper thingy

I go back to the video and see that it's actually called a pry bar. I add *pry bar* and *pliers* to the list. *Great. Spectacular.* I don't think I've ever set foot in a hardware store in my life. My dad bought me a basic tool kit in a zippered canvas bag when I moved into my first apartment, and yes, the bag was pink. I picture it, sitting on a shelf above my washer and dryer back home. I wish I had it now. But more than I want my pink tool kit, I want to collapse into a useless puddle. What was I thinking?

Resting my forehead on the glass tabletop, I seriously consider changing my mind. But what would that mean, really? Swallowing my pride and asking Daniel to hire someone? No. I can do this. So nothing in my skill set has done anything to prepare me for manual labor of any kind, let alone home renovations. I can at least try.

I'm full of dread as I force myself to get in the car and map out the route to the nearest hardware store. Forty-five minutes later, I'm back in the house with a broom in one hand and a plastic bag full of supplies in the other. The hardware store wasn't too bad. Yes, I felt like an impostor, and yes, I expected someone to ask what I was buying all these things for and was slightly disappointed when no one did. But I got what I needed and now comes the actual hard part.

I carefully set the broom and tools against one wall and extract the X-Acto knife from the bag. Now all I have to do is cut out a corner of the carpet and start pulling.

I can't.

What if I do it wrong and mess it up? What if I literally, physically can't?

My chest feels tight. I could fly home tomorrow. Email Daniel from the plane and tell him I changed my mind.

This idea feels both comforting and nauseating.

I pick up my phone—no texts from Daniel—and search for flights to Seattle. And then I'm immediately filled with a sense of self-disgust. *Come on, Mallory.*

"Argh!" I slide my phone across the carpet, and it skitters into the kitchen. "Fine!"

I use the knife to remove a neat square of carpet from the far corner of the room. The knife cuts smoothly. I'm actually surprised it worked. This tiny victory eggs me on. Tentatively, I work my fingers under the edge of the carpet and pull. I have to pull harder than I thought, and then I hear it: a satisfying ripping sound as the carpet comes free from the pad underneath. A surprised whoop of laughter escapes me, before another yank sends me sprawling flat on my back. *Ow.*

It takes me a minute to recover—I'm pretty sure I'll have a huge bruise on my tailbone—but then I keep tugging, pouring all my frustration into the physical task, and before I know it I've pulled up the carpet from the entire side wall of the living room.

My heart pounds as I stop to survey my work. I can't believe it. It looks like this room is under construction, and *I* did that.

The video I watched said to cut the carpet as you go to avoid having to roll up huge swaths of it. I cut a long line, grab the fresh roll of duct tape, and roll up my first piece of carpet.

Holy shit. I did it. Well, one-quarter of one room. And only the first step of many. *But still.*

I keep going, and it gets progressively harder as my muscles grow tired. By the last stretch, it takes all my mental energy to keep tearing up the old brown carpet. I think about Kat being up in my business, about losing Lottie, about Daniel not responding to my text, about Maeve being a fulfilled wife and mother while I'm alone down here in Florida sweating to the roots of my hair.

It works. The anger gives me strength. After a couple hours, I'm surrounded by four rolls of carpet, neatly duct-taped, standing on a weird beige carpet pad. If it weren't for YouTube, I wouldn't even know that I have to rip out the carpet pad next.

I decide that can wait until tomorrow.

One by one, I lug the carpet rolls out to the curb. Trash day is a couple days from now, so I hope the neighbors don't mind. By the time I set the last roll down, my limbs are quivering with exhaustion. I stand in my yard, hands on my hips, gazing at the carpet rolls like a proud mother gazing at her four children. The evening air is mild and smells of salt water and grass. Cicadas chirp from somewhere nearby. My body and mind both feel deliciously loose, like I've just gotten out of a hot yoga class. I wonder if this is how Daniel feels after riding his bike around all day.

"Looking good, Rosen!"

I spin around.

Daniel's hopping off his bike in the cul-de-sac. "You did all that yourself? Maybe you don't even need me!"

"What are you doing here?"

"Didn't you get my text?"

"No, I—well, I haven't checked my phone in a couple hours."

He wheels his bike over to me. "I would've come sooner, but I was helping out at a house showing."

"That's okay!" I'm glowing. Under the sheen of sweat, I feel like I'm literally glowing with delight that I couldn't suppress if I tried. He didn't ignore me! He came!

I try to morph my facial expression into something relatively neutral—and normal.

"I really appreciate you coming, but"—I gesture to the carpet rolls—"I think I'm done for the day. I need to rest and maybe, like, carbo-load or something."

"Nah." He waves my words away. "We could paint? Or have you done the carpet pads yet?"

"How do you always have so much energy? I swear I can barely lift the pliers at this point."

He takes me by the shoulders and guides me, firmly yet gently, toward the front door. "We'll order you a pizza, how 'bout that?"

"Pizza?" I perk up.

"I can start on the carpet pads while you carbo-load."

I beam at him.

"See?" He laughs at the look on my face. "Are you glad you called me or what?"

Chapter 21

Twenty minutes later—one perk of small-town life: the pizza place is very close by—I'm sitting on the floor, biting into a hot, cheesy slice of spinach pesto pizza, watching as Daniel rips up a carpet pad.

I'm distracted from his biceps by a droplet of sweat rolling down the side of his face. He stops and, without so much as a warning, whips off his T-shirt.

"Um..." My pizza slice droops forgotten in my hand.

"Hot in here." He gets right back to work, now shirtless.

"Oh...sorry..." My gaze flicks toward the thermostat. I am deeply *not* sorry. "Do you want me to crank up the AC?"

"Nah, this is fine." He shakes his sweaty hair back from his forehead.

"Okay." I bite off another piece of cheesy goodness, wondering if I'm in a dream. A yummy, yummy dream.

"Want some help?" I offer after a few minutes.

Daniel glances at me, lounging on the floor and reaching for my second slice. He shakes his head, laughing.

"Good. I need to regain my strength, anyway."

"You did a lot," he says, kneeling down to scrape up some staples from the subfloor. "Did I mention that I'm impressed?"

"You did. I mean, I'm impressed too. I've never done anything remotely like home renovations before."

"If you get really into it, I might be able to offer you a job." He sweeps the staples into a garbage bag. "Picture it: McKinnon and Rosen, partners in home management."

I guffaw. "I better stick to my own home for now. You know, for liability reasons."

I wipe my hands on a paper napkin and sit back against the wall, sighing contentedly.

"Feel better?" he asks.

I nod. "Have some pizza before it gets cold."

"Yeah, let me just finish this up." He grunts and pulls out the final piece of the carpet pad, then rolls it up. He reaches for the pry bar, but I stop him.

"I'll do the staples. You eat."

"Thanks." He wipes his hands on his shorts and takes my spot on the floor, tearing off half a slice of pizza in one bite.

I dig out the staples, fighting the urge to curse under my breath.

"How did you make this look so easy?"

"I've done it before," he says, his mouth full.

"Do you help all your clients like this?" I ask before I can stop myself.

"Yes." His voice is deadpan. I shoot him a suspicious look. "No, Mallory. Obviously I've been giving you special treatment. My gold-star level of service, if you will."

"Why?" I pry at a bent staple that won't budge. "Because you feel bad for that first night?" *Making out with me before you knew I was a client?*

"Bad?" Daniel pauses before selecting his next slice. "The opposite."

"What?" I sit up on my knees, suddenly wishing we were using straightforward language instead of joking around. Because I'm confused.

"I don't feel bad that we kissed, Mallory."

I blush furiously. I guess that's pretty straightforward.

"Would I have done it if I knew who you were?" he continues. "No. I do pride myself on being professional. But am I helping you out because I feel bad about all that? Also no." He gives me a level look, as though he's wondering if he needs to spell it out. "I enjoy hanging out with you."

The empty room seems to echo with those words. So sweet, so uncomplicated. *Don't ruin it, Mallory.*

"Oh." I look down at the pry bar in my hands, then say slowly—as normally as I can—"The feeling is mutual."

He claps his hands together, stands, and grabs the broom. "Glad we cleared that up."

I watch as he sweeps up the staples.

"I guess I'm just not used to it," I say.

"Used to what?"

"Making new friends." I regret the words the instant they leave my mouth. "Because, I mean, back home I don't really make new friends all that often. I have Carmen and my family and my co-workers and..." I shrug. "It's different here."

"Small-town friendliness?" he suggests.

"Maybe."

"For what it's worth, it seems to come naturally to you. You don't come across as someone who doesn't know how to make friends."

I smile, embarrassed. "Thanks. All right, can we be done talking about me now?"

He ties up the garbage bag and teases, "Makes you uncomfortable, doesn't it?"

"Just a little."

"Well, come on." He taps his bare chest and spreads his arms like he's an open book. "Fire away. I love talking about yours truly."

"Okay," I laugh. "Who's your best friend?"

"Jones."

"Favorite movie?"

"Pirates of the Caribbean."

"Do you dress up for Halloween?"

"Last year I was Lucille Ball." He gestures to his hair. "The redhead thing."

"I have got to see pictures of this."

"Come on, keep 'em coming."

"Favorite meal?"

"Breakfast. Banana pancakes."

"Ice cream flavor?"

"Cookie dough."

"Me too!"

"I knew I liked you, Rosen."

I'm momentarily flustered, beaming at him. Why does it tickle me so much when he calls me by my last name? Like we're teammates on the high school track team.

After a long pause, Daniel seems to remember that he's shirtless. He clears his throat, pulls his shirt on, and says, "Well, I should get going. I've got an early client meeting tomorrow."

"Thank you for your help. And the pizza."

"Anytime."

"You know, I saw that movie four times the summer it came out in theaters."

"Hmm?" He looks confused.

"Pirates of the Caribbean."

"Ah. See? We would've been friends even back then."

We look at each other, the moment long and sticky. Nothing can happen between us. Our conversation about his ex-girlfriend confirmed that. But still...

And then he starts to sing. "Duh-duh dun dun, duh-duh dun dun..."

It's the *Pirates* theme song.

I burst out laughing and smack him on the shoulder. He runs outside, still singing as he snaps on his helmet and swings a leg over his bike. I chase him, weak with laughter, which only makes him sing louder.

I shout after him, "You are without doubt the worst pirate I've ever heard of!"

"But you have heard of me!" he calls back, just before he disappears down the dark street.

When I wake up the next morning, my first thought is *ouch*. My muscles ache, my hands ache. The walk to the dining room for breakfast is slow and painful. Somehow my quads are sore, as well as some muscles around the backs of my shoulders that I didn't know existed.

In my victorious haze last night, I'd thought maybe I could return to the house in the morning before work and devote an hour or two to ripping up carpet in one of the bedrooms. Now I realize that was wildly optimistic. I am completely exhausted, as though I ran a marathon yesterday. There is no way I'll be recovered by tonight; the only thing I'm going to want to do after work is soak in the Jacuzzi and then crawl into bed. Which means I'm wasting an entire day when I should be working toward my goals so that I can eventually, someday, *go home*.

As I'm lingering over my plate of scrambled eggs and potatoes with ketchup, staring absently out at the beach, my phone rings. It's my mom; she must have heard my thoughts from across the country and now wants to make sure I am actually coming home.

"Hey, Mom."

"Darling, did I wake you?"

"No, I—" Why does everyone keep assuming I sleep until midmorning, like I'm a teenager? "I'm eating breakfast. What's up? And why are you up at the crack of dawn?"

"Pickleball, darling, pickleball!"

"Right." I take a sip of my now lukewarm coffee.

"Anyway, listen, is Gramps with you?"

"No, he's back at his place. He eats Grape-Nuts at five A.M. I guess that's where you get it from."

"Oh, hush. Well, I am calling because Trish and I had a terrific idea. You know his birthday is coming up?"

"That's right. June tenth, isn't it?" I somehow pluck the date out of my memory and instantly feel bad that I haven't thought about his birthday until now.

"Yes, which is six days away. You will still be there, I assume."

"Um…" I picture Pebble Cottage: its brown, brown walls, one room now devoid of carpet. I mentally combine these images with the fact that I, apparently, can't do two days of manual labor in a row, and that I still have to purchase and install flooring, not to mention paint the walls.

I groan and shove a forkful of eggs in my mouth. "Unh-hm."

"Yes, we figured. I hope you're using sunscreen. So here's our idea: surprise birthday party!"

"Oh. Wow."

"Your father and I will fly down, arriving the evening before his birthday, and check into a hotel. Maeve and Blake are still TBD, since one week is short notice for them."

"Okay. Wow," I say again. I don't know why, but the idea of an impromptu visit makes me feel defensive. Gramps and I have a decent rhythm going, and I don't want my parents to mess it up.

"And we'll need *you* to help with the logistics." She says this in the same tone of voice she might use to tell me I'd won a shopping spree at Nordstrom.

"Logistics?"

"Booking the party room, ordering a cake from Publix, buying decorations. Trish will handle the caterers for the dinner buffet. Of course, we can sneak in and help you set everything up before the party."

"Party room?" I repeat, feeling ten steps behind.

"The party room there at the condo, Mallory. Inquire today because it sometimes books up well in advance."

"Inquire today."

"Are you feeling all right? You seem a little slow this morning."

"I'm fine, I just ripped up some carpet yesterday," I say, as though this reason would make sense to anyone other than myself.

I expect Mom to skim right over this detail—she's not usually one for details—but she snags on it instead.

"You—what? Carpet? Where? Pebble Cottage?"

"Yeah. It needs new floors. And paint." *Don't laugh*—I really need her not to laugh. If one more person laughs at my attempts, especially now that I feel like I did the hardest workout of my life, I might just give up.

"Look at you taking initiative!" Her voice surprises me by sounding like it's full of admiration instead of hilarity. "Mallory is taking initiative!" This last bit sounds like she yelled it at my dad in another room.

"I've taken initiative before," I grumble. "I think."

"What kind of flooring are you going with? Because I think a nice vinyl plank would really—"

"Mom," I snap, pressing my fingers to the bridge of my nose. An elderly couple a few tables away looks up at me in alarm. I lower my voice. "I can handle it."

"Of course you can, darling. So, the family guest list will be Trish and co., your father and me, Lenore, and Eddy. Make sure you invite Gramps's friends from Sandy Shores, too—you know, Angela and whoever else he's spending time with these days."

"You want *me* to invite his friends?"

"Yes! You live there now, don't you? Text me after you've secured the party room. I have to run. Love to you and Gramps!"

So now I have this on my to-do list on top of everything else. I wish my mom hadn't surprised me with this on a Monday morning. My Mondays are always packed full of meetings, and I'm finding it hard to concentrate. What did she mean by decorations? Balloons and streamers? What would Lottie have done? Probably something sophisticated, but I can't for the life of me think what that might be.

Sometime after lunch, as I'm listening to a drip-voiced co-worker drone on about the "learnings" from an all-hands last week and then something about "solidifying the asks that we're bringing to leadership," a tidal wave of resentment crashes over me. Do I resent that I have a steady, decently paying job? No way. But I do resent that I'm sitting here right now, bored to numbness, when I have so many other things that need my attention. Things that, frankly, I would much rather be doing. Active, tangible things, like running around town to organize a party, and using my own two hands to beautify a house. Things that seem a lot more interesting and rewarding than sitting through meetings full of corporate jargon, tapping out notes so I don't instantly forget what people say.

I have a break from meetings at three o'clock. (I have my calendar permanently blocked for lunch at noon Seattle time, and people occasionally respect that.) The rest of the afternoon is full of meetings that I only have to listen to. Sitting cross-legged on my seashell-covered bed, I wish I could work on the house while listening to these meetings, but there's no internet at Pebble Cottage.

Maybe I should fix that. I mean, it is my house. I could get it hooked up to the internet, and then my future tenants could pay me for the internet instead of having to set it up themselves.

Two hours later, I've gone down a rabbit hole of internet service providers in the Tampa area. Somehow, I haven't absorbed a word of the meetings I've been in, nor have I made any progress toward planning Gramps's party. *Nice.* But I did manage to make an appointment with the internet guys, so at least I have that.

It's almost five, so I decide to try to figure out the party room situation. If only I could ask Gramps where the party room is—but he's not supposed to know about the party. I vaguely remember where it is from family reunions past, so, after setting my Slack status to "BRB," I take the elevator to the ground floor and wander toward the building that contains the gym and the library.

My sandals slap against the cold tile floor as I walk through the empty lobby. It's sumptuously—and thematically—decorated with watercolor paintings of egrets and whales, huge mirrors framed with borders of milky-green sea glass, and aquamarine floor vases overflowing with tufts of dried ornamental grass.

At the end of one hallway is a door with a helpful placard that reads, PARTY ROOM. The room is empty. I half expected there to be some sort of party room receptionist manning a desk. But there is no desk, just a large room full of couches, a TV, a pool table, some scattered tables, and a kitchenette.

I sigh. Why didn't my mom tell me *how* to book the party room? That detail would have been helpful. I'm just thinking that I could ask Angela next time I see her, when I spot it: a bulletin board in the kitchen. It contains a few flyers and notices, and right in the middle is a sign-up sheet titled PARTY ROOM RESERVATIONS. *Perfect*—so I don't even have to talk to anyone. I can just add my name.

I scan the sheet to see how it's done. At the top, the short instructions say that the room can be reserved up to twice a day, for a minimum of two hours and a maximum of four hours. The cleaners come by once at the end of each night, so morning parties are responsible for their own cleanup. Works for me.

Running one finger down the list, I find the date of Gramps's birthday, June 10. My heart sinks. In small, cursive handwriting, someone has written, "Susan Goodwin, 5–9 P.M." So that means either we can have the party in the morning or we have to choose a different date. Why didn't Mom tell me about this sooner? Would she and Trish be opposed to a brunch party instead of a dinner party?

I glare at the paper. The day after Gramps's birthday is available. But what kind of surprise birthday party would that be? And then I realize that each row has a space for the person to put their phone number. Susan Goodwin's phone number is right there, in her neat penmanship. The idea of cold-calling a stranger sends uncomfortable prickles down my neck. But it's for Gramps's birthday.

Phone pressed to my ear, I stand at the window overlooking the path to the beach where sea oats sway in the light breeze. Susan answers on the second ring.

"Hello?"

I clear my throat. "Hi, is this Susan Goodwin?"

"Yes, who's calling?"

"My name is Mallory Rosen, I was just, ah—" I really should have planned what I was going to say ahead of time. I try for some authority. "I was hoping to book the party room for June tenth, but I see you beat me to it. Is there any chance you might be able to change the date of your party? See, we were hoping to throw a surprise birthday party for my grandpa, and—"

"Who's your grandpa?" Susan interrupts brusquely. I get the sense she's wondering how much cachet my grandfather holds in their community. I consider lying and saying the name of the condo president, Arnold Engelhorn.

"Leonard Gilberstein."

"Leonard!" she says happily, and my heart lifts with hope. "Send him birthday wishes from me! But no, dear, there's nothing I can do. It's the twentieth anniversary of my book club's inception, and we have an author coming to talk with us about her book. It's all set."

"Could…" I try, knowing it's pointless, "could you have it in the morning instead?"

"Wine, dear. Book clubs are about the wine first, gossip second, books third. It has to be in the evening. I'm sorry. Have a nice day, now." She hangs up.

Well, crap.

I sit heavily on the nearest couch. If only Mom had had this idea sooner. Now I feel like I'm the one ruining Gramps's birthday party—a party that was only conceived of a day or two ago. Could we have it in Gramps's condo? No, that place can't comfortably hold more than eight people at a time. What about Trish's house? It's a bit out of the way, and she has two huge Dobermans, but I could ask her. Or I could research community parks, local restaurants with party rooms to rent.

Or…

I sit up straight, struck with sudden inspiration. Or I could host the party at Pebble Cottage. Outside, obviously, and in the sunroom. There's literally no way the inside of the house will be ready before then. But if it's a dinner party, that means we'll be there at dusk—I could make the garden extra magical with twinkly lights hidden in all the bushes, patio lights strung above an outdoor table.

This could work.

I text Mom impulsively: *Party location secured.*

Once I'm back at my computer, with meetings droning on in the background, I start a list of all the things I'm going to need for the party.

It also occurs to me to text my neighbor, Sam, that I won't be home for at least another week or two.

Your package count continues to grow, Sam replies.

I laugh guiltily. *I'm sorry! You can open them if you want. To get rid of the boxes. Or to see if you want anything. They're mostly skin-care products, I think.*

All I get back is a thumbs-up emoji.

But a little while later, Sam texts again: *Oh my God, this blue candle smells amazing.*

Keep it! I reply. *As a thank-you gift!*

They send a thank-you emoji, but I can see they're still typing.

Why do you buy all this stuff?

It makes me happy, I send. And then I add, *Or it did. For a long time. I guess I should cancel my auto orders.*

Please do. I'm running out of space here.

I laugh again and try to focus on work. A few minutes later, Sam sends one last text. It's a picture of a Bath & Body Works foaming hand soap.

Holy shit, this stuff is nice. Remind me to package-sit for you anytime!

I heart the message, and then I cancel all my auto shipments.

Chapter 22

On Tuesday afternoon, I head to Pebble Cottage to meet the internet people. Unfortunately, they've given me a window between one and four P.M. So I change my Slack status to a broken signal connection that says "Internet problems." It's a common enough status that no one will question it, and it's kind of true. I do my best to keep up with messages from my phone, and aside from that, I paint a bedroom. That's how the blue-polo-wearing internet guy finds me: holding a paint roller, my limbs splattered with paint. It's not my most flattering image, but in a weird way, I like that this is this stranger's first impression of me: a woman who's not afraid to work hard and get messy. I don't think I've ever felt like that kind of woman before.

As I'm sitting in the sunroom, drinking water and catching up on messages while the guy finishes his work, I get a new one from Kat:

Kat White: *Still having internet troubles?*

Mallory Rosen: *Yeah, so annoying. But there's a guy here now fixing it.*

Kat White: *Sounds serious. Glad you're getting it fixed!*

I wonder if that's all she had to say, but then she types again.

Kat White: *You know, you could always come into the office if you need more reliable internet. A few of us have been coming in occasionally. It's nice.*

What the...? Like most people at my company, I haven't been

into the office since early 2020. They sent us home for quarantine, and we've never returned. I remember the newly hired version of me who was so excited to have a job again, navigating the congested downtown streets to a dark, glossy office tower, and she seems like a different person. As grateful as I still am for this job, I have no desire to sit in an overly air-conditioned cubicle, to make forced elevator small talk, to eat a sad lunch in a sad office kitchen, ever again.

But to Kat I type: *Thanks, I'll keep that in mind!* Vaguely, I wonder if she suspects that I'm working from out of town and lying about it. But as the internet guy helps me connect my laptop to my shiny new internet, I don't give Kat's words a second thought.

Now that I can work from Pebble Cottage, I stay for the rest of my workday, headphones on to join meetings while I finish up the bedroom walls. By eight o'clock, I've finished two coats of paint. My hands are stiff and aching, but I'm ridiculously proud of myself, and I want to keep going. I text Daniel to let him know that I want to choose the new flooring.

I'm all yours Thursday morning. We can meet at the Floor Emporium.

You're a lifesaver! I don't even know the difference between linoleum and tile.

All you need to know is that you won't be choosing either one. Daniel replies so quickly, I imagine he's staring googly-eyed at his phone, watching my typing bubbles, just like I'm doing. This makes me giggle.

I send him a picture of the painted bedroom.

Nice work, Rosen!

I reply with a smiling angel emoji.

The next morning, I return from breakfast with a couple hours to spare before my workday begins. Since Gramps's surprise party is only a few days away, I decide to make some invitations for Angela and the others. I wonder if there's any chance they'll be available on such short notice.

I consider making them on my computer, but that would involve figuring out how to connect to Gramps's ancient printer. So instead, I decide to get crafty. In the hall closet, I find a box of arts-and-crafts supplies, the same box Maeve and I used to scrounge around in when we were kids, looking for glitter glue and scissors and construction paper.

The construction paper is still there, as are markers, colored pencils, and more. Some of the markers appear to be twenty years old, but some of them are newer. My youngest cousins are basically still arts-and-crafts age, so Lottie probably kept the box stocked for them.

I'm sitting cross-legged on my bed, surrounded by sparkly half-finished cards that read YOU'RE INVITED, when Gramps knocks.

"Yes?" I scramble to pile the cards behind me without messing up the wet ink.

Gramps lets himself in. "What's all this?" He gestures to the colored pencils, paper, and glittery gel markers littering my bed.

"It's, uh..." I think fast, trying to decide whether "new hobby" or "making a postcard for Mom" sounds more believable. But then I glance up at Gramps's face. He looks brightly curious, as though he's sure the answer will delight him. And he also has folds of skin around his eyes that will forever hold his grief.

I picture finagling him to somehow come down to Pebble Cottage the night of the party; this will require lying to him. I, for one, have never been a fan of surprises. They feel almost like pranks to me: a grand joke for the group who's in on it, at the expense of the one person who's not. Worst-case scenario would be Gramps bursting into panicked tears. Best-case scenario, I'm pretty sure, would be

Gramps mildly pleased to see all his loved ones, but taken aback by all the noise.

I take a deep breath. "Gramps, Mom and Trish are planning a surprise birthday party for you."

His lips purse into a comical O. "For me? Why, how splendid." He pauses. "Did you not just foil their plans by telling me?"

"Yes, but I thought you should know. I wasn't sure if you would appreciate a surprise. Would you?"

"Oh no." He shakes his head with a dismissive wave of one hand. "Dreadful, surprise parties. You might have saved me from a heart attack."

"Okay, good." I'm pleased with myself. Maybe I really am getting to know him.

He picks up one of the cards and makes soft noises of approval, like he's my dad and I'm a kindergartner.

"So, who do you want at this shindig?" I ask. "Other than family. I'm going to invite Angela, but I wasn't sure who else."

"Ah." He holds up one finger, bustles off to the kitchen, and returns with a notepad and pen. "I can give you some names and their unit numbers." He jots down several names and then pauses. "It'll be nice to reconnect with some old chums."

My chest fills with a warm glow. I definitely made the right decision by telling him.

"Remember," I say with a stern voice, "you have to act surprised. Mom and Trish would kill me if they thought I ruined their surprise party."

"You mean like this?" Gramps drops his pen, his hands flying to his cheeks as he utters a small scream.

I double over with laughter. "That's perfect. Do it just like that."

Chapter 23

I'm sitting in Gramps's car, applying a coat of a CVS lipstick that's supposed to be a Charlotte Tilbury dupe, when Daniel rides up on his bike. I glance at the clock on the dashboard: It's exactly nine o'clock. Impressive. It feels early to me—the breakfast room had been bustling when I arrived there an hour earlier than usual—but the parking lot of the Floor Emporium is as crowded as though it were midday.

I step out of the car, clutching my Starbucks iced coffee in one hand (an actual Starbucks: one of the perks of driving all the way into St. Pete).

"I cannot believe you biked all the way here."

He flashes a grin as he removes his helmet, his red hair sticking up.

"Easy ride. Barely took more than half an hour." I follow him as he locks his bike to the rack outside the automatic doors of the Floor Emporium. He's wearing his usual black biking shorts and white T-shirt. It takes all of my self-control to prevent my gaze from flicking down to his thighs.

"Aren't you afraid of..." I twirl my iced coffee for embellishment. He gives me a quizzical look. "Like, getting flattened by all the cars?"

He presses his lips together like he's trying not to laugh at me.

"It's not high on my list. Poisonous snakes, climate change, riptides, cancer. Those are higher."

I have no response to this. All I can manage is a small "right."

"You should really try it," Daniel continues. "If only to get around our little town. Isn't this your grandpa's car?"

"Yeah, but he never uses it. Besides, if I were biking, where would I freshen my lipstick?"

Daniel gestures to the round rearview mirror clipped to one of his handles, showing it off like a game-show hostess. This makes me laugh.

"And the helmet hair?" I press. "I don't know, Daniel."

"I don't think you have anything to worry about in the hair department." He says it nonchalantly, leading the way into the store. I'm glad he's ahead of me, because now I'm blushing furiously, and simultaneously very pleased that I wore my hair down this morning.

"Oh my..." As soon as we walk in, I'm overwhelmed. This place is huge, filled with slabs of tile and planks of wood and rows and rows of linoleum squares. If I had come here by myself, I would've just turned around and walked out.

"You've done this before?" I confirm.

Daniel slows his pace next to a gorgeous slab of white marble. "Of course. I help clients with stuff like this all the time. And I redid my own place a few years back."

"Did you hire someone to do your floors?" I ask.

He gives me a look that somehow insinuates that this is a silly question and do I really think he wouldn't do his own floors?

"No," he answers. The look, and the one-word answer, are filled with so much manly confidence that I have to suppress a nervous giggle. I slurp my iced coffee.

"I like this one." I drape myself over a block of pale, creamy marble with pink highlights.

"Oh yeah?" He smirks, probably at the fact that I've chosen the girliest floor they have. "Do you have an extra five hundred grand lying around?"

"What?" I spring up as though the marble has burned me.

"I guess I should ask." He turns to face me, and I can't help but notice the full-frontal body language. I brace myself for a flirtatious question, but then he says, "What is your budget?" and my excitement deflates.

Picturing my bank account minus my rent, a couple of plane tickets, the rental car, and the insurance on Pebble Cottage, I say, "Small. Cheap."

"Got it." He strides forward and beckons for me to follow. "Your section is over here. Forget you ever saw that marble."

"But..." I stroke it lovingly, picturing how nice it would look with my Pottery Barn couch, my off-white chunky crochet throw blanket, the enormous, creamy pink Anthropologie candle I could buy to go with it.

"Say goodbye, Rosen." Daniel grabs my hand and drags me away.

"I'll never forget you," I call. I can tell he's trying not to laugh.

"Now, your square footage is small—reasonable—so you really don't have to spend too much," Daniel says. He suddenly realizes he's still holding my hand and drops it. I snort with laughter. He continues his spiel. "But you should be prepared to spend around two thousand dollars."

"Does this include paint?" I ask hopefully.

"No. But since you're doing it yourself, the paint will only set you back a few hundred."

"Excellent."

An older salesman with a white mustache and a red vest pauses beside us, holding a clipboard.

"Help you find anything?"

"Yeah, we're looking for vinyl hardwoods, light neutral shades, something mid-range," Daniel says. I give him a sideways glance—shouldn't he have said *cheapest possible*? But he doesn't look back at me.

"Or," I interrupt the salesman's response, "what about a ceramic tile with sort of a faux-marble look?"

Daniel touches me lightly on the elbow. "I don't think you want to get into installing tile. It's harder than you'd think."

"I'm sure I could—"

He cuts me off. "Plus, tile is impossible to replace, and I bet good money you want to redecorate again in five to ten years."

This shuts me up; I bite back a smile. Seems like Daniel McKinnon somehow, sort of, knows me.

"Your husband is right," the salesman continues. "Tile is tricky, especially if you're going for self-installation. I can show you a selection of vinyl that's made to look like tile, or even marble."

Daniel briefly closes his eyes as though praying for patience, holds up one finger, and starts to say "We're actually—"

But I twine my arm around his. "Hubby is *always* right. Aren't you, smoochikins?"

The salesman's cheeks turn rosy with delight above his mustache. "Newlyweds?"

"Just back from our honeymoon." I nuzzle against Daniel's shoulder. He stiffens with discomfort.

"Enjoy this time," the salesman says indulgently. "I remember my honeymoon like it was yesterday. Niagara Falls. Been married almost thirty-six years now."

Suddenly, Daniel leans into me and ruffles my hair, somewhat aggressively. "Any advice?" he asks.

"You know what they say." The man tucks the clipboard under one arm. "Happy wife, happy life!"

"Well, that's easy. Give this one another clown figurine to add to her collection and she's happy as pie. In fact, she loves clowns so much, I should let her join the circus." Daniel tilts his head to smile down into my face. I'm still gripping his arm, my face locked into a smile that's now more like a grimace.

"Oh." The man clears his throat. "Well, the LVPs are thataway." He points and then hurries off.

As soon as he's gone, Daniel and I spring apart.

"Clowns?" I hiss.

"Some might find it strange, but what can I say? My little missus is a special one." He strides off toward aisle 17.

I scurry after him and smack his arm.

"Anyway," I say, "I know you think vinyl is cheap, but I really might want to consider one that looks like marble."

"Well." He stops and spreads his arms at the selection around us. "I think you're going to like LVPs. Luxury vinyl planks."

"Ooh. *Luxury* vinyl?"

"Includes the word *luxury*, but still in your budget," Daniel confirms.

I beam at him, then slowly pace the aisle, taking in my options. I'm stopped in front of a gorgeous plank that's made to look like antique black-and-white tile when my phone buzzes with a new email. I check it out of pure reflex, and then I re-read it three times, my brain fuzzy with confusion.

It must show on my face, because Daniel asks, "Everything okay?"

"Uh...I need to..." I grope around behind me for a place to sit, but I don't want to send tile samples tumbling, so I just sit cross-legged on the floor. Daniel immediately crouches down next to me.

"Is it your grandpa?"

"No." Startled, I look up and see that his face is serious, one line creased between his reddish eyebrows. "It's a work thing. I..." I exhale, set my empty coffee cup down, and read the words from the email itself. "All full-time employees must return to the office no later than Monday, July second. Attendance in the office will be expected five days a week."

Daniel's face merely crinkles deeper with apparent confusion. I realize that he's so far removed from corporate tech life, he just doesn't understand.

"I've been working from home for years," I explain. "Now, with no warning, they're saying we all have to go back to working in the office. They don't even know I've been in Florida the last few weeks."

"Will you get in trouble if they find out?"

"I don't think they'd be happy about it." I scan the rest of the email; the tone is stern and doesn't mention any exceptions to this new rule.

"When were you planning to go back home?"

An unexpectedly heavy weight fills my chest.

"Honestly?" I realize the truth as I say the words. "I wasn't. I mean, not for a while. I kept kicking the can down the road, because things kept coming up, and—well, because I like it here. I feel different here."

"Different how?" Daniel cocks his head. This man who lives so vibrantly in the world, staying active and busy and talking to people all day long. How could he understand what my life is like at home? Solitary. Quiet. Absolutely devoid of humidity.

"I feel...useful here." I leave it at that for now.

He nods. He knows all about Gramps and Pebble Cottage, so I suppose this makes sense to him.

"And now you have to go back," he says.

"By the end of the month."

We don't say anything for a long minute. My butt is getting

uncomfortable on the hard floor, but I want to curl up and stay right here. The idea of leaving Gramps, of leaving Pebble Cottage unfinished, of leaving the beach...of going back to my lonely apartment, of being forced to commute to a sterile office building to do my boring job under Kat's watchful eye...it's too much. It's way too much.

Boldly, I look up at Daniel, still crouching in front of me. There's no denying that part of me wanted something to happen between us. I mean, that kiss outside the mermaid bar is not something I'll easily forget. Deep down, I'd thought that maybe, as we worked together on Pebble Cottage, something would unfold naturally. And I know it was unlikely, because of his history with a failed long-distance relationship. But now, it's absolutely impossible. It's taken me years to get over my last ex; there's no reason for me to start something new when it has no chance of going anywhere. I'm not going to do that to myself. Or to Daniel.

I have three weeks left. Now is the time to get things done, not to fantasize about what might have been.

Daniel has held eye contact as these thoughts raced through my head. I can't tell what he's thinking. He offers me a hand and helps me up.

"Well," he says, letting go quickly and dusting his hands on his shorts. "Then we better get cracking. No time to lose, right, Rosen?"

"Yeah. No time to lose."

The mood of our shopping trip has changed noticeably. We deliberate between a few options, and within fifteen minutes I've chosen the new flooring for my house. Daniel helps me place the order, calculating how much I'll need. Outside, we pause at his bike. The hot, humid air feels like a hug after the air-conditioning inside.

"Mallory." He fidgets with his helmet. "I don't want to overstep, but..."

My heart gallops, and I know that it wouldn't take much for me to toss out the resolution I just made. If Daniel wanted to start something, I might be powerless to say no.

"When you leave," he continues, "I would be happy to drive your grandpa to appointments. If he needs help."

This is so far from what I was expecting, I don't say anything for a moment.

"It's only that I did the same thing for my dad," he rushes to explain. "When he was sick."

"Oh, I'm so sorry." My hand lands on his. "Is he okay now?"

Daniel looks down at the helmet in his hands. "He passed five years ago."

"Daniel, I'm so sorry," I say again. What else is there to say? I can't imagine losing my dad.

"Me too," he says. "But I know what it's like to help someone in that situation. I know your grandpa has friends and other family around here, but I wanted to offer. Maybe it'll take some of the stress off your plate if you know that's taken care of."

It's so thoughtful, I don't know what to say. My throat fills with tears and I feel hot color flooding my cheeks. Just knowing that, without Trish and without me, Gramps will have someone nearby to help him out...it means a lot. Suddenly, I'm tossing my arms around Daniel's shoulders.

"Thank you," I say into his chest. He squeezes tight—he gives good hug, which does not surprise me one bit. And then he lightly taps my waist and takes a step back.

"You're welcome."

I exhale shakily, and he gently chucks me under the chin.

"Chin up," he says.

I nod. Chin up.

Chapter 24

Publix cake: ordered. I almost went with the cake Mom would've chosen—a tasteful vanilla buttercream, white with a colorful border of confetti-like dollops of frosting. Instead, I ordered a dark-blue cake adorned with planets. Probably meant for little boys who love the solar system, but equally fitting for a telescope-loving grandpa.

I muddle through work on Friday, too upset about the return to office email to really focus. I mostly work on the house while periodically checking my laptop for messages. Having internet at Pebble Cottage has been great for my productivity—house-related productivity, that is. I've pulled up the carpet in one of the bedrooms already. After this, I need to focus on the backyard. The party is the day after tomorrow. I still need to get decorations, but the guest list is shaping up. Angela and all of Gramps's other friends called me to RSVP yes, except one guy who's getting a colonoscopy that day. I did not ask any follow-up questions.

There's one person I wish I had invited. I still could, even though it's super last-minute and he probably already has plans.

It seems a little off the wall to invite Daniel to a family party. Do I really want to expose him to my parents and extended family? They're...a lot. But on the other hand, he offered to drive Gramps to appointments, and he's never even met him. So maybe he should. And maybe I'm just looking for excuses to invite him.

I table that thought for now. It's almost dinnertime, and I want to get back to the condo. I feel like I've been neglecting Gramps the last few days.

It's such a gorgeous evening that I drive back up Gulf Boulevard with the top down. The air is balmy and briny. The sky spans endlessly blue in every direction, and as I drive and sing along to the radio, zipping past palm trees, I experience a moment of pure disbelief that this is where I live. Only for a few weeks, but still. Compared with my life back home—the well-worn walks around my overcast neighborhood—this is paradise. People dream all their lives of retiring to a place like this, and here I am.

Pulling into Sandy Shores, I'm waved in by the parking lot attendant, and I smile and wave back at him. If this were a movie, I would cheerfully call out, "Hey, Carl, looking good! That CrossFit is paying off!" But I haven't moved that far out of my introvert shell yet, and I probably never will. Also, I have no idea what his name is. I do, however, pass by one of the friends I invited to Gramps's birthday party as I stride across the grassy lawn.

"Hi, Tom!" I call as he walks in the other direction with a swim towel over his shoulder.

"Evening, Mallory."

This puts a little spring in my step. See, I practically am living in a movie now. Or an episode of *Gilmore Girls*. Upstairs, I greet Gramps, who's listening to classical music out on the balcony, and then start on dinner prep. My laptop is open on the counter beside me, but it's blessedly quiet—no pings or emails.

I follow a recipe I found in an old, well-loved recipe box of Lottie's. I can just barely make out her scrawl on the index card titled CINCINNATI CHILI, but I figured I might have better luck with Lottie's tried-and-true recipes than random ones I find on the internet.

Half an hour later, we sit down to eat. Gramps digs into his steaming bowl of chili served over spaghetti and takes several large bites without stopping, which I take as a good sign.

"How is it?" I ask. Cooking for someone else has given me an unexpected respect for my mom's cooking—she may not be the world's greatest chef, but cooking for other people is hard.

"Delicious," he says with his mouth full.

"It's Lottie's recipe."

"Oh." He looks down at his bowl in surprise. "So it is." He twirls more spaghetti around his fork and then adds, as though realizing he'd been remiss, "It's just the way she always made it."

I smile to myself. I know he was just being polite, but it's still nice to hear.

We eat in silence for a minute, and then I ask something that's been on my mind. "Hey Gramps, what do you want for your birthday?"

"Cake," he says decisively.

"I mean, yeah, there will be cake. I meant for a present."

"Oh!" The question seems to take him by surprise. "You know, Mallory, we old men don't typically expect a gift on birthdays."

"Why not?"

"That's a young man's game. Or a young boy's game, rather."

"Everyone gets presents on their birthday. Didn't Lottie get you gifts?"

"Yes, she did. Every birthday and every Hanukkah. But everyone else stopped buying me birthday gifts ages ago. After all"—he gestures around to the condo at large—"what do you get the man who has everything?"

I smile at this. "Okay, well, what did Lottie used to get you? What were some of your favorite birthday presents ever?"

"Ever?" He leans back in his chair thoughtfully, hands folded over his stomach. "Let's see. Last year Lottie got me a porcelain bowl for my shaving soap."

I feel my eyebrows flick up quizzically, and Gramps chuckles. "It might not sound like much, but I use it every day. And it was the last birthday present she ever got me. So I'll never forget it."

"Of course," I say quietly.

"Other than that, let's think. There have been ties. Many, many ties. I only ever wear ties to weddings, or to conferences back in my working days. Most of them I've never had occasion to wear."

"So you're telling me I shouldn't get you a tie."

He shakes his head and takes a sip of iced tea.

"When I was thirteen, my aunt Mills got me a bicycle. A cherry-red Schwinn Phantom. She was a spinster with no children of her own, so she doted on us quite a bit." He smiles dreamily, and I refrain from calling out his use of the word "spinster." "I rode that bike for years. Gave it to a neighbor kid when I went off to university."

"Sounds like the perfect gift."

"It was. Other than that, my birthdays included a lot of sports equipment, books, and clothing. My mother was always giving me shirts and socks. We only got new clothes once or twice a year."

I suppress a shudder at the thought.

"Although..." Gramps continues, sitting up straighter and holding up one finger. "There was one year—my ninth birthday—that my mother got me something entirely different."

"What was it?"

"It was—" He breaks off, grinning widely, and suddenly stands. "Wait here."

Very mysterious. I finish my chili, wondering if he's going to bring back some ancient, beloved telescope or maybe a wristwatch. When he returns five minutes later, however, he's holding an old photograph. He carefully moves my bowl aside and sets the picture down in front of me.

I gasp. It's the most precious thing I've ever seen. Smiling up at me in black and white is Gramps as a young boy, his face beaming and dimpled, a cap perched on top of thick black hair. He's sitting on a stoop with one arm around a dog. The dog's tongue is hanging out happily, his head cocked to one side, dark eyes glittering. His fur looks wiry and light, although I can't tell what color it was from the black-and-white photograph. He has the sweetest black nose and perfect floppy ears.

"Waldo," Gramps says.

"Your mom got you this dog for your birthday?" I'm getting emotional, and I've never even been a huge dog person. The picture is just so cute; Gramps and the dog both look so happy.

He nods. "I wanted a dog my whole life, and she thought, at nine, I was finally responsible enough. Or that's what she told me. Now that I'm old, I can't imagine a nine-year-old being responsible for anything. But I sure loved Waldo. We did everything together. He slept on the foot of my bed." He pauses, his eyes distant and nostalgic, and then laughs fondly. "His favorite toy was this great big stick he found in the woods one day. He insisted on bringing it home, carried it around everywhere."

"How long did you have him for? How . . . how old was he?"

"Eh." Gramps waves a hand and looks away, like it's unimportant. "About a year later, Waldo chewed up one of my dad's shoes."

I wait for him to say more, but he doesn't. "And?"

"And"—he raises both hands as though it's obvious—"my dad got rid of him. Gave him away."

I feel my mouth drop open in horror. "Gave him away just for chewing up a shoe?"

"Back then, a shoe wasn't just a shoe. It was your only pair of shoes until the soles fell off. And besides, that was my dad's nature. He was the paterfamilias, it was his house. No one ever dared to argue with him."

It's so sad, I can barely believe it.

"Did you ever get another dog?"

Wordlessly, he shakes his head.

"Why not?"

"Lottie never wanted a pet. She preferred a clean house."

Lottie! You never let the man have a dog?

"Well, you could get one now!"

Gramps laughs. "I think those days are behind me, Mallory."

"The days of what? Loving another creature? Having someone around to keep you company?"

"And giving that creature baths, lugging him or her to the vet?"

"We could get you a small one. One that doesn't need much grooming."

"Waldo was small. That was one of the reasons my mom chose him." He pauses. "And what about exercise? Dogs need that. I'm too old."

"Gramps. You know perfectly well that you're supposed to be taking a walk every day. A dog would make sure you don't forget."

He brings our empty bowls to the dishwasher. "Look. Forget what I said. Just get me a tie for my birthday."

But it doesn't escape my notice that, instead of putting the photo of Waldo back in its album, he carefully hangs it on the fridge with a seashell magnet.

I spend Saturday preparing the backyard for the party. The first thing I notice is that some of the flower bushes are overgrown, with branches sticking out into walkways. And then I see that the walkways themselves are being overtaken by little spiky green plants—weeds, I assume. I know nothing about plant life. I crouch down and tug out one of the weeds. *Look at me! I'm gardening!*

I pull out a few more, wishing I had gardening gloves, and then wonder how I'm going to trim the flower bushes.

Back to the hardware store I go.

I return with some promising-looking shears, gloves, and a little pronged tool that was labeled WEED PULLER, so I bought it. With the shears, I clip at a branch experimentally. It falls easily to the ground. *Okay! I'm doing it!* I make a few more snips, and then a few more, until the bushes look like they've had their hair cut by an overenthusiastic barber. But at least no one will get their eye poked by a rogue branch.

After digging up a few more weeds with the weed puller tool, I'm at a loss. I don't know enough to identify any other weeds that need removing. What else does one do in a garden? How on earth did Lottie make the garden look so lush and magical? I suppose I could water the plants.

I find the hose, turn it on, and spray all the flower bushes and trees.

There. I gardened.

Next, I drape string lights across the bushes and scatter solar-powered lanterns around the patio, near the pool, and along the pebbled paths.

I get overly ambitious at the party store and purchase a kit to make your own balloon arch. This ends up taking me two hours. By the time I finish it, I'm both pleased with the festive blue-and-silver arch and also starving. It's almost eight P.M. and I haven't eaten since lunch. Feeling like I've earned a nice drink, I head over to the mermaid bar.

It's buzzing now, much busier than it was the last time I came. There are a few open seats at the bar, so I take one and grab a menu. Amanda is mixing a drink down at the other end. She sees me and waves, then sidles over after she hands the customer her drink.

"Hey!" she says, wiping her hands on her apron.

"Hi! Looks like you're staying busy here."

"Guess so." She looks around the place, buzzing with chatter and the clink of cutlery. "Saturday-night rush, I guess. I don't know if it'll be a normal thing, but I'm liking it."

"It will totally be a normal thing! This is the perfect place to hang out!" I sound a little too enthusiastic to my ears, but I'm excited to have a new friend. It hasn't happened in way too long.

"Thanks." Amanda smiles in what I'm pretty sure is a genuine, grateful way. "What can I get for you?"

"I'm starving." I glance down at the menu. "What do you like? I mean, I'm sure it's all delicious."

"The burger," she says decisively.

I read the description: a quarter-pound burger topped with Gruyère cheese, red onion, arugula, and a secret sauce.

"That sounds great. I'll have one of those and an Andrina, please." I decide on the spot, remembering the delicious purple gin and cava cocktail I had last time.

"You got it."

Amanda bustles off to put in my order, and I pop in my earbuds, figuring she'll go on to chat with other customers. But a few minutes later when she drops off my burger, she strikes up a conversation again. I am beyond tickled.

"What are you listening to?"

"Oh." I swallow my bite of burger, removing my earbuds. "Just a podcast. This is freaking delicious, by the way."

She juts out her chin in a told-you-so kind of way.

"Which podcast?"

"It's called *Elementary*. It's—"

"No kidding? I listen every week!"

"Really?"

"That episode where they analyzed classic movies from the '90s and why they're actually unhinged had me crying."

"Yes!" I grin wildly. I've never met a fellow *Elementary* fan in real life before.

"And the one where Samantha talked about adopting a senior dog? Dang, that was sweet," Amanda continues.

"So sweet," I agree. "Actually, I've been looking into where to adopt a dog around here."

"Did you move here? I thought you were just visiting from Seattle, right?"

"I was—I mean, I am. I have to go back to Seattle in a couple weeks. But I want to get my grandpa a dog for his birthday. Is that crazy?"

"I don't know your grandpa, so I don't know. But it sounds cute to me. Although…" Amanda adjusts her headband—chartreuse today—and continues thoughtfully, "I read a post on Instagram once that said you shouldn't get people pets as surprise presents. Because they might not be prepared to care for them. Or they might give them back to the pound? I forget the reason exactly."

"Hmm." I ponder this over another huge bite. This burger is seriously hitting the spot. "I wouldn't want to fly in the face of conventional Instagram wisdom. But I think my grandpa is prepared. He had a dog when he was a kid, and his dad made him get rid of it, and he's never been able to have another dog since then."

Amanda makes a small sound of dismay, and then says, "Mallory, I don't know how old your grandpa is, but you cannot let this man die without having another dog."

"Do you have one?" I ask, taking a sip of my delicious fizzy drink.

"I do. That's probably why I feel so strongly about this." She whips out her phone and shows me the photo on her wallpaper: It's a tiny, fluffy white dog with the most adorable black button eyes and nose.

"Shih tzu?" I hazard a guess.

"Bichon." She pockets her phone. "His name's Draco."

I snort. "Okay, so you're supportive of my plan. Where did you get Draco?"

She seems suddenly embarrassed. "Oh, it was a whole thing."

"What? Now you have to tell me."

"Well." She's interrupted by a server who comes up to whisper urgently in her ear. Amanda nods, her face serious and thoughtful. I see the real businesswoman side of her. I wonder what it's like to be in charge of a place like this—to be in charge of anything, actually. She has authority. She has freedom. She had a vision and brought it completely to life. I'm suddenly, inexplicably, jealous. My job has never required me to have a vision. I'm never expected to be creative, never given any freedom—and besides, what would I do with creative freedom at my job, anyway? Dream up a new format for our spreadsheets?

Amanda is here day and night, consumed by this job—this calling. It reminds me of how I feel about Maeve—not that I want to be a lawyer, but that it has to feel good, in a way, to have to use all of your brain at work, to solve problems and think on your feet and work closely with other people. My job is so sterile. Unimportant. Lonely.

"Send them dessert—chocolate cake—and comp it. They'll get over it," Amanda tells her server.

"Thanks, boss." He glides away, skirting around the bar and in between customers.

"Everything okay?" I ask.

"For sure. People will complain about anything. Okay, so, where was I?"

"About to tell me where you got Draco."

"Right. I actually drove up to Georgia and bought him from a breeder. I paid…a lot."

I wait a beat, and when she doesn't add more, I say, "That's not embarrassing."

"Maybe not, but in the context of adopting dogs from the shelter, it kind of is. I could have adopted a dog from somewhere local, a dog that they found abandoned on the side of the highway or something, but I really wanted a bichon."

"And I can see why." I scoot my now empty plate away from me and wipe my hands on my napkin. "He's precious."

"Thanks. But back to your grandpa. There's a Humane Society not too far from here, in Clearwater. You could try there."

"Perfect! I guess I'm spending my Sunday looking for a dog. His birthday party's tomorrow night."

"Do you want help?"

I tilt my head, caught off guard.

"I have the morning off." She laughs. "I give myself half a day off every week."

"Um. I mean I'm sure you have other things to do, but that would be amazing."

"I would love to. It's not every day you get to help someone find a dog."

"Okay, great! I can pick you up in the morning? Maybe ten?"

Amanda agrees, and we exchange numbers.

A couple wanders up to the bar, and Amanda says, "I better go make some drinks. You want another?"

"No thanks, I'm driving. Go do your thing!" I feel warm and fuzzy from the alcohol and the absolutely foreign concept of a new friend. Riding high on these feelings, I impulsively start typing a message to Daniel. I re-read it once, quickly, and then hit SEND before I have time to talk myself out of it.

After I pay my bill and head out to the car, Daniel texts me back.

I would love to come to your grandpa's party. Thanks for thinking of me! See you tomorrow.

A swoop of elation rushes through me, which I am so not going to analyze right now. I drive home, music blaring, the balmy night air whipping through my hair.

Chapter 25

"Remember, you have to act surprised." I open the passenger door for Gramps and hold out my hand for his.

"I feel like the belle of the ball." He daintily accepts my hand and steps out of the car.

"You are! And you look the part, too."

Gramps and I had rummaged through his drawer full of unused ties and found the most extravagant one: deep plum with colorful parrots printed on it. It's absurd.

"A gift from my niece," Gramps said with a grimace. I laughed. Gramps's niece is Lenore's daughter, Sheila, whom I've always thought of as my most glamorous cousin. She currently lives on a beach in Thailand, running a hostel.

We'd built the rest of Gramps's outfit around the tie: a lavender dress shirt paired with a navy-blue two-piece suit. He only owns one pair of dress shoes: black patent-leather wingtips, which he had polished to a high shine right before we left the condo.

I'd decided on my black wrap dress and strappy nude sandals. I didn't pack many suitably festive outfits. (The carefully winged liquid eyeliner and sparkly lip gloss may or may not have been applied with Daniel in mind.)

My heart pounds as we approach the front door of Pebble Cottage. Partly because of the "surprise" about to take place, but also because of a certain something—someone—I left in the back bedroom. I left him with food, water, toys, and a bed. But still, I'd been anxious about it ever since I closed the door and promised to be back soon. What if I was causing him additional trauma by bringing him to a strange location and leaving him all alone? What if he destroyed the bedroom in his anxiety? Not that there is anything in there to destroy. What if—

Breathe. Focus on getting Gramps to the party first.

I lead the way inside and Gramps marvels at the bare, floor-less floors. I open the back door and say loudly, "This way, Gramps. I want to show you something."

He pokes his head out and says (a little too theatrically in my opinion), "Ooh, what can it be?"

"*Surprise!*"

Even though I know it's coming, I'm startled by the sudden noise and the sight of my extended family jumping out of the shrubbery.

Gramps utters a high-pitched shriek. I'm pretty sure he missed his calling as a thespian. The guests apparently buy his over-the-top reaction; they're eating it up, clapping, cheering, and whistling.

"Happy birthday, Dad!" My mom bustles forward and plants a kiss on his cheek.

"What a surprise to see you, my dear girl!" Gramps grabs her shoulders and kisses her back. I elbow him lightly to tell him to take it down a notch.

Other relatives and friends swarm to greet him, and I hang back, surveying the faces. I don't think Daniel's here yet—not that I am looking for him. Not at all. But, you know, he doesn't know anyone else here, so I should greet him and introduce him to people, to be polite.

The backyard looks perfect, if I say so myself. The sun is just setting, casting a golden-orange glow over the pool and garden, the lanterns and twinkly lights adding little spots of warmth to the scene. The balloon arch is mounted over the dessert table that Trish brought. The balloons look fabulous arching over the blue solar system birthday cake. Trish also set up a makeshift bar cart, which I predict is going to cause some trouble with this crowd.

After they greet Gramps, my parents and Trish pull me in for hugs, oohing and ahhing about the house.

"It looks absolutely perfect out here," Trish says. "Lottie would be proud."

"Did you really tear up all those floors by yourself?" Mom asks.

"Will you hire someone to put in the new floors? Because, you know, Mal, the sooner you can get tenants in here, the better." Dad gestures emphatically with his gin and tonic.

"Everything will be fine." I try for a soothing voice. "I have it under control."

"Yes, Hugh, can't you see that she has it under control? I've never seen you rip up a carpet."

"Thank you, Mother," I say. "Now I need a glass of wine. Excuse me for a sec."

At the bar cart, I pour myself a plastic cup of Chardonnay. My cousin Ellie is helping herself to vodka and cranberry juice. I glance at her sideways.

"What? I'm twenty-one now," she says, by way of greeting.

"I know. And hi." I take a sip of the slightly chilled wine and feel the relaxation spread through me instantly. "How's the ice cream shop?"

"Best job ever. I get a free scoop every shift, and the customers are always happy, because, like, they're getting ice cream so why wouldn't they be?"

I lean against the dessert table. "When I was a senior in high school, I worked at a bakery, and it was kind of the same. No one can be rude when you're handing them a frosted cinnamon bun."

Ellie nods, gives me a tight smile that may or may not be sarcastic, and walks away to talk to her brother. Of course. Kids these days have no time to make polite chitchat with their elders.

I glance around, looking for either someone else to talk to or some sort of hostess duty to perform. There are plenty of cups and beverages, and the guests all appear to be enjoying themselves, including Gramps, who is laughing with Lenore and one of his friends from the retirement village. Maybe I should go check on the surprise I left in the bedroom, make sure he's okay. But then I see a tall head of red hair: Daniel is standing near the pool, holding a can of seltzer and talking to Angela.

"You're here!" I sidle up to them.

"You invited me," Daniel says, and there's an adorable edge of nervousness in his voice, as though there's a chance he wasn't actually invited.

"I know! I just didn't think you were here yet."

"You can't be late to a surprise party. You'd miss all the fun."

"Hi, Mallory." Angela smiles at me. She's wearing a short skirt and a silky pink blouse, sort of the party equivalent of her usual tennis attire. "Love what you've done out here."

"Thank you! I'm glad you could make it."

Angela glances from me to Daniel, and I realize how close I'm standing to him. I shuffle half a step sideways.

"I must go say hello to the birthday boy," she says, and slips away.

"Did she accost you?" I ask Daniel, my voice low.

"Angela? No," he says, laughing, "we were catching up. I manage a house for her. For her son, mostly, but Angela shows up a lot."

"She does, doesn't she?"

"She's a hoot. And she sends the best Christmas baskets."

"Christmas baskets?" I lean in conspiratorially. "What are we talking? Pears? Cheese and crackers?"

Daniel nods with a look that says, *All that and more.* "Flavored popcorn, sausages, chocolates, fruit, you name it."

"Wow." I sip my wine. "I should get into a field where people send you holiday baskets."

"Absolutely. It's why I got into this business."

This makes me laugh. "Really?"

He looks at me, deadpan. "Yes, Mallory, I chose my career purely based on the number of gift baskets I might hope to receive." His jaw twitches a little, and I can't help but notice the cleft in his chin. I want to press my finger into it.

"Makes sense to me. Working in tech, I never receive so much as a mug for the holidays."

"Aw, you poor thing. But no, my dad was a handyman and my brother's a real estate agent, so it just worked out. I had a lot of connections right off the bat just from the people they worked with."

"What does your other brother do?" I ask, remembering that he mentioned two of them.

"He's a middle school science teacher."

"Ha! From catching lizards to teaching science."

"Hey now, I don't remember telling you we caught lizards." He pauses. "But we absolutely did."

We're skating perilously close to discussing the first night we met—when we swapped saliva but not names. Part of me wants to toe the line and push the conversation further in that direction, but I decide to be nice. I don't want to make him uncomfortable.

"So, your family is, like, super enmeshed in the community here," I say.

"Enmeshed? I mean, I guess we are."

"You really are. *You* obviously know everyone in this town. And one brother is a teacher and the other a realtor. It's cute."

"Cute?"

"I mean, this is like your Stars Hollow. And you're Lorelai Gilmore."

"You lost me at Stars Hollow."

"From *Gilmore Girls*?"

"Ah." He takes a sip of his seltzer. "We were always more of a *Sopranos* family."

"Fair enough." I fidget with my nearly empty cup. "Anyway, it's nice, that's all. I'm kind of jealous."

"What, are you saying you're not enmeshed up there in Seattle?" He gives me a playful nudge with his elbow.

"Not at all. I'm completely un-meshed."

He doesn't reply for a moment, and I worry that I'm sounding a tad pathetic.

"Well, hey," he says, gesturing around the garden, "look what you've done here. You've only been here a few weeks and you can pull together a crowd like this."

"They're all here because of him. The star of the show!" I nod towards Gramps, who's clearly having the time of his life in the center of a cluster of friends and family. "Speaking of Gramps, I should introduce you."

Daniel straightens up and nods dutifully. "Lead the way."

Walking with Daniel across the yard, I immediately realize the impact this has on my relatives. I should have seen this coming. My parents, Aunt Lenore, even Ellie stop and watch us with avid curiosity, exchanging meaningful looks with one another.

"My property manager," I explain to Mom and Dad as we pass by. "He manages the house. In a professional capacity."

Daniel doesn't seem to notice. When we reach Gramps, he sticks out a confident hand and shakes Gramps's warmly.

"Gramps, I wanted to introduce you to Daniel McKinnon," I say. "He's managing Pebble Cottage for me."

"Nice to meet you, sir, and happy birthday." Daniel has turned on the Southern charm, and it does not *not* charm me.

"Nice to meet you, Mr. McKinnon." Gramps's eyes are wide and mischievous as he turns to me. "Mallory, you never told me your property manager was so..."

I hold my breath, bracing for him to say *young* or *good-looking*.

"Red-haired," Gramps concludes. I groan and start to chide him, but he continues, "A red-haired McKinnon. Are you, by any chance, related to the late Callum McKinnon?"

Daniel's face relaxes into a warm smile. "He was my dad."

"I knew it. He was our jack-of-all-trades for many years. I was never very handy myself, and Cal never minded coming over to change a single lightbulb."

"Sounds like Dad."

"I was sorry to hear about his passing. He was no age to go."

"Thank you, sir."

Gramps's attention is pulled away by Lenore's husband, who is demanding to know Gramps's opinion on the latest political debate. I shrug at Daniel as if to say, *Well, that was your introduction.*

"By the way"—Daniel pulls me to one side, up against a rosebush—"is there a place to put presents? I didn't know what to get, but..." He pulls a small, neatly wrapped package out of his pocket.

"Is it a tie?" I ask.

"It's socks."

"Adorable." I look around and notice a few gifts scattered around the dessert table, which is already full of plates, cups, and cake. "Let me grab something from inside."

Without hesitation, Daniel follows me through the sunroom and into the dark, bare living room.

He lets out a low whistle. "Sure looks different than the last time I was here. Did I mention that I'm impressed, Rosen?"

Thank goodness the dark room hides the furious blush that colors my cheeks. What is it about him using my last name that gets to me?

"Yep, once or twice." I try to keep my voice casual as he follows me down the hall. I flip on the light in one of the bedrooms and grab the small stepladder I'd left in there the other day. "There's no furniture in the house, but I think this should be big enough for people to put a few gifts on."

"Good thinking."

As we head back down the hall, a distinct bark comes from behind the closed door of the other bedroom.

Daniel freezes. "What was that?"

"Oh, uh..." The dog barks again, a small, questioning sound. Something fiercely maternal rises up in me, and I absolutely have to check on him before we go back outside. "It's Gramps's present."

"You got him a dog?" Daniel sounds dumbfounded.

"Um. Yeah. It's a whole thing. We discussed it first. Kind of." I lean the stepladder against the wall, then skirt around Daniel to the closed door. "I should probably check on him while we're here."

Curiously, Daniel pokes his head over my shoulder as I open the door.

"Hey, buddy," I croon, bending down and holding out one hand so the dog can smell me. I have no idea how to act around dogs. He seems okay, though—his tail wags so hard it makes his whole butt move side to side. "It's almost time for your big debut. You doing okay in here?"

"He's a cutie, ain't he?" Daniel offers the dog a hand, too, and then scratches behind his ears. "What kind of dog is he?"

"I don't know, but he's absolutely perfect." Finding this dog earlier today felt truly meant to be. Amanda and I walked through one shelter full of Chihuahuas and pit bull mixes—and don't get me wrong, they were sweet—but none of them felt like the right dog for Gramps. And then the second place we tried, Happy Paws, only had three dogs: a Lab mix, a cross between a Chihuahua and a Yorkie, and this fellow. My heart nearly jumped out of my skin when I saw him, because he's the spitting image of Waldo. He's some kind of terrier mix, with wiry, sandy-colored hair, floppy ears, shiny black eyes, and the friendliest pink tongue I've ever seen.

"This one," I'd said immediately to Amanda.

"He is the cutest!" she'd agreed. "And he does look like the picture."

I'd taken a picture of Gramps's photograph to use as a reference.

"Don't you want to play with them all a bit first?" the volunteer had asked, surprised.

"No. It's this one. He's perfect. It is a he, right?"

"Yes. His name is Rex."

"Waldo," I whispered.

"What was that?"

"Nothing," I said, and knelt down to introduce myself to Gramps's new best friend.

The rest of the afternoon had been a blur of acquiring all the necessary dog equipment at the pet store—Amanda had texted me a list before she headed home to prepare for her shift: food, a bed, toys, a collar, and a leash—and then taking him on a chaotic walk around my neighborhood to make sure he went potty before I put him in the back room. I hadn't been able to stop thinking about him all day, hoping he was okay all alone. Now, giddy relief flutters through me: He is, in fact, just fine, and it's almost time for him to meet Gramps.

"You know," Daniel says, now rubbing the dog's belly, "some

people would say it's a bit...ill advised to get someone a dog for their birthday."

"And other people would say it's ill advised to let a dog lover go his entire adult life without ever having a dog." I wait to see if he'll challenge me again, but he just grins.

"I like you, Rosen." He walks past me and grabs the stepladder on his way down the hall. "Just let him open my socks first, all right? Before your gift ruins him for everyone else's."

I whisper goodbye to Rex/Waldo and follow Daniel, trying not to read into what he said. But still, *I like you, Rosen* replays in my head more times than I care to admit.

Everyone gathers around near the dessert table as Gramps opens his presents. It's dark now, stars just starting to peek through dusky clouds, so I turn on the light in the sunroom so Gramps can see what he's doing. He makes appreciative comments as he opens a fitness tracker watch from my parents, a calendar from Trish, a shirt from Angela, some books, pens, and multiple pairs of socks. I exchange an amused glance with Daniel.

After Gramps opens the last present, a coffee mug with constellations on it, he starts to thank everyone for their generosity. Daniel clears his throat.

"There's one more thing," he says. Gramps looks around in surprise.

"I'll be right back," I say. Inside, my hands tremble as I hook the dog's brand-new leash onto his collar.

"Come on," I whisper. "It's time!"

We trot out to the backyard, where people instantly start cooing about how cute he is. Gramps, however, just looks stunned.

"Gramps," I say, "I would like you to meet your birthday present. He's a very good boy."

Gramps stares, mouth open, for such a long moment that my heart begins to sink. He doesn't want a dog. This was a horrible idea.

Poor Rex. Now he'll be stuck with me, because there's no way I'm bringing him back to—

But then Gramps falls to his knees and hugs the dog to him. "Waldo!"

His stunned look has morphed into one of boyish delight as he rubs his face into the dog's wiry fur. My heart seizes when I realize that Gramps's eyes have filled with tears.

Tears spring to my eyes too as I kneel down beside them. "I thought he looked like him, too! His name is Rex."

"No." Gramps shakes his head, beaming and rubbing the dog's jowls. "I will call him Waldo Two."

I laugh. "You can't call him that, can you?"

"Wally, for short."

"Okay. That's better."

My cousins and a few of Gramps's friends rush forward to meet Wally. Angela shrilly asks, "Who's a good boy?" over and over, scratching Wally's hindquarters. I step back to make room.

"Well done," Daniel says in my ear.

I turn to smile at him—and then I notice my mother charging forward, Trish trailing behind her. Their expressions are incongruous compared with the heart-eyed crowd around the dog. It takes me a second to realize that they look...mad.

"Mallory, can we talk to you for a minute?" Trish says, just as my mother hisses, "What on earth were you thinking?"

I glance at Daniel, who looks mildly alarmed. He shrinks back into the shadows. I don't blame him.

"Umm...what?" I ask my mom.

"He can't have a dog!" She gestures wildly to her dad. The way she says it is as though he's an invalid, or perhaps someone who has completely lost touch with reality.

"What are you talking about? Why not?"

"How is he going to care for him?"

"Well, I imagine by giving him food, water, walks, love…"

"Walks! The man can't even take himself on a walk."

"He can, he just doesn't like to," I say defensively.

"And you thought giving him a dog would magically fix that?"

"Yes?"

Trish elbows her sister aside and tries for a more understanding tone. "It was really thoughtful. He's a precious little thing. But I'm worried that most of the care will fall on—well, on Ellie. After Ron and I move and you've gone back to Seattle."

I glance at Gramps. He is still on his knees hugging Wally while Ellie feeds the dog treats that she procured from somewhere. The little-boy-like look of wonder on Gramps's face is worth this whole argument.

"I'll make sure he has a good handle on it before I leave," I say.

"How long do you have?" Trish asks with a little laugh. "That could take forever."

I exchange a look with Daniel, who's sitting on a nearby bench, sipping from a fresh can of LaCroix and pretending not to eavesdrop. Right now, Daniel is the only person who knows I have to return to the office—in Seattle—in two weeks.

He points to his chest and mouths, *I can help.*

I tilt my head with a grateful, sad smile. I can't exactly tell Mom and Trish that everything will be okay because my property manager can help walk Gramps's dog. The two of them are arguing with each other now—weirdly, since they're on the same side of the argument, but they've been known to fight over less. The right way to cut tomatoes, for instance. Or how old they each were when they learned how to tie their shoes. That particular argument ended with a broken water glass and Mom crying in a locked bathroom.

As I listen to them discussing Gramps's inability to take a ten-minute walk, how he could possibly get the dog to the vet in an emergency, how he'll know what to feed him, something red-hot wells up inside me. I'm the one who's been living with Gramps. I'm the one who's seen the hole in his life where Lottie used to be. I'm the one who saw his eyes shine when he talked about his childhood dog. And I'm the one who has to leave him alone. The one who can't bear to leave him alone.

"Stop, both of you." I don't yell the words, but I've never spoken to them like that in my life, so they both freeze with identical faces of surprise. "Gramps needs this. He needs Wally. He needs a friend."

Mom rolls her eyes and says, "He has human friends," just as Trish says, "So get him a goldfish."

"He needs a dog." I am yelling now, and multiple people stop talking and look at me. "He needs this dog. Lottie never let him have one, and he's wanted one his whole life. Did you know his dad gave away his childhood dog for chewing on a shoe?" Mom and Trish exchange sad looks at this—they must have heard the story before. I lower my voice so Gramps doesn't hear the next part. "I have been living with him for almost a month now, and nothing—nothing—has made him look this happy the entire time I've been here. You saw his face when he saw Wally. You see his face right now. Just let him be happy. We'll figure out the logistics."

We all look over at them. Gramps is now standing, holding up a treat and politely asking Wally to sit. When he does sit, a cheer goes up through the crowd and Gramps bends down to kiss Wally's head.

"What a clever boy you are!"

Mom and Trish look at each other, knowing they're beat. They don't apologize to me, and I don't expect them to. Mom goes over to greet the dog, and Trish says, "I'll give you the name of the vet we take our dogs to. Local. Great gal. You'll want to make an appointment, just an initial checkup, since he's been in a shelter."

"Thanks, Trish."

"Yeah." She heads toward the bar cart and then turns back to me. "You're a good kid, Mal."

"I know."

Chapter 26

The party ramps up before it winds down.

As expected, the self-serve bar cart situation gets a little out of hand. There's a raucous game of twenty questions, where every answer turns out to be something about Gramps—his name, the city he was born in, lasagna (which is apparently his favorite meal; not sure I'll ever be brave enough to attempt making it for him). Then there's an impromptu round of karaoke, because Lenore just learned that you can pull up an instrumental version of any song from your phone. This starts strong, with Lenore and Eddy performing a decent Frank Sinatra duet; slips into questionable territory with Ellie belting out an off-key Taylor Swift song; and ends on a major cringe when Dad decides, for reasons best known to himself, to sing "Baby Got Back."

Around nine, after we've cut the cake and the patio is littered with blue-frosting-stained paper napkins, my mom holds up her phone and announces that Maeve has joined the party. My sister's grainy face shouts happy birthday from the iPhone screen. She then holds up the camera to baby Adam, whom Gramps has no interest in trying to speak to over the din of the party. This offends my mom, who then tries to get everyone to sing "Happy Birthday" again with Maeve on the phone, but only three people actually hear her, and then everything devolves into chaos. Mom admits defeat and hangs up on her eldest daughter,

Ellie and the rest of the cousins say goodbye, claiming that they have another party to go to, and Angela turns up the volume on the music and convinces Gramps to dance with her. Soon Daniel and I are surrounded by elderly people wiggling their bodies to an MC Hammer song. Wally has curled up underneath the dessert table.

We sit on a bench near the glowing, kidney-bean-shaped pool.

"You're still here," I say.

"Shouldn't I be?" He spreads his arms across the back of the bench. I sit ramrod-straight.

"You tell me, is this the best offer you got for a Saturday night?"

He considers this for a moment. "Of course, I did have to disappoint an awful lot of folks tonight. What with all the other parties and engagements I was invited to." He flashes a quick grin and then holds eye contact so long I wonder if I should blink or not. "But yes, Mallory, this was the best offer."

"Oh." I'm so startled by this change in direction—by the stark, heartfelt sound of these words—that I have no idea what to say next.

Daniel seems to sense this and fills the silence with, "Your grandpa can dance."

"You should see him do the mashed potato."

I actually consider changing the song to "Mashed Potato Time," but it might make Gramps think of Lottie. I don't want to ruin this moment for him, when he's glowing with sweat and joy and dancing with a beautiful woman.

"He looks happy," Daniel says, reading my mind.

"So happy. My mom was right to plan this party for him." Speaking of my mom, we both turn to look at her. She and my dad are loudly cajoling Trish and her husband to join them for a game of chicken in the pool.

"Nobody brought bathing suits," Trish points out, sipping from a cup of white wine.

"Trish!" Mom's voice is shrill, and then it changes to a loud stage whisper. "It's called skinny-dipping."

Dad laughs so hard at this that his laughs stop making any sound at all other than labored wheezing.

"Oh boy," I mutter.

"If your parents get naked, I might have to leave. Just out of politeness, you know. Wouldn't want them to be embarrassed, knowing I'd seen their—you know—the next time I see them. I mean, if there is a next time. Not to say that there would be, necessarily, but I—"

I give Daniel a long, straight-faced look, long enough to make him realize he's been rambling. It's cute. Kind of reminds me of me.

"Daniel." I place a comforting hand on his knee. It's warm, and I can feel the soft, curly hairs on his thigh. "I'm not going to make you sit here and watch my parents play naked chicken."

I cross the yard and put an arm around my mom's shoulders.

"Hey, Trish, what do you say we pour these guys into an Uber back to their hotel?"

"Abso—" Trish hiccups and waves her cup. "—lutely."

Mom and Dad pay no attention, still giggling with their heads together like a couple of first-graders.

"And what about you? Did you drive here?"

Ron scoffs. "I've got her, Mallory. I know my wife and I know when I'm the designated driver for the evening."

The four of them coordinate, drunkenly gathering their belongings—aside from my uncle Ron, who stands there, feet planted firmly, arms crossed, watching the scene as though curious to see if they can pull themselves together. Meanwhile, a similar scene unfolds with Gramps, Angela, and the two senior-citizen friends who remain.

Gramps isn't drunk—he stuck to his usual "cocktail" of seltzer and lime—but he's loopy from the party atmosphere and from being up past his bedtime. I watch for a moment as he tries to convince everyone to dance to one more song, and then I turn sadly back to Daniel.

"I better get him home."

Daniel stands and spreads his hands as if to say, *You gotta do what you gotta do*.

But then Angela calls to me, clutching Gramps's elbow, her tiny purse slung over her shoulder.

"Mallory, please, don't worry yourself. I can get the birthday boy home."

"It's okay, I mean, I have to bring all of Wally's stuff, too, and—"

"Mallory." Angela crooks her bony, manicured finger at me. Frowning, I walk over to her. She whispers in my ear—her breath smells like lipstick. "That young man has been patiently waiting for some time alone with you. I'm only trying to help you out."

"Huh?" I whisper back.

"Don't make me spell it out for you, child. That Daniel is a gem. Don't break his heart, you hear?" She straightens up and raises her voice again. "Now, just show me what all I need to bring for Wally. And help me wrap up that cake to put in Leonard's freezer. There's a good gal."

Daniel dutifully boxes up the leftover cake as I walk Wally and all his accoutrements out to Angela's car. Before he gets in the passenger seat, Gramps grabs me and smacks a kiss on my forehead.

"Thank you for a wonderful birthday, my girl."

"Glad you had fun, Gramps. See you back at home."

I stand in the driveway, waving as they drive away for longer than is strictly normal. Because, frankly, I don't know what I'm supposed to do once I turn around and find myself alone with Daniel McKinnon. My instinct is to assume that he's about to leave, too, now that the party's over. But on some level, I know he's not planning to leave quite yet.

I lower my arm and hug myself, gazing out at the dark cul-de-sac, palm trees stirring gently in neighbors' yards. The air is so warm and fragrant, so different from the damp, chilly night air back home.

"I think they're gone," whispers a voice in my ear.

I startle and then laugh. "Yeah. They are." Facing him does not help my dilemma. What do I do with my arms? They're itching to twine around his waist, because they're arms and hence have no brains; that would obviously be an extremely weird thing for me to do right now. To his credit, Daniel doesn't seem fazed by the moment's awkwardness. He stands, an inch or two away from me, hands in the pockets of his shorts (real shorts tonight, not bike shorts), face turned toward the lone tree in my yard. In the last week, the buds have bloomed into big, creamy white blossoms.

"Nice magnolia."

"Is that what it is?"

"Oh yeah. You didn't know?"

"I know nothing about plants. I was wondering what it was."

"Southern magnolia," he says. "Beautiful."

"Thanks," I say, as if I can take any credit. "So, um, I would invite you in, but as you know I have no furniture."

"The backyard was pretty comfortable."

"Yeah?" My heart flutters annoyingly. "May I offer you another drink? Perhaps some chips?"

"I would love another drink and perhaps some chips."

I give his arm a playful nudge, and if that sounds like it was just an excuse to touch his rock-hard arm, that's because it was.

We weave around to the back of the house in silence. At the bar cart, he scans the wet cans of beer sitting in melting ice and the half-empty bottles of wine and then selects a can of seltzer. I follow suit and also grab a bag of Lay's, then lead the way to the side of the pool. We kick off our shoes and sit on the edge with our feet in the warm water.

"Do you not drink?" I ask, hoping it's not a rude question.

He crunches on a chip. "I do. Just not often."

"Ah." I nod. Usually when guys say something like this, it's because they had a problem with alcohol, or their dad did, so I don't ask any follow-up questions.

"Having two brothers and a lot of guy friends, I've seen too many guys turn into complete assholes when they drink. It's like they can't control themselves. I decided a long time ago that I wanted to be able to control myself. And, you know, not to be an asshole."

I hold up my can of seltzer to clink against his. "Cheers to that."

We swish our feet back and forth. Like magic, a pair of fireflies zips over the pool, zapping and blinking. The evening breeze makes a gentle rushing sound in Lottie's flower bushes.

"This is nice," Daniel says.

"It is, isn't it?"

"Whoever gets to live here sure will be lucky."

I don't say anything to this.

"Tell me about your house," I say after a minute.

"Hmm." He leans back, planting his hands on the cement behind us, and doesn't apologize when a couple of his fingers land on mine. I straighten up and put my hands in my lap, clutching my cold, sweating drink.

"It's a condo," he says, "on the first floor of a three-story building over on Pleasant."

"On the beach?"

"On the beach. It's a one-bedroom with a big balcony. I added faux-wood floors and a shiny new IKEA kitchen and bathroom. Big project, but it needed it. It was my parents' first place together. They bought it in the early eighties for, you know—"

"A thousand bucks and a spit handshake?"

"Basically. They kept it for various reasons over the years, but I think it was mostly sentimental. They lived there as newlyweds. But they told us they kept it for the rental income, and then later for us kids to crash if we ever needed a place for a few months. Summer break from college, that kind of thing."

"Did you go away to college?"

He leans back at the faint surprise in my voice, scrutinizing my face as though I might be making fun of him.

"Not that you don't seem like you went to college," I add, "but I got the sense that you grew up here and never left."

"Nah." He relaxes and looks up at the stars instead. "I was up in Gainesville for four years. Four wild years."

"Florida State?" I hazard a guess.

He lets out a low whistle. "Don't let people hear you say that. University of Florida. Gators."

"Gators. Not Seminoles. Got it."

He shakes his head in amazement, like I've had a close brush with danger.

"What did you study?" I ask.

He adjusts his posture and gazes evenly at me, silently telling me to go ahead and assess him, give it my best guess.

"Hmm, okay." I feign deep thought, but really I'm using the moment as an excuse to drink him in. His dusky-red hair—I can't tell if it would feel soft or prickly—and the faint freckles across his face that somehow seem more pronounced in the moonlight. The dimple in his chin, the slight smirk creasing the corner of his mouth. He has a freckle right in the center of his bottom lip. I really should not be noticing these things, not if I want to keep myself together. Nothing can happen with this person. This man sitting so close to me that I can feel the warmth of his body and smell his woodsy soap.

Keep your pants on, my brain hisses at me.

"Business," I say decisively.

He drops his head back and howls with laughter. "You sure got my number."

"I bet you were in a fraternity, too."

"I am offended. And yes, I was."

Now it's my turn to laugh.

"You were not in a sorority, I take it. Up there at..."

"University of Washington."

"Huskies."

I nod, impressed.

"I know my college football," he says. "I can see you up there, pretending to study in the library but really just reading your American Girl doll catalogs."

"Hey!" I swat at him, but really I'm tickled that he remembers that detail from our first conversation. And here we are again, referencing that night.

"Look." His tone is serious all of a sudden. Here it comes: He's going to say something about that kiss and about how we can't let it happen again. "I've been meaning to ask you." I swallow and nod, bracing myself. "How do you react to getting pushed into a pool?"

"What?" I barely have time to say the word before his hand is on my waist and he nudges me—gently, really, but hard enough to do the job—and I feel my bottom slipping over the edge. A guttural shriek escapes me right before I crash, fully clothed, into the water.

"You—" I sputter once I've come back up for air. "You pushed me in! I can't believe you just did that." I push tangles of wet hair out of my face. It's not cold, but it's still shocking to be suddenly submerged. Daniel roars with laughter.

"You should've seen your face."

"I hope it was worth it," I say, and then I grab hold of both of his legs and drag him in with me.

He's still laughing as he goes under and then pops back up, spitting out a fountain of water.

"You know, I could have had my phone in my pocket," I say.

"I *do* have my phone in my pocket," he says, and I gasp in horror. He pulls it out and places it on the pool deck. "It's okay, it's waterproof. And I knew you didn't have yours on you."

"How did you know that?"

"Trust me." His eyes rove down to where my legs are treading water under the rippling surface of the pool. "I didn't see any pockets in that dress. And I looked."

The way he says it sends a sudden jolt through me.

"Speaking of my dress." I hoist myself out of the pool, and he groans.

"Party's over already, huh?"

I stand up, far above him, and shake my head. "I didn't get my hair wet just for ninety seconds in the pool. But this dress deserves better." With some difficulty that probably negates any possible sexiness, I tug the sopping black dress over my head and drop it on the nearest chair. I'm wearing black cotton cheekies and a black bra—one of only two bras that I brought on this trip, but there's no need for Daniel to know that.

He's gazing up at me in stunned silence, the lower half of his face underwater.

"That's better," I say. Daniel makes a choking sound. I slip back into the water and swim sedately to the other side of the pool.

He follows me, doing a slow backstroke.

"I met a guy from Seattle once," he says, "who didn't know how to swim. That common up there?"

"I guess, kind of." I hang on to the edge of the pool. "I know plenty of people who never learned."

He shakes his head. "Isn't that dangerous?"

"Maybe not if you never go on vacation. We have lakes, but they're freezing cold."

"You learned, though."

"Well, yeah. My parents are both from here. We came to Florida every year when I was a kid."

He puts an elbow on the pool edge beside me. His eyes are a strange reddish blue in the glowing light.

"Did you ever consider moving here?"

"Never. I always had a life up in Seattle. Until recently."

He chooses this moment, for reasons unknown to me, to take off his soaking-wet polo shirt. He tosses it onto the deck, and I don't even pretend not to look at his gently chiseled chest, covered in reddish-brown hair.

"Until recently, meaning you had a life until recently? Or you never considered moving here until recently?" As he speaks, he moves closer, and I can't tell if it's on purpose or not, but suddenly he's so close I could touch his foot with mine if I flexed my big toe.

"Both," I whisper. Gazing up at him, I realize that I probably have mascara pooling under my eyes. Still, something comes over me and I cover his foot with mine, down at the bottom of the pool. He doesn't flinch.

"Can we talk about how this is a terrible idea?" I say.

"Terrible might be overstating it a bit." One of his hands finds my bare waist. He doesn't pull me closer, just leaves his hand there.

"Because I'm leaving soon. And if we start something, it's not going to go anywhere. It's just going to end."

"I've heard they have this nifty thing called email now."

"You don't want another long-distance relationship." I'm instantly mortified that I used the word "relationship." Seems like a stretch.

"So if—just following your logic—if it can't go anywhere, that means there's no point in it at all?" Slowly, he brings his other hand up to the other side of my waist. Somehow, despite the bathtub temperature of the water, his hand is warm against my skin. "No point in one night, just because there might not be another?"

I feel like a stunned little goldfish. My heart is pounding, with Daniel's nearly naked body so close to my own, surrounded by fairy lights and the ripple of the glowing pool all around us. My logical mind is summoning up weak reminders of why I decided this would be a bad idea: saying goodbye soon, possible hurt on both sides, opening myself up to another heartbreak, another man who might prove impossible to get over.

"Because if that's how you feel," Daniel continues, "I will respectfully remove myself from the situation. Just wish I had some dry clothes."

He removes his hands and takes a step backward. And then my logical mind is utterly silenced by the swift decision of my body. I lunge toward him and wrap my legs around his waist and my arms around his shoulders.

Due to some apparently ultra-strong self-control on his part, we're not immediately kissing. He swivels me around so my back presses against the side of the pool, his hands digging into my thighs harder than is strictly necessary given that I'm weightless underwater.

"Is this a green light, Rosen?" he asks, and it's not at all lost on me that his voice is suddenly raspy.

"A green light for tonight," I confirm, and our mouths meet before I've finished saying the words, both slick and wet from pool water.

He pushes himself against me, our kiss feverish and desperate, just like the first time. There's no room between us other than our clinging, wet clothes, and he's not shy about grinding into me, so I grind back and work myself into a frenzy, my back rubbing against the edge of the pool so hard I know I'll have a scrape there.

After minutes that seem like an hour, Daniel pulls away, looking as shaken and breathless as I feel. I'm looking around for a pool chair or someplace comfortable enough to turn this party horizontal, but he's thinking something different.

"Okay," he gasps, holding up a hand. "Okay."

"Okay?"

"Red light," he says, swimming backward, away from me. "For tonight."

"Red light? After all that?" I cock my head at him, my brain blurry from the cocktail of hormones racing through me.

"*All* that"—he waves a finger through the air in my general direction—"was more than enough to—" He stops and runs a wet hand over his face. "It was more than enough. Trust me."

I'm legitimately confused for a second.

"I don't know about you, Mallory, but that... You know, I'm not a monk; I have had hookups before, but they don't usually feel like that. Again, I don't know about you." He seems a little embarrassed to be admitting this. But I know what he means.

"No," I agree. "They don't usually feel like that."

"So. You might have been right."

"Right? That we shouldn't have?" I deflate at this.

"Maybe." He gives a nervous laugh. "I don't know. I don't know anything right now."

"Me neither," I say. "Except I wish we had a towel."

With an unspoken agreement not to touch each other again, we sprawl out on pool chairs and spend the next hour and a half talking as the balmy night air dries us off.

When we finally say good night, I have to admit to myself that the talking might not have been such a great idea, either. If he hadn't suggested going home, since it was past one in the morning, I could've kept talking to him all night long.

Chapter 27

So, that happened. And I don't know how to feel about it. On the one hand, I am basically floating on cloud nine. On the other hand, I'm slightly mortified by the way Daniel pulled back, and I feel like an idiot for getting carried away. Saying goodbye to Gramps and the beach and Pebble Cottage will be hard enough...did I have to go and add an extra layer of emotional complexity to it all?

I can't help replaying every moment again and again, from the moment in the driveway when we found ourselves alone, to the feverish groping in the pool. I replay it all while I'm sitting in planning meetings, while I'm stirring a pot of soup, while I'm walking on the beach at night after my workday is over and Gramps is asleep. As I walk, I catch up on the latest episode of *Elementary*, but I haven't been paying attention for the last few minutes (my mind got snagged on the memory of the look on Daniel's face when he said, "Red light"). But something the podcast hosts are talking about catches my attention. One of them is moving to another city soon for a new job, and she's saying that she created a bucket list of things to do before she moves. Touristy things that she never got around to doing in her own city.

And suddenly I'm counting the days I have left. Only eleven. Eleven days before I have to go back to Seattle—home to a place that doesn't even feel like home right now.

Staring out at the dark water—so dark I can only tell where the gulf begins by where the bank of purple clouds on the horizon ends—I realize there are so many things I still want to do. Not only do I need to finish the floors and walls at Pebble Cottage, I need to soak up every minute of life here. Because I don't know when I'll be back. Once I go home, my job here will be done: The cottage will be rented out, and Gramps will be in a better place than he was when I found him. And once I'm home, there will be no beach walks, no Jacuzzi, no mermaid bar, no dinners with Gramps. No cottage. No Daniel.

Before I know what I'm doing, I stand up and strip off my jogging shorts, tank top, sports bra, and underwear. I leave them in a pile on the sand with my phone and earbuds on top, and then I jog out into the dark waves. Naked.

I'm not a naked person. Even when I'm changing in front of my sister, or in a gym locker room, I always cover myself with a towel. But right now, swimming naked in the Gulf of Mexico under a thin wafer of moon just seems like the right thing to do. I swim out to the sandbar, reveling in the feel of the silky salt water on my skin. Until I step on a slippery stingray that swims away before I can scream. Maybe next time I'll try morning swimming. Sunrise swimming, even. I'm pretty sure sharks come out at night.

The next morning, I hear Gramps bustling around pouring himself cereal—but only after he scoops some food into Wally's bowl—and I'm instantly awake. Like, freakishly awake given that it's before six A.M.

"Morning," I say, stepping into the kitchen as I slip on a cardigan.

"Ah!" Gramps nearly drops the carton of milk. I can't tell if he's joking or not. "What are you doing up?"

I shrug. "Seizing the day."

He squints at me suspiciously.

"I know, weird, right?" I still haven't told him that I'm being summoned back to the Seattle office. "How about a beach walk?"

I watch as he and Wally eat their breakfasts—even with my newfound energy, it's too early for me to eat—and then the three of us troop downstairs.

"Wow." I stop in my tracks, halfway down the grassy path that leads to the beach. "Look at the sky."

It's awash in color, gentle pastel shades that remind me of orange sherbet and farm-fresh butter. Gramps places his hands on my shoulders and steers me around to face the other direction, away from the beach. I gasp. The eastern sky is swathed in fluffy pink clouds, the horizon gilded with sunlight.

"Sunrise, my dear," Gramps says. He sounds amused but also pleased.

"It looks different than sunset."

"Indeed, for it is the exact opposite." With that, Gramps turns and leads the way toward the beach.

It's the absolute perfect temperature, warm but not yet humid or blazing hot. We walk in silence for a few minutes, nodding hello to the other early beach walkers: people walking their dogs, joggers with earbuds in, and one middle-aged couple walking barefoot and collecting shells at the water's edge.

Gramps stops to let Wally sniff a clump of seaweed.

"You know," Gramps says suddenly. "I was wondering if you might do me a favor."

"What is it?"

He coaxes Wally forward. "If you would attend one of Angela's aerobics classes, it would mean a great deal." He sees the stunned look on my face and continues, "She's mentioned a few times that she would like to get to know you better. And I know how much you enjoy your—" He waves a hand as though he's forgotten the word.

"Yoga?"

"—so I thought it might be the perfect combination."

"Um, okay. Sure, Gramps."

"They meet at eight A.M. on Monday, Wednesday, and Friday, under the gazebo."

We turn around to head home; Gramps's endurance still needs some work.

"Will you be joining me?" I ask, giving him a sly look.

"Oh no, I will have already done my kickboxing training before then, so no need."

"Of course." I laugh.

Okay, so on top of everything else I want to do while I'm here, I need to add Angela's workout class. I should really make a list.

On Tuesday, Gramps successfully drives himself to his therapy appointment and home again. He seems more chipper this time, so I take that as a good sign, although when I ask how it went, he just says, "Fine," and shuts himself in his room with a book, Wally trotting at his heels.

My calendar is snarled with meetings, but I have the evening to look forward to: Daniel and I are planning to meet at Pebble Cottage to paint. Or we were. Around three in the afternoon, he texts me, saying he needs to reschedule. He sounds genuinely apologetic, but a gloomy part of me guesses what this is: It's regret and awkwardness about what happened between us last weekend. My mood is dismal for the rest of the day, but I force myself to go to the house that evening anyway and paint without him.

Wednesday morning, my primary concern is that I've agreed to go to Angela's workout class. I'm so used to doing my workouts alone—my virtual yoga class back home, and now my solitary beach-walks-turned-swims—that I feel apprehensive approaching the gazebo. I still got up early for a swim in the Gulf, because I only have nine more morning Gulf swims. But even those endorphins don't calm my nerves entirely.

"Mallory, you came!" Angela flings her arms wide, and I don't know if she's expecting a hug or just expressing herself in the most energetic way possible. I give a little wave in return. This doesn't seem to faze her.

"Everyone, you know Mallory, Leonard's granddaughter."

I'm greeted by a chorus of "Hello, Mallory"s from a group of startlingly tan and scantily clad senior citizens. The men are dressed in sweat shorts, T-shirts, and white sneakers with tall white socks. The ladies are all dressed like Angela, in little brightly colored skirts and tank tops. I'm wearing copper-red bike shorts and a matching crop top, and I've brought a beach towel, because I noticed they all have a yoga mat during these classes and a towel is the best I've got.

"So, what is this class, anyway?" I ask.

In response, they laugh. I mean, they *all* laugh, as though I've made a hilarious joke. *Okay...*

One of the elders moves to the front of the group, waving his hands to get everyone to quiet down. He's short and squat, with a round, freckled face and a big white smile that reminds me of Gramps. Unexpectedly, the voice that comes out of his mouth is loud and booming with a heavy Boston accent.

"All right, everyone, let's get started."

"That's Ace," Angela whispers to me as I spread my towel next to her mat.

"Is that his real name?" I whisper back.

"No."

There's no time for further explanation, as Ace has started the music, using an iPhone and a Bluetooth speaker with absolutely no technical difficulties. His competence leaves me feeling unbalanced. The music is a sort of instrumental power rock, which only adds to my confusion.

Following Ace's instructions, we sit cross-legged and begin with some gentle stretches. This, I'm okay with. He leads us through neck stretches and wrist rolls, gradually transitioning into cat cow. Music aside, moving through the familiar yoga stretches against the backdrop of bright white beach and sparkling water is downright pleasant.

I'm starting to loosen up, when Ace calls, "Now that everyone's back is warmed up, we'll move straight from cat cow to scorpion walk."

Scorpion walk? I cast a bemused look at Angela, but she's looking at her friend on the other side, raising her eyebrows like, *Oh, here we go*. Suddenly, everyone is on their hands and feet, butts in the air, flipping one leg over the other, followed by one arm, doing a sort of extravagant sideways crab walk. I do my best to follow their lead, getting dizzy as we scorpion-walk across the gazebo and back to our mats. I'm a little out of breath, but the move definitely got my heart rate up and stretched my shoulders and hips.

"Duck walk!" Ace calls.

There are some appreciative murmurs as everyone finds a deep squat position and then waddles, hands on hips, like a duck. I can't help but laugh as I waddle unsteadily along with them.

That one was kind of fun. And also, how are they all doing this with their elderly knees?

"Gorilla!"

There are a few groans and a few whoops. I whoop along with them, getting into it. The gorilla walk turns out to be similar to duck, except you swing one leg out in front of the other while the other stays in a deep squat. It looks hilarious, but my quads and glutes are on fire by the end of it.

"Okay," I mutter to Angela, "I can see why you're all so toned. Ouch."

She just gives a little laugh. An ominous little laugh.

"Bunny hops!" Ace says. That sounds cute—but no one whoops this time. I glance around uneasily.

We're back in the deep squat, hands behind our heads, and we're hopping. After two hops, it becomes apparent that I absolutely do not have the stamina for this. I barely make it, doing tiny squatting bunny hops with my feet barely leaving the ground. Back on my towel, I'm panting, ready for a break.

Someone calls out, "My knees, Ace, my knees!"

"Yeah, can we move on, please?" another man agrees.

"Yeah, yeah, we're done with the squats," Ace says, and I can't help but notice that his stout body isn't as round and squishy as I previously thought. It's more... round and rock-hard, like a boulder. I'm about to settle into child's pose when Ace booms, "Crouching tiger!"

Quickly, with no complaints, everyone finds a plank position and crawls across the gazebo with their knees extending to their elbows. I can do it without too much difficulty, but I'm definitely getting a cardio workout from all this.

"Not too bad," I whisper to Angela when we're back on our mats.

She shushes me. I take this as a bad sign.

"Chameleon!"

At first glance, the chameleon walk appears to be similar to crouching tiger. Except, I realize, everyone is pausing for a beat in the middle to do a one-armed push-up before crawling onward.

"Uhhh..." I kneel on my mat, watching these old folks move their bodies in ways I could never hope to achieve.

"Mallory!" Ace barks.

Everyone else "ooohs" like we're in second grade and I just got in trouble with the teacher. So I do my best to follow the moves, wobbling like a drunken lizard instead of a muscular chameleon.

I half crawl back to my spot and gulp down some water. Ace gives us a thirty-second rest break.

"Is it almost over?" I ask Angela.

She simply shakes her head, delicately mopping her hairline with a small white towel.

"Okay, people," Ace shouts. "Inchworm jump!"

The woman on Angela's other side utters a small scream. Ace demonstrates the move: from a wide-armed plank position, he sticks his butt up and then propels himself into the air, landing back in plank position with the grace of an acrobat. What fresh hell is this?

I'm not alone in my sentiments: There are a few audible groans.

"Would you rather do jumping spider?" Ace asks threateningly.

Whatever jumping spider is, it must be scary, because everyone immediately lurches into the inchworm jump.

We go through a few more animal walks, each more torturous than the last. I have to sit out the last exercise (angry piranha). My limbs are jelly by the time the class ends. And yet, for some reason, when everyone has rolled up their mats and trooped off in small groups to hit the sauna or jump in the pool, as I'm sitting on my towel unable to move, I find myself laughing. Once I start, I can't stop. I've just completed what was simultaneously the hardest and the most ridiculous workout of my life. I might not be able to walk tomorrow. And also, I might have to come back next week. If Ace's animal workout class isn't making the most of my time here, what is?

As expected, I can barely walk the next day. I mostly hobble. But the kernel of energy inside me isn't dimmed by my physical limitations. There's one thing I haven't tried yet that I suddenly can't stop thinking about. Over breakfast, I waver back and forth. Things feel strained with Daniel right now. He hasn't reached out again since canceling on me on Tuesday, and I haven't, either. But I have to at least ask—if I don't, I know I'll regret it.

I want to ride bikes before I leave.

After I send it, I hurry to add: *As friends.*

He replies minutes later saying that I can borrow his spare as long as I want. To my delight, he offers to meet me this evening.

Chapter 28

I go through my new daily routine: a post-breakfast swim that feels heavenly on my sore muscles; a walk with Gramps and Wally; a couple hours of work at Paradise Coffee; and some manual labor at Pebble Cottage. I almost can't manage painting, given how sore I am from the animal workout, but I can't afford to lose a day working on the house. How embarrassing would it be to have to leave before it's finished, to have to ask Daniel to finish it for me? Or to hire someone else after all the effort I've put in? No, I'm determined to finish it, even if my limbs ache to the point where I can barely lift a paint roller. Anyway, I'm almost finished with the walls—tomorrow I start on the floors.

At six, I stop work—putting an "Away" message on Slack—and head over to Daniel's. It's my first time seeing where he lives, and I'm strangely nervous as I drive up to the modest white building, standing on stilts like so many of the beachfront buildings around here. It's only three stories and has a tidy little garage underneath.

I park in a visitor spot and then dither at the call box. It's in front of a locked door that leads to an elevator and stairwell. He didn't tell me whether I should text him or buzz from the call box, so I scroll through the residents' names on the ancient machine until I find M—McKinnon.

"Hello?" Daniel's voice crackles through the speaker.

"It's Mallory! Mallory Rosen? I'm here!" *Very smooth.*

"Okay, I'll come down."

This comes as an unexpected disappointment. I thought this might be my one and only chance to see his place, but I suppose—since we're just *friends*—the garage is as far as I'm going to get.

A minute or two later, he bounds through the stairwell door, a grin plastered on his face. He looks like Wally before Gramps takes him on a walk.

"Hey." I almost laugh at the excitement on his face.

"Mallory, how are you? I'm so glad you decided to bike!" He's wearing his black-and-yellow biking onesie that leaves absolutely nothing to the imagination, holding a helmet under each arm.

I'm taken aback by his open enthusiasm. Maybe I misinterpreted things when he bailed on me the other day. Maybe I should have taken his words at face value, that something came up unexpectedly. On top of my surprise at his attitude, I'm just not used to the stark contrast between the people here and the people back home. Seattleites don't express their enthusiasm—they might twitch their mouths upward in a pseudo smile, but that's about it.

"I couldn't leave without trying it." I reach for the spare helmet. "You talked it up enough. Where should we go?"

He leads me over to his bike, which is chained up next to a few others. "We can ride around here. There's a trail along the bay."

"Sounds pretty."

"And, like I said, you're free to take the bike for as long as you want. Until you leave, I guess."

"Oh, thanks." I can tell that my skepticism comes out in my voice.

"What?"

"I'm just not sure if I'll use it again. After our ride today."

"Why not?"

"Where would I use it? Where would I go?"

He stares at me blankly. "Wherever you go with your car. Your grandpa's place, your house, the shops."

"Those places are miles apart."

"Only two or three miles, and it's all flat here."

"Right. Okay." Now that he mentions it, it is flat here. Seattle is full of hills. "Maybe I will."

"Wonderful." He draws the word out, sounding so Southern it makes me smile. "So, this one's yours. It's my spare." He unlocks a yellow bike that's slightly smaller than his.

He wheels his own bike toward the street. I snap my helmet on and hurry to follow him. The yellow bike feels rather large and unwieldy.

He gives me a sharp look. Suddenly, he stops short.

"Do you need a lesson?"

"Um." I examine the bike. Looks pretty standard. "I think I'm good. This is the part I sit on, right?" I point to the handlebars. He laughs, and I get a heady sense of accomplishment from the sound.

A few minutes later, we're cruising down a paved path lined with boats docked at the edge of a canal. It was ninety degrees out today, but it's almost dusk now, and zipping along with trees on one side and water on the other feels amazing. The warmth of the evening air and the fresh breeze in my face melt away all my worries. It's magical.

Daniel's riding ahead of me, and he looks back at me to give me a thumbs-up. I grin, remembering him saying—what feels like forever ago—that he would get me on a bike eventually. Like he knew I needed it, even though he barely knew me.

We're not talking, just zipping along, Daniel in front of me, and the scenery is doing something to me. It's the glistening water, the colorful boats—some of them are canal boats that appear to be lived in, with people lounging on deck chairs, waving as we whiz past. It's the smell of grass and tangy, fishy water. It's the feeling of going fast, being propelled by the strength of my own legs. It's the man riding in front of me and the way I can't stop looking at the back of his neck, strong and freckled and lightly sheened with sweat. All these things add up and make me think, *How did I get here? How did a solitary girl from Seattle go from lonely, rainy days to all this?* And I know it's not forever, but right now that doesn't matter. Because right now it *is*. Right now I'm here, doing this.

And I'm happy. So ridiculously happy.

After twenty minutes or so, Daniel takes a right turn that spits us out onto a street. I think we're near the downtown area, but I'm not sure exactly where.

He pulls over on the side of the street and I stop next to him. "I thought we could grab a bite and something to drink before we turn around."

I blink at him, getting emotional whiplash as I picture us sitting down at a little café together—because that would totally be a date, right? But then I see where he's pointing. It appears to be a farmers market of some kind, rows of white tents and a covered area of picnic tables. Very cute—and definitely not a date, unless explicitly stated. Which it won't be.

We wheel our bikes among the tents, where vendors are selling everything from pastries to antiques. The first thing I notice is how un-crowded it is here. A similar market back home would be swarming with people, but here the vibe is relaxed, just a couple dozen people milling about. Also, strangers keep saying hello to us, even going so far as to make friendly comments about our bikes or the weather. It's bizarre.

"This place has the best pretzel dogs." Daniel nods toward one of the tents. "And fresh-squeezed lemonade."

"Lemonade sounds perfect." I hesitate, scanning for a menu. "Do you know if the dogs have pork in them?" I brace myself for a confused question, prepared to give my standard answer—*I'm Jewish*—and hoping we won't go into the intricacies of the different levels of kosher. But he doesn't ask.

"I always go for the veggie dog myself. Says the other ones are one hundred percent beef, though." He points out the menu, a laminated piece of printer paper taped to the cash register.

"Excellent." I unzip my belt bag to pull out my wallet, but he covers my hand with his.

"My treat."

"Thanks." I am so not going to read into this. He's a Southern gentleman; he can't help it.

He orders, and as we wait for our pretzel dogs, I ask, "Are you vegetarian, then?"

He nods. "Going on fifteen years."

"Wow. I'm surprised. You seem so…" I don't even know what I'm going to say. Manly? Floridian?

He just laughs. "Yeah, well, I visited a slaughterhouse on a high school field trip and that was that. The trip was supposed to get us interested in agriculture and farming, but it certainly had an unintended effect on me."

"Yikes." Our order's up, and I look sadly at my paper-wrapped pretzel dog, wishing I'd gone for the veggie one, too. But after one bite of the salty, juicy goodness, I forget about it. The lemonade is incredible, too, super fresh and not too sweet.

We lock our bikes together against a tree and wander, munching our pretzel dogs and sipping our iced lemonades.

"I can't get over how good this is," I say.

"What did I tell you?" Daniel balls up his paper bag and tosses it in a garbage can.

We pass a flower vendor, someone selling ocean glass jewelry, and a tent full of beach-themed knickknacks.

"Clearly, they have everything here," I say, pointing to a pair of oven mitts shaped like mackerel.

Daniel nods. "All your sea creature paraphernalia. If you can imagine it, they sell it."

I gently brush my finger along a sand dollar wind chime.

"Now, I would feel remiss if I didn't buy you a going-away present."

I whirl around to look at Daniel, and then burst out laughing. He's holding up a toilet brush that has apparently been superglued to a gulf-themed snow globe. I can only assume you're supposed to hold the snow globe as you clean the toilet and the swirl of glitter inside will make you feel a sense of peace with the unpleasant task at hand.

"That would make cleaning day more interesting, for sure."

"Are you a cleaning-day-type person?" Daniel asks as we move on to the next vendor.

"What do you mean?"

"Just trying to gauge what type of personality I'm dealing with here. Are you a 'clean the house top to bottom every Saturday morning with music blasting' type of person? Or a 'it's been so long I can't put it off another day' type of person?"

"When I'm home, I clean my apartment every other Sunday. Sometimes more frequently if I have people coming over. Often with music blasting."

"Ah. So not quite an every-weekend gal, but close." He pauses, slurping down the last of his lemonade. "I won't tell you which kind I am."

"Gross," I laugh. "Is that why you didn't invite me upstairs?" I ask before I can stop myself.

"Hmm?" He's distracted by a sudden squeal from a group of teenage girls nearby all looking down at one phone.

"Earlier, you didn't invite me up to see your place." I'm half wishing I could shut up now, but my curiosity won't let me.

He doesn't answer right away. Looking at me out of the corner of his eye, he doesn't apologize or act embarrassed about it. Finally he asks, "Did you want me to?"

"I won't lie, I am dying to see how you've decorated your bachelor pad."

"What makes you think I've decorated it at all?"

"You have opinions about floors and paint. And you told me you renovated it yourself. Are you telling me you haven't put up a single picture? Curtains? A plant?"

His mouth quirks. "You may never know."

"Hey!"

We're being lighthearted and playful, but there's some seriousness behind my complaint. Because at this point, there is a good chance I'll never see inside his place. I don't even know if I'll see Daniel again at all after I leave. We'll probably just communicate via email about house things, and I won't need to visit again anytime in the near future, and that will be that.

I try not to dwell. I'm hanging out with him now, so might as well enjoy the moment. For his part, I can tell Daniel's not about to fold. As much as I wish he would say, *Actually, I was going to ask if you wanted to come to my place for dinner*, I know he won't. He has too much damn self-control.

But then something catches my eye that fully distracts me. It's a mirror. It's gilded around the edges and has a sort of baroque shape. If I saw the same mirror on the Anthropologie website, it would be five hundred dollars, minimum. But there's a little tag fluttering on it that clearly says seventy-five dollars.

Daniel stops to look at me. "What's wrong?"

"Wrong?"

"You gasped."

"It's..." I point. "It's just so cute."

"The mirror?"

I nod.

"Yeah, it's nice."

But *nice* doesn't explain it. The mirror is making me see things. I see, instantly, where I would put it. It would go in the entryway of Pebble Cottage, and I would find the perfect curved-back, Shaker-style bench to go under it. Shoes would go underneath the bench. A colorful rag rug inside the front door.

"Earth to Mallory." Daniel waves a hand in front of my face, making me realize I've been staring, spaced out, at the mirror all this time.

I blink. It's a strange feeling—wishing I could make my vision come to life but knowing that I can't. Would I even be thinking about this if I didn't have a ticking clock? Is the fact that I'm leaving making me cling to improbable fantasies?

Still, even if it's just my brain rebelling, I have to have it. I literally can't imagine leaving this market without that mirror.

"Where would you put it?" he asks.

"Pebble Cottage," I say instantly. "Can we get that home on a bike?" As soon as I ask the question, I regret it, because I can predict how he'll react. He will scoff and try to talk me down. He'll tell me it's impossible and that we'll look ridiculous.

I have experience in these matters. Like the time Alex and I were walking back to his place from the grocery store, bundled up against the chilly November air, him carrying a paper bag of kale, garlic, chicken breasts, and spaghetti. On a street corner not too far from his apartment, there was a dresser with a FREE sign taped to it. It was small, more of an accent cabinet than a dresser, with three drawers and a cabinet. It had turned legs and sweet little dragonfly knobs. The paint was badly chipped, but the possibilities grabbed me, and I was already imagining what color I would paint it.

"I need that," I gasped to Alex. He gave a little snort laugh.

"What?" he asked, like he didn't see the gorgeous piece of furniture right in front of us.

"The dresser. I have the perfect spot for it in my living room. I've been looking for something for linens."

"Linens? Don't you have a towel closet?"

I looked up at his skeptical, annoyingly handsome face. "Will you help me carry it?"

He shifted the grocery bag from one arm to the other. "Carry it?"

"We could bring it back to your place. And then I could borrow my sister's car later to come pick it up."

"Um." I could tell he was about to laugh, and I saw the moment he adjusted his expression to one of pacifying good sense. "Mal. How would we get it up the stairs? I live on the second floor." He puts an arm around my shoulder. "You'll find a better—"

"It's not big," I press. "We could definitely do it."

He just stared at me, his mouth a straight, emotionless line. I couldn't find the words for what I was trying to say: that people do this, carry furniture up two flights of stairs. Ideally not often, but when they have to. That it's not a crazy idea. That I'm not one of his students with a harebrained scheme. That he could at least humor me, give me a little respect. After all, I hardly ever asked him for anything.

But his face wasn't budging, and neither was his decision. Feeling stupid and frustrated, I shook my head and said, "Yeah, it's dumb. Never mind."

"And she sees sense," Alex said, ruffling my hair.

Now I shudder slightly at the rankling memory. I'm about to tell Daniel to forget about it, that I obviously know we can't carry a large mirror home on a bike. But before I can say a word, he's walking up to the vendor, an older woman with curly white hair. He asks her something, gesturing with one hand from the mirror to our bikes over by the tree. She listens, holds up one finger, and rummages around in a clear plastic bin.

I hurry over to them just as the woman produces a roll of paper and some bubble wrap.

"That should work perfectly," Daniel says. "How much do we owe you?"

"I got this," I say, dying with curiosity about his plan as I tap my credit card. He and the saleswoman wrap the mirror carefully. We thank her and head back to our bikes.

"Um," I say. "So, how are we going to carry it? Are we walking? Because I can hold it if you—"

"'Course not." Daniel leans the mirror against the tree and rummages around in his panniers. He extracts a bright-orange bungee cord. Before I know what's happening, he straps it around his back and then instructs me to slip the mirror inside the cords.

"Are you serious?" I ask. There's no way this could work.

"Trust me. I carry stuff like this all the time."

Well, no point in arguing. I finagle the mirror into the bungee cords, he makes sure they're tight enough, and then we kick off. He rides a little more slowly and carefully, but with a surprising amount of confidence for a man wearing a mirror as a backpack.

As we ride back in the rosy dusk, I can't help the grin that takes over my entire face.

Chapter 29

Apparently, all I have to do to have a magical time at the beach is announce my intention to leave. Saturday morning, I park my bike—my bike!—in the shady parking lot of a public park. I'm meeting up with Amanda and a group of her friends to kayak through the mangroves. I've never been kayaking before, but Amanda didn't seem worried about that. She'd invited me last night when I stopped by her bar for a drink after a few hours of painting. I told her about how I'm living a bucket list of sorts in the less than two weeks I have left, and she invited me to join her and her friends without hesitation. I didn't even consider the physical exertion required when I accepted, I was so excited to be included.

It's eight thirty on a weekend, but there are quite a few people milling around the park, walking or schlepping paddleboards over to the dock. I take it in my stride when strangers call out hearty good mornings to me.

A mini van pulls up and Amanda waves to me from the passenger seat. She and a guy she introduces as her brother, Francis, jump out and unload two kayaks. One of them is a double. As we deposit them in the shallow water by the dock, we're joined by her other friends, three girls and one guy. It's a lot of kayaks. After a round of introductions, we're off.

Amanda instructed me to join her in the double. I didn't argue.

I'm seated in the front, Amanda behind me, and we glide easily through the clear green-blue water of the bay. I have a feeling it wouldn't be quite so easy if I were trying to paddle myself.

After a few minutes, we find ourselves in a tunnel of mangrove trees.

"Wow," I breathe. It's so otherworldly, I'm speechless. Tree roots rise out of the water, crisscrossing in midair. Above us, the tree branches form a leafy green canopy. It smells incredible—mossy and verdant and alive.

I turn around to shout at Amanda, "This is so cool!"

She grins. "I couldn't let you leave without experiencing this."

"You guys do this a lot?"

"At least once every month or two." Amanda's arms look intimidatingly strong as she dips the oar back and forth.

"Come on, slowpokes!" Her brother, Francis, cruises past us. I face forward again and add my paddle to the water.

We skim through the glowing mangrove tunnels in near silence, the only sounds our oars sloshing through the water and the calls of birds, frogs, and some chittering creature I can't name. A sense of peace settles over me, so profound I don't know if I've ever felt anything like it. I think I came close to it after that first day of ripping out carpeting—but that was a sense of calm caused by physical exertion. This is more like a calm bestowed on me by the environment itself. I can't stop grinning, and I already know I'm going to go overboard with how many times I thank Amanda for inviting me.

We turn back into open water for a while, the sun beating down on us, before turning into another thicket of mangroves.

"Alligator," one of the girls calls matter-of-factly.

"What? Where?" I shriek and clutch my paddle to my chest.

Amanda points it out: There's not just one but two alligators lounging among the tree roots.

"They're just chilling," Amanda says.

"Chilling to save up the energy required to eat us?"

"Don't worry, they only eat people stupid enough to swim in these parts," Francis calls back. This must be an inside joke, because everyone erupts in laughter.

"What?" I ask.

"It was me," Amanda says. "I swam here one time. It was really hot. And I didn't see the gators."

"Until it was too late," Francis says in a menacing voice.

"Oh my God, what?"

Amanda shakes her head at her brother. "Quiet, fool! He's just messing around. I mean, yeah, I didn't see the gators until after I'd jumped in. But they didn't actually try to eat me. I got right back in my boat."

"That is... terrifying."

We glide past the alligators, who don't even open their eyes, and continue on for another half hour or more. Time doesn't seem to behave the same way in the quiet of these watery tunnels. Suddenly, one of the girls up front is calling back, "It's eleven. Shall we?"

"Yes, please," Amanda says.

"Shall we what?" I ask.

"You'll see! I can't ruin the surprise."

"Does this involve swimming? I didn't bring a towel."

The others just laugh.

"Did you bring your appetite?" Francis asks.

Wondering if they somehow packed a picnic without me noticing, I nod eagerly. "I could definitely eat."

But they don't stop on a sandy bank and reveal a picnic basket; we keep paddling toward some small buildings on the water's edge that I never would have looked at twice. They're ramshackle, to say the least. One of them appears to be a boat repair place, which makes sense given the location. It looks like these places can only be reached by boat, but that wouldn't make sense, would it?

I am so confused. But still optimistic. There used to be a famous poke bowl place in Seattle that was hidden inside a gas station, so. Anything could happen.

Francis is the first one to tie his kayak to the dock and hop up the ladder. "Honey, we're home!"

"Does he live here?" I whisper.

Amanda bursts out laughing. "No, he's just a clown."

We all follow Francis inside the place. I'm expecting an office building or something, but it's a restaurant. A tiny, hole-in-the-wall restaurant. (Maybe hole-in-the-marina would be a more apt description.) It smells vaguely of Lysol and fish. But I decide to put on a brave face and be game for anything.

An older gentleman who towers above all of us, with a mop of thick gray hair and a face that's never been touched by sunscreen, gestures to a table by the window. For all Francis's familiarity, the man doesn't seem particularly familiar with the group as he hands around some menus and lists the two daily specials. Until Francis asks about the weather, and his eyes animate.

"Seen the storm forecasts, have you?" he asks in a gravelly smoker's voice.

"I know you have, Buddy." I internally cringe at Francis calling him buddy—seems a little too try-hard—before I realize that that's his actual name.

They trade a few back-and-forths about the likelihood of seeing the season's first hurricane this weekend. I'd forgotten about hurricane season. That's one rather large silver lining to my situation: leaving town before hurricane season starts in earnest.

Before we have time to look at the menu, let alone discuss it, one of the other girls—Melissa—orders for the table. I'm a little shocked, but also a little relieved. I'm not expecting much, so I'm fine with whatever other people are eating.

A few minutes later, Buddy drops off a veritable feast of seafood. A shrimp cocktail, fried scallops, a huge platter of raw clams, and a whole crab surrounded by piles of steak-cut fries. He returns with a dozen little silver cups of ketchup, mayonnaise, and tartar sauce. And maybe I'm extra hungry from the kayaking, or maybe it's because my expectations were so low, but this is without a doubt one of the most delicious meals I've ever had.

"Oh my God," I say repeatedly, slurping down clams topped with vinegary hot sauce, and dredging morsels of crab through melted butter.

"I think she likes it."

"Don't they have seafood up in Seattle?"

"Of course, but it's different. We don't have clams like this, that's for sure. I've never had clams, actually."

This gets some appreciative hoots, and Amanda asks Buddy to bring us another dozen. As we demolish the food, I'm awash with the group's easy conversation and laughter. I haven't asked how Amanda met these friends—I'm not even positive about a few of their names—but that doesn't seem to matter right now. It's just the atmosphere. The easy way their chatter flits from kayaking, to triathlons, to family drama, to a concert they saw recently, to Fourth of July plans. There's nothing stilted: no awkward pauses, no introductory questions, no effort to catch up on recent events in each other's lives. It's just *easy*. I wonder if—not like this would ever happen, but *if*—I lived here, whether I would be part of this friend group. Amanda seems to like me enough to invite me to hang out with them. I imagine it for a minute: what my life would look like. Catching up with Amanda at her bar, spending weekends doing outdoorsy things with this group, being invited to their birthday parties and barbecues. I see myself riding my bike to work in the perennial sunshine—to some hazy, imaginary job—and returning home in the evenings to drink a glass of chilled rosé in the sunroom of Pebble Cottage.

Okay, Mallory. I straighten up, wipe my mouth with a paper napkin, and chug my tall glass of lukewarm water. No point going down that imaginary road. I'll just enjoy the moment now and not worry about the fact that it won't be repeated.

Chapter 30

It's Sunday afternoon and I have made an enormous mistake.

I decided to work on the flooring without Daniel; after all, he has a life, and I can't keep spending hours with him one-on-one. It's not good for my sanity.

But I must have already lost my mind when I decided to attempt this myself. I've fastened down the vinyl boards across almost the entire living room—feeling obnoxiously proud of myself all the while—only to realize that I completely screwed up. The room isn't entirely rectangular, and the way I started the planks along the longest wall means I'll have to cut the remaining ones and finagle them to fit the room and it will look completely wrong. Frantic googling has led me to understand that the only solution is to start over, and that I was supposed to start laying the planks in the doorway—not along the opposite wall.

All I can do is sit down and cry. Four hours of work, wasted. And now I'll have to pull up the planks and who knows how long that will take? Not to mention that I might damage them in the process, which means I would have to reorder them, wasting time and money I don't have.

I decide to call it quits for the day. I can't face pulling up the floor I spent all morning laying. I'll just go back to the condo and spend the rest of the evening with Gramps. Maybe a cold mocktail on the balcony will make me feel better.

But Gramps doesn't want a mocktail on the balcony. He surprises me by saying that Angela and some of the others are going to a PowerPoint night down in the dining room and he thought we might join them. I can only assume he means that someone is here to teach the senior citizens how to use PowerPoint, to which I ask...why? But I'm encouraged that Gramps is expressing an interest in joining group activities, so I say yes.

The dining room is packed when we arrive. Angela waves us over to her table. She's already sitting with five others—popular much?—so Gramps and I drag over some nearby empty chairs.

"What's going on?" I hiss.

"PowerPoint night," Angela whispers back helpfully. Her eyes are politely fixed on the woman at the front of the room. She's a stout woman with a halo of grayish-brown curls, pointing a clicker at the projector screen. The screen currently shows a blurry photo of half of the woman's face, framed by the hood of an electric-blue rain jacket, with a steely-gray gulf behind her.

"This is when we crossed over into the Prince William Sound," she says, in a slow, long-suffering voice. "It was pretty rainy that day. It rained the whole trip. It was June, so you would have thought—but, well..." She heaves a sigh, then clicks to the next photo, which shows a group of men onstage wearing black suits with what appear to be LED lights all over them. "This was night two's entertainment. As you can see, it was the same as night one. These singing cowboys again. It was supposed to be a magician, but he was sick, I believe. Not food poisoning, though, I asked, because that happened on a cruise I was on back in 2015, and let me tell you—"

It is taking all of my strength not to laugh. I lean over to Gramps and Angela. "I thought this was going to be a lesson of some kind?"

"Lesson?" Gramps asks, his eyes still on the presenter. "What do you mean?"

"It's presentation night," Angela says. "We started doing these earlier this year and they've been such a hit, we do them monthly now."

I am fascinated. So not only do these seniors already know how to use PowerPoint, they are PowerPoint fanatics. I wish I had some popcorn.

The Alaskan cruise slideshow continues for another ten minutes, and then after a polite round of applause, the next presenter shuffles to the front. There are a few minutes of general chatter as the staff member sitting at a laptop by the projector opens the correct file.

"Hi, I'm Tabitha," the presenter says in a voice that crackles like a paper bag. She's diminutive and white-haired, and the deep wrinkles on her face make me wonder if she's the oldest resident here.

With no further preamble, she launches into her presentation. The first picture is a grainy close-up of dog poop on the grass.

"Anyone know what this is?" Tabitha scans the audience with rheumy eyes.

A man at the table next to ours raises his hand. "Dog shit."

"Correct," Tabitha says with a terse nod. "And—" Before she can continue, another woman calls out, "Donny Egan's dog's dog shit."

"*Hey*," comes a plaintive voice from the far corner. A man with a dark mop of hair that I strongly suspect is a toupee looks wounded.

"That is correct," Tabitha says again. "This is the third time I have seen Donny Egan fail to clean up his dog's mess. After the second time, I reminded him. He said he ran out of dog bags. Guess he's still out." Something about Tabitha's ancient, brittle voice makes her words extra scathing. She clicks to the next slide.

"Now this, this is when Maggie Barnes took out her dentures at lunch." It's a photo of a woman sitting at a dining table with a glass of water beside her, inside which I can barely make out the shape of dentures.

"Oh, really," comes an exasperated whisper from Maggie herself. "I told her it's unseemly, but she didn't listen."

"I didn't even *hear* you," Maggie calls out.

"Lost my appetite," Tabitha continues, glaring at the picture on the screen.

The crowd begins to mutter and laugh behind their hands. Tabitha goes on to berate Patrick Zhang for taking an overlarge helping of mashed potatoes, Ken Teeson for taking a phone call during movie night, and, finally, Angela for laughing too loudly during last month's PowerPoint night.

"Pfft." Angela rolls her eyes and whispers, "Now, Tabitha."

To wrap up, Tabitha simply says, "Thank you for your time," and hands the clicker to the next person.

The final presentation is a soft-spoken gentleman's thorough explanation of why he believes there are alien civilizations living at the bottom of our oceans.

After a thunderous round of applause, including some wolf whistles, everyone stands and stretches and breaks into conversation.

"That was...wow," I say.

"Told you it would be good, didn't I, Leonard?" Angela beams.

Gramps nods, his cheeks flushed with enjoyment.

"You better not leave Wally's poop lying around," I stage-whisper. "You'll end up on Tabitha's next slideshow."

As we join the crowd trooping outside onto the grassy lawn, Gramps says, "You know, we could do a presentation about Wally! With some photos of him doing tricks—oh, and the photo of the original Waldo, too."

"Excellent idea," Angela says briskly. "People always love anything about dogs."

"You could help me make it," Gramps continues.

I make a noncommittal noise in response, my cheerful mood dissipating. I won't be here for the next PowerPoint night, but Gramps doesn't know that yet.

I hang back and tell them that I'm going to go for a walk on the beach. I watch Gramps and Angela continue on, the pale dusky sky arching overhead. I can't avoid it forever; I have to tell Gramps that I'm leaving.

Chapter 31

I walk longer than I normally would, and deep down I know it's because I'm waiting for Gramps to go to bed. If he's asleep when I return to the condo, that will be one more night that I don't have to tell him the truth.

When I get back upstairs, I hear snores rumbling from behind his bedroom door. It takes me a long time to fall asleep; I toss and turn, my mind going over every possible way that I can prolong my stay here, or at least put off telling Gramps for a bit longer. But there aren't a lot of options, really. I can't quit my job when I worked so hard to get it. I already used up most of my vacation time. I could take a leave of absence. But when I open my laptop at two A.M. to check the leave-of-absence policy, I learn that I would be forfeiting my health insurance, and my job would not be guaranteed to be waiting for me upon my return. That's too risky for me.

I finally fall asleep, promising myself that I'll tell Gramps before the end of the week.

The next morning, I'm barely online long enough to check my calendar and respond to a couple of Slack messages when an ominous email lands in my inbox.

It's from someone I've never heard of named Chelsea. My eyes jump down to her signature: She's from the HR team. My first thought is that it's something generic that was sent to everyone—but from the first sentence, I can see that it's not. It's just for me.

Hello Mallory,

As we prepare for our employees to return to the office, we are gathering data about who may or may not have trouble complying with the policy. It has come to our attention that, although you have a home address and an assigned office in Seattle, your recent VPN logins have occurred from an IP address in the State of Florida. This flagged our attention, so we took a look and found that you have been logging in from Florida for several weeks now.

Your manager is CC'd on this email. She will schedule a time to discuss this with you. Please be aware that you are still assigned to a Seattle office and will be required to meet the in-office requirements starting next week. Also, please note that working from an unauthorized location can be grounds for termination.

Thank you for your cooperation.

Chelsea Hudgeons
HR Connections Team

This is my nightmare. It's like I'm reliving what happened with my first remote job. How could I let it get to this point? I'm going to be fired... *again.*

I pace my bedroom, my hands shaking. The abruptness with which Kat schedules a one-on-one meeting only adds to my anxiety. I'm certain she's going to fire me over Zoom. And then what? *Then I won't have to leave*, a small voice in my brain says. But this tiny voice is quickly shut down by the louder voice, the one that's always been there, shouting, *I need this job*. I somehow got this job after being fired from my last one. There's no way I could pull off the same trick twice.

The good thing about Kat scheduling such a last-minute meeting is that I don't have to dread it for long. The bad thing is that it's as uncomfortable as I could have imagined. Kat's tone is terse, disappointed, as she expresses her dismay that I could lie about something like this for so long. I desperately want to point out that I didn't lie, I just didn't explicitly tell her the truth. Instead, I opt for the pity angle, telling her all about Gramps and how he needed family support after Lottie's death. I don't know if she had been planning on firing me before, but my little sob story softens her a bit. She ends the meeting by saying that as long as I'm there in the office next week, and I don't pull something like this again, it will all be water under the bridge.

So that's it, then. I got away with it. But now it's over. Now I am really, truly leaving Reina Beach. Because coming this close to losing my job has firmly squashed any dreams I had of staying here. The concept of staying here, unemployed, with no idea where my next paycheck will come from? It's terrifying.

As soon as work wraps up, I meander into the living room, where Gramps is watching TV in the dark, Wally curled up on the couch beside him. I'm surprised to see it's not the news, but a baseball game.

"Whatcha watching?" I ask, sitting in the armchair beside the couch.

"Rays game," he replies.

"So..." I scan the game happening on TV, looking for a conversation topic, but all I can come up with is, "Are we winning?"

"Mm." Gramps nods, his eyes glued to the screen.

"I didn't know you were a baseball fan."

"I'm a fair-weather fan," he says, uncrossing his legs and glancing over at me. "The Rays have been known to be terrible. But right now they're all right. It'll be nice to see them win." Gramps scratches behind Wally's ear, then continues, "My parents took us kids to see a baseball game about once a year. The Reds were pretty good. Some of the time."

I nod encouragingly. I would rather keep talking about this than broach the subject of my departure.

"I enjoyed the game, but it wasn't so much about that, really. It was about the atmosphere. Enjoying something that my father was enjoying at the same time. Also, the Cracker Jacks."

"Have you been to a game recently?"

He lets out a short laugh that makes Wally look up curiously. "Not in recent decades."

We both watch the game in silence for a minute or two. When a commercial comes on, I take a deep breath and mentally put on my big-girl pants.

"Gramps..." The commercial for an erectile dysfunction medication blares. I reach for the remote and turn the volume down. "There's something I've been meaning to tell you."

"Oh?" He turns to me. Wally sighs sleepily and curls up even more, like a little croissant.

"It's...about..." I'm finding it nearly impossible to get the words out. But I have to. "Actually, my work just told us that everyone is required to return to the office. Like, the office-office in downtown Seattle."

There's a long pause. "Oh my. That does sound serious. No more remote Zooms for you, then?"

I shake my head. "No more remote Zooms."

An even longer pause. I'm about to open my mouth to say that I have to leave this weekend, but Gramps beats me to it.

"When will you be flying home?"

Home. The word feels incongruous with how I'm feeling right now. Because I'm feeling like this small living room with the humongous TV, the white noise of the gulf rising up through the glass balcony doors, and Gramps and Wally cuddled on the couch—this feels more like home than the apartment I've lived in for years.

"This weekend," I say. "I think Sunday."

Gramps looks down at Wally with a sad smile. "Well, we knew this couldn't last forever." His voice becomes more robust as he continues, "It's been lovely having you here, Mallory. I feel as though I've really gotten to know you."

I just nod, my head bobbing as I try to think of something to say. "Me too," I finally choke out.

"Don't worry about us. You've got your own life to go back to. You're leaving me in good hands with Wally and Dr. Mellors."

"And Ellie will be around if you need anything…And Daniel McKinnon, too, he said he—"

"Yes, yes. Don't worry about a thing, all right?"

"Okay, Gramps."

He stands. Wally jumps up to follow him.

"Well, good night."

"What about the baseball game?" I ask.

He looks around at the TV like he'd forgotten it was on.

"I'm a bit tired now. I'll read the highlights in the morning paper."

"Oh. Okay." I watch as Gramps and Wally disappear down the hall, the triangle of light spilling from the bedroom shrinking into nothingness as the door closes behind them.

"Good night," I whisper.

I'm not going to cry. I'm not. I'm going to take a shower and watch *Outlander* in bed. Except I feel so jittery with emotion that I don't know if even *Outlander* will calm me down. Maybe a dip in the Jacuzzi downstairs.

No. I need to move my body, to breathe fresh air. I hop on the yellow bike, even though it's dark outside. The headlight is strong and bright, because of course Daniel would optimize for safety when outfitting his bicycles. That's how he is.

I ride fast, with no destination in mind. There's a bike path off the main road that I never noticed from my car. I pedal so hard my thighs burn, the humid evening air like hot breath on my face. The pounding of my heart distracts me from the racing thoughts in my head, until all I'm thinking about is breathing in and out. So *this* is why people exercise.

Without warning, the sky breaks open. At first, the rain pounding against my cheeks and my bare arms is exhilarating. But it quickly becomes too much. The rainwater thuds deafeningly against my helmet and streams into my eyes too fast for me to blink it away. The path in front of me is blurred and filling up with puddles quicker than I would've thought possible. My bike tires splash through puddles that soak through my sneakers and socks—within minutes, I'm completely drenched from head to toe. Another biker passes me in the other direction, his headlight glaring into my eyes, and I have to swerve to avoid a collision. I pull over to the far side of the trail and steer my bike under a tree. This doesn't do much to protect me from the rain, but I can't keep riding in this. A huge clap of thunder makes my teeth vibrate, and I know I made the right decision to pull over—although I can't remember if it's a good or a bad thing to stand under a tree during a lightning storm.

The tree I stopped under is right next to the canal. The normally calm water is choppy and dark. The houseboats rock hard enough to make me wonder why anyone would choose to live in one. I shiver; the air is still warm, but I'm so soaked that I'm chilled all the way through.

Staring out at the canal and the lightning flashing between heavy, purple clouds, I tell myself that everything will be okay. Gramps will be fine. So he seemed put out by the news that I'm leaving. It would have been strange if he'd been happy about it, right? He has Wally. I'll call him every week. I can even teach him how to FaceTime.

The thunderstorm moves on—the rain slows to a drizzle and the thunder rumbles faintly, miles away now. I look around, shivering, and realize where I've been heading. My subconscious led me to a three-story white building on the beach. I wheel the bike across Gulf Boulevard and right up to the door. I don't try to talk myself out of it as I jab the button to dial Daniel. Waiting for him to answer gives me time to regret this choice slightly, as I catch sight of my reflection in the glass door: I look like I swam here. But he answers and rings me up with no questions asked, so I don't have time to change my mind.

"Mallory." He opens the door to his condo, his expression alarmed. "Are you okay? Come in."

I follow him in, embarrassment surging through me as my clothes drip onto his floor, forming a puddle underneath me. I step out of my sopping sneakers with difficulty.

"What's going on?" he asks, taking in the state of me.

"I..." I start, not knowing what I'm about to say. But then I stop, forgetting my embarrassment and the fact that I need to explain my waterlogged presence somehow. "Wow."

He follows my gaze—I'm staring into his living room slash kitchen area.

"This is..."

"What?" He gives a little laugh that betrays his nervousness. He's *nervous* about what I'm going to say about his place. This delights me.

"Not what I expected," I finish. It's not, not at all. I mean, for starters, there's no galloping horse print anywhere. Maybe there'll be one in the bedroom—I'll hold out hope for that.

"What did you expect?"

A black leather couch, a bar cart... my imagination stops there. Whatever I had in mind, it wasn't this. Daniel's living room is like something out of a Scandinavian design magazine. It's gently lit by well-placed globe lamps. There's a light-gray sofa that's all soft angles, a modern bent-wood coffee table with two magazines and a black knot sculpture artfully displayed on top. A black-and-white rug that looks extremely soft and extremely expensive.

"A plant!" I point out a graceful potted tree. I don't know what kind it is, but its pointy leaves are a gentle green with almost gray undertones. He must have chosen the type of tree as carefully as he clearly chose everything else here.

"And you thought I wouldn't have one."

"What's that?" I point at the painting above the couch. If I could have guessed, based on the rest of his decor, I would have imagined a monotone work of inscrutable modern art. But it's a sort of impressionist painting in pale pinks and blues, so pale they're nearly white.

"Beachgoers," Daniel says.

I can see it now, the forms of two people sprawled on the sand, the effervescent sea in the distance.

"It's beautiful."

"I thought so, too. I found it at a gallery downtown."

I beam up at him; I can't help it. It's so endearing to think of him browsing art galleries and choosing this painting.

We seem to realize at the same moment that my teeth are chattering.

"God, you're soaking wet. Let's get you dry." He pushes one hand into the small of my back, guiding me across the living room and toward the hallway.

He ushers me into the bathroom, which is right next to a little laundry nook with a stacked washer and dryer.

"We can put your clothes in the dryer," Daniel says, handing me a neatly folded, fluffy white towel.

"Um, okay. Sure. Thank you." I look at the towel in my hands; I guess I could wear this while we wait for my clothes to dry. Because it would be weird to ask to wear a T-shirt of his, right?

He starts to close the door of the bathroom to give me some privacy, but then he stops. "Then you'll have nothing to wear."

"Ha. Yeah. But I'll just—" I hold up the towel.

"You want to take a bath?" he says suddenly.

"A bath?"

"Look at you. Your lips are blue. You can warm up in there while your clothes dry."

I glance at the tub behind me. It's a large, built-in Jacuzzi-style bathtub that I'm guessing was here when his parents bought this place. The rest of the bathroom is neat and inviting, with pale-gray walls decorated with a large, framed ink drawing of a stingray.

"I do love a bubble bath. But I don't want to put you out. I just showed up here without—"

"It's fine. You're here until your clothes are dry, anyway." He crosses to the bathroom closet and pulls out a new bar of soap. "No bubbles or salts or anything, but I do have soap."

I take the small box from him. My fingers are truly very cold. He turns on the tap and checks the water temperature with his hand before plugging the drain.

"Thanks, Daniel."

"Oh, wait." He procures a bottle of Old Spice shower gel. "This might work for bubbles."

I press my lips together, holding back a laugh as he pours some of the shower gel into the running water. I feel so cared for. It's adorable.

"Look at that," I marvel, as bubbles foam up in the water. "Works perfectly. Now I feel swindled by the bubble-bath industry."

"Those bubble tycoons will take you for all you're worth." We stand there awkwardly for a second, and then he says, "Well, enjoy," and gives a funny little salute as he closes the door.

I hang the towel on the rack, put my wet clothes in the dryer, and gingerly step into the bath. The water is steamy hot; it feels so good on my cold skin that I let out a sigh as I sink into it.

"This was a good idea," I mumble to myself.

The rumble of the dryer and the sliver of night sky outside the narrow window create a very relaxing ambience. I sink down until my chin is submerged in bubbles, and then I startle up again when I hear Daniel's voice.

"By the way, there's shampoo and conditioner in the shower. You can use those, too."

I laugh. "Thanks, but that's okay. I don't need to wash my hair."

"All right, just wanted to offer."

"Yeah. It takes a long time when you have this much hair," I call back.

There's a pause, and I figure he's gone back down the hall. But then I hear, "I could do it."

"What?" I sit stock-still, staring at my toes sticking out of the bubbles.

"I could wash your hair. If you want."

I wait for a laugh or a *just kidding* or a *never mind, crazy idea*. But he doesn't say anything else. I'm dying to know what expression is on his face right now as he waits for my answer.

"Okay," I hear myself say.

The door opens slowly, and a flushed Daniel peeks around it. Then he mutters, "Probably need a cup," and retreats again. He returns a moment later with a white coffee mug.

Wordlessly, he gathers the shampoo and conditioner, then sits on the edge of the bath.

"Have you always wanted to be a hairdresser or something?" I ask.

"Nah." He doesn't look embarrassed anymore as he dips the mug into the bathwater. "I just have a thing for your hair."

Now I'm the one with flaming cheeks.

"Oh." Because, really, what else is there to say to that?

"Lean back," he says.

I do as he says, extremely grateful for the Old Spice–scented bubbles hiding my naked body from view. I feel a gentle hand smooth my hair back before he slowly pours the water. My scalp tingles with pleasure.

He works shampoo into my hair, strong fingers massaging my head.

"That feels amazing."

He continues his massage, and then says, "So, you want to tell me why you biked here in the rain?"

"Right. That." I savor the feeling of the warm water slowly rinsing away the shampoo, of Daniel's hand sweeping the hair back from my forehead. "Where do I start."

"At the beginning?"

"Well. Yesterday, I went to Pebble Cottage and laid the new flooring in the living room."

"You did?"

I nod. Daniel smooths conditioner down the lengths of my hair. I close my eyes, enjoying it probably more than I should admit. It's like the heavenly feeling you get at the salon when the stylist washes your hair, times a thousand thanks to the dash of chemistry between us. I mean, maybe some people feel that way at the salon, in which case, more power to them.

"Why didn't you call me? I could have helped."

"I don't know, but I should have. Because I messed it all up. We'll probably have to redo the whole room now."

"What happened?"

"I started on the wrong side of the room and the planks got all wonky."

"Ah. Well, that sucks, but it is fixable."

"That's the next part. I don't have *time* to stay and fix it." I explain about the HR email. "So, they found out that I'm not in Seattle, and they'll fire me if I stay here."

"Harsh." He finger-combs my hair, his touch the opposite of harsh. "They already told you that you have to go back to the office. Did they have to threaten to fire you, too?"

"Guess they really wanted to drive the point home."

"Well, point taken."

"And then there's Gramps." I sigh, opening my eyes to stare morosely at the ceiling light. I can tell that even that, a cute little brass fixture, was chosen with care. "I'd been putting off telling him that I have to go home. But I told him earlier, right before I came over here."

"How did he take it?"

"Um, he seemed fine, but—" I stop, my lips trembling as I try not to cry. "He was watching baseball. Which he never does. He seemed pretty into the game. And then I told him, and he acted fine, but then he went to bed."

"You think he was broken up about it?" Daniel rinses my hair one last time and then twines it in his fist, gently squeezing the water out. I want to ask him to wash it again, but that would be weird.

I sit up a little, crossing my arms over my chest, just in case.

"I think so. But he would never admit that."

Daniel peers into my eyes, his elbows on his knees. "You really care about your grandpa. I'm sure he can feel that. And I'm sure he appreciates the time you've spent with him."

I shrug. "It just sucks that I have to leave. But this was supposed to be a quick weekend trip, and it's already been over a month. It's not like I was going to stay here forever."

I lean back again and close my eyes. The water is still deliciously warm. If only I could stay in here forever, soaking my troubles away. Daniel doesn't say anything, probably because there's nothing more to be said. So my little vacation has to end, so I have to go back to my life and my job. It's a privileged problem to have. I'm happy I had this time here. And now it's time to move on.

I heave a sigh that may or may not be a touch dramatic.

Wordlessly, Daniel slips his hands back into my hair and rubs my scalp. I let out an involuntary, embarrassing moan.

He snickers.

Cracking open one eye, I say, "You could charge three hundred bucks an hour for these hands."

"That much? I should get new business cards." He massages some more. "Hands for hire."

"Sounds dirty."

"Hey, please don't sully my professional name." He sits back and I feel his fingers disappear from my hair.

"Don't stop!"

He grins wickedly—and ridiculously—and I flick water at his face. He grabs my wrist.

"We're not making a mess in here, young lady."

I point at my head and he laughs, resuming my head rub. His strong fingers stray down to the nape of my neck and my shoulders, but—other than the fact that he's massaging me while I'm naked in the bath—he keeps things strictly respectable.

"I just had a brilliant idea," I say.

"Do tell."

"Baseball games happen all the time, right? Like every day?"

"Pretty much."

"I could take Gramps to a Rays game before I leave. Cheer him up a bit. He said he hasn't been to a game in decades."

"I bet he'd enjoy that."

There's a pause as Daniel shifts his position to massage my forearms and hands. Screw three hundred—this man deserves five hundred an hour.

"You know, the Rays stadium is pretty big. It might help to go with someone who's familiar with it."

I turn to raise an eyebrow at him.

"Are you saying you want to come hang out with me and Gramps?"

"Mallory, please." He gives me a look, like he's about to say something like *Of course I want to spend more time with you*, and my heart speeds up, but then he says, "I'll take any excuse to go to a Rays game."

I laugh. "That would be great. I mean, I barely know one end of the baseball bat from the other. I'm sure Gramps would appreciate having someone there who knows what's going on."

"It's a deal." The dryer buzzes, and Daniel hands me the towel. "I'll let you dry off. Come through to the living room when you're done."

I do as he says. My shorts and tank top are nice and toasty. Daniel's sitting on the couch, but he stands and hands me a glass of water.

"Thanks."

He motions for me to sit, taking a seat beside me.

I sip my water, my damp hair against my neck a potent reminder of what just happened in the bathroom. *Daniel washed my hair.* A hot flush creeps up my chest and neck.

We settle back against the couch, leaving a full foot of space between us. I stare around his place, my curiosity getting the better of me. It's so minimalist chic.

"You didn't have a professional designer do this, did you?"

He lets out a surprised laugh. "Flattered. But no."

"Well, I can tell you have an eye for this kind of thing."

"Thanks, Rosen."

"You're welcome, McKinnon." I drain my water glass and set it on the coffee table. "Am I going to get in trouble for not using a coaster?"

"Yes," he says seriously. "You will be punished."

My hand flies to my chest in mock fear. "What's my punishment?"

He tilts his head as though considering something, then gives a little laugh and changes tack. "It's getting late. Are you riding home, or am I driving you?"

"I can bike. Should be fine as long as there aren't any more downpours."

"You never know," he says.

"Yeah. You never do."

He promises to text me about the baseball game. I thank him for everything and say goodbye, then let myself out into the starlit night.

Chapter 32

"Peanuts! Peanuts here!"

The peanut vendor strolls down the aisle of the stadium. Gramps is contentedly munching on Cracker Jacks. I'd found the one snack counter that sells them, to Gramps's delight.

He and Daniel don't even notice the peanut guy—I mean, really, how adorable is it that someone is walking around selling peanuts in little paper bags?—because they're deep in conversation about the third inning.

"I haven't seen a bases-clearing triple like that in years."

"And the way Ramirez shot that line drive straight to center field!"

I sip my lemonade and watch them chat, not exactly listening, their baseball terms floating gently over my head. And then I check Slack on my phone for the hundredth time, because it's the middle of the afternoon and I'm playing hooky from work.

After a while, Gramps notices that I'm typing messages every few minutes. "If they fire you, you can stay with me, rent-free." He says it nonchalantly, squinting out into the field, grinning as he pops another handful of Cracker Jacks into his mouth.

"Thanks," I laugh. It's too bad that shacking up with your grandpa isn't an actual life plan.

Not much happens for the next hour, it feels like, but Gramps and Daniel don't run out of things to talk about. Gramps didn't ask me any questions about why we brought Daniel to the game with us. Trish would be asking why the property manager's here; my mom would be asking when we're going to send out save-the-dates. But Gramps is just happy to be here, and happy to talk baseball with Daniel.

And I am, too. I'm rather pleased with myself for having the brilliant idea to take Gramps to a game. It feels like the perfect last hurrah.

Not to mention that it gives me a few extra hours to stare at Daniel. I have fully accepted that nothing is meant to happen between us, but that doesn't mean I'm oblivious to the way I feel about him. I have a huge crush. I enjoy looking at him and talking to him and being with him, and that's okay. A crush doesn't hurt anyone. Not when you have realistic expectations about what can or can't happen.

After several more innings, I'm starting to get a bit restless, sitting in the stands with no action to pretend to pay attention to. The other team scores, then more things happen or don't happen (I'm not sure), and then the game is over and the Rays have won, six to one. I silently thank the baseball gods that I just happened to take Gramps to a winning game.

As we're filing out of the stands, Gramps says, "I can't thank you both enough. Taking an old geezer like me out to a ball game is a mitzvah, that's for certain. And it was nice talking to you, young man. You remind me a lot of your father."

Even as we're jostled by the crowd around us, one glance at Daniel's face tells me how much this compliment means to him. As we reach the end of the stairs, Daniel reaches out to steady Gramps by the elbow, somehow communicating compassion and respect with a single, wordless touch.

Daniel interrupts these thoughts by saying, "Leonard, if you feel like getting out again this weekend, my mom is having her annual family barbecue. She'd be happy for you to join us."

"I'm sure Mallory and I would be delighted." Gramps beams. "Thank you."

Daniel looks around at me sharply. "You'll still be here?"

"Leaving on Sunday. But if you don't want—"

Daniel waves away my protests. "The more the merrier. It's Saturday at noon. Wally's welcome to come, too."

"Can we bring anything?"

"Please. My mom would be insulted."

We find our way back to Daniel's car. As he drives us back to Sandy Shores, the two of them discuss baseball, real estate, local gossip, and more baseball, and I lean my head against the back-seat window, smiling to myself. At least I know that Gramps will have a friend in Daniel after I'm gone.

It's Friday, my last day of virtual work, and there's no way I can focus. I'm torn between the desire to spend time with Gramps and the desire to work on Pebble Cottage. In the end, I dither around, not really doing either.

I've put off booking my ticket home, so now it's painfully expensive. But I finally rip off the Band-Aid and buy a ticket to Seattle, leaving Sunday morning.

Gramps finds me in my room in the early afternoon as I'm folding my clothes and slowly stacking them into my suitcase.

"Packing already?" he asks. Then he spies my laptop, which is open on top of the dresser with a Zoom meeting on the screen, the volume so low it's barely audible. "Oops." He holds one finger to his lips.

"It's okay," I say. "We're muted, and I'm not really listening anyway." I fold the black dress from Bettina's, then take it out and roll it up instead.

Gramps sits on the edge of the bed. "Lottie always rolled her clothes when she packed. Said it kept things from wrinkling."

"She told me the same thing. She always had clever little tricks." I sit back on my heels. "She told me about boot shapers back when I went through a riding boot phase. And she got me these tiny sachets filled with lavender to put in my dresser drawers."

"To keep away moths," Gramps says.

"And to keep your clothes smelling fresh."

"Lavender still makes me think of her," he says quietly.

"I miss her."

Gramps just smiles, as if at a distant memory, gazing into the other room, where Wally sleeps on the couch.

"I bet she would have some sort of pep talk for me right now," I continue. "Something to get me pumped up to return to work."

"Oh, let's think. What would she say about it?"

"I don't know." I don't want to speculate, really. I just wish, with a bone-deep heaviness, that I could have one last conversation with my grandmother. And I'm sure Gramps does, too. I try to lighten the mood a little. "I'm sure if she could see the state I'm leaving Pebble Cottage in, she'd regret leaving it to me."

Gramps doesn't laugh. He gives me a shrewd look and says, "Have I ever told you the story of how she found that house?"

I shake my head. "I didn't know Lottie was the one who found it."

"We had moved here from Cincinnati a few years before. We'd been living in an apartment over a butcher shop—now, that wasn't a problem, because Stan, the butcher, gave us discounted cuts on Shabbat—but the apartment had a shared bathroom at the end of the hall, which was used by two other families. We'd been saving every penny we could—darning our socks, making one pot of soup last three or four days—to someday buy a house. When Lottie was pregnant with your mother, she took to riding her bike around different neighborhoods on her way to work—"

"I thought her boss wouldn't let her work while she was pregnant," I interrupt.

"That's true. So she hid both of her pregnancies until the very end, when she looked like she was smuggling a beach ball under her dress. The doctor advised her on how not to gain more than fifteen pounds or so."

"Yikes."

"Your mom and Trish turned out fine. Anyway, one morning she rode past Pebble Cottage. The next-door neighbor was out watering his grass, and she stopped to talk to him. Asked if anyone on the block would be moving soon. Said he had no idea. But she liked the look of that street, so she kept coming back. Struck up a conversation with whoever she met. One day, a woman on the other side of the cul-de-sac told her that the owners of Pebble Cottage were moving to Scottsdale to be closer to their grandkids. The woman didn't know if they'd be selling the house or keeping it, and she wouldn't give Lottie their phone number when she asked. Lottie knocked on their door, but they weren't home that morning, and she didn't want to wait around. So when she got to work, she looked up the local realtors in the phone book and called every one of them. Finally, one of them admitted he was familiar with that address, that the owner was planning to list it the following week."

Gramps shrugs and makes a little *poof* sound as if to say, *That was that*. But I'm on the edge of my seat—metaphorically speaking, since I'm still sitting on the floor. "So how did she get it?"

"She talked the realtor into selling it directly to us. Laid it on thick about how we were a young, hardworking couple with a baby on the way, said we had enough cash for a down payment, and that we'd take excellent care of the house. He conferred with the owners, and it turned out they were delighted to sell the place to a young family. It had been their family home, too, see. They liked the idea of the house getting another chance at life, at watching a family grow up."

Suddenly I'm blinking back tears—I'm getting emotional for a house.

"I can't believe I didn't know that story. I knew Lottie loved the house, but I didn't know the lengths she went to in order to get it."

Gramps strides across the room and picks up the oval picture frame, the one with the picture of a young Lottie and my mom on the beach.

"She never did anything by half measures," he says. "She had conviction. It was one of the first things I loved about her. If she wanted something, she got it. And if she didn't care for something, or someone, well, she wouldn't waste a minute on them. Life was for living, she said, more than once—not for twiddling your thumbs."

Someone on my work meeting coughs loudly. I glare at the computer. Gramps looks at it too, and wordlessly shakes his head.

"What?" I ask, hearing an edge of defensiveness in my voice.

He raises his fluffy white eyebrows, mildly surprised. "I didn't say a word."

"Oh. Sorry."

"Anyway, I'll let you pack." Gramps retreats down the hallway. I hear him sigh as he settles next to Wally and flips open the newspaper.

I turn the volume up slightly on my laptop so I can hear the end of this meeting. I finish packing the clothes I know I won't need this weekend. As voices drone on about metrics and quality standards, I gaze at the little photograph. Lottie was so beautiful—her beaming smile, dark curls floating above her shoulders in the breeze—and I realize with a jolt that she was around my age when the picture was taken. Mother of one with another on the way, a woman with enough conviction and courage to become a public defender when nobody wanted her to. Not her parents, not the professors who graded the female students harsher than the men in the class, not her bosses and co-workers. But she didn't let that stop her. I picture her living in a run-down apartment, stretching her grocery dollars to the limit, hitting the streets day after day to find a house for her family, not taking no for an answer.

Guilt and regret settle heavily on my shoulders as I picture the state I'm leaving that house in. Unpainted walls, unfinished floors. Empty, abandoned.

I barely register what I'm doing as I close my laptop and gather my phone and keys. I tell Gramps I'm going out. Half an hour later, I'm wheeling my bike up to Pebble Cottage.

Chapter 33

I stop to gaze at the magnolia tree in the front yard, thankful that I got to be here to watch her bloom. The creamy white petals stir in the salty wind coming from the west. I'll miss this tree, and this tidy patch of St. Augustine grass, and the quaint carport.

I park Daniel's yellow bike in the carport and let myself into the house, the surfing Obama key chain jingling cheerfully against the lock.

The house smells like paint and dust.

I know I don't have time to finish anything, but I can at least give it a few more hours of my time, this house that my grandmother loved so much.

In the main bedroom, I turn on some music and crack open a can of paint. I'd impulsively chosen a sage green for this room, though I'd stuck to a safer eggshell white for the rest of the house. I'm glad I chose this color; it makes me happy just looking at it as I roll it onto the walls.

I paint the entire room in under two hours. My arms ache, and I roll my shoulders and stretch my triceps as I walk from room to room. The two small bedrooms remain unfinished—one painted, one not, both with no floors. In the living room, I stop to survey the damage I've done: half the room has new flooring, laid the wrong direction. It looks so pathetic that I sit down on the subfloor and wrap my arms around my knees.

As I sit here knowing that I won't be able to finish this room, something wells up inside me, a big dark wave; before I can stop it, it crashes down all around me. I don't know why I bothered starting all this. I don't know why I thought I could handle such a big project on my own. I should have just paid someone to do it all. I've never, *ever*, been the type of person to follow through on something like this. I'm the type of person who has an idea and abandons it at the first sign of potential failure. Like when I attempted a cross stitch for my nephew's nursery before he was born. The stitches were too complicated; I knew it was going to take me way longer than I had bargained for—and so it's still sitting, unfinished, in a bag in my closet. And the time I decided to start a blog—abandoned after two entries that were only read by my mom. Same with the book club I joined after a former co-worker invited me—I was convinced, for one shining evening, that I'd finally found a group of girlfriends, a group I'd carry with me for my adult life, sharing gossip about bad dates, wedding planning, husbands, pregnancy, kids. And then I'd failed to read the next month's book and silently disappeared from their midst as suddenly as I'd joined.

These thoughts make a bitter taste rise in the back of my throat. It's over. I'll just add Pebble Cottage to the list of things I've failed at.

An afternoon rainstorm starts suddenly, pattering on the roof. I let myself out into the sunroom and take a seat at the old Scrabble table, letting the humid, rain-soaked air hug me, listening to the rhythmic rush of rain falling in the garden.

I try to make peace with goodbye. I never wanted to live in Florida. I'm not a fan of hundred-degree weather, not to mention their politics. I've always been a Pacific Northwest girl. It's where I grew up, where my family is, where my friends are—or were. It's been a nice vacation from my real life, that's all. It's been a change of pace that I didn't realize I needed. But that's all it was: a break. Now I'm going to go home, and that's okay. Things will be different there, too: No more holing up in my apartment day after day. Back to a commute, an office. Making myself presentable enough to interact with real humans. Maybe different will be a good thing.

By the time I've given myself this pep talk, the rain has stopped. That's the funny thing about rainstorms here: They're intense and short-lived. Kind of the opposite of the constant drizzle in Seattle. There's probably a metaphor in there about my time here. I just have to appreciate it for what it was: short and sudden and entirely different from what I'm used to.

The sharp scent of earth after the rain makes me feel...something. Alive. My thoughts stray to Daniel. I'm not going to ask him to come help me with the house, not now. He's helped me so much already, and there's just not enough time.

Sitting in the sunroom, feeling the sticky warmth of the metal chair under my thighs, the prickle of sweat at the nape of my neck, I think about that bath. His finger pads pressing into my scalp. Gazing out at the kidney-bean-shaped pool surrounded by flower bushes, I remember that night, too. The weightlessness of my body as I treaded water with his hands whispering against my waist. The slick warmth of his open mouth on mine.

I send him a message: *Can you meet me at Pebble Cottage?*

I barely have time to exhale before he responds: *I'll be right there.*

Twenty minutes later, I'm still in the sunroom, staring dreamily out into the backyard when I hear the doorbell.

I open the front door to find Daniel, slightly out of breath and running one hand through his sweat-damp hair.

"Hey," he says. "Everything okay? Did you want me to help with some last-minute house stuff?"

"No. I know you're busy and I—"

"Mallory." He drops his arm, and a crease appears between his brows. "I think I've made it pretty clear by now that I'm never too busy for you."

"Right." I shift from one foot to the other, my hip bumping against the doorknob. I seem to have forgotten how to stand like a normal human. Dimly, I'm aware that I should invite him inside, but I feel like I don't know what will happen if I leave the shelter of this doorframe.

He looks confused, and, if I'm honest, completely delicious, standing there in his formfitting bike shorts and clinging T-shirt. I look from his red hair, to the freckle on his lower lip, to his muscled thighs, dragging my gaze back up to meet his.

"Mallory?"

"I—" My voice rasps. I clear my throat and try again. "Before I leave, I just wanted you to know."

He reaches back to scratch his neck, and I don't even bother trying to keep my eyes from following the swell of his biceps.

"I wanted you to know that I appreciate everything you've done for me these past weeks," I continue. "And I know nothing can come of this, but I feel—I mean, you're—" I lose the thread. I really should have planned what I wanted to say, but I had texted him without giving a thought to what would happen next.

"Yes?" One side of his mouth curls upward, and there's a look in his eye that I haven't seen there before. He takes a half step forward, and I notice how very broad his chest is. As if it would take up this entire doorway. My breath catches as I look up and realize what the look in his eye is: It's confidence. He doesn't move any closer, just stands perfectly still, like a predator who knows that all he has to do is wait.

Ridiculous. He's not a predator. I'm in control; I'm the one who invited him over, this is my house, and I'll be the one who decides if and when to let him inside.

I shake my head to clear out these swirling thoughts.

"No?" he asks.

"No," I say quickly. "Not no. I just—I wanted you to know." I take a shaky breath. "And I think you do."

He looks at me, unblinking, with a question in his eyes. I nod.

With one unhurried movement, he curves his face down to mine as one arm curls around me. He buries his fingers in my hair at the back of my head and gently tugs so that my face turns upward to meet his.

"I do," he says.

And with a noise deep in his throat, so low it's almost a growl, he kisses me. As I kiss him back—simultaneously starving for the taste of him and wanting to savor the moment so that it lasts forever—every particle of my body relaxes. It's as if I've been tensed, waiting for this, wanting this, and I've finally succumbed, and it's bliss.

He backs me up into the doorframe, his body molding to mine, his hands gripping my hips now. I break away just long enough to say, "Maybe we should close the door."

He laughs gruffly, glancing out at the empty cul-de-sac. I grab his hand and pull him inside, shutting the door behind us. He wastes no time pressing me back against the wall, caressing my jaw, gently clinching my earlobe between two fingers as he kisses me softer than before.

"Damn, you're good at this," I mutter.

He smiles down at me. "Should we stop?"

I hesitate. My hands are on his chest; one of his legs is in between mine. I rest my head on the wall behind me.

"I leave in two days."

He nods, removing his hand from my face, taking a step back. The sudden air between us physically hurts.

"Don't stop," I whisper, and then I laugh because I said the same thing in the bath, and now it sounds like I'm begging, and maybe I am.

"Rosen?" The crease between his brows deepens. I reach up and smooth it away with my thumb.

"Green light," I say.

He needs no more encouragement. And as it turns out, we're fine without furniture.

I help him out of his clothes—what can I say, I want the visual image to take home with me—before stepping out of mine. There's a fluidity about the way we come together, as if we've done it before. And there's an ease with which he holds me, presses me into the wall, my legs wrapped around him, as if I'm floating again, only this time I'm weightless with ecstasy and wondering why the hell I waited this long to let him in.

When we've both finished, our foreheads pressed together as we catch our breath, Daniel doesn't loosen his grip on my thighs. Instead, he says, "Come here," and carries me across the empty living room and into the kitchen, where he lays me down on a bench in the breakfast nook.

"Again?" I laugh.

"Again." He hovers over me, and words cannot express my delight at being caged in by those biceps. "I've been thinking about this for a long time."

This time I'm the one who growls as I reach up for the back of his neck and pull him toward me.

Chapter 34

The sky outside melts from strawberry sorbet into a deep huckleberry purple. Daniel proposes that we paint one of the smaller bedrooms, since we're here. So we do—after putting our clothes back on—and it's a movie-montage-like hour of painting and giggling and screeching as we chase each other with paintbrushes. We admire our handiwork, and I wipe a dot of eggshell paint from his chin, and we kiss in the middle of the empty room.

"Worth it, even though it can only be one night?" he asks, his arms around my waist. I know he's referring to the conversation we had in the pool, when we forced ourselves to stop, but the words still send a pang of disappointment through me.

"Worth it," I say. "Even if it can never happen again." I say it lightly, teasingly, secretly holding my breath and half hoping he'll say that it can.

"Hey, never say never. I sure hope you'll call me next time you're in town."

"Yeah." I remove myself from his arms. I have no idea when that will be, but I don't want to get into all that right now. "We better get out of here before we get lightheaded from paint fumes."

Outside, the dark sky flecked with stars, we share one last kiss under the magnolia tree.

"Well," Daniel says, "see you at the barbecue tomorrow." This makes us both laugh way too hard. We bike down the street together, and then he goes his way and I go mine.

Gramps and Wally and I arrive at Daniel's mom's house around one the next afternoon. We agreed it would be a faux pas to arrive at a party early when we barely know anyone there.

Arriving fashionably late was a good call; people are swarming in and out of the house, chattering and laughing, so we slip in basically unnoticed.

I'm excited to meet Daniel's family, but I also don't want to make a big deal out of, well, the fact that I'm meeting his family.

Gramps, on the other hand, appears to be brimming with excitement, calling out a robust hello to everyone we pass. We've barely reached the kitchen before he's surrounded by people who want to pet Wally.

I find Daniel pulling water glasses out of a cabinet and stacking them on a tray.

"Hey, Mallory," he says lightly.

"Hi. Thanks again for inviting—"

"You brought the girl home!" A woman I can only assume is Daniel's mother joyfully clasps her hands over her bosom, which is wrapped in a KISS ME, I'M A CHEMIST apron.

I widen my eyes at Daniel. *The girl?*

He answers his mother with a laugh. "Mom, this isn't—there is no—I mean, Mallory *is* a girl, yes, but—"

He's interrupted by two slightly older guys, each holding a bottle of beer, who clap him on the shoulder and then bombard me with a chorus of "Mallory!" All I can do is gape at them as they shower me with "Finally"s and "We meet at last"s. Daniel's protests go completely ignored by his brothers. As they carry on, Daniel's eyes meet mine with a knowing twinkle. I'm pretty sure if anyone caught the smile passing between us, they would know our secret immediately. As his brothers elbow one another, each trying to shake my hand first, his mom swats them with a dish towel, shooing them away.

"Sorry about them," she says to me. "I'm Annette." She covers my hand with both of hers, which are small and warm. "Very nice to meet you, Mallory."

"Nice to meet you, too. Thank you for inviting us."

"I've heard all about you and your grandfather. Where is he?" She turns to her three sons, all of whom tower over her, and says, "What are you all standing here for? Someone needs to get the burgers on the grill."

"I got it, Mom."

"Leave it to the master."

"Give me the tongs back!"

Daniel grins at me as his brothers retreat to the backyard, arguing all the way. "So yeah, those are my brothers."

Gramps manages to extract himself from the group of dog lovers.

"Annette, this is my grandpa, Leonard."

"Thank you for having us in your lovely home," Gramps says, shaking her hand.

"Of course." Annette reaches up and grips Gramps by the shoulders, giving him a motherly squeeze. "I'm sorry for your loss."

"And I'm sorry for yours. I knew Callum—not well, but he was a kind man."

Annette nods gratefully, and then resumes bustling around behind the kitchen island.

"Anything I can help with?" Gramps asks as Wally sits alertly at his feet, watching us with his dark, shining eyes like he's part of the conversation.

"Yes," Annette says. "You can get yourself a cold beverage and settle into a chair out back. And help yourself to some food, too. It's all out there."

"You don't need to tell me twice."

"See you in a minute," I say to Gramps, and he and Wally trot off to the back door.

Annette arranges pita chips around the perimeter of a chip-and-dip tray with what appears to be baba ghanoush in the center. Daniel ducks around her to grab a drink from the fridge.

"Mallory, can I get you a—" he begins, but he's interrupted by one of the brothers, returning from the backyard.

This one has dark-brown hair and a deep, Florida tan. The other one—the grill master, apparently—looks more like Daniel, though his hair is a darker reddish brown.

The dark-haired brother waves Daniel away and says to me, "Can I make you a cocktail, Mallory?"

"That sounds amazing," I say. "What can you make?"

"What *can't* I make?"

Daniel rolls his eyes.

"My wife likes a Dirty Shirley." He gestures across the room with his beer bottle; I turn and see a pretty woman with shiny black hair wearing a Lilly Pulitzer dress, talking to an older relative. "Can I make you one?"

"Sounds delicious." I lean my elbows on the kitchen island as he pours grenadine, Sprite, and vodka into a cocktail glass.

"I'm Jeremy, by the way."

"Nice to meet you. I've heard a lot about you." An exaggeration, but it feels like the right thing to say. They seem to have heard about me, which is weird.

As he mixes my drink, Jeremy makes small talk, asking about where I'm from and what I do. It becomes apparent that despite his rowdy-older-brother act when we first arrived, Jeremy is a serious, earnest guy who's only too happy to discuss his job as a realtor in extreme detail.

Daniel hovers, and once I have my syrupy-sweet drink, we cross through the living room to the back door. The McKinnons' house has cool tile floors underfoot, a giant TV surrounded by brown leather couches (they're the biggest sectionals I've ever seen; I imagine Annette bought them to accommodate three enormous teenage boys and their friends), and a back door leading out to a screened-in pool. There are a handful of kids splashing and shrieking in the pool—Daniel's nieces and nephews, I suspect—while three grown-ups sit in lounge chairs sipping drinks and talking, occasionally glancing around to make sure the kids are still alive.

Daniel leads me across the pool deck to the other door, which opens onto a paved patio that's decked out with a gas grill and built-in countertops, with a huge teak table, a red-and-white-striped umbrella open above it. I follow Daniel to the food spread, where he hands me a paper plate. I quickly realize that this is not your average family barbecue. These people are foodies.

There's a platter of sticky-looking ribs that give off a heavenly aroma; a huge piece of salmon on a wooden plank, topped with some kind of green pistou sauce; a plate, resting on a bed of ice, containing scallop crudo surrounded by thin slices of lemon; a bowl of pale-orange gazpacho with diced cucumbers and chives on top; a platter of caprese salad made with juicy, colorful heirloom tomatoes and plump, hand-pulled shreds of mozzarella cheese. And that's only one half of the table.

"Wow. Your family likes food," I say.

Daniel spoons some caprese salad onto his plate. "Doesn't yours?"

"Eh," I shrug, "my mom likes lentils, beans, any and all pulses really, plus mushrooms and kale, whatever vegetable has the most prebiotics in it. Anything with the word *flax*, she loves. She uses agave instead of sugar, no matter the recipe. Adds chia seeds and walnuts to everything."

"For the omega-threes?" Daniel ventures, now selecting an ear of corn.

"Exactly."

"May she outlive us all," he says.

"She will."

"And your dad?" Wordlessly, Daniel offers me a scoop of pineapple and melon fruit salad. I nod, and he adds it to my plate.

"My dad would be content to eat scrambled eggs and toast for every meal for the rest of his life."

"Hmm. Can't say I feel the same."

"Yeah, he's a special duck."

We find Gramps sitting in one of the many folding chairs that have been set up in the grass. He's happily tucking into a plate of caprese salad and chatting with an older man with a handlebar mustache.

"Bet you'll be happy to see your parents again," Daniel says as we settle into chairs near Gramps.

"Yeah." I try to keep my voice light and breezy. "I do love them, silly as they are." Remembering that Daniel lost his own dad, I add, "And I'm lucky to live close to them. I bet you miss your dad."

He chews, swallows, and nods. "Every day."

"What was your favorite thing about him?" I pop some salmon into my mouth—it's buttery, rich, and perfectly seasoned. I almost feel bad for Daniel that he's a vegetarian.

He thinks for a moment. "He was a pretty reserved guy, except when it came to sports. He knew everything about our home teams, even trivia about things that had happened before he was born. He taught me how to play catch and how to bat—and when my brothers and I played sports in school, he was there for every single game. Literally, never missed any of our games from elementary school through high school. And he never got upset with us if we lost or did something dumb. He was always willing to talk strategy, to rehash a certain play over and over."

He takes a long drink of his soda and then continues, "I think my favorite memory with him was when I was eight. August seventh, 1999, it was just Dad and me at a Rays game, and we saw Wade Boggs make his three thousandth hit. We'd been going to the Rays games since before I could remember, but that day, we felt like we had a real victory, like there was hope for our little team yet." He pauses, looks up at the puffy white clouds overhead, and then blinks. "The next big moment for the Rays came almost ten years later. Dad and I watched that game from his hospital room."

I'm about to reach over to squeeze his knee consolingly, but the man with the mustache comes over and says, "Did I hear you talking about Callum and that Rays game? Do you remember the time he got thrown out of a game for yelling at the umpire?"

Daniel groans at the memory. After the man has finished his story, Daniel introduces him as his uncle Terry. Other family members gather around and add their own stories, until I have a pretty good idea where Daniel got some of his personality traits from—namely his mischievous sense of humor and his gentlemanly manners.

The party grows a bit rowdier as the afternoon wears on. The way his family shrieks with laughter and interrupts one another in their eagerness to share stories reminds me of my family, the way they behaved at Gramps's birthday party. It makes me think Daniel's clan would get along with mine. But I squash that thought, because it's pointless.

Daniel gets swept up in a lively conversation with his cousins. Wally is curled under Gramps's chair, fast asleep. Gramps and I look at each other.

"How would you feel about making dinner together and then watching an old movie tonight?" *Our last night*, I think but don't say.

"Watch what you're calling old. To me, they're just movies." Gramps grins.

"We could stop by Foxy's for dinner stuff on the way home. Maybe I'll try out Lottie's recipe for broccoli cheddar soup."

"Sounds wonderful. And I'm sure Foxy will be delighted to see you."

"Hey," I laugh. Then I glance over at Daniel. A pang zips through me. *It's not really goodbye. I'll be back to visit, I just don't know when.*

Gramps stands and says, "I'll meet you at the car. I'll take Wally for a little walk to let him do his business."

"Okay. Be right there."

Daniel notices me hovering and excuses himself from the group.

"Heading out?" His voice is low, and I wonder if I'm projecting my own feelings or if I detect sadness in his words. I nod.

"Thanks for—" I break off. It seems silly to keep thanking him for everything. For all that he's done for Pebble Cottage, both as the property manager and as a friend. For inviting me to his friend's party and this one. For befriending Gramps. And for...

His hands are in his pockets, and the few inches between us feels palpable. I would like nothing more than to reach out, even just to nudge his arm with mine, but I get the sense that he prefers it this way. Whether to avoid giving his family something to gossip about, or to avoid the temptation of anything more happening between us, I don't know. As for me, I'm weirdly relieved that we're saying goodbye here, in front of an audience. I don't know what would happen if we were alone. It's going to be hard enough to leave, holding on to the memory of last night, and if anything else were to happen, I don't know if I'd be able to say goodbye.

"We'll be in touch," Daniel says, and my heart lifts annoyingly. "About the house."

"Oh, right."

"I'll reach out when I have a lead on possible tenants," he continues.

"Okay." *So I guess this is it.* "Talk soon, then."

"Definitely," he says, and I feel a weighty meaning behind the word, but I know that's all I'm going to get. Before I can overthink it, I reach up and wrap my arms around him. He squeezes back, and I think I can feel his relief that I didn't leave without a hug.

"Bye, Rosen." His breath riffles my hair. I don't want to let go, but I feel like the longer I hold on, the harder it will be. I pull back, gripping his hands for a fraction of a second. Something in me is fighting against this, against saying goodbye. It feels wrong. But I have to go back home; I have no choice. And dragging it out will only make it hurt more.

I rip off the Band-Aid: "Bye, McKinnon. See you around."

Chapter 35

My alarm goes off at five thirty. After splashing some cold water on my face and swapping my pajamas for a matching lounge set, I zip up my suitcase and wheel it out to the kitchen. Gramps is sitting at the kitchen table with a half-eaten bowl of Grape-Nuts, a glass of orange juice, and a newspaper in front of him. Wally snoozes at his feet.

"And she's off," he says, smiling up at me.

"And I'm off." I try to match his cheerful tone. "Be good. Don't throw any wild parties without me."

"Wouldn't you know, I have a DJ and a keg booked for tonight."

"Of course you do." I slip an arm around his shoulders and plant a kiss on his head. "Love you, Gramps."

He pats my hand and squeezes it hard. "Love you, too, Mallory. Have a safe flight."

I notice that he doesn't ask me to tell him when I land. Because, I guess, that's not how this is going to go. We're not going to keep in touch every day, maybe not even every week. Things will go back to how they used to be between us. I'm just one of his several grandchildren, once again.

I place his keys on the table and give the Barack Obama key chain a fond pat goodbye.

"If you forgot anything, I'll FedEx it to you," Gramps says. "Overnight express." He winks.

I give a little laugh. "I got everything. My Uber will be here in a second. Bye, Gramps."

"Goodbye, my dear."

I crouch down and rub Wally behind his ears, nuzzling my nose to his.

"Bye, Wally."

He perks up and wags his tail, looking expectantly at me. Probably wondering if it's time for a beach walk.

"Sorry, boy. I have to go," I whisper. "I'll miss you."

I don't look back as I close the door behind me. I don't want to see how very alone Gramps looks. I have never been more grateful for a dog than I am at this moment.

My apartment smells different after a month away. Like Volcano candles, old food, and damp.

I unpack quickly, not wanting to drag out the process, and start a load of laundry. The state of the refrigerator is depressing—the old food smell is clearly emanating from a bag of apples and a bunch of carrots, foods I thought would still be good when I returned after a weekend. But using my own shower—that makes the cross-country trip worth it. The water pressure, my arsenal of bath products, my own fluffy towels instead of Gramps and Lottie's threadbare ones from before I was born. It's heavenly.

My parents invite me over for dinner tonight, but I decline. I'd rather not schlep all the way over to the Eastside after my long flight. And I have to mentally prepare myself for commuting into the office in the morning.

I do some quick math and realize that if I have to be in the office by nine, I won't have time to do my virtual yoga class beforehand. This almost makes me cry. The one good thing about coming home is the return to my beloved routine. But of course, I can't even do that.

Monday passes in an uncomfortable haze. The bus is full of silently suffering commuters, plus one guy who shouts into the void and smells of pee. I circle the overly air-conditioned office until I find a desk with my name taped to it. Kat pops by "just to say hi" about five minutes after I sit down, so I'm ninety-nine percent certain she was waiting for me to arrive. During lunch, as I unwrap my Subway sandwich in the office kitchen, a guy from my team wanders in, wearing a mask—he was one of several people hired in 2021, so I never met him in person. "Hi, Mallory," he greets me. "Hey, Jace." I wave. He pauses in front of the microwave. "I'm not Jace." And then he leaves. I still don't know who he was.

If the lunch encounter is the lowlight of my day, the highlight is when, around three P.M., I get an email from Daniel. My pulse skips and I bite back an excited grin as I open it.

Mallory,

I hope you had an easy trip home. My mom keeps asking about "that lovely Mallory Rosen." (Her words.) I told her you had to return to your high-flying, big-city career. I checked the weather in Seattle. Looks nicer than here! A pleasant eighty instead of a painful ninety-eight.

Anyway, wanted to let you know that I have a couple of parties interested in seeing the house. I know it's not finished yet, but it's not unheard of for me to show a house while it's still in progress. Let me know.

Best,
Daniel McKinnon

My smile melts away. It's all business. There's nothing for me to read into here. Other than the fact that he checked the weather in Seattle—that bit is cute. But the part about his mom calling me lovely—did he have to immediately clarify that those were her words, not his? In fact, the email dredges up a sense of unease. Until now, I'd been confident that we were on the same page: we'd had a fun fling, and if it weren't for the fact that we live across the country from each other, it might have been something more. But what if I'm wrong? What if he hadn't felt that way at all, and he'd only let the fling happen because he knew there would be no strings attached?

I roll my eyes at myself. *Calm down*. It doesn't even matter, because it's over now. No point in reading between the lines of his email, imagining how he does or doesn't feel, just to hurt my own feelings.

I tap off a quick reply: *Let's hold off for a bit. I'm not sure yet. My cousin Ellie might want the place for a few weeks this summer.*

A big fat lie. But I don't want to keep going back and forth with Daniel about the house, about possible tenants. Talking to him hurts too much—way more than I thought it would. So let's just leave it there for now.

Carmen, forever loyal, texts me within twenty-four hours of my arriving home to ask me to meet up. Tuesday after work, we meet at a new place in Fremont where we sit on a shaded patio, too close to the DJ, eating dumplings and ordering cocktails with names like The Joker You Wish You Never Met. They're pretty good; I have three.

Carmen asks me about my time in Florida, and she's so intent on asking for all the details about Gramps and Pebble Cottage and Wally that she doesn't think to ask if I met anyone there. Any other time, I would have been touched by all her questions—about

Gramps's health, how he spends his time, and what he gets up to with his senior-citizen friends—but I'm strangely disappointed that I can't easily drop Daniel into the conversation. It's not Carmen's fault that she's not psychic. And I obviously *could* tell my best friend all about Daniel. But the hurt that surfaced unexpectedly from his email is clouding my senses. Part of me doesn't want to talk about him or even think about him. And part of me wishes that Carmen had been there for all of it so I wouldn't have to explain it all from the beginning.

By the time I'm on the last half of my third cocktail, Carmen is telling me about the incredible sex she had with her latest date, a guy named Hernando, and I feel my descent into moody restlessness. Darkness is gathering around us, and our fellow bar patrons are talking louder to compete with the DJ's volume. My mind skips like a broken, drunken record. She had this apparently mind-blowing sex with Hernando. And I had it, too—with Daniel. But it already feels like a dream. Like it might have not really happened. I feel so far away from Reina Beach and Daniel and the house—my house—where it happened. Maybe if I were more like Carmen, putting myself out there more often, mind-blowing sex wouldn't feel so impossible. Because I have had it before... Before Daniel—literal years before him—I had Alex. Alex, Mr. Edelman, he of the chest hair and the books scattered around his apartment and the low, confident voice that makes you lean in closer to catch every word. Eleven years my senior, with the age and experience and emotional intelligence to bring a woman to orgasm slowly, expertly, repeatedly.

"Are you okay?" Carmen asks. I'm sucking my straw, even though my cocktail is gone, and I can feel the frown tugging my eyebrows together.

"What if it was Alex?" I ask.

"Mr. Edelman?" She grins as I glare at her. "What about him?"

"What if it's him? I mean, what if I've been an idiot, and he's the one I'm meant to be with?"

"Meant to be?" Carmen begins to smirk, but then she sees my face and rearranges her face to get back on my level. "I mean, I always thought you were good together. And he's so fucking hot."

"*Carmen.*" She snickers. "Do you think I was stupid, letting him go?"

"No way."

"What do you mean?" I eat the last dumpling, cold now.

"Mallory. Please." She covers my hand with hers and gives me a level stare. "Yeah, he was hot, but that's, like, it? He never really let you in. Don't think I've forgotten about you complaining that he didn't want to meet your family."

I grimace. Even years later, the memory rankles.

"He hurt you," Carmen says.

"You're right. But I hurt him, too."

"Yeah, well." Carmen sits back and swings one leg over the other.

I snort. I could easily list five guys who Carmen has made cry. Maybe ten.

"We had a real relationship, you know? And I ended it with a text." I knew it was wrong, but it hits home now. Now that I've just said goodbye to Daniel without so much as an *I miss you* since.

"You know he still texts me sometimes?"

"Really?"

"Every once in a while, he asks if I want to meet for coffee."

"You think he wants to get back together?"

"I don't know. I doubt it. It's not like I think that he's been pining after me this whole time."

"Maybe he wants closure," Carmen says.

"Closure." I ponder this for a moment. "Has anyone ever told you how wise you are?"

"Not often enough."

"I think I'm going to go talk to him. I think, maybe, we both need the closure." As I say this, I'm checking the time, pulling my denim jacket on, opening my Uber app.

"Mal?" Carmen says casually, using her phone as a mirror as she applies lip gloss. "Maybe wait until you're not drunk."

I sit back down, deflated. "Right. Good idea."

I dither back and forth about it for a couple of days. Is it worth going down that path again? Can I handle seeing him? Do I even want to see him? There's a chance that seeing him will ignite some forgotten spark between us. Or that he will be completely over me and confused about why I'm there at all. I suppose there's also the chance that he won't live in the same place anymore. But he'd already lived there for eight years when we started dating, so I'm relatively confident he'll still be there.

I decide Friday is the day. He used to head straight home from work on Fridays, or go for a quick happy-hour drink with his fellow teachers before heading home at a reasonable hour. So, after work, I take a quick body shower to wash the bus commute off me. My hair is cooperating today, so I let it tumble over one shoulder, which works well with the plunging neckline on the shirt I chose. Even if I'm just planning to apologize, I feel like it's a requirement to look your best when you're going to see an ex. I pair the top with some hip-hugging jeans in the style all the cool kids are wearing these days. I missed my jeans while I was gone. There's no need for pants of any kind in Florida in June.

Around eight, I step out of the car in front of Alex's complex. I'm thankful his building doesn't have a call box like Daniel's—here, I can just walk around the back, climb a flight of stairs, and knock on Alex's front door. This makes me remember when I showed up at Daniel's unannounced and the way he let me in, no questions asked. But I wasn't showing up on him after literal years apart. I push thoughts of Daniel out of my mind. I don't know why, but I don't want to think about him right now.

When Alex answers the door, my heart is pounding so hard I can hear it in my ears; I'm too flustered to read into the expression on his face. He stands there in the same clothes he wore to work that day, I assume: a blue checkered button-down and dark-wash jeans. The shirt, and his wavy black hair, are rumpled, like he's had a long day. He's so handsome it makes my chest ache.

"Mallory." His eyes widen the slightest bit, but as always, he holds his emotions close, revealing almost nothing. Or perhaps he's just truly unruffled—I could never quite tell with him.

"Hi, Alex."

He stands in the doorway for such a long moment that I'm afraid he actually does have someone with him, or that he's not going to invite me in.

But finally he blinks and says, "Do you want to come in?"

Inside, he gestures stiffly to the living room. He doesn't sit, so neither do I. It occurs to me how different his place is from Daniel's. There are framed travel posters on the walls and books shoved onto every possible shelf, toppling in piles under the end tables. I take this all in over the span of a second or two, and then I gather my courage and look him in the eyes.

"Long time no see." I try for some awkward charm. He simply looks bemused.

"You look..." He sort of gestures to me and then lets his hand swing down to his side. "Tan." He clears his throat. "What are you doing here?"

"I just wanted to..." I glance behind me at the couch, desperately wishing we could sit, but I don't feel like I can suggest it. So I just stand there. "I wanted to talk, and...apologize."

"Okay." His heavy, dark brows furrow ever so slightly. That minuscule change of expression makes me feel the full force of the guilt I've been harboring for the past couple of years. Like I had the power to hurt this grown man, and I did. For someone so confident and stoic, he still had a heart to break, and I broke it.

"I..." I reach for his hand but then can't bring myself to touch it. "The way I ended things was wrong. It was cowardly." It almost hurts me to say it—*cowardly*—because I've thought of myself that way for so long, it's like a dirty secret.

He sort of scoffs, and for a second I think he's going to say it was no big deal.

"A text. A text, and then nothing. You never granted me so much as a phone call." There's a bitter twist to his voice.

"You're right. You didn't deserve that."

It occurs to me that I half expected a sense of chemistry to still exist between us. But there's a definite chill in the air. No spark.

And, honestly, how could I have expected anything other than a chilly reception after what I did?

"Was there anything else?" He asks it in a wooden voice that throws me off balance. "Any other reason you showed up here with no warning?"

"Alex, come on. I wanted to apologize. And you asked me if I wanted to have coffee sometime, so, I thought..."

"You could have apologized anytime in the last three years. And a normal person would have scheduled coffee with me first. Why show up now?"

I can't find the words to explain what I'm doing here. Probably because I don't even know, myself. I spent the last few days thinking about whether or not I should, without asking myself why. What is the point? It's not like Alex has been waiting for me to show up out of the blue. This isn't a movie where I show up one day to find that he still loves me and I still love him. I just...I just finally understand how I must have made him feel. How it feels to care about someone and then have them disappear from your life like it was no big deal.

And also—the thought dawns on me all at once—I understand now that the way Alex made me feel wasn't right. I don't deserve to be hidden away. So I might come off as shy sometimes, I might not always be the life of the party, but that doesn't mean I deserve to be hidden. The man I'm with should be proud to introduce me to everyone in his life. Like Daniel was.

"I just wanted..." *An apology.* But I can't bring myself to say it. "I wanted you to know that the way you treated me wasn't—I deserved better. I wanted you to meet my family and vice versa. You shouldn't have hidden me like a dirty secret."

He stares, and for a moment I think he might argue.

But finally he says, "I know. I realize that now."

"You do?" It's not an apology, but he rarely apologized for anything—perhaps I should have seen that for the red flag that it was.

"Yeah. I've been seeing a new woman for a while now, and I won't make that mistake again."

"Oh." *Of course he's seeing someone new.* I wait for anger or hurt, but, unexpectedly, something inside me softens. It takes me a second to realize that I'm happy for him. We didn't work out, but he deserves to be with someone who's right for him.

"What is she like?"

"She's a speech therapist. She loves board games. And backpacking."

I grin, and after a moment he grins back, laughing a little. Because those are Alex's hobbies that I could never get into. The board games were fun sometimes, but usually I spaced out while he tried to explain the rules. And backpacking? Just the thought of hiking up a mountain with camping gear strapped to my back makes me shudder with horror.

"She sounds perfect for you. So you're going to introduce her to your parents, then?"

Slowly, he nods, with an apologetic shrug.

And even though I'm certain that I'm over Alex, even though I'm glad that he's found someone, a part of me breaks open. Because, three years ago, I wanted so badly to be the person he brought home to his parents—and now, I am that person, for a different someone. Or I was a week ago.

Tears well up from deep inside my chest, and my throat aches with the effort of keeping them inside. The memory of how joyfully and unreservedly Daniel introduced me to his family hits me. I wanted that for so long. And I had it, for one brief, shining moment.

"I'm happy that you're happy, Alex."

"Hey. Same to you. Are you? Happy?"

Faking it is the only option right now. Because I didn't come here to pour my heart out to Alex about how much I miss Daniel. I just wanted to end my last romance on a high note, instead of the low note that's been lingering for too long.

"I am." I beam at him, smiling through tears.

He finally reaches for me and pulls me into a hug. It's the embrace I've thought about countless times, but right now I'm vibrating with the effort of trying not to cry and I just want to leave.

As soon as I'm a block away, I pull out my phone and call Carmen. Because I *do* want to pour my heart out about Daniel. To someone who will understand and care about every single interaction, every up and down, every kiss. To my best friend.

That night—after crying buckets of tears to Carmen as we drink chamomile tea on my tiny patio, the chill of the Seattle summer night cooling our skin as music pours out of a neighbor's window—I feel cleansed. Now the whole story of Daniel McKinnon is out there—in my best friend's brain, at least—and I can accept it for what it was, and move on. I feel like something has been wrung from my heart, leaving me lighter, with more room to breathe.

Chapter 36

After talking to Alex—after finally putting my memories of him to rest—a sense of acceptance settles over me. I'm in a new phase of my old life. It could be a good thing. Seattle is gorgeous this time of year, with the kind of weather that makes some people want to go camping and makes me want to sit at sidewalk cafés sipping icy cocktails. It also makes me wish I could take Daniel on a bike ride here, winding through a forest trail with an evergreen canopy over our heads. But I squash that particular wish.

I finally give in to my mom's requests and go to their house for dinner. It's exactly the same as ever. My mother prepares recipes from a cookbook called *Nuts About Health*, my dad spends the evening discussing sports with Blake, and everyone mostly pays attention to baby Adam. He's sitting up now, so. Very exciting stuff.

I'm used to feeling like the spare—how very Prince Harry of me—so it doesn't bother me too much. I'm just excited to get back to the sanctity of my apartment afterward. As much as I love my apartment, a stray part of me wishes that I could come home to Gramps, sitting on the couch with a knowing smile and a wry remark, and Wally, thumping his tail in wild excitement.

Work drones on the way it always does. The meetings are the worst part, because now I have to sit in the same room as people, and I can't figure out how to make or avoid eye contact at socially acceptable moments. I do my best to quell the feeling of vague panic at the idea that I'm going to have to do this day in and day out for years and years and possibly forever.

On Wednesday, I return to my desk from an hour-long planning meeting and see that I have a missed call from Mom. There's no voicemail, but she texted me.

Gramps in hospital. Getting latest from Trish. Will keep you updated.

The air dissolves from my lungs. The text was sent forty-eight minutes ago, and she hasn't followed up with any details yet?

I text back as fast as I can: *What's going on? Is he ok?*

When I don't immediately see any typing bubbles, I call her. It goes to voicemail. I call two more times, but she doesn't answer.

I try Trish: no answer, so I send her a quick text, too, begging for details.

After five and then ten minutes with no updates, I spiral.

Did Gramps have health problems? He never complained about anything, health-wise. Was he hiding something from me? Or was this sudden and unexpected? A heart attack or stroke? Oh my God, I should have booked him a doctor's appointment, too, not just therapy appointments. How could I have overlooked that?

I'm sitting at my desk, struggling to get enough air, staring at my computer screen with eyes blurred from tears. I should have asked him when was the last time he had a checkup. No, I should never have left. Was he alone when something happened? Was he, perhaps, crumpled on the floor for hours before someone found him and called 911? *Please, not the kitchen floor, it's so hard and cold.*

The thought of Wally sniffing around Gramps's body, confused and whining, almost makes me sob. I muffle my cries with the palm of my hand. Everyone around me is glued to their computers, headphones on, paying no attention to anyone around them, including me and my breakdown.

The minutes tick by. I call Dad, Maeve, even Ellie. Maeve is the only one who answers, and she doesn't know any more than I do. Turns out Mom didn't even think to text her, so I'm the one breaking the news to her.

"But did he—was there anything wrong with him? When you were there, I mean?" Maeve sounds scared.

"I don't know, Maeve, I don't know! I didn't think there was." I'm pacing the halls now, trying to keep my trembling voice down as it climbs higher and higher.

"I've heard of elderly couples who die within months of each other," Maeve continues in a whisper. "Like they can't bear to live without each other."

"So not helping," I say. "Just—call me if you hear anything, okay?"

The panicky part of my brain threatens to go numb with shock. But then there's another part of my brain that's fighting mad. I should be there. I should be there helping Gramps, talking to his doctors in person, getting as much information as I can. *I should be there.* What the hell am I doing here in this office building across the continent?

I call every hospital within a twenty-mile radius of Sandy Shores. They refuse to tell me anything over the phone. I call Angela, but she doesn't answer. Is she with him? I hope she's with him.

I've just opened the Alaska Airlines website to search for immediate flights to Tampa when my phone rings.

"Mom?"

"Sorry, sweetie. Hectic day," Mom says. Her voice is not nearly as frantic as mine.

"What's going on, is Gramps okay?"

"Oh! Yes." She sounds like her mind was elsewhere. How is that possible?

"'Yes'?" I repeat, desperate for more information.

"He had a scare. His friend put him on an ambulance. They thought maybe a heart attack."

"I knew it." I take a deep breath. "How's he doing now?"

"Apparently it was angina. So they've given him a new prescription and sent him home."

I pause, struggling to let go of the pent-up panic. "That's it? So it wasn't a heart attack?"

"No, darling."

"And he's fine?"

"Absolutely fine."

I pause again. "Then why didn't you respond for the last hour?"

"I was in court," she says simply.

"Oh my God." I press against the bridge of my nose, my hand shaking with adrenaline. "I thought he was dead."

"Oh no. I'm so sorry, sweetie." She sounds distracted; I can hear someone talking to her in the background. "I've got to run. Sorry again!" She hangs up.

I sit there for a long minute, staring at nothing. I have several unread messages on Slack: an engineering manager arguing about something on the monthly project schedule I sent out this morning, and a UX designer asking me to review something that I'm absolutely not the right person to ask about. A new one pops up, this one from Kat.

Kat White: *Hey Mallory, thanks for speaking up in the OP meeting earlier today. Julie and I were discussing the new XR project. It aligns with one of our top Q4 goals, and it would look really great on your performance review if you were to take the lead on it. What do you think?*

I stare at her message. I start to type a reply, something along the lines of "Sounds good, thanks for thinking of me!" But I can't bring myself to type the words. Finally, I get up and walk across the hall to her desk. Our company doesn't believe in private offices, but she has a large corner cubicle surrounded by windows. Still, she's also surrounded by co-workers clacking away on their keyboards.

"Kat, hi."

"Hey! Good idea to come chat about the project in person. Because we can do that now, ha!" She swivels around to face me, her body language easy and open, clearly expecting me to accept her offer with boundless gratitude. And I consider it, seriously, because it's so ingrained in me to say, *Yes, please, thank you!* Whatever it takes to keep my job. But I am quite literally unable to form the words.

"Kat..." I start slowly. "I can't."

"Oh?" She straightens up, blinking at me through her trendy glasses. "Because I took a look at your Jira workload and it seems like you have availability. Is there something else on your plate?"

I press my thumbs into my fingers, cracking them one by one.

"No," I say finally. "It's not my plate necessarily. Or not my work plate. It's more, my life plate." Kat just stares at me. I need to do this better. I take a deep breath and let it out slowly. "I quit."

This does not seem to register. "Quit what?" Kat looks for all the world like she's expecting me to say I quit smoking or something irrelevant to work. Of course, that's because I'm going about this all wrong, like the main character in a movie. What people do in the real world is send a well-written email giving their two weeks' notice. But I can't back out now. And weirdly, instead of feeling like an anxious, guilty mess, I suddenly feel light, like a fresh, sunny breeze is blowing right through me.

"I quit...this."

The people around us have started poking their heads up like gophers with headphones dangling from one ear. So they can look up for office drama but not for someone sobbing at her desk over a potentially dead grandpa. I almost laugh, realizing that I won't have to deal with this passive aggressive—no, aggressively passive—office culture anymore. Good riddance, gophers.

Kat pouts her lips out, like she's confused and slightly hurt.

"Did something happen? We can schedule a meeting with HR if—"

I cut her off. "Nothing like that. It's just me. I need to move on."

"Did you get another offer? Because typically people give us the option to match whatever—"

"No." She is really not getting it. "I don't want to do this anymore. I quit."

I think it finally sinks in. Kat's posture crumples the slightest bit; she looks disappointed to lose me, which is oddly gratifying.

"So, your last day is two weeks from today, then?" she asks hopefully.

I shake my head, removing the badge from around my neck.

"No, Kat. It's today."

I leave the badge on her desk and walk away, trying my best to hold my head high as the gophers gawk openly, watching me every step of the way.

Chapter 37

Sitting on my couch, the jubilant feeling of victory has disappeared. It's been replaced by a hollow what-have-I-done feeling as I scroll through my bank accounts, seeing how much I have left.

I'm not going to starve immediately. But it was undoubtedly reckless. I've been clinging to that job for dear life for such a long time, it's terrifying to suddenly be cut loose. But—I pause in my mental calculations—I can take my expensive Seattle rent out of the equation. Which means the little money I have will last a bit longer.

Because that was part of this decision. (Maybe *epiphany* would be a better word, since most of the decision-making was subconscious.) Leaving my job means I can leave Seattle. For real this time.

Just because I've lived somewhere my entire life doesn't mean it's home. Living here these past few years, I've been anonymous, overlooked, superfluous, and many variations on the word *lonely*. Living in Reina Beach for just a month, I felt seen, important, needed. My life felt fuller, and it wasn't even my real life. But it could be.

I've been thinking of myself as a coward for such a long time. Maybe it started with the way I ghosted Alex instead of breaking up with him properly, or maybe it started years earlier when I got rejected from law school and couldn't bring myself to apply again. And I know that staying with a job I hated just for the paycheck was a sensible financial decision—but I also realize now that it was cowardly. And I'm shedding that part of myself. I'm ready to be brave.

It turns out that breaking up with your life is easier than you might expect. The first call I make is to my landlord. I expect him to tell me I'll have to find a sub-leaser to finish out my lease, but as it happens he's happy for me to leave so that he can list my unit at what he calls "current market rates." Yikes.

I contemplate getting a storage unit for my stuff—just in case—but decide I don't want a fallback option. I want a fresh start. So I list my prized possessions online for sale at dirt-cheap prices, hoping they'll sell quickly. It works. I spend the next three days letting strangers carry off my furniture in exchange for a Venmo transaction. I keep two boxes' worth of stuff I don't want to part with—my favorite mugs, blankets, art prints, gadgets—to ship across the country to Gramps's condo. The clothes and shoes and personal items that I'm keeping, I'll stuff into my two suitcases. By the end of the week, my place is all packed up. Even my bed is gone, so I spend my last night at Mom and Dad's.

"Are you sure you want to do this?" Mom keeps asking. "Florida is so far away. It's so hot. And so...Republican."

I give her a sardonic stare over my toothbrush. This is the third or fourth time she's given me this spiel today. I spit out toothpaste and wipe my mouth.

"I'm sure. Like I've said a hundred times."

"And what are you going to do for work? I can ask Trish if she has any leads."

I consider this as I zip up my toiletries bag.

"I was thinking of asking Ellie if her ice cream shop is hiring. Could be an easy gig while I figure out what I want to do next."

Mom whimpers and covers her mouth with her fingertips.

"Mom. Please."

"You don't really want to work at an ice cream shop, do you? You don't want to get too comfortable there and forget to, you know, go back to your real career."

"What career?"

"Technology!"

I can't help but laugh. "I'm not going back to tech. I never really liked it."

"But..." Mom stands behind me, smoothing my hair and staring mournfully at my reflection in the mirror.

"It's okay," I say. "I'm never going to be a lawyer like Maeve and...all of you. I don't know what I'm going to do. But I'm still me. And I'll figure it out."

I can sense that she wants to keep arguing her case, but apparently she decides to save it for another day.

"At least I know Gramps will be happy to have you back. Was he thrilled when you told him?"

I freeze. The thing is, I haven't exactly told Gramps. I thought about it; after all, there's probably some type of etiquette around informing someone before you show up to crash at their place. But ultimately, I decided that I don't make huge, life-changing decisions often—this might be the only one in my entire life—so I want to have some fun with it. Make a grand gesture. It's fun to imagine the look of stunned delight on Gramps's face when I show up unannounced. Even if he doesn't normally like surprises, I know he'll like this one. But I know my mom wouldn't find it cute; she would make me call him first. In fact, she would probably freak out at the idea that I've packed up my whole life here without even okaying it with the person I'm going to live with.

"Yeah," I lie. "Thrilled."

Mom turns suddenly emotional, her eyes filling with tears as she smiles and touches my cheek. "You're a good daughter, Mallory. And a very sweet granddaughter."

"Thanks." My voice is muffled as she squeezes me to her.

"I'm going to visit all the time."

"Good."

"I'll let you get some sleep. We're leaving for the airport bright and early."

I say good night and then shut the door to my childhood room, now a guest room slash my dad's sports-themed man cave. Despite the clutter of sports paraphernalia, and despite the fact that I'll be waking up to jump into a whole new life, I drop quickly into the heavy sleep of someone with no regrets.

I arrive in Tampa at five P.M. and pay for a taxi to take me to Sandy Shores. This time, instead of brutal afternoon sun beating down on the freeway, there's a purplish-gray sky crackling with lightning and distant rumbles of thunder. It feels electric, hot, and steamy, so different from the place I left behind.

I drag my two suitcases across the grassy lawn. In the stormy light, the gazebo glows bright white. As the rain starts—deceivingly gentle at first, but I know it'll be pounding down soon—I gaze across the beach at the choppy waves, filling my lungs with salty air. This is home now. I get to jump in those waves tomorrow morning, and every morning if I feel like it.

I take the elevator to Gramps's floor and knock gently on his door before realizing that it's unlocked.

"Helloooo," I say quietly, suddenly worried about giving him a heart attack. "Gramps? It's Mallory!"

I hear a happy bark and rush into the kitchen to greet Wally. I'm on my knees scratching behind his ears before I realize that Gramps is sitting at the kitchen table, and that he's not alone. Angela sits across from him, and the table is laid with a tablecloth and the remnants of dinner, with two taper candles flickering between them. Flickering *romantically.*

"Oh my gosh." I stumble back to my feet. "I'm interrupting!"

"Mallory!" Gramps breaks into the huge smile I'd imagined he would have when I showed up. "What are you doing here?"

Angela is bustling around, telling me to sit down, pouring me a glass of water, microwaving me a plate of food before I can say a word.

"I'm—" I'm finding it impossible to say, *Surprise, I'm back to live with you!* in the midst of this development. "Really, I'm so sorry to interrupt, I'll just—"

"Please!" Angela slides the plate in front of me, along with a fork and knife. "It's wonderful to see you. Now tell us, what brings you back?" She sits back down and refills her own glass from a pitcher of water with ice and lemon slices floating in it.

"I..." What do I say now? I'm here to stay? I'm here to permanently cramp your style? "I'm moving to Florida."

"Wonderful!" Gramps looks like he really means it. I smile back at him.

We don't address the fact that I obviously crashed a date. The conversation flows easily as I devour Angela's cooking—some kind of slow-cooked meat and potatoes. Gramps asks me about my "computer job" and looks proud when I tell him that I quit.

"My son owns a snorkel company," Angela says instantly, "and he's always hiring. Instructors, salespeople, and I think he's looking for someone to do their website. Let me give him a call."

I thank her and put a hand on hers to stop her from grabbing her phone. "Maybe tomorrow."

She nods graciously and then fills me in on some funny retirement village gossip. Gramps and I never had a problem finding things to talk about, but the conversation is certainly lively with Angela in the mix. After I eat, I clean up as much as they'll let me, and then I tell them that I'm tired and going to get ready for bed. This is not strictly true, seeing as how it's barely five P.M. Seattle time. But I'm determined to give them some privacy.

After I shower and settle into the seashell bed to start a new TV show—I'm all out of *Outlander* episodes—I start to have some misgivings. I mean, clearly Gramps is trying to start a new phase of his life here. I never thought he would be able to move on from Lottie, and I'm delighted for him. There's no way I'm going to stick around to doom his budding romance.

I try to focus on this episode of *Ted Lasso*, but I can hear the low voices of Gramps and Angela in the other room, and I can't shake the awkwardness of feeling like I'm intruding. And then it hits me—like, how did I not think of this before?—I have a house. I literally have my own house, a couple of miles away from here, empty, waiting for someone to live in it. Waiting for me.

Chapter 38

After breakfast with Gramps—he slept in and I woke up early, so our schedules lined up for once—I borrow his car and drive to Pebble Cottage. Gramps had protested, saying there's no need for me to go anywhere else, but I convinced him that we're both too old for a permanent adult roommate. This made him laugh. I also promised that I would see him every day, so often that he would get sick of me.

As I drive up to the house, I savor everything, from the way the car tires crunch over gravel pulling into the carport, to the heady fragrance drifting from the magnolia tree, to the bright morning sun pooling on the front doorstep. It may not be a grand front porch, but the little stoop is just big enough to display a few pumpkins in the fall. And a festive doormat. The thought of decorating for Halloween, of still being here in three months and watching the seasons change (or not, maybe, since this is Florida), thrills me.

I take a deep breath and unlock the door, the Obama key chain rattling. *Home.* That thought will take some getting used to.

My first impression as I step inside is that it smells like fresh paint. My second is that the mess of floorboards that I left here, piled in the entryway and the living room, is gone. Odd. I walk farther inside, my sandals slapping gently against the brand-new floors. It's finished. Every room has a new floor and freshly painted walls.

Even the planks that I messed up in the living room have been relaid correctly. I spin around to take it all in, and then I notice something I missed when I walked in. My mirror—the one Daniel carried home for me on his bike, the one I never got around to picking up before I left—is hanging near the front door, exactly where I had envisioned it.

I touch the gilded frame and smile at my reflection. I like the way I look here, in the sunny entryway of my very own house. I look sun-kissed and relaxed and happy. I wonder when Daniel was going to tell me about all this. My fingers itch to grab my phone and call him immediately to thank him. I will, of course, but thanking him would mean telling him that I'm back in town. As eager as I am to see him again, a part of me wants to wait. I want to make this perfect.

It's amazing what one can accomplish in one day with a credit card, a rented U-Haul, and a cousin who is happy to have something to do "other than watching ferret trainers on TikTok." I didn't ask any ferret-related follow-up questions; large rodents are not really my thing. Ellie is uncharacteristically excited to see me and proves extremely helpful in hauling things into the truck—like the rattan queen-size bed frame and the vintage, navy-blue velvet love seat that we found at Goodwill. "I deadlift," she explains.

By that evening, the place is decently furnished. The living room looks cheerfully minimalist, and so different from my cozy, neutral Seattle living room. I paired the navy-blue sofa with a bold yellow-and-white rag rug and a kitschy lamp with oyster shells and sand dollars dangling from it—both from the flea market Daniel introduced me to. The walls are empty, but I'm waiting until I find the perfect art piece. I have plenty of time—and I happen to know someone who likes perusing art galleries.

There's something very satisfying about filling my brand-new closet in my brand-new bedroom. Like the rest of the house, the closet also looks pretty sparse, because I left most of my cold-weather clothes at my parents' house. But I like it this way. It's calming.

In the kitchen, the built-in breakfast table is set with handwoven place mats and a cut-glass vase full of fresh flowers. I shipped my trusty Nespresso machine and Vitamix blender; they should arrive next week. I unwrap a new-to-me set of colorful Fiestaware and a full set of utensils that I got for pennies. As I'm opening and closing cabinets and drawers, trying to decide where to put everything, a small sheet of paper flutters down onto the countertop.

It's a letter—to me.

Dear Mallory,

So, my little house is yours now. I hope you know how much this place meant to me. It was a place of security, of love. Over the decades, it was full of friends in the kitchen, the laughter of little girls, and flowers from the garden.

Here's what I hope for you, my dear granddaughter: I hope that this house can be a place to plant deep roots. And I hope that those roots give you both the stability to reach out and grow, to flourish, and also a safe place to which to retreat. I feel the need to care for you the way I cared for Leonard. In you, I've always seen him. And in him is a tendency to retreat inward. I know that there's nothing wrong with this. But I also want to remind you to look toward the sun. We need other people, just like we need sunlight.

Take care of my house, dear one. Take care of my Leonard. And take care of you.

I know you will.
All my love,
Lottie

I'm sitting cross-legged on the kitchen floor, wiping away tears.

An overwhelming relief surges through me. Lottie did want me to live here. It took me a while to realize it, but I made the right choice in the end.

"I promise I will," I whisper.

At dusk, I do a few laps in my little pool (my pool!) and then I swim to the edge and grab my phone. Legs kicking languidly in the warm, glowing water, I think about what I want to say to Daniel.

Finally, I type: *Hi Daniel! Hope you're doing well. I have a prospective tenant who wants to see the house. Can you meet them there tomorrow?*

I put my phone down, suddenly nauseous with nerves. What if he's not happy to see me? What if we're totally not on the same page and he's just confused? Before I can duck my head under the water, my phone lights up.

Happy to. How's 6 P.M. tomorrow? Busy day. If that's too late for them, I can do noon or 3 the following day.

For some reason, this response fills me with affection. He's so professional. So prompt. So thoughtful.

I reply: *Tomorrow at 6 is perfect. Thanks!*

It's slightly killing me not to thank him effusively for all the work he did on the house in secret. But I don't want to let him know I'm here, not yet. I slip back under the water and swim until my anxious brain has quieted down, until my limbs feel like jelly, and then I take a long hot shower in my very own bathroom before falling instantly asleep on my very own couch. (I'm ordering a new mattress for the bed frame—one thing I didn't feel like buying secondhand.)

The next day, I meet Gramps for lunch and then swim in the Gulf. I savor the sensation of feeling like I've actually used my muscles over the past few days. Amazing how I never felt this way back home in my old solitary routine, and yet I've felt this way frequently during my time here. I may not be a backpacking type, but I see a future full of swimming, kayaking, and biking in the hot sun. In the afternoon, I visit an antiques mall in St. Pete for more furniture and odds and ends.

A few minutes before six, I do a final walkthrough of the house. The bedroom still looks unfinished with no mattress, but the living room and kitchen are warm and inviting.

I really didn't want to have Daniel over with no furniture in the house yet again.

I slip outside to wait on the front stoop. Daniel will recognize Gramps's car in the carport, so I might as well be out here to see his reaction. Like the professional property manager he is, he shows up at two minutes to six, tooling slowly up the driveway on his red bike.

"Mallory?" he shouts, his face slack with disbelief. "What—?"

I give a little wave, unable to contain a smile.

He hops off his bike, still rolling, and then stops a few feet away from me, clutching the handlebars suspiciously.

"What are you doing here? What about the tenants I'm supposed to meet?"

I stand and dust off the back of my denim shorts. I kind of like the way this feels, standing in front of my own front door, having a man look at me like...that.

"It's me. I'm the tenant."

He still looks suspicious, so I explain. "I went back home to Seattle, but it didn't feel right. I quit my job and sold all my stuff and... Here we are."

"Okay..."

My heart plunges. This is it; this is what I was afraid would happen. I try to surprise him and I make a fool of myself, because he actually didn't want this, and he's not happy I'm here.

I take a deep breath. "Daniel. Before we talk about anything else, I have to ask. Did you finish the floors and walls yourself?"

He grins guiltily. The lopsided smile and the flush coloring his freckled cheeks make it nearly impossible for me not to run over to him immediately.

"I did," he admits.

"Why?"

"Because I wanted to get the place rented." He says it stoutly, defending himself, but he can't quite hide the laugh in his eyes.

"I would have paid Alan for that, though." I step through the open front door and point at the gilded mirror inside. "And what about this?"

He takes a few steps closer. "That—well, you left it at my place. It doesn't exactly match my decor."

"I see." I appraise him, still not entirely sure if we feel the same way. Not sure how he'll feel about the fact that I may or may not have moved across the country for him. I mean, it was obviously for Gramps, but...

"Want to see what I've done with the place?" I say.

He climbs the steps with his helmet under one arm. "How long have you been in town?"

"Just two days."

"Two days, huh?" He gives me a once-over as he passes over the threshold, as if he's wondering why I waited two days to see him. But I'm probably imagining it.

"Wow." He stops in the living room. "You've done a lot. So you're really...?"

"Living here? Yep." He doesn't immediately squeal for joy—I'm *really* wishing we had discussed our intentions before now—so I beckon for him to follow me.

"I found this at the antiques mall today."

He gazes around the kitchen, taking in the new dishes, the dish towel on the hook, the soap bottle beside the kitchen sink—all signs of someone living here. And then he looks at the kitchen table, where I'm pointing.

"Is that tabletop shuffleboard?"

"It is!" I'm a little too proud of myself. I didn't even know tabletop shuffleboard existed, so when I saw it, I had to have it.

"I kind of thought there'd be a home-cooked meal when you brought me in here." Daniel picks up one of the little blue pucks.

"My cooking is still a work in progress. I wouldn't subject you to that. Not yet."

"Yet?" Daniel looks around, his hand closing around the puck.

"Yeah." I lean against the kitchen table, the memory of what happened on this very bench suddenly flooding my mind. "Not when I'm—"

"Not when you're what, Rosen?" He does that unwavering-eye-contact thing again, like he might be able to read the words in my mind before I say them out loud.

"Not when I'm trying to make you like me." I let out a slightly hysterical laugh.

He sets the puck down on the board and sighs, like he's disappointed. But I've said it, and I can't take it back now. All my cards are on the table—or my pucks are. Or something.

"I'm sorry to say," Daniel says slowly. *Oh God—I would like to disappear now.* "I think that ship has sailed."

"It...has?"

He looks at me, and there's a disbelieving twinkle in his expression as he points to the breakfast nook bench. "I believe I showed you, just a few weeks ago, right here on this very bench, exactly how I feel about you."

"Oh." *Right.* All the blood has rushed to the lower half of my body. But I don't move. Because I want to be very sure that we're on the same page about what my being here means—what it means about us.

"You're here for good?" he asks.

I nod.

"Guess you won't need a property manager anymore."

I shake my head. He closes the distance between us. I put both hands in his hair, sticking up at all angles, and I wonder if this sensation, and the salty smell of him, will become something I get to experience day in and day out.

"Ma'am." His hands find my waist. I can feel the warmth of his palms through my tank top. "You've just put me out of a job."

"I'm sorry. And I'm sorry about the other thing, too."

He tilts his head. "What other thing?"

I lean in and whisper, my lips grazing his ear, "How badly I'm about to beat you at shuffleboard."

He hoots with laughter and proceeds to roundly kick my butt in the first match. I demand that we play best two out of three, but we get distracted.

And that's how I discover that my new blue couch is good for more than just sleeping on.

Epilogue

Two weeks later

My head pops out of the water and I push my soaking hair out of my face.

"Grab hold!"

With one hand, I grab the ladder at the back of Angela's son's boat; with the other, I grab Daniel's hand. He helps me hoist myself up.

"How was it?" Daniel beams from under the brim of a Rays cap.

"So fun!" I wrap a beach towel around myself, momentarily chilled although I know I'll be sweating again in three minutes. "I haven't done that since I was a kid."

Angela and her son had invited us—and Gramps—to join their family on their boat outing, which is just something they do most weekends (mind blowing to me). He has a tube that he tows behind the boat. His two kids, both in their late teens, are constantly telling him to crank up the speed and do more zigzags.

"You wanna go again?" Angela's son, the captain, asks me from his spot at the steering wheel.

"No, thanks!" I'd rather sit up here, drying off in the sun and chatting with Gramps and Angela.

"Sounds like it's my turn!" Daniel sounds like a big excited boy as he kicks off his flip-flops and jumps feetfirst into the water.

"He's a good egg, that one," Angela says. She's sitting with her ankles crossed, wearing a bright-purple bathing suit underneath a white caftan, a wide-brimmed sun hat keeping her hair in place, one hand holding Gramps's. I agree with this.

"Mallory, when are you going to join my workout class again?" she shouts over the noise of the engine.

Gramps gives me a knowing, uh-oh sort of look. I'd joined her class again last week and I don't know if my core muscles or my dignity will ever recover.

"You guys are too intense for me," I admit.

She shrugs, like she's heard this before. "And what about that job opening at the cybersecurity firm in St. Pete?" It had turned out that her son only had openings for snorkel instructors, which I was in no way fit for, but Angela had put out her feelers for other jobs. Like Mom, she thinks of the ice cream shop as a stopgap measure.

Again, Gramps looks at me.

"She's on sabbatical," he says with a grin.

I smile back at him. The cybersecurity job seemed like it would pay well and like it might be something I could finagle my way into. But, as I had confided in Gramps, I'm not ready to tie myself to another corporate job quite yet—or maybe ever. I need some time to breathe. I might even do some traveling.

But for now, I'm soaking up the moment I'm in, in the place I'm meant to be.

The next evening, I FaceTime Carmen from my sunroom. I will never get tired of coming home from a shift at the ice cream shop and kicking my feet up with a cold drink in hand. It's comfortable out here now, with some new wicker chairs and ottomans and a bright-blue outdoor rug.

"I am so jealous of that pool," Carmen says. She's currently walking down a busy Seattle street. I can hear the rush of cars and see the crowds of commuters around her. Meanwhile, the only sound on my end is the rustle of the breeze in nearby trees, punctuated by the chirp of crickets.

"It's pretty great." I sip my rosé.

"And you can bike to the beach from there?"

"Yep. I went swimming in the ocean this morning." The doorbell chimes. "They're here, I have to go."

"Don't let your new friends replace me! Don't forget about me," Carmen cries dramatically, clutching her phone closer to her face.

"How can I when you're coming to stay with me for two weeks?"

"I mean, when you told me you have two extra bedrooms, I realized I had no choice. I can't just let you be all alone down there."

"Of course not." I wave at her through my phone. "See you on Friday!"

She squeals and then hangs up.

Daniel and Amanda, along with Francis and some of the other friends I met kayaking, are here for game night. My first time hosting friends in my new house. I put out bowls of chips and decked out the living room with some throw pillows and candles—I can't get over how cozy it looks in the evening light.

I look around, savoring one last minute of solitude, and then I open the door.

Acknowledgments

Thank you to everyone who helped make this book possible. Thanks to Kimberly Whalen, my amazing agent, for making my dreams come true. Thank you to Sabrina Flemming, editor extraordinaire, for bringing out the best in this story.

To the wonderful team at Forever, thank you for all that you do!

To all the writers I've connected with, both online and in person, over the last couple years: thank you! Having people to turn to for advice and solidarity, people who get it, is truly invaluable. I am so grateful for the support the author community provides, even to its newest members.

Thank you to Tara Nieuwesteeg, for being my accountability buddy during the writing of this book, and for your support and friendship.

Thank you to Judy Owen and Callie Nettles, for showing me around St. Pete and Tampa over the years, for answering my questions, and for all your support.

To all of my friends: What would I do without you? Thank you for shouting about my books, but thank you especially for being there for me. The laughs, the vent sessions... they are essential. You never cease to inspire me.

Mom and Dad, thank you for believing in me and rooting for me, and for telling all your friends to buy my books. Seriously...

keep it up! And thank you to my sisters for catsitting, babysitting, and being so awesome. To the rest of my mishpocha, thanks for the outpouring of love and enthusiasm about my books. I'm so lucky to have you all in my life.

This is the part where I try not to cry: My grandparents aren't here to read this, but I have to acknowledge them, because they were with me in spirit while I wrote this book. Iris and Rafi, Carol, Richard: They were each so different, and so wonderful. I'm lucky to have had close relationships with all of them well into my adult years. The character of Gramps was inspired by both of my grandfathers, Rafi and Richard, both of whom were kind, funny, and alarmingly intellectual. Iris and Carol: I expect you'll get your own books someday. I love you. I miss you.

Dave, thank you for figuring this out with me. Becoming an author while also becoming a mother of two, with a full-time job, has not been easy. You've been nothing but supportive, even when there's nothing you can do except give me a really long hug in the middle of the kitchen after the kids are asleep. Every romance I write is inspired by you.

Caroline, my girl, becoming your mother has made me feel all the feelings, so much stronger than I felt things before. I want the world for you so fiercely. Becoming an author is my Big Dream, and I hope to show you that you can achieve yours, too. I can't wait to see what yours is.

Evan, you were with me the whole time I wrote this book. Literally. Thanks for letting me finish writing it before you were born!

Finally, thank you to all the readers. Reviews and articles are great, but I'll never get over the thrill of a simple message from a reader who wanted to tell me they loved my book. Thank you from the bottom of my heart.

About the Author

Lauren Appelbaum works as a technical editor and has been writing fiction since she could hold a pencil (usually when she's supposed to be doing other things). She lives in Seattle with her family.

You can find out more at:
LaurenAppelbaumBooks.com
Instagram @LaurenAppelbaum

RAISING READERS
Books Build Bright Futures

Thank you for reading this book and for being a reader of books in general. As an author, I am so grateful to share being part of a community of readers with you, and I hope you will join me in passing our love of books on to the next generation of readers.

Did you know that reading for enjoyment is the single biggest predictor of a child's future happiness and success?

More than family circumstances, parents' educational background, or income, reading impacts a child's future academic performance, emotional well-being, communication skills, economic security, ambition, and happiness.

Studies show that kids reading for enjoyment in the US is in rapid decline:

- In 2012, 53% of 9-year-olds read almost every day. Just 10 years later, in 2022, the number had fallen to 39%.
- In 2012, 27% of 13-year-olds read for fun daily. By 2023, that number was just 14%.

Together, we can commit to **Raising Readers** and change this trend. How?

- Read to children in your life daily.
- Model reading as a fun activity.
- Reduce screen time.
- Start a family, school, or community book club.
- Visit bookstores and libraries regularly.
- Listen to audiobooks.
- Read the book before you see the movie.
- Encourage your child to read aloud to a pet or stuffed animal.
- Give books as gifts.
- Donate books to families and communities in need.

Books build bright futures, and **Raising Readers** is our shared responsibility.

For more information, visit **JoinRaisingReaders.com**

Sources: National Endowment for the Arts, National Assessment of Educational Progress, WorldBookDay.org, Nielsen BookData's 2023 "Understanding the Children's Book Consumer"